Red Treasure

How One Man's Passion for Adventure Drives Him to Build a Copper Empire

George E. Smith

First published by Dog Ear Publishing
4010 W. 86th Street, Ste H
Indianapolis, IN 46268
www.dogearpublishing.net

ISBN: 978-145750-406-8

This book is printed on acid-free paper.

This book is a work of fiction. Places, events, and situations in this book are purely fictional and any resemblance to actual persons, living or dead, is coincidental.

Printed in the United States of America

Chronology

1875-1900	Rockefeller, Carnegie, Ford, and Morgan lead the industrialization of America
1879	Edison perfects the incandescent light bulb
1880	The Southern Pacific Railroad crosses Arizona into New Mexico
1881-1900	5.2 million immigrants enter the United States
1886	Geronimo surrenders, signifying the end of the Indian wars
1889	Phoenix becomes the permanent capital of the Arizona Territory
1891	The University of Arizona is established at Tucson
1893	Labor strife hits the copper mines, disrupting production
1898	The Spanish-American War
1901	Railroad linkage between the United States and Mexico is completed at El Paso, Texas, and Douglas and Nogales, Arizona
1903	Daniel Jackling establishes open pit copper mining in Utah and develops new metallurgical techniques to recover metal from low-grade ores
1909	The Yuma Territorial Prison is closed; all inmates are transferred to Florence, Arizona
1911-1916	Diaz removed as President of Mexico; Madero, Huerta, and Pancho Villa struggle to become the new leader of Mexico
1911	Salt River Dam #1 (Roosevelt Dam) is completed
1912	Arizona becomes the 48th state of the United States of America

CHAPTER 1

A Surprise Letter

MIDMORNING SUN STREAMED INTO THE dining room of the hotel as Konrad set his empty cup into a saucer, then twisted an unlit cigar in his mouth as he stared across the expanse of bright white cloths on unoccupied tables. The engineer was bored. His Ocotillo Silver Mine was producing a steady one hundred tons of ore a day, and placer gold reserves near Tent City seemed good for at least three more years. His next venture, as yet undetermined, was gnawing at him. Gold discoveries in Oatman and Prescott Valley were of moderate interest; Ed Schieffelin's silver discovery at Tombstone sounded like a major find. Rumors of something big going on at a copper prospect in Morenci could demand some follow up. But copper mining is a different sort of mining.

Archie, the dining room attendant, who presented him with a note from a visitor waiting in the hotel lobby, interrupted his musings. As Konrad opened the folded paper, he noticed the well-dressed Mexican, holding a wide brimmed hat in his hands. The man seemed familiar but Konrad couldn't come up with a name. Where have I seen that man before? he wondered. The note read, "I'm here, Mr. Bruner, with a message from Senor Amelio Rodriguez of Zacatecas, Mexico. May I join you, please?" As Konrad nodded a welcome to the man, he slowly recognized the courier as none other than Lumberto Villegas, his shotgun companion of over ten years ago. Both men brightened as they met, shaking hands, then embracing each other.

As Lumberto joined the German, he carefully handed Konrad a heavy parchment envelope embossed with a dark red wax seal. Calling

Archie for more coffee, Bruner cut open the seal to examine the message handwritten in Spanish. " Dear Konrad: It has been far too many years since you left Zacatecas and our hacienda. It pains me to tell you that our Luisa died in Barcelona, Spain, six weeks ago. Her body is being shipped to our ranch and should arrive here by the end of the month. At that time, Father Petrillo will conduct a funeral mass for our only child. I know you had special feelings for Luisa and hope that you will be able to join us for this memorial. If you are able to do so, Lumberto will escort you on the trip. We have missed you all these years and look forward to seeing you again. Respectfully, Amelio Rodriguez."

Konrad, tears welling in his eyes, read and reread the letter. Rubbing his hands over his chin and cheeks, he slowly shook his head. Old memories were revived. Looking into Lumberto's eyes, he murmured, "This is terrible news for the Rodriguez family and also for you and me. I have many, many questions but first, be assured that I will attend Luisa's funeral. Give me the afternoon to take care of a few odds and ends and we can leave first thing in the morning. You must be tired, my friend, so let me get you settled in my suite so you can get some rest."

As Konrad packed his saddlebags and clothing, he pondered questions that Lumberto would not be able to, or want to answer. What was Luisa doing in Barcelona? Was she on a trip? Had she been living there permanently? Had she married? What caused her death? It had been over ten years since he left Mexico, why hadn't the Rodriguez family contacted him? At the same time, Konrad Bruner recognized that he had never written to Luisa, as much as he had wanted to.

The next day, Konrad and Lumberto rode the stagecoach to El Paso, and then provisioned themselves with food and horses for the long trip south. The Mexican produced pistols, rifles, and ammunition; they could easily encounter marauding Apache Indians, renegade Civil War veterans, or Mexican bandits. The war had ended twenty years ago but remnants of the armies still remained criminals, ignoring the laws of both Mexico and the United States.

It took Konrad the better part of a week to get accustomed to saddle travel, trail food, and sleeping on hard ground. Lumberto did everything possible to reduce the strain but even his excellent cooking and guiding could only slightly reduce the roughness of cross-country travel. The two travelers followed the eastern slope of the Continental Divide, exchanging horses with friendly ranchers along the way. Virtually nothing was discussed about the loss of Luisa and the upcoming funeral. Lumberto led the party well; after two weeks of steady riding they reached the Rodriguez estate on the outskirts of Zacatecas. On arrival, the patron quietly embraced Konrad and instructed a servant to lead the German to his old room. " Sleep well, my friend. We'll talk in the morning after you have rested. Thank God you're here."

Konrad slept fitfully, tossing and turning, as he mulled over Luisa's death. Last seen, she was a beautiful, healthy woman. Even with the passing of time, she couldn't have been more than thirty or thirty-two years old when she died. While anxious to talk with Senor Rodriguez, an actual meeting with the man unsettled him. Something was missing; he could not explain his uneasiness.

On arising, he joined the senior Mexican at a breakfast table set for three. It overlooked a large patio festooned with potted ventana of yellow, violet, and red. Deep purple and red bougainvillea vines covered the adobe pillars supporting a second floor of the hacienda. A female servant brought steaming plates of fried eggs, beans, strips of beef, and tortillas to the two men and poured strong, chicory-laced coffee. The third chair and table setting remained unoccupied while Konrad and the wealthy landowner ate in conspicuous silence. Respectfully, Konrad waited patiently for his old friend to open the conversation, knowing his grief must be overwhelming.

As the maidservant cleared the dishes and refilled the coffee cups, Amelio looked at Konrad, finally breaking the silence. "Konrad, we have much to talk about and I am having trouble deciding where to begin. I'm sure you realize that my various business interests have done well over the years. Carlos Ortega has developed our silver mines into an empire; we are now the largest producer of silver in all of Mexico, and probably the world. He is anxious to see you again and show you how far we have progressed. My nephews have taken over my operations in Tampico and the fishing fleet in Guaymas. Many other talented people keep track of my factories in Mexico City. I am still very much involved with the ranch, cattle breeding, and farming. My greatest concern is the political unrest in our capital and deciding who will take over my interests when I leave this earth."

Konrad, noting the somberness of the patron's remarks, replied "Senor, you have accomplished much and nurtured many good people. I'm very much aware of the problem of getting and holding on to responsible workers but you seem to have succeeded quite well. It's good to hear that Carlos Ortega and your nephews have helped you build your businesses." Refusing a third cup of coffee, Konrad ventured further. "Your message of Luisa's death in Spain still has me in a state of shock. May I ask about the circumstances that took her from us at such an early age?"

Sighing heavily, Amelio Rodriguez played with his empty coffee cup and said, "While my business interests have helped me build a great fortune, my family circumstances have not fared as well. First, my wife died shortly after you left Mexico. Luisa was devastated and decided to join the Sisters of Magdalena. Her mother's untimely death was only part of the reason, however." Staring intently at Konrad, the older man pointed to the empty chair at the table. "You see, my friend, I am a grandfather."

Studiously, Konrad blinked his eyes, bit his lower lip and responded "Senor Rodriguez, I am happy for you but I don't understand what this has to do with Luisa joining a convent. Are you saying that Luisa was the mother of this child?"

"Konrad Bruner, I am trying to tell you that Luisa gave birth to a son twelve and half years ago and asked that he be named Carlos after his father, Konrad Bruner. I planned on having him join us for breakfast but decided that the shock to both of you would be too much. I decided to tell you first. Forgive me for keeping this secret for so long but Luisa insisted on it after she became pregnant, had young Carlos, and left Mexico for Spain."

CHAPTER 2

The Grandson

KONRAD SAT IN STUNNED SILENCE. He could not believe that his brief episode of lovemaking with Luisa had produced a child and that he would be kept unaware of the event for over twelve years. Excited, his heart pounded and the palms of his hands moistened. He searched for words to express his shock but none came. He had more questions than answers. At last he collected himself and asked the older man, "Why wasn't I told, even if I was hundreds of miles away in a different country? You surely knew where I was. What right did you have to keep this a secret?"

Senor Rodriguez exhaled heavily. "We have much to talk about, Konrad. Try to understand. Luisa was thrilled to know that she was going to have your baby and was not ashamed to tell her mother and father. She told us how much she loved you and how she went to you, hoping and praying to conceive a love child, as she called the baby. She was also adamant that you were not to be told; she assumed complete responsibility for the seduction. In the beginning, I was ready to send vigilantes after you but Luisa quickly changed our minds. Her love for you and the expected child was overwhelming. Also, bear in mind the complication of a forced marriage between a Catholic and a Protestant Lutheran, a topic you and Luisa discussed many times."

Konrad interrupted, "I still cannot understand why you would not have contacted me in Arizona. We could have come to some kind of arrangement."

The elder slowly smiled for the first time. "Yes, you have a point. But remember, I was dealing with a pregnant daughter, a distraught wife, and an extremely rigid Mexican Catholic attitude that insisted that I do everything right to deliver a healthy child for Rome. When Luisa gave us the news, she also told us of her plans. Believe me, she had given her future plans a great deal of serious thought. She'd spent a lot of time with Father Petrillo, the Mother Superior at the abbey in Guadalupe, and Anna Maria, her longtime maid and chaperone. When she broke the news to us of your love affair and her pregnancy, she was committed to leaving the ranch and Zacatecas."

When he finished his story, the patron sighed with exhaustion. "I need an hour or so in the saddle to clear my mind," he told Konrad. "I also need time to prepare to introduce my grandson to his father tonight at dinner. Please excuse me."

Konrad decided that a ride before dinner was a good idea and had a horse saddled for a trip to the escarpment where he and Luisa had shared many hours in conversation, always under the eyes of Anna Maria. He tried to analyze the information given to him by Senor Rodriguez. He started at the beginning, when he and Lumberto had departed for Texas and the New Mexico Territory.

At her Friday visit to Father Petrillo for confession, Luisa had confided her affair with Konrad Bruner and assured the padre that she was pregnant. The priest advised waiting a month for further proof; when sixty days had passed he conceded that the girl was indeed with child. He also advised Luisa that she should break the news to her parents, immediately.

A healthy baby boy was born in Tampico on April 17, 1872. Luisa was allowed to spend three days with her son, and then parted with the boy to join a group of novices preparing for the ocean voyage to Spain and the Monastery of Santa Maria. She was never to see her son again. When Esteban Carlos Rodriguez was six months old, he and his governess were transported four hundred miles west to the estate of his grandfather, where he would reside permanently.

Young Esteban became Carlos to the ranch staff and eventually to his family, Father Petrillo, and the locals. As the boy grew up, he and his grandfather became inseparable riding companions and friends. By the age of nine, young Carlos was an expert horseman who thoroughly enjoyed the routine of a working ranch. The women in the boy's life also made certain that he was schooled in English and French, knew his sums, and was conversant in history and the classics. Between the elder Rodriguez, his governess Florina, and the household servants, the boy grew up in a disciplined but loving environment. At twelve years of age, Carlos Rodriguez had developed into a strong, well-balanced young man.

Earlier, Luisa Rodriguez had completed her novitiate and become a nun, taking the name of Sister Alicia. She joined a group of city medical missionaries who tended poor and destitute Catalonian women, many of whom had borne illegitimate children. Sister Alicia and her fellow nuns Sisters Marguerite and Juanita toiled endlessly to establish a home and orphanage for women and children in Barcelona. Sister Alicia became a legend, working tirelessly as a midwife and manager of a clinic for downtrodden women.

Under the rule of her order Sister Alicia was allowed to write one letter a year to her family. She was also permitted to receive one letter a year from them but only after it was censored by the Mother Superior. Any detailed information about her son, with the exception that he was in good health, was purged from these correspondences. Then came a letter from the Mother Superior, informing the Rodriguez family of their daughter's death. A wave of influenza had swept through Barcelona, killing off hundreds of residents of the port city. It had been particularly severe in the barrio where Sister Alicia spent most of her time. Her death was a shock to her community of lost souls who looked up to her as a source of hope and forgiveness. Her body was embalmed and stored in a crypt at the monastery where it would remain pending her family's wishes for permanent burial. In a fog of grief, Senor Rodriguez requested the body of his only child be shipped home to Mexico for internment.

CHAPTER 3

Konrad Meets His Son

A WAGON MASTER HAD DELIVERED the sold mahogany casket to the hacienda several weeks ago. Final internment would take place when the mausoleum, crafted by skilled stonemasons, was completed. As Konrad digested the events of the past few days, he fought unsuccessfully to forgive Senor Rodriguez for keeping Luisa's instructions intact. The prospect of meeting his son only fortified his feelings toward the older man. All the same, his thoughts were tempered by his conversation with Florina, the governess, as they sat at a table enjoying the warmth of a sunny morning.

Florina was a tall, attractive woman who had devoted her life to raising Carlos. Her dark eyes and quiet beauty reminded Konrad of Luisa. He admired Florina for her love of the boy and her composure in describing his upbringing. "Senor Bruner, I have been with your son since he was three days old. He has been a good boy, attentive to his lessons and devoted to his grandfather. He is also a smart young man and at that stage where he is beginning to ask all sorts of questions. He knows his mother died in Spain, not all the details of course, but enough to satisfy his curiosity for now. I hope you can understand that he knows nothing about you, his father. You have a clean slate to work with. I can only warn you that he's a little confused about where you fit into his life." With a subtle smile, Florina glanced over Konrad's shoulder. "Ah, here he comes now."

Konrad stood up from the hardwood table as Esteban Carlos Rodriguez walked across the fieldstone patio accompanied by the elder Rodriguez. Both the boy and his grandfather, attired in vaquero riding clothes, removed their flat brimmed dark leather hats as they approached Konrad and Florina. The boy embraced Florina with a warm smile, then turned his gaze to Konrad as the patron introduced the German. Composed, Amelio Rodriguez looked at the boy and declared, "Esteban Carlos, this is your father, who has come from America to honor the memory of your dear mother." Young Carlos hesitated momentarily, and then stepped forward to shake his father's hand. "Sir, I am very pleased to meet you. Grandfather and Florina have told me about your adventures in America; I hope we will be able to spend some time together while you are here. I mean, before you leave for your home."

Suppressing an urge to smile, Konrad took in the boy's maturity and presence of mind. Looking directly at his son, he replied, "I am pleased to meet you, my son. I thank God for the loving care you have received from your grandfather and Florina. I must also apologize for being an absentee father all these years. I can only hope to make it up to you and your family here in Mexico." The introductions accomplished, Senor Rodriguez suggested they sit down at the table while servants roasted a calf over a mesquite carboncillo fire pit. The aroma of the roast, basted with herbs and spices, was tantalizing.

While a servant poured an estate-bottled red wine for the adults, Carlos sipped a concoction of orange, lemon, and lime juice. Innocently looking at his grandfather he confessed, "You know, Gran Pa Pa, I have tasted the wine processed at last year's harvest. Might I have a sip to celebrate this occasion?" The elder Rodriguez passed his glass to the boy, who took a swig and chimed, "Thank you, Gran Pa Pa. I think you and Senor Bruner will enjoy this wine as much as I have." Somewhat uncomfortable by being addressed as Senor Bruner, Konrad also realized that the boy had only met him a few minutes ago. Instinctively, Florina suggested, "Carlos, perhaps you should consider calling Senor Bruner father in the future." The youngster looked at his grandfather and Konrad, smiled sheepishly, and murmured, "Yes, Florina."

That evening the Rodriguez family and Konrad Bruner dined on a roasted calf, rice, beans, and squash as a group of troubadours serenaded them with traditional Mexican music. As the platters of food and bottles of wine were passed around, young Carlos gradually relaxed and opened up to the group, describing how he'd spent the afternoon with the ranch hands as they branded cows born the previous spring. With a grimace, he rolled up his shirtsleeves and showed off the cuts and bruises from the day's work. Shortly before sunset, Florina suggested to Carlos that it was bedtime, and while he protested mildly, he excused himself from the party. Wearily, he hugged his grandfather and turning to Konrad, offered his hand. "Goodnight, father." As Carlos turned to join Florina, Konrad Bruner watched in silence as tears filled his eyes. The evening had erased any misgivings he had over Luisa and her father keeping the boy's birth a secret. While he disagreed with their pact of silence of twelve years, he understood and accepted their decision.

When Senor Rodriguez suggested an after dinner drink, Konrad readily accepted. As the cooking fire slowly spent itself, the two men clinked glasses and toasted the health and well being of young Esteban Carlos. Cubano cigars were lit and a second round of the sweet liqueur was poured. Before the patron could say anything else, Konrad lifted his glass and offered, "Amelio, I must apologize to you, Luisa, and Florina for my thinking poorly of you for not telling me about the boy until now. I can only thank God and your family for raising such a fine young man. I am also sorry for not staying in touch with you all these years. I hope you will forgive me."

Surrounded by the darkness, illuminated only by the dying embers of the cooking fire, Amelio listened to Konrad's words with quiet emotion. "Thank you, my friend. Helping Florina raise the boy has been a particular joy for me. Having him in my household has given me a reason to live. The death of my wife and Luisa's decision to join the convent left a terrible void in my heart. Understand, I did my best to convince her when I suggested we contact you in Arizona. I should have been stronger; I made a bad decision but that is water over the dam as they say. So, compadre, we will forgive each other and start anew. We must think about the boy and how best we can shape his transition to manhood. Father Petrillo will not prevail this time."

Pouring a third round of drinks, Amelio and Konrad toasted Carlos and their beloved Luisa. The two men lifted their glasses one more time, drank, and then walked slowly back to the hacienda, their arms over each other's shoulders. Sister Alicia and her mother would have been pleased with the events of the day.

CHAPTER 4

A Plan for Carlos

ENCOURAGED BY KONRAD'S PRESENCE, SENOR Rodriguez prevailed upon Father Petrillo to perform the burial mass for Sister Alicia in Spanish. Initially, the padre had demanded that the service be conducted in Latin, but realizing that the senor was seriously considering a service in the cathedral at San Miguel, the priest relented. The memorial service was held in the family chapel, with the overflow of attendees standing on the patio of the hacienda. Father Petrillo conducted the service, honoring the "Saint of Barcelona." After the internment of the body in the newly constructed mausoleum, family members and guests adjourned to the courtyard for servings of food, wine, liquors, beer, and a multitude of toasts to the departed nun.

Esteban Carlos Rodriguez, accompanied by his grandfather and father, witnessed the ceremony in subdued silence. He understood the words but could not relate to a mother he had never met, let alone knew, and a mysterious father who had suddenly appeared out of nowhere only a week ago. Perplexed, he turned to Florina and his grandfather for an explanation of what had transpired. An attempt by Father Petrillo to explain the meaning of the service to the boy was thwarted by Florina who took Carlos by the hand saying, "Come with me, my son. We can talk about this later; it's been a long day for all of us." The padre smoldered, recognizing the influence the governess had over the boy. "Someday, when Carlos becomes a priest, that woman will understand that God takes a back seat to no one."

The ceremony of Luisa's burial behind them, Senor Rodriguez and Carlos, sometimes joined by Konrad Bruner, rode and talked together as they toured the ranch holdings. At times, the two older men conversed about political developments in Mexico and the United States, sharing their thoughts about the turmoil in Mexico City and America's emergence as an industrial power. While seemingly disinterested, Carlos listened closely to the conversation. "I am soon going to be a teenager," he thought. "Why are they being so protective? When will I have the opportunity to say something about my future?" He was not to be disappointed.

Periodically, Konrad received mail from Barney Pryor in Ribera, assuring him that his business interests were being well taken care of. Trusting his partner completely, the German gradually relaxed and began to enjoy the hospitality of the ranch and the friendliness of the patron and Florina. Quiet evenings on the patio with the charming governess were particularly enjoyable. Notions of romance entered the mind of the visitor. And why not?

Three weeks after Konrad's arrival in Mexico, the patron suggested a meeting in the elder's private study. Sitting before a crackling fire, Konrad was asked if he would like coffee, English tea, or a mixed drink of tequila. After pouring coffee for himself and his guest, the patron opened the conversation. "Konrad, I have spent much time looking to the future since Luisa left us. I'm pretty well finished with the business interests I have built up over the years. I have also studied the political problems here in Mexico and watched the Americanos north of here grow in ambition and strength. We accepted Maximilian as our leader; he couldn't deal with the various factions and paid for his ineptness with his life. I love my country dearly but we are a corrupt, politically immature rabble that may never learn how to govern ourselves. I am not optimistic that someone will emerge to lead our country into prosperity and international respect. I am personally part of this flawed system and pay a lot of people in Mexico City to look after my interests. Mordida is alive and well in our country and I don't expect to see things change in my lifetime."

The patron paused and glanced at his guest. "Ah, but I am straying from the subject I wish to talk to you about. The centers of my interests are the silver mines, cattle herds, and the rancho and hacienda where we are now sitting. They are my heart and soul. While I believe I'm in good health, I will die some day. I must make plans for the future and how you and Carlos fit into this considerable wealth. The boy has done well with his studies and loves working on the ranch. I'm prejudiced of course, but justly proud. But now we have important decisions to make to prepare him for his inheritance. As you well know, there are many people who depend on working for me to support their families. I wish to continue providing them with work. I believe we should consider having Carlos spend a couple of years in a military academy, followed by exposure to life in Mexico City, and then a college education in the United States. In this process, my friend, he must also get to know his father. There's one other thing, Konrad. The boy must be raised in the Catholic Church but away from Father Petrillo. That man sees Carlos as Mexico's next cardinal."

Konrad knew that the subject of inheritance and Carlos's education was inevitable but he'd hoped it would come at a later time. He'd thought about inviting Carlos for a visit to Arizona but hadn't planned much beyond that. One thing bothered him, though: the boy's name. If Carlos was indeed his son, shouldn't his legal name be changed to Esteban Carlos Rodriguez Bruner? He decided to bring up that question later.

"Senor Rodriguez, I've been so busy concentrating on getting to know Carlos that I haven't given much thought to the next five or ten years of his life. I agree with you that he speaks nicely and handles mathematics well and, of course, he's strong and looks older than he really is. I think he's also mature for his age and that perhaps we should ask him what he thinks about his future. Amelio, you know Carlos best. Why don't you present the subject to him? He may have some good ideas for us."

Senor Rodriguez hadn't considered involving his grandson in a discussion about his future but warmed to Konrad's suggestion. It was a radical departure from what most Mexican families did but maybe the German's approach could turn up something the two older men had not even thought about.

The next morning after breakfast, Senor Rodriguez suggested to Carlos that they look over the herd of bulls destined for the corrida in Mexico City. The boy always enjoyed watching the vaqueros move the animals from their winter pasture to the confinement of the inspection pens. He also liked mingling with the ranch hands while they feasted on spicy burritos, rolled tortillas filled with onions, spices, and pinto beans. In turn, the cowboys enjoyed teasing Carlos about schoolwork replacing riding and roping. There were limits to the joking, however. The hands recognized that someday the young boy would be their new patron.

Sitting on the top rung of a corral, Senor Rodriguez started the conversation by talking about the ranch. "Carlos, you seem to enjoy being with the vaqueros. Do you think you'd like to run the ranch someday?" The boy was startled by his grandfather's question but wasted little time in replying. "Gran Pa Pa, it would fulfill my wildest dream! You seem to be reading my mind. I've enjoyed fishing in the Sea of Cortez and working with Senor Ortega in the silver mines. And I loved my vacation trips to the big city. But my heart and soul is here at the ranch. I cannot imagine being anyplace else when I grow up. You see, Gran Pa Pa, you and Florina are my family."

"My dear grandson, those are fine words to hear but try to understand that your father is also family and will have something to say about your future. Spend some time with him while he's here. You will find that he is a very fine person."

Carlos nodded his consent. "Yes, sir. I will." But he knew his response was mainly an effort to please his beloved grandfather.

Over the next few days, Senor Rodriguez arranged for Konrad to spend time alone with Carlos. Father and son filled the hours talking about the ranch operations and the animals and crops that supported the surrounding villages. The boy was polite and friendly but uncomfortable talking about a mother he never knew with a father he'd just met only a month ago. Konrad sensed his son's awkwardness and switched the conversation. He listened with interest as Carlos told him about his cousins who were scattered in various parts of Mexico.

Late one evening, Konrad brought up the subject of his return to Arizona with the elder Rodriguez. "We could take a ship via Mazatlan to Guaymas, where we can enjoy a few days at the capital of western Mexico's fishing fleet. From Guaymas, we can coach our way to Hermosillo and Nogales. From there, we can hire horses and ride to Ribera. I think Carlos would enjoy the trip and it would give him a chance to see what his father's been up to all these years. I think it would be good for all of us. And I hope you will join us, Amelio."

Before the trio left Zacatecas, Konrad dispatched Lumberto to the Arizona Territory with a letter for Dr. Ben Lawson in Ribera. In the letter, Konrad asked the physician to look for appropriate housing for his traveling companions. He did not mention his relationship to Esteban Carlos.

CHAPTER 5

A Hospital for Ribera

BEN LAWSON, M.D., LEFT BRAD Scoville's office shaking his head in disappointment. He was sure his proposal to build a private hospital in Ribera was sound. But the banker didn't like Lawson's answer to "How are you going to pay back the loan of $5,000?" Taken aback by Scoville's rebuff, Lawson really wanted to ask, "Where the hell is your community spirit?" But he kept his thoughts to himself, figuring he'd come back to the banker with a revised plan on a better day.

Returning to his four-bed clinic, Lawson was greeted by Doc Gilroy. "Good morning, Ben. Why the sour face?" When Lawson explained his unsuccessful meeting with Brad Scoville, Gilroy removed his bifocals and began cleaning them, preparing an answer for his good friend. "Son, there's surely a need there. Between Ribera, Tent City and other folks within ten miles or so, we've probably got a population of 1,800. That's a lot of responsibility for one doctor, even if he has emergency help from an old sawbones like me. Your idea of an eight- or ten-bed hospital with a separate operating room makes good sense to me. Hell, times are changing and we've got to keep pace with what's going on. And I know as well as you do that Kate would like to have a house for herself and the kids. And don't jump all over Brad Scoville. He's a banker and they just think differently than most. He's got the responsibility for protecting his depositors and can't shell out money because some local has an idea. Were I in his shoes, I'd probably ask the same question. So, tell me Ben, how would you pay back the loan?"

The younger man looked at his friend in dismay. "Doc, the hospital idea isn't just about dollars and cents. You know damn well that medicine has made huge progress since the Civil War. Better facilities, better equipment, and a full time trained nurse would help us save more lives and reduce pain and suffering. I figured if I take 75 percent of my fees for the practice and 25 percent to pay off the loan, I'd likely have the money paid back in five years or so."

Doc scratched his chin and paused before responding. "I'm not so sure I agree with that, Ben. And anyway, I don't think it's the way to go. Sure, we read about doctor-owned hospitals in big cities that apparently do well but this is a frontier town where people barter for services. I don't think Brad Scoville would be happy to receive a ton of alfalfa or a butchered sow in place of a cash payment."

As Ben Lawson simmered, Doc Gilroy continued. "Look, Ben, don't get all riled up because I'm not agreeing with you. What about making the hospital a public hospital with directors, like our present water conservation board? Now, take it a step further. We approach five or six Ribera people who would like a hospital and be willing to put up some money to support it. You'd be the medical director and the others would oversee buildings and grounds, the nursing staff, medical supplies and equipment, and finance and administration. As proof of their interest and commitment to the plan, people would pledge $1,000 over a three-year period so we can acquire the land and start construction. With four or five other directors, you'd have your new hospital and be free to practice medicine without the burden of stuff that doesn't interest you. What do you think?"

Lawson sighed, crunched his knuckles, and looked Doc Gilroy in the eyes. "Why, you old schemer. Don't try to tell me that you just came up with that idea. Seems to me you've been dreaming up something like this for quite a spell. So, now that you've got me hooked on the idea, who else can we talk into coming up with the money and being a director? And paying over $300 a year for the next three years."

"Well, Ben, I'll start by volunteering myself to be one of the directors. I'll even work on the board. I've got the time and I think, the energy. We can also approach Barbara Casey, Garland Newport, and Brad Scoville. Ain't no way money bags can turn us down on this one. The town's folk would shame him into it. Then, we can talk to Konrad Bruner when he gets back from his trip to Mexico. There's no reason we can't approach others for lesser amounts to buy beds, furniture, and medical supplies. I think the town would rally around the idea of a new hospital. By the way, do we have any idea when Konrad plans on getting back this way?"

"Funny you asked, Doc. A Mexican courier came by yesterday with a letter from Konrad. He's on his way back and is sailing from Mazatlan to Guaymas. Then he's taking a coach to Nogales where he'll rent or buy horses to do the final trip overland. He's bringing a Senor Amelio Rodriguez and his grandson with him. I don't know what the plan is, but Kate has arranged for his guests to stay at the Volunteer Ranch. I have no idea who this Rodriguez person is or why his grandson is accompanying him. Maybe it's got something to do with the Ocotillo Mine. I'm thinking Konrad worked for this guy some years back before he came to Arizona. Anyway, let's talk to the people you mentioned and also make up a list of secondary donors."

Doc Gilroy got up from his chair and with a satisfied grin, shook Ben Lawson's hand, muttering, "Sounds good to me. Let's get on with it."

During dinner that evening, Ben explained Doc Gilroy's plan to build a public hospital supported by public funds to his wife Kate. "I don't know where you plan to build this hospital," she responded when hearing the news. "But don't tell me you are going to expand our house to fit in eight or ten beds. It's time we had some privacy, Ben. We need some space so the girls can be separate from the boys. And, one other thing: I'm tired of people coming and going here as if they own the place. So, getting the clinic and medical equipment out of our house will suit me just fine."

The doctor was surprised by his wife's reaction but realized how much the clinic and her job of nurse had intruded on their personal life. Maybe it was time for Kate Lawson to give up her career.

The next day, Ben Lawson and Doc Gilroy called on Garland Newport to explain their plan to build a new hospital and hopefully, gain her support. Garland listened attentively and, after a brief period of silence, offered, "I like the idea but I'm leery of committing a thousand dollars in cash at this point. But I will do this for you: I'll contribute five acres of land near town that will be worth more than a thousand dollars. But I want to run it by Dolores and her husband, Don, first. I expect they'll go along with the idea." A few days later, Garland informed Doc Gilroy that papers were being drawn up to complete the agreement.

Discussions with Barbara Casey and Brad Scoville were equally successful. Any proposal to Konrad Bruner would have to wait until he arrived in Ribera but recent developments virtually assured the doctors that they would have a new town hospital in the near future.

Lawson and Doc Gilroy then approached Dan Sullivan, spokesman for Tent City. The Irishman was skeptical at first, arguing that Tent

City wasn't part of Ribera. When the doctors provided a list of Tent City diggers treated at the Ribera clinic, Sullivan eventually agreed to hold a fund raiser a month or so in the future. With the endorsement of the miners, the project was formally announced in the *Ribera Territorial*. The same issue of the paper announced the arrival in Ribera of Mrs. Sophie Kaminski of Silverton, Colorado, and the new owner of the Whitman Hotel. The announcement declared Mrs. Kaminski's plan to build new rooms and refurbish the saloon so that traveling light opera companies and minstrel shows would have a place to perform for the town's citizens. Mrs. Bascomb, president of the ladies' garden club expressed her displeasure with the news of an improved saloon. Secretly, her husband and his fellow poker players smiled and looked forward to the new diversion.

While Ribera grew and prospered as the 1880s drew to a close, conditions at the San Carlos Indian Reservation worsened. The U.S. Army, acting on a directive from Washington, D.C., was about to move Chiricahua Apaches from a large area of good hunting to the already crowded and disease-ridden confines of San Carlos. Some of the weary, hungry families would make the move but a small group of warriors and their wives and children had other ideas. They decided to take an armed stand against the treachery and broken agreements of the politicians in the East.

CHAPTER 6

Corruption on the Reservation

CALEB BENSON CAST AN APPROVING eye over the warehouse stocked with flour, dried beef, beans, and shiny new shovels, rakes, and hand tools delivered by the army from Santa Fe. His trading post, one of four supply points on the San Carlos Reservation, was producing profits that would embarrass most frontier traders. Sure, it was a little risky shortchanging the Indians and having the post executive officer as a partner, but another year or so of this effort and Caleb Benson would be able to retire and return to New Orleans in style. Making his own whiskey and selling it to the Indians was a bonus.

In 1865, the Navajos surrendered at Canyon de Chelly, a travesty facilitated by Kit Carson, a friend of the tribe for many years. Carson and the army burned the Navajo crops and forced the tribe to walk to a reservation. Hundreds of Indians starved and died during "the long march." Kit Carson's treachery virtually destroyed the Navajo Nation as a fighting force. Adding to the misery, President Ulysses S. Grant established a policy whereby Arizona Indians were to be trained as farmers under the administration of the Dutch Reformed Church. The fact that many of the Indians were sheepherders or hunters and gatherers was totally ignored by the policy-makers in Washington. A few warriors, mainly those belonging to the Chiricahua Apache, refused the government order to take up farming.

The Chiricahua Apache chieftain, Aguijador, a distant relative of Geronimo, was one who refused to cooperate with the army. He was one of the few Indian leaders who recognized the white man's goal: to squeeze the heart and soul of the Indians into submission or extermination. Most tribal leaders were tired of fighting and wanted peace; they hoped the White Father in Washington would provide adequate food and clothing for all Arizona Indians. Unfortunately, the federal government managed to effectively send mixed messages to the frontier West. Army orders were inconsistent, top generals were transferred frequently, and vigilante groups, inflamed by Indian atrocities, declared open war on the tribes.

In 1871, three hundred Aravaipai Apache tribesmen and their families surrendered to the U.S. Army near Fort Grant, Arizona. Believing that the peace commission was sincere, they relaxed their guard only to be attacked by a Tucson citizen army. The whites tore through the Apache encampment, killing and wounding most of the Indians. The history of the massacres at Canyon de Chelly and Camp Grant were burned into Aguijador's memory. Embittered, he reminded the elders of the white man's dishonesty and vowed to fight the army and the white settlers to the death. "There will be no more compromises, no more surrenders; and we, the last of the Apaches, will protect our land, our families, and fight to our deaths, if necessary," he exclaimed.

Chanting their loyalty, more than seventy of Aguijador's warriors drank tiswin, an alcoholic concoction made from desert plants, and circled a huge bonfire, working themselves into a frenzy. Retiring to his wikiup, Aguijador remarked to an aide, "From now on, we will be on the attack; no more waiting for food to be rationed out by crooked government agents, no more hiding from the troopers, and death to the turncoat Indians who are the eyes and ears of the pony soldiers."

Not many Apaches sided with Aguijador. When the army, following orders from Washington, shut down the allocated Apache territory of over fifty square miles, most of the tribe moved to the San Carlos Reservation, already crowded with White Mountain Apaches and Yavapai Apaches. This move eventually cost the lives of hundreds of Indians as corrupt traders, misguided missionaries, and the U.S. Army did nothing to alleviate the spread of disease that decimated the tribes.

A few people profited from the move of the Indians to the reservations. Local merchants supplied food, blankets, and mules to the tribes, government agents doled out rations from their trading posts, and dishonest soldiers stole food and pillaged Indian camps while indifferent officers looked the other way. Other whites were happy to see an end to Indian uprisings; to them, the crowding of the tribes on the reservations was simply a necessary evil.

Lieutenant Vince Booker was one of the few frontier cavalrymen who respected the Indians and did everything in his power to treat

them fairly. Booker had been promoted from sergeant to second lieutenant after exhibiting brave, disciplined conduct in several battles.
Now stationed at the San Carlos Reservation, he could readily see that
while Washington may have had good intentions, the system of dealing
with the tribes was deeply flawed. Crooked traders and soldiers pilfered
food and equipment procured for the Indians. Well-meaning missionaries were unable to deal with the problems. Experienced thieves who
had no interest in the welfare of the Indians outfoxed them at every
turn.

When Booker recognized Caleb Benson on the San Carlos Reservation, he knew that the trader was almost certain to be involved in the
profiteering of government goods. Proving it was something he had
failed to do at Fort Gore, however. The unsolved mystery of Limping
Bear's death reminded Booker that he was dealing with a shrewd criminal, capable of almost anything. With a new commanding officer and
an unknown executive officer, Booker knew he would need ironclad
evidence before making any accusations against Benson. The real problem was that Lieutenant Booker was frequently called on to chase down
Indians who left the reservation in the hope of a better life. At least he
saw to it that when captured, the runaways were properly fed and
clothed. His exploits did not go unnoticed by tribal leaders, who
learned to trust the soldier.

During the cold, wet winter of 1884, Aguijador was challenged to
keep his followers and their families together. Rather than attacking to
kill, he resorted to stealth, sending out small patrols to steal horses, cattle, or mules. On one occasion, he led a group of warriors that made off
with three, fully loaded pack mules while soldiers were having breakfast.

With the onset of spring, his band made their way back to the Dragoon Mountains where they set up camp in a well-protected, secluded
canyon. Thick branches, up to four inches wide and eight feet long,
were cut and formed into a circular skeleton and tied down with strips
of flexible green bark. The domed structure, resembling an upside
down bird's nest, was then covered with thin branches and secured with
more thongs that circled the structure horizontally. The completed
wikiup was secure from all but the worst weather. With his camp hidden deep in the rugged mountains, Aguijador was prepared to lead his
warriors to virtually anywhere in southern Arizona and northern Mexico. His fighters were well-rested and itching for combat.

Replenishing food and supplies for the encampment was their
first priority, so the main body broke up into small, mobile units and

pillaged the Sulphur Springs Valley. They attacked farms and ranches, burned the buildings, and killed the families without mercy. The Indians took very few prisoners. One exception was the capture of Sunny, a young blond girl whose brother and parents were slaughtered. Her light hair and fierce resistance enabled her to survive the rampaging Apaches, who respected bravery in the face of attack.

The Apaches brought Sunny back to Aguijador's camp where she was renamed Soleado and assigned to the care of an elderly squaw who protected her from the young, curious males who were still too young to ride with the warriors. At the insistence of the chieftain, Soleado became part of the tribe and was raised as an Apache.

The murderous attack on Sulphur Springs Valley caught the attention of the press and stirred up anti-Indian demands for the extinction of the marauders. Additional troops were sent to bolster garrisons at Arizona forts, including Fort Gore.

When Lieutenant Booker was transferred back to Fort Gore, he accepted the order from Major Garrison with suspicion. Over the past few months, Booker had discovered that the executive officer and Caleb Benson were close friends and likely involved in the shorting of food that was allocated to Section A of the San Carlos Reservation. Government food and equipment was being sold to settlers and miners, the cash being pocketed by Benson and probably Garrison. The lieutenant felt that he was close to linking Benson to a specific theft but was thwarted when his sole witness, a trusted Indian trading post clerk, was discovered dead with his throat cut.

At post headquarters, Major Garrison handed Booker his written orders. "Mr. Booker, Apache tribesmen have overrun Sulphur Springs Valley. Settlers, miners, and ranchers are being killed and chased off their land. Fort Gore has requested help and, because of your extensive field experience dealing with the Indians, the general himself has requested that you lead a reinforced platoon to render assistance. A contingent of six men, led by Sergeant Parry, is being assigned to you. Parry and his squad have recently completed training on the new Gatling gun, which will give you unprecedented firepower. I suggest you meet with the sergeant as soon as possible and get ready to move out. You will report to the executive officer at Fort Gore. Unless you have any questions, you'd best get moving. We've got a lot of angry people in the Valley screaming for army assistance."

Lieutenant Booker saluted, did a smart about face and left Major Garrison's office. His story sounded authentic, but he wondered if

Caleb Benson had something to do with his transfer. And just as he was getting ready to spring a carefully planned trap on the wily trader.

Booker's detective work into missing stores had been supported by Hugh Packard, the Methodist minister in charge of over four hundred Indian men, women, and children. Packard knew food was being stolen, but had little time to deal with the problem; his main concern was the overall poor health of his charges. "Mr. Packard, I've been transferred to Fort Gore and I really don't know who my replacement will be. We both know that Caleb Benson and possibly Major Garrison are involved in food and blankets being stolen and sold off the reservation. I'm hopeful I'll be back here in a couple of months, but that's up to the army. When I do get back, we'll pick up the investigation again. Be careful; Benson is a ruthless crook and murderer. Good luck and keep your eyes open."

Vince Booker then checked in with the post armorer, who gave him a rundown on the Gatling gun and the crew serving the weapon. "We've only got two of these things; they just got here a few weeks ago. I've watched the crews train on them and I've got to admit, that gun can throw out more lead than I've ever seen. You really have to see it in operation, Lieutenant. It's still experimental and tends to jam, but if fed properly and cranked right, it's one helluva piece of weaponry."

Booker looked at the Gatling gun and wondered how it would fight off Indians on horseback who could move quickly and fire accurately. He decided to reserve judgment until he'd met Sergeant Parry and his crew and witnessed a firing drill on the range.

The cavalry troop left San Carlos, forty-two men strong. A pair of mules pulled the Gatling gun in the bed of a wagon, so going was slow. And vulnerable to attack, thought Booker. Late on the third day, the troop arrived at Fort Gore. The fort was in far better shape than a year ago, when Lieutenant Booker was sent up to San Carlos. The executive officer, Major Griswold, welcomed the cavalry contingent and showed particular interest in the awkward looking Gatling gun.

The major gave Booker an appraisal of the military situation. "When Washington closed down the Chiricahua enclosure, most of the Apaches moved north to the San Carlos Reservation, but not all of them. This animal Aguijador convinced more than seventy warriors and their followers to stay behind and fight, and that's what they're doing. In the last month, they've attacked ranches and farms all over the Sulphur Springs Valley and have killed at least fifty people; some were women and children. Normally, with the help of Apache scouts, we would have his hideout spotted by now, but our scouts fear capture and torture and won't venture very far without army protection. The enemy seems to be able to watch us and stay clear of us. So, we're at a Mexican standoff, only the civilians are scared to death, screaming for protection and we've lost our Indian eyes and ears. The general has suggested we try negotiating with this guy, but honestly, I wouldn't know where or how to begin. Lieutenant, you know the territory. Do you think it's possible that Aguijador would sit down and consider stopping the attacks?"

"Major, I've been away from Fort Gore for over a year. I've never had a personal run in with Aguijador, but I sense from what you tell me that he will not listen to any talk from the U.S. Army. He doesn't trust us, and with good reason. We've broken just about every treaty we've agreed to with the Indians."

Griswold listened intently to the younger man's statements. "Are you siding with the Indians, Lieutenant?" he asked.

"No sir, I'm just giving you my thoughts on why it's going to be difficult to subdue this Indian. He's a lot like Geronimo: crafty and ruthless but genuinely concerned for the welfare of his people. He knows how his people are being treated at San Carlos and is convinced that we're out to destroy his nation. In my judgment, we are wasting our time thinking we can solve this problem by horse-trading. He's past that stage."

A few minutes of silence passed as the major pondered what he had just heard. "In view of your position Booker, will you have a problem following U.S. Army orders to fight or capture these criminals?" Lieutenant Booker looked at his superior officer with a glint of steel in his eyes. "Major, I've been in this man's army a good part of my life and if you'd read my fitness reports, you wouldn't ask that question. Rest assured sir, I will do my best to protect my platoon and carry out the major's orders."

Without a dismissal, Lieutenant Booker saluted, did an about face, and left the room. Major Griswold, stung by the fierceness of Booker's reply, returned the salute and remained silent.

Booker was nearly certain that Aguijador wouldn't make a frontal assault on the fort but decided that a demonstration firing of the Gatling gun would help dispel any such thoughts. He set up a field exercise outside the fort and instructed Sergeant Parry and his crew to fire at targets about three hundred yards away. The NCO set up the Gatling gun and peppered targets with serious accuracy. The discovery of the weapon and the noise and demolition of the targets did not go unnoticed by Apache scouts.

Back in the Dragoon Mountains, Aguijador and his men rested after three weeks of tearing up the countryside. Their camp was fully stocked with food and provisions, most of the families were healthy again, and casualties had been minor. The arrival of additional pony soldiers concerned the chieftain, but he would shift attacks to Sonora, Mexico, for a period, while he studied just what the army troops had in mind. Confident that the soldiers wouldn't follow him across the border, Aguijador prepared for his next expedition. "The war is just beginning," he thought.

CHAPTER 7

Don Richmond Visits Phoenix

THE KILLING OF GREG NEWPORT at the Bowie River Dam and the natural death of his father, Dale Newport, created a huge leadership void on the River Bend Ranch. While Dale's widow, Garland Newport, owned the ranch outright most chores were handled by her daughter Dolores and her husband, Don Richmond. A native of Illinois, Richmond had earned a degree in veterinary medicine. He and Dolores had a brief courtship in Chicago where she was studying law. Shortly after their marriage, they moved to Ribera to help run the ranch, tend the stock, and manage the irrigated acreage that produced hay, wheat, corn, and garden vegetables. In spite of Don Richmond's significant contribution to upgrading the cattle and horse population, he never felt part of the family. His mother-in-law Garland was always polite and friendly but Dale and Greg Newport ran the ranch, made all the decisions, and kept Richmond at arm's length. With father and son now buried in the ranch cemetery, Dolores and Don gradually assumed responsibility for the family holdings. When Don formally became ranch foreman, exercising control of fifteen hands, Dick Canton, lead wrangler, readily accepted Don's new role and fully supported him.

By the mid-1880s the ranch was again running smoothly under the supervision of the Richmonds and their children, Dale and Elizabeth. Both youngsters were healthy and outgoing and loved ranch life. The success of the ranch, due mainly to the sale of cattle and horses to the U.S. Army, actually forced Don Richmond to look at his long range plans. He chatted with Barney Pryor about a Ribera-Tucson transportation link, but after close examination, decided not to pursue the scheme. Barney also offered Don an opportunity to start up a commercial building company but that didn't appeal to Richmond either. Then an article in the *Ribera Territorial* caught his eye.

Farmers in central Arizona were beginning to build irrigation canals to support the growing of wheat, barley, and vegetable crops. Mormons had established a community called Lehi east of town and were already busy farming the land. The newspaper article also mentioned how periodic droughts upset the normal availability of river water, a situation that required cooperation between the farmers to finance construction of dams. To the north, the town of Phoenix was growing, only recently having changed its name from Pumpkinville. The Salt, Verde, and Gila River basins offered a huge opportunity for agriculture on a grand scale. When asked for her opinion, Dolores Richmond encouraged her husband to look into the irrigation problems of Phoenix. She knew Don was bored now that the ranch was under control and felt that future growth would someday make Phoenix a major city. Her keen business instincts told Dolores that Phoenix would outpace Tucson and Prescott and might even become the state's capital one day.

Garland Newport looked out her kitchen window and observed Don Richmond as he issued instructions to their ranch hands. It had been years since the death of her son Greg and two years since her husband had passed away. She sorely missed Greg, who ran the ranch on a day-to-day basis for his father and frequently joined his mother for midmorning coffee and conversation. She never got over his untimely death during the Bowie River wars and still kept his room in the ranch house the same as the day he died. Even though she knew that needy people in town could use his clothes, she couldn't bring herself to dispose of them. Garland's daydreaming was cut short as her daughter Dolores entered the kitchen. "Good morning, Mom. I think I'll just have some coffee and a biscuit for breakfast. I want to have a good, two-hour geography lesson with Dale and Elizabeth. I want them to know more about the eastern United States. They're pretty good on the West and Mexico, but have no idea where the big cities are." Don Richmond, who poured himself a mug of rich, black coffee, joined the women. "It looks like we're going to have a good day," he announced. "I'm going into town shortly so if there's anything you need, let me know and I'll pick it up for you. I'll be taking the stage to Tucson and Phoenix later on. I plan on visiting Henry Dempsey in Tempe to talk to him about Salt River irrigation. Remember, I talked with him a few months ago. It was right after his appointment to the state legislature to organize some sort of a co-op to allocate and control water availability. He looked me up to find out how we had settled our problems on the Bowie between the miners and ranchers. The Salt River basin is a much, much larger problem of course, but maybe I can be of some help. I'll be meeting with Henry and others to look at a few of their irrigation projects and get an idea of just what the problems are."

In 1875, Phoenix was a town of about 1,800 people. The territorial capital was in Tucson but, once again, was to be relocated to Prescott. The distance between Tucson and Phoenix—a straight line of 125 miles—was normally a three-day trip by horse and buggy. In the early 1880s, Phoenix was growing rapidly as farmers wisely figured that irrigation projects would eventually provide protection against droughts and floods. It was this development that drew Don Richmond's attention.

Richmond's coach pulled into the stopover settlement of Casa Grande shortly after dark. Rising early the next morning for a hearty breakfast, he climbed aboard the coach for the final leg of the trip north. Henry Dempsey was waiting for him when he entered the lawyer's Tempe office. Both men were anxious to study the valley's problems and work out a solution to the conflicted views of organizing and funding a master plan.

Using a large table in his well-appointed office, Dempsey spread out a map showing the several rivers that comprised the valley water district. The Verde from the north and the Gila from the southeast joined the Salt, rising in the mountains of northeast Arizona. Snowmelt and rainfall for all three rivers was unpredictable, restricting well-planned planting and harvesting. With an adequate water supply, double and triple crop plantings were possible. But torrential rainfall could wreck havoc and destroy the farmers' investment.

"Don, I don't want to bore you, but I think a little history will help you appreciate this area before we start our tour tomorrow," Dempsey began. "Hohokam Indians settled this valley around 300 B.C. We think there were about 400,000 of them living in an area of about 45,000 square miles. They built and maintained more than 300 miles of major canals and another 1,000 miles of smaller waterways. I know this sounds amazing but archaeologists from Yale and Princeton insist that these numbers are pretty accurate. So, for the moment, let's assume that the professors know what they're talking about. The Hohokams occupied this land expanse for over 1,750 years then mysteriously disappeared around 1450 A.D. Some say they were forced to move because of a prolonged drought; others suggest internal squabbling over who would grow what crops, where, and how much water would be allocated for irrigation. The Hohokams are possibly the ancestors of the Pimas and the Papagos, but we don't know for certain. That's more than you wanted to know, but I'm sure you can appreciate the extent of the canals, all hand-dug with primitive tools, by the way. Anyway, what you'll see tomorrow are the remnants of an ancient civilization that supported a population of several hundred thousand people."

"We've re-dug many of the original Hohokam canals to create a network of interconnected waterways that works fine most of the time," Dempsey continued. "Wheat, barley, corn, squash, and some tobacco and cotton are the main crops in the valley. But when we get heavy rains in a short period, like in January, flooding can wipe out farms, particularly in certain areas. But, back to the Hohokams for a moment: They were skilled irrigation engineers and equally expert farmers. The largest of their canals were 15 miles long and up to 33 feet wide and perfectly calibrated to drop 2.5 meters of water per mile, enough distance to sustain a flow rate that would flush out unwanted silt. They built miles and miles of lateral canals and ditches, all with hand labor and elementary tools. It's really incredible when you think about it."

That evening Henry Dempsey continued his presentation, but only after he and Don Richmond dined on a dinner of corn tortillas, rice and beans, liberally washed down with local beer. Dempsey brought along some Indian artifacts to illustrate the afternoon history lesson. "Take a look at these tools, Don. They are ancient Hohokam stone knives, planting sticks, and digging tools made from slate and pieces of broken pottery. I still can't comprehend the number of man-hours required to construct the network of canals. I could go on for hours on how they lived but like everyone else, can't tell you about how or why they disappeared. Let's turn in for the night, so we can get an early start in the morning." Exhausted from the coach ride, a hearty meal and several steins of beer, Don readily agreed.

Before the day was out, Dempsey and Richmond had visited the confluence of the Verde and Salt rivers and the place where the Gila joined up with the two. While the Gila was almost dry, Richmond could see how high the water reached at flood stage by spotting pieces of debris still clinging to low tree branches. It was not hard to imagine the toll a rapidly flowing, flooded river could take on the surrounding farmland. Riding back into town, Henry Dempsey commented, "Mother Nature can be unpredictable, and we survive because we seem to have three good years to one that's poor. The real problem we have is individual canal owners who fight one another over water rights and refuse to look at the big picture. We've got a bunch of independent growers who worry about their own investment and say 'the hell with anyone else.' Or we have the cotton farmer who needs thirty inches of water to grow his crop, while the guy planting wheat or barley needs much less. You'll meet some of these people tonight at our grange meeting. Most are skeptical that we can agree on anything, but a few believe a regional approach to irrigation control is the only way to grow. There's no question in my mind that we'll need federal money to build containment reservoirs and a major dam. That's a long way off, but we have to start planning or it won't happen. This is my meeting to run, so I hope you don't mind my calling on you for a few comments."

The saloon where the grange meeting was being held filled rapidly as Henry called the meeting to order. "Gentlemen, we're here tonight to see if we can create an organization that will manage the flow of water through our canal system, so that all growers are treated fairly. We also want to prevent speculators who are not farmers from buying up acreage strictly for resale and quick profits." There was minor grumbling from the audience but most attendees nodded in agreement.

Del Landry was the first one in the crowd to make a comment. "Henry, your idea makes sense but there are too many variables to contend with. I suppose you can point to the Mormons as a way to establish a good cooperative but we ain't Mormons. Hell, most people in this room don't even bother to attend church on Sundays." Laughter ensued, then the room quieted down again. Henry Dempsey plowed ahead. "Look folks, we all know that different crops need different amounts of water and that soil conditions vary a lot. But unless we band together to regulate the availability of irrigation water, we're going to have chaos. Some of you have heard about the ruckus down south over water rights on the Bowie River. Well tonight, we have the man who helped solve that problem. Please listen to him, because the solution he's going to talk about worked out well for all parties. Gentlemen, here's Don Richmond of Ribera, a veterinarian turned rancher, farmer, and politician."

Don rose and stood in front of the table. Looking out over the audience, he began, " The fight over water rights came to a head when five men died in a gun battle over the construction of a dam. Now, the Bowie River flows year round most of the time and we get more water than you do. The River Bend Ranch needed water early in the day, just like the miners. So, we built a system of floodgates whereby we could shift water back and forth to satisfy each party. We also built a couple of small lakes on the ranch property to store water. The system isn't perfect but it allows the miners to prospect and the ranch to feed the animals and grow wheat, corn, and some vegetables. We have a five-man board that meets monthly to oversee the needs of the community, including drinking water."

Dan Perkins, leaning against the bar, shook his head and spoke, "With all due respect, Mr. Richmond, but we're looking at thousands of acres of ground, several hundred farmers and three untamed rivers. And we bounce back and forth between drought and flooding."

Don listened calmly and then replied, "Mr. Perkins, you're right. The River Bend Ranch dispute with the miners doesn't come close to what is involved here. However, I truly believe that our spirit of cooperation, driven by the loss of five lives, can be duplicated in your setting. My point is this: The men in this room have to want to develop a government structure that will be fair and equitable to all parties. I plan to spend the next few weeks studying the area, talking with several growers, territory officials, and others to see if perhaps there is a solution. You all recognize the present situation is a temporary one. Let's see if we can come up with something that we can all live with permanently. When I have a plan that is worth talking about, I'll come back here and present it to you."

During the following week, Don Richmond and Henry Dempsey reconnoitered the Salt, Verde, and Gila River systems. They reviewed existing documents that enabled them to produce a preliminary map of the valley, showing farmland ownership, major canals and tributaries, and the location of floodgates. They made a duplicate of the map and stored the original in Dempsey's office. Don took the copy back to Ribera for further study and consultation. "Henry, give me a month or so to study this information and talk with folks who know something about weather, river flows, farming, and irrigation. When I feel confident I have a worthwhile package to talk about, I'll come back here and let you take a look at it. This is a project that could lead to the creation of a major agricultural region and help us on the road to statehood." Henry looked at his partner with an admiring grin: Don Richmond's enthusiasm was infectious.

CHAPTER 8

Sophie Arrives in Town

SOPHIE KAMINSKI BREATHED A SIGH of relief as her private coach, battered and dusty after 800 miles of travel, slowed to a halt in front of the Whitman Hotel, the only hotel in Ribera. Eyeing the structure with an experienced gaze, she decided that at least from the outside, it looked to be in reasonable shape. It was early evening, in the middle of the week, and only a few people were walking on the boardwalk that stretched from the hotel to Barney Pryor's livery stable. Lights flickered in several houses on the main street as people were beginning to turn in for the evening.

Her driver, Nick Lacy, helped Sophie out of the coach and walked with her to the lobby of the hotel. Nick, a strapping hulk of a man, had been Sophie's escort and security for more than ten years, when she first went to Silverton, Colorado. While he was now pushing sixty, Nick Lacy was still a formidable protector, well schooled in fisticuffs and equally capable with a pistol or sawed-off shotgun. His friend, Lonnie Gomez, had proven to be an excellent cook and guide on the trail through northeastern Arizona Indian country. Sophie was grateful for their protection and companionship of the lengthy journey.

Straightening her hat and removing her gloves, the new owner of the Whitman Hotel strode to the front desk and asked for Mr. Harvey Cartwright. The clerk arched his eyebrows and considered asking the lady the purpose of her visit, but the presence of two male companions with side arms told him it really wasn't part of his job to screen visitors, particularly one as pretty as this young lady. It wasn't long before Cartwright came down the stairs to introduce himself. "Ah, Mrs.

Kaminski. It is a distinct pleasure to finally meet you. You must be weary from the trip. What can I do for your comfort?" Sophie thanked Cartwright for his offer and suggested a supper for Nick Lacy and Gomez. All she wanted for herself was a private room and a hot bath. Tea and a sandwich in her room would also be welcome. "Mrs. Kaminski, we have a reserved suite for you in the rear of the hotel, where it will be quiet. I'll send Mary up to help you get settled in. I'm at your service at any time, but will plan on seeing you in the morning at your convenience. Good, evening, Mrs. Kaminski." Sophie was tempted to correct Cartwright on her marital status but decided perhaps being a widow would deflect prying questions about her past.

Harvey Cartwright was pleased that the new owner of the Whitman Hotel had finally arrived to take over the operation. He was anxious to get his ailing wife to Tucson, where she would receive better care in one of the sanitariums. He'd received a very good price for the hotel and saloon; only Brad Scoville knew the details of the transaction. If the people of Ribera had any idea who Sophie Kaminski really was, the ladies' guild would raise cane. "She sure is a looker," Cartwright thought. He anticipated lots of tongue wagging when Sophie started visiting around town.

At thirty-five years of age, Sophie Kaminski was a "looker" and she knew it. Of medium height with light brown hair, she had a firm, well-proportioned figure and a smile that attracted men like bees to honey. As an orphan from Chicago, she had moved west to Denver as a housemaid to Mr. and Mrs. Hobart Bartholomew, he a mining baron with properties in Leadville, Cripple Creek, and Silverton. When Sophie and Hobart were discovered in bed together by the tycoon's wife, Sophie had been terminated with a month's salary and a note of introduction to Maude Pauley, owner of Silverton's upscale bawdyhouse. Sophie had resisted the opportunity at first, but soon found out that entertaining wealthy gamblers and mine owners was a lot better than working in a laundry or being a saloon barmaid. Within a few years, she had saved enough money to buy the establishment. On leaving, Maude offered, "Its time to stop being a working girl, Sophie. Your new job is to build a good clientele and manage the place."

Over the next five years, Sophie expanded the operation and cashed in on two prospecting investments that had made her a wealthy woman. When she learned that the Whitman Hotel in Ribera was for sale, Sophie decided it was time to start a new career in a new location where, hopefully, her past would remain a secret.

Her meeting with Harvey Cartwright the following morning was cordial and, after conversing with banker Scoville, Sophie informed him that with the hotel staff already in place, Nick Lacy would be the new manager, starting immediately. "I thank you for your hospitality, Mr. Cartwright," Sophie declared. "You've answered most of my questions, so please feel free to leave things to me and depart for Tucson at your convenience." Cartwright sensed he was being forced out of town but after ten years as the owner of the hotel he was happy to move on as quickly as possible. His wife, Bessie, would also be pleased with the news.

After introducing Nick Lacy to the cooks, dining room servers, and housemaids, Sophie donned casual western clothes and made her own inspection of the town, general store, clinic, and livery stable. She was very pleased to see that Ribera had a church, a new school, and two doctors. On her return to the hotel, she inspected the lobby, dining room, kitchen, and guest rooms and decided that they were more than adequate. After a lunch of Chinese pork and noodles, she returned to her suite. As she lay down for a brief nap, she decided that she'd made a good decision in buying the hotel. She also decided to let Lonnie Gomez investigate Tent City by himself.

Sophie was confident that hotel operations were well under control with Nick Lacy running things, so she decided to accompany Gomez on his visit to Tent City. They rode down river to watch the miners panning for gold before entering the village. In spite of her experience in Silverton, Sophie was shocked by the mud, filth, and squalor of the place. Tent City was typical of highly transient mining towns. There was no sanitation system or signs of permanence. Buildings consisted of tents; some resting on platforms, to roughly constructed shacks of wood and tarpaper, and many lean-tos. She pulled her hat brim down as she viewed two wooden buildings under construction. Nearby, in a kitchen covered with a canvas canopy, workers served food and a saloon dispensed beer and liquor, while a handful of card players occupied a few gaming tables. Tent City reminded Sophie of other western mining camps but she had no interest in participating in the raucous environment, even though there was money to be made with the miners, gamblers, and prostitutes. Men gawked at her but made no gestures or uttered words in her direction. One half-drunk miner by the name of Burr Tilden, sipping whiskey, did take notice though. "Damn, that's a fancy looking woman," he thought. "She sure reminds me of someone I'd like to meet again. Now, who in hell was that?"

Riding into Ribera, Sophie heard someone calling out. "Hello, Miss. Can we talk about that coach you left here a week or so ago?" Directing Gomez to continue on back to the hotel, Sophie squinted into the sun where she saw Barney Pryor standing and wiping his forehead with a red, cotton bandana. She couldn't place him at first or understand what he was talking about, but then remembered that Nick had taken her coach to the town's livery stable. "Pardon, me. I'm Barney Pryor. I own this here barn, stables, and horses. I've been hunting for a genuine Concord coach for a long time. I'm hoping you might be interested in selling me the one you left here. If you were to put a fair price on that road warrior, I'd be mighty pleased to take it off your hands."

Sophie shifted in her saddle as she looked down at Pryor. She quickly glanced at his large frame, strong hands, and smiling face. Was this Barney something getting fresh with her? Or was he really offering to buy the old, stiff coach that had nearly ruined her back on the trip from Colorado? Then she saw the sign over the door, "Barney Pryor, owner." Thinking it was probably a good guess, Sophie replied, "I'm so sorry, Mr. Pryor, but I'd almost forgotten about that wreck of a coach. I'm curious. Just what do you plan on doing with it?"

"Well, Miss, come into the barn and I'll show you what I have in mind." Good with horses, Sophie slid down off the gelding and followed Barney into the barn. Off in a corner, she could see the coach now polished clean. "You probably know this, Miss, but your coach was built in Concord, New Hampshire by the Abbott-Downing Company, I'd guess in the late 1860s. This one has a few miles on her for sure, but the white oak wheels and body are in very good condition. New, a Concord would sell for $1,050. I'd probably replace all the leather suspension braces and the same with the interior seats, but the real fun would be in repainting the body." As Barney spoke, Sophie could see that he knew what he was talking about and was more interested in the coach than her. Inwardly smiling, she decided to question the stable owner. "Just what colors did you have in mind, Mr. Pryor?" Barney stroked his chin and replied, "Oh, yellow spokes and wheels, dark red exterior paint with green trim, brass lamps, and all new cloth and leather inside. I'd get one of the ladies at the boarding house to help me with the fabric and sewing."

Convinced that Mr. Pryor was sincere, Sophie responded, "It sure sounds like an interesting project, but I don't think I can sell it to you." Crestfallen, Barney asked the lady to reconsider her decision. "Mr. Pryor, fixing up that old coach sounds like a labor of love for you. What

I mean is this: I want to give it to you as a gift. I have my hands full working on the hotel and I don't see when I'd have a use for it. So, please accept the old girl from me, free of charge."

Barney was flabbergasted. He expected a spirited negotiation over the price but instead this beautiful woman was handing it to him for free. "I don't know what to say, Miss. I was prepared to pay you $500 for the coach. Your offer is most generous."

"Mr. Pryor, you don't have to say anything," Sophie exclaimed. "I will be your first passenger when you've finished the renovation. And I'd just as soon we keep our arrangement to ourselves." With that, Sophie placed one boot in the stirrup, swung her leg over the saddle, and trotted her horse in the direction of the Whitman Hotel.

Barney watched Sophie Kaminski as she rode up Main Street. He'd been blown over by her friendliness, beauty, and generosity. "Ain't she something," he thought as he tripped over the threshold of the barn where the coach waited, now destined for better days.

CHAPTER 9

Carlos Meets Rachel

BARBARA CASEY AND AMELIO RODRIGUEZ were enjoying morning coffee on the porch of the Volunteer Ranch. "Senora Casey, you have made our visit to Arizona most pleasurable. I'm sure my grandson will not be happy to leave here to return to Zacatecas. Then, at times, I think it would be best for Carlos to stay here with his father for a while. I go back and forth on what we should do to prepare the boy for the future. He's going to have big responsibilities when he gets older. Ah, perhaps I worry too much."

It had been two months since Konrad Bruner, the elder Rodriguez, and young Carlos had arrived in Ribera. They had stayed briefly at the Whitman Hotel, and then moved to the ranch where they enjoyed larger, more comfortable quarters. The open spaces, horses and cattle, and Betty Ortiz's cooking had relaxed the senior Rodriguez. As he saw Kate and Rachel Lawson ride in, he waved and greeted them with a hearty "Buenos dias." He had grown fond of Barbara Casey and Kate Lawson but was in love with Rachel Lawson. The youngster was an accomplished piano musician, spoke fluent Spanish, and could ride and rope like a veteran vaquero. She was also self-confident and poised beyond her years. She was also beautiful. The Mexican viewed her as a treasure and wondered if his reserved, sometimes withdrawn grandson was aware of such a gem.

His concerns were unfounded. Young Carlos worshipped the girl; he just hadn't been able to figure out a way to express his feelings toward her. He was afraid that she might laugh at him and turn him away. Even when riding alone together in the high country, Carlos held back revealing his true feelings. Most of the time, he simply dreamed about Rachel.

For her part, Rachel surmised that Carlos might need help in developing a relationship. A week earlier, while scanning a herd of cattle near a water hole, Rachel asked Carlos if he enjoyed his visit to Volunteer Ranch. The young boy had looked into Rachel's eyes and replied, "I am pleased to be at the ranch with you, Rachel. You have made my visit very pleasant." Jokingly, Rachel smiled and commented, "Carlos, is that the best you can say about how you feel about me?" Blushing heavily, Carlos summoned his courage and taking the young girl's hand, said in a halting voice, "You are the most beautiful person in the world to me. Someday, when I am older, I will come to you with serious intentions. In the meantime, be patient and just be my best girlfriend."

It was Rachel's turn to be embarrassed, but she recovered quickly. She flashed a smile, squeezed the boy's hand and kissed him tenderly on the cheek. "Carlos, I want you to know that I like you very much and that you will always have a special place in my heart." They looked at one another silently, smiled, and heeled their horses for the ride back home for supper.

That evening, Betty Ortiz served up a sumptuous meal of spit-broiled pork, fried potatoes, and a mixture of corn, beans, and squash. Betty and her husband Sam had built up the herds of horses and cattle and also cultivated a garden plot that was the envy of every visitor to the ranch. Government contracts with the U.S. Army for beef, horses, and hay had brought prosperity to the Volunteer Ranch far beyond Barbara Casey's expectations. She had expanded the original ranch house by adding a wing that consisted of a great room with bedrooms on a second floor. She was also studying ways to spend more time at the ranch by either selling or finding a manager for the general store. Kate Lawson was the most qualified person to own or run the store, but her obligations to her husband and children erased that possibility.

While Senor Rodriguez and Konrad Bruner retired to the great room, the two women relaxed in the kitchen while Betty Ortiz and Carlos played with Tom II, Rachel's brother. Dr. Ben Lawson had been invited for dinner but failed to appear because of an emergency at the clinic. It was at such times that Kate Lawson felt that their involvement with patients in town was beyond their control.

"Barbara, please forgive me for boring you, but I'm feeling put upon again. Ben needs a nurse's help, which I provide when I can, but I'm trying to raise four children. He's always busy and we don't have time for ourselves. What's worse, we've been here over twelve years and have very little to show for it. Ben doctors a lot of people, but always seems to come up short on collections. Frankly, I think the townspeople are taking advantage of him."

Mrs. Casey listened quietly before replying, "Kate, in spite of what you say, I'd trade places with you tomorrow. You have a fine, devoted husband, four healthy children and are still an attractive woman. When Doc Gilroy and Ben came to me to discuss building a hospital, I thought that this was an opportunity that might help a lot of us, including you. The hospital would enable Ben to provide better medical services and perhaps help people understand that the doctor and his wife are entitled to a private life. Your house would become your home again, Kate. Of course, we'd need another doctor and several nurses to fully staff the place. But, in time, we'd be able to provide for all sorts of care. And I suspect, it would give you and Ben time to get your lives back together. Why, we just might anticipate another Lawson as a result."

Kate raised her eyebrows at this last comment but replied laughingly, "Oh no you don't, Barbara, not in a month of Sundays. Four children are my lifetime limit."

Meanwhile, a bright fire burned in the huge fieldstone fireplace of the great room where Konrad and Amelio revisited the subject of Carlos's continuing education. The older man, puffing on a Cuban cigar, began. "The boy has adjusted well to Arizona. Of course, I think he would be happy anywhere as long as Rachel Lawson was around to go riding with. She has him stumbling around like a love sick cow." Konrad sipped his pony glass of cognac and smiled in agreement. "Yes, he will surely miss her, whether he returns to Mexico with you or goes on to college in your country or the United States. Whatever is decided, I believe he is mature enough to leave home and begin university training. But not grown up enough to handle Rachel Lawson."

The patron gazed into the fire, adding, "Konrad, I think you are right. I also think he should go to New York and Columbia University to study law or engineering. New York offers outstanding academics and an urban environment he has little experience of. I'm reluctant to send him to Mexico City because of the political strife that seems to have the city and Mexico in permanent turmoil. And, school in Germany or elsewhere in Europe might be better suited for graduate work. Plus, it's a long way from home."

"Well, it's something we should talk to the boy about," Konrad offered, knowing full well that the time of Carlos's departure was not far off. "These past few months have been glorious, but we must move on," Konrad concluded.

When the two men opened the subject of his future with Carlos, the young boy explained his position. "I have thought much about the university, but I really want to stay in Zacatecas and become a full-time rancher. I love the animals, the smell of leather, and working with the vaqueros. I know I'm not ready to run the ranch today, but with the help of Grandfather and Lumberto, I believe I can grow into the job. When I'm ready to run things, I'm sure that my teachers will know and allow me to change my relations with the men and women of the ranch. You both mean very much to me, so I must think about what you have told me. I will think through what we have discussed and come back to you in a week or so." Surprised but pleased with the maturity of Carlos's remarks, the two men nodded in unison.

The next day, Carlos rode into Ribera to pay a surprise visit to Rachel. When he walked into Dr. Lawson's office, the young woman was submerging the doctor's instruments in boiling water, a practice now insisted upon by her father. Turning to greet Carlos, she said, "Are you here to see the doctor or to take me on a picnic?" Her directness startled Carlos at first but he quickly regained his composure. "I'm here to do both, Rachel. I'm going to talk to your father about a career in medicine. Then after you've made lunch, we can go upriver and maybe even take a swim. Why don't we meet here about 11:30?"

Dr. Lawson relaxed in his overstuffed leather chair and looked at Carlos inquisitively. "So, you want to talk about medicine as a career? My nosy daughter also tells me you are considering law and perhaps engineering. They're all good fields, of course. I couldn't be a lawyer; it never appealed to me. You probably know that I partnered with your father to develop the Ocotillo Mine, but I was never involved with the heavy stuff. I'm still a silent partner and have to admit the money we receive in dividends has been very helpful over the years. The death of my brother at the mine hit me hard. He'd worked hard as hell for three years at that mine and was ready to enjoy the fruits of his labors when the accident happened. I've never been back to the mine since then. It's not the safety issue, Carlos. His death shattered a dream that my father had: that someday we'd all be together. Speaking of safety, frontier doctoring is probably more dangerous than mining, particularly here in Indian country. Cholera and the plague have devastated many tribes. I knew I was going to be a doctor when I was a young kid traveling around with my father on some of his house calls. Dad never pushed me to be a doctor, but he was very pleased when I told him I wanted to go to medical school. As a family practitioner in the West, you'll work long hours and never be a wealthy man, but the satisfaction of helping others makes up for it."

The more Dr. Lawson talked, the more Carlos began to think that he was far more interested in other career choices, especially engineering. Maybe it's in my blood, he thought. He thanked Dr. Lawson for his time and turned his thoughts back to the doctor's beautiful daughter.

Rachel showed up wearing riding jeans, a white blouse, and dark leather boots. A yellow ribbon held her dark hair in place. Carlos gazed at her slim figure with stirring emotion. His gaze didn't go unnoticed. After a picnic lunch, the two youngsters sat on the riverbank, their feet dangling in the cool water. Rachel broke the silence. "Carlos, I couldn't help but overhear most of the conversation you had with my father. I really think that law or engineering would be good fields for you. So, being as smart as you are, why don't you take up law and engineering at the same time? And besides, it would keep you away from the girls, at least part of the time."

Carlos was amazed at the girl's outspokenness. "Rachel, are you jealous that I might see someone else?" Reaching over to embrace Rachel, his hand gently brushed across her breast. As he kissed her on the lips for the first time, Rachel whispered, "Remember me always." "I will," he replied.

After dinner at the ranch that evening, Carlos told his grandfather and father that he had decided to go East to attend Columbia University and study law and engineering. Both men were pleased with the young man's decision, and told him so. After returning to Zacatecas for another year, Carlos packed his belongings for the trip to New York City.

CHAPTER 10

Tombstone

THE STAGECOACH RIDE FROM RIBERA to Tombstone had been uneventful but tiring. Senor Rodriguez and Konrad Bruner checked into the Silver Saddle Hotel, nodded to one another and agreed to meet for dinner at eight o'clock.

Both men had heard a lot about the tremendous wealth created by Ed and Al Schieffelin and had wanted to visit the district as possible investors. A courtesy tour had been scheduled through an exchange of letters; those familiar with the silver mines of Mexico knew that Rodriguez was an important figure in world silver production. Young Carlos remained behind at the Volunteer Ranch to ride with the ranch hands and see more of Rachel Lawson.

While the era of precious metal mining was beginning to wane, several discoveries had recently been made. Henry Wickenburg founded the Vulture Mine, fifty miles outside of Phoenix, followed by Isaac Copeland's silver discovery at Silver King. But the biggest breakthrough had happened when the Schieffelins made their 1877 silver strike.

Satellite mines followed their bonanza find. By 1882, Tombstone had an estimated population of 15,000 and was the largest city between San Antonio, Texas and San Francisco, California. Silver production rejuvenated farming and ranching in the area and enticed the Southern Pacific Railroad to choose a southern route through the territory. Fifty miles west of Tombstone, significant but smaller properties were founded at Harshaw, Duquesne, and Mowry in Santa Cruz County. All these mines contributed significantly to the economic welfare of the southern part of Arizona. They also attracted their fair share of gamblers, swindlers, prostitutes, and gunslingers. Due to its proximity to the border with Sonora, Mexico, the area was heavily populated with people of Mexican descent.

As Konrad and Amelio feasted on steak and a fine French wine, they talked about silver mining in Tombstone. The town was bisected by the San Pedro River, which when running, supplied a modest amount of water to the mines. Unfortunately, demand for water for Tombstone and Contention, twelve miles to the northwest, exceeded supply. Several mill sites, two well-populated towns and service industries all needed water to function. The threat of fire and destruction to the community was ever present. In the early 1880s, an explosion and fire destroyed over sixty-five stores, saloons, restaurants, and businesses. Ironically, it was the flow of underground water that eventually caused the death of silver mining in Tombstone.

After a night's rest, Konrad and Amelio accompanied general superintendent Peter Holly on an underground tour of several mines and a discussion of mining practices at the Tough Nut, Lucky Cuss, and Contention mines. They also heard an explanation of the heavy flow of water at the 500-foot level of the Sulphuret mine. By 1882, flooding had become a serious problem, requiring the purchase and installation of steam-driven Cornish pumps. The ore grade held reasonably well, despite the need to forage for wood to fuel the pumps and the constant threat of fires. The district remained a major producer of silver for over fifteen years.

Over dinner that evening, Peter Holly gave his outlook for silver mining. "Gentlemen, the first thing we need in this neighborhood is consolidation of all the mines into a single operating unit. Right now, it's just too damn complicated to manage. We continue to have too much claim jumping and disputed ownership rights. We need control of our surface water and the means to finance the capital costs of the British pumps and their cost of operation. Then we have the problem of unexpected flows of water that flood the mines and, as I mentioned, the cost of dewatering. That said, I believe there's enough good ore to last another ten to fifteen years if we bring all the owners together. If not, we've got a much shorter life to look forward to."

Konrad listened attentively and replied, "Peter, we appreciate your comments. We can see many of the problems you've mentioned, but also agree that without better administration, there are too many difficulties to overcome. We're tempted, but after serious thought, have decided not to become investors. Amelio has extensive holdings in

Mexico that are completely under his control and my limited gold and silver operations have provided me with a comfortable life. I have one question though, Peter: What is your take on the future of copper mining in Arizona?"

As cigar smoke curled from his mouth, the Englishman smiled and replied, "I've been involved in silver mining all my life, but I honestly feel copper production will be more important than silver to Arizona in the next fifteen to twenty years. We know there's copper here. Why, they've been digging the stuff off and on at Ajo for over fifty years. Down the road, Bisbee is starting up an underground operation and we are hearing that the Clifton area is a hot spot. If the army can control the Apaches, those people from Silver City will make a go of it, I believe. Unless the federal government supports silver coinage, long-term prospects for silver are not very good. The big question for copper is this: How fast will electrification take place? We're past the hobby stage, gentlemen. If a place like New York City were to go electric, it would start a demand for the red metal like we've never dreamed of. If that's what you're thinking about, you'd best look for yourselves up in Pinal County."

As the coach rumbled back westward to Ribera, the two men reviewed their visit to Tombstone. "Disappointing perhaps, Konrad, but it's good we saw it for ourselves," Rodriguez offered. "And I agree with the Brit. Without consolidation, there's not much of a future for Tombstone in the long run. Now, if it's silver you're interested in, you know that I would be very pleased to have you join me in Zacatecas. I'd make you president of the company. It would provide you with a good life and most important, give you a solid connection with your son. I don't expect an answer today, but I hope you will give it serious thought."

Konrad thanked Amelio and replied that he certainly would consider the offer. At the same time, he knew in his heart that he enjoyed being his own boss and running his own business. The Tent City placer gold and Ocotillo Silver Mine had given him a net worth of over $500,000 and should continue to generate at least $100,000 a year for at least five more years. He also liked Ribera and Barbara Casey. Somehow he'd never taken the time to romance the pretty widow properly. Perhaps, this time he'd get around to it.

Peter Holly's comments about copper did get his attention, however. "I have a feeling that something big is about to start in copper mining," he thought. And with that, he resolved to travel to Pinal and Graham counties for a look.

CHAPTER 11

Aguijador Attacks

AGUIJADOR'S FORAY INTO THE MEXICAN states of Sonora and Chihuahua had been rewarding. Mining camps and isolated ranches had yielded horses, but most important, the young warriors in training had conducted themselves admirably. Their leader, Red Arrow, had responded well to tactical orders from the chieftain and executed attacks with skill. Aguijador was pleased that he now had a fresh, well-trained group of warriors to resume operations in southern Arizona.

He noted that the expedition into northern Mexico had again revealed the weakness of the Mexican army troops. Inadequately equipped and poorly commanded, they easily succumbed to his riders in combat. He also confirmed that the lightly armed peasantry offered little resistance to his warriors. Grudgingly, Aguijador accepted the fact that an attack on Fort Gore would be far more difficult. But first, he had to find out more about the new, wheeled gun that fired many bullets.

The lack of Apache activity east of Fort Gore did not go unnoticed by Lieutenant Vince Booker. He had battled many times with the Apache tribes over the past ten years and narrowly escaped with his life on one occasion. He also knew that with warmer weather the Indian horsemen would be on the move again. Not expecting a direct attack on the fort, Booker nevertheless drilled his platoon every day and made plans for a firing demonstration of the Gatling gun outside the fort. He knew the Apache scouts would hear it and perhaps see the weapon in action.

Booker had his men set up three straw bales covered with red, blue, and yellow bulls eye cloth on a rise about 150 yards away but well within sight of the fort. On an order to "fire," Sergeant Parry and his crew sequentially destroyed each target in a matter of seconds, sending straw and cloth flying in every direction. Ordering the crew to cease fire, Booker shouted a "well done, men" as the troopers wheeled the gun wagon back toward the fort.

Just as the lieutenant hoped, two Apache scouts witnessed the demonstration and returned to Aguijador's camp to report what they had seen. Even after questioning the scouts for half an hour, Aguijador was uncertain what the pony soldiers had that was different from previous engagements. He recognized the firepower of the new weapon but was experienced enough to realize the limited mobility of the horse- or mule-drawn gun wagon. The chieftain also decided to get inside information on the new weapon from Spotted Pony, an army scout who was also a spy for the Apaches. One evening, disguised as a friendly Apache, the chieftain met Spotted Pony near the fort. "Tell me what you know about this Gatling gun the army has, my friend."

"The machine, when it operates properly, can fire rapidly and accurately, up to 250 yards," Spotted Pony began. "That would be from here to the bottom of that oak tree at the base of the rise. The soldiers have been training on the gun for the past two weeks, learning how to set up quickly in case of an attack on the fort. The demonstration the other day was an exercise to show a few of the officers how fast the crew could set up and fire the gun. I can tell you they were impressed with the weapon and its firepower. So was I. Worse still, it's been assigned to Lieutenant Booker, probably the best desert field soldier in the Southwest. I advise the tribe to stay away from Booker and his Gatling gun. In open country, they could be difficult to deal with."

Sensing possible discovery, Aguijador left Spotted Pony and rode quickly toward the Dragoon Mountains. Later on, when the scout was questioned about whom he had been talking to, Spotted Pony replied, "Oh, just an old friend, amigo."

The visit with Spotted Pony also revealed to Aguijador that the army was reinforcing the fort. Returning to his camp, he was disturbed by the thought of a larger army force and their new equipment. He was also concerned over the attention his young warriors were paying to Soleado, the white girl abducted during the raid on Sulphur Springs several years ago. The novelty of her resistance and capture was wearing off and the young tribal maidens were jealous of her. He'd have to address what to do with her soon. And the old squaw wouldn't help; she had become too attached to the girl.

After his meeting with Aguijador, Spotted Pony was assigned to Lieutenant Booker, who was preparing a scouting patrol into the Chiricahua Mountains. The rugged peaks and sharp canyons were perfect hideouts for renegade Indians, including the main battle force headed by Aguijador. The lieutenant had decided to take a full strength platoon on the trip, using Spotted Pony as lead scout since he knew the terrain and the location of water holes and springs. Booker also decided to leave the Gatling gun and its crew at Fort Gore.

The reconnaissance force was provisioned for two weeks in the field and had mapped out a trail that would include a stop at a spring in the Dragoon Mountains. Spotted Pony was worried that the soldiers might venture too close to Aguijador's camp, which was located only two miles north of the water source. Did Booker have some secret information? Or is the route just a lucky choice on his part? Spotted Pony liked the lieutenant but knew in his heart that he had to protect the Apache camp first. But he could see no way to warn the chieftain unless he deserted the troop.

On the way to the only water source that flowed year round, Lieutenant Booker moved steadily but cautiously, sending cavalry scouts forward of the main body and flanking both sides of the column. An experienced Indian fighter, Booker knew that the best way to prevent an ambush was to keep on the move and keep an eagle eye out for the Apaches. At night, he doubled guards on short shifts to prevent any theft of horses or supplies.

Aguijador grew increasingly nervous as the army column approached the spring and his camp. He also began to suspect that Spotted Pony had betrayed the tribe and was leading the soldiers to him.

The day before Lieutenant Booker's platoon was to reach the mountain spring, Aguijador decided to attack. Splitting his horsemen into two groups of twenty-five warriors each, the chieftain hit the soldiers' bivouac just after sunrise. The first assault had the element of surprise but alert troopers sounded the alarm before Aguijador's warriors made contact with the main force. Coffee mugs and mess gear flew in every direction as the troopers ran to designated protection areas, firing their pistols and rifles on the run.

The Apache attack plan was based on surprise and a weak response from the blue coats. After the initial attack, the Indians realized that the soldiers had neutralized their strategy. They hadn't panicked when attacked and regrouped quickly into a strong defensive unit. Aguijador recognized that the battle had turned to the advantage of the cavalry with the soldiers killing and wounding too many of his men. Signaling retreat, the chieftain led his bloodied band back to their camp, believing the troopers would not follow. He was terribly mistaken.

In the early afternoon, Lieutenant Booker's platoon reorganized and was on the attack and only half an hour away from Aguijador's camp. The chieftain's priority was to establish a rear guard force to slow down the advance of the army offensive. He also had the wounded and the women and children to take care of. Aguijador instructed Red Arrow to lead the fittest group of women and children deeper into the canyon where a new hideout would be established. Gritting his teeth, Aguijador surveyed the abandoned campsite, and then joined his warriors in a delaying action against the troopers. He was shocked to see how well the soldiers were organized in pushing through his men. Understanding the precarious state of his situation, Aguijador ordered his men to break off the fight and signaled a withdrawal. As the Apaches rode away, the troopers shouted and cheered in victory.

Booker was uncertain of the Apaches' withdrawal and decided to follow them into their hideaway. Accompanied by three men, the lieutenant rode slowly into Aguijador's camp, weapons at the ready. They were surprised to see fires still burning and a large cache of food, blankets, and several survivors. One was an elderly squaw who held the hand of her companion, a white girl dressed in buckskins and moccasins. As Booker got off his horse and walked toward the two, the older woman pointed at the girl, calling out her name, "Soleado, Soleado." Cautiously, Booker approached the two and in sign language, told them that the army meant no harm and that they were now in safekeeping.

The lieutenant then summoned Spotted Pony to ask him where the Apache war party might be heading. Before he could utter a word, rifle shots rang out and the Indian scout fell forward, clutching his chest. Spotted Pony was dead before he hit the ground. Two fatal slugs from a Sharps rifle had avenged the spy, whom Aguijador believed had betrayed the tribe. The sight of dust from a long distance away gave the soldiers a general direction of the Indian withdrawal.

CHAPTER 12

Konrad Meets Colin Barksdale

THE TWO MEN SAT IN a pair of overstuffed chairs, looking at one another, glancing from time to time into a spitting mesquite fire. Konrad's office, newly constructed as a stand-alone building, was cluttered with mining equipment, wall to wall bookshelves, and unusual mineral samples taken from the Ocotillo Silver Mine. A vial of gold platelets reminded a visitor that the Bowie River was an important source of placer gold. Wide planked hardwood floors were covered with expensive Oriental rugs. On one side of the room, framed mining certificates and hand woven Navajo rugs adorned a wall. A large oaken desk, retrieved from a decommissioned U.S. Navy warship, had two green-shaded kerosene lamps to provide illumination.

"Mr. Barksdale, it is indeed a pleasure to welcome you to Ribera. It's been quite a while, perhaps six to eight years, since hearing from Sir Clarence Bingham. I'm pleased to hear that he's enjoying good health and that Cornwall Tin is still prospering. His letter of introduction describes you well: "Mr. Barksdale (you should call him by his first name, Colin) is six feet tall, weighs about two hundred pounds, and has brown hair and blue eyes. He should be wearing a gold signet ring with two engraved lions. Colin will explain the intention of our syndicate and can be completely trusted as a representative of our firm." Pouring coffee into a pair of matching cups, Konrad invited the Englishman to explain the purpose of his visit.

"Mr. Bruner, I represent Sir Clarence Bingham and three Scottish associates interested in the finding and development of U.S. mineral deposits in the Southwest. We might also be interested in investing in railroads supportive to the discovery and development of these ore deposits. You come to us highly recommended by Senor Amelio Rodriguez, and of course, by your own successes with the Ocotillo Silver Mine and the Tent City gold operations. Your credentials are indeed impressive. I have been a partner with Sir Clarence, Geoffrey Gibbons, Clyde Hawkins, and Clifton Barnes for about five years. Our consortium is called Britsco Mining and Smelting. The name is a bit "corny" as Americans might say, but it does represent the combining of British and Scottish interests into a well-financed investment group. Incidentally, I might add what you may already know: The Cornish tin mines are getting deeper with lower grade ore, hence, operating costs are beginning to pinch profits."

"What you say is interesting, Mr. Barksdale," replied Konrad. "I wonder why with Sir Clarence's contacts in Mexico, you haven't invested in that country."

"You bring up a good point. May I call you Konrad?" With a nod from Bruner, Barksdale continued. "We have two exploration teams in the Fresnillo area, looking for new prospects. We're also examining a few situations where we would feel comfortable legally and where the missing key ingredient is capital. But we are being very cautious because of the political situation, which we feel is unstable. A small number of families run Mexico, and while we have good relations with them, any revolutionary faction could easily confiscate foreign-owned businesses. Besides, the United States appeals more to us for obvious reasons: We share the same language, our legal systems are similar, and your mineral industry is in its early stages of development. I have spent the last few months in New York and Washington, talking with mining people, legislators, and confidants to be sure we are on the right track. Additional conversations with a few friends in Silver City, New Mexico have confirmed that Colorado, Utah, New Mexico, and Arizona are excellent targets for exploration, discovery, and mine development. We're playing catch up with the Guggenheims but will accept the challenge. That's why we want you to lead our exploration team in the western United States. We need someone who knows exploration and mining and has the business experience to avoid propositions that are, shall we say, less than legitimate."

Konrad appreciated the flattering remarks but wondered if Barksdale was giving him the whole story. "You mentioned meeting with people in Silver City. What did you learn from them? What do they see on the horizon?"

Now we're getting somewhere, thought Barksdale. "Our contacts tell us that the Goldsmith brothers are very active in the Morenci area. I don't think there's any question that they're mining silver, but the Apaches are giving them all kinds of trouble. It's proving extremely difficult to get mining equipment and supplies into the area. Abe and Ira are tough men and are doing everything possible to get material to the mines. I've heard they've asked the army for convoy protection. What's really interesting though is their re-discovery of copper ore on the surface that's running fifteen percent copper or better. And I guess you've heard the news about the electric lights at the Chicago Exposition. If population centers like New York, Boston, and Philadelphia were to switch over to electric lighting, the demand for copper wire would be huge. In a nutshell, we believe this change is going to happen and we want to be in at the beginning."

Konrad mulled over Barksdale's comments before answering. "From everything I've heard, the Goldsmith brothers have made a major discovery. In addition, there are rumors of major copper finds in Bisbee and up north in Jerome. These are unconfirmed reports, but I believe the stories of unusually high-grade ore are true. Too many respected people are getting involved for it not to be true. I also hear that there is gold and silver associated with the copper that may be recoverable. It's very possible that someday Arizona will be a major producer of copper; the gold and silver would be sweeteners."

"Konrad, my partners and I are in this part of the country for the long haul. We know that Arizona gold and silver production has flattened somewhat. We expect copper to take over and be the metal of the future."

"Well, I won't disagree with you," replied Konrad. "But gold and silver still have a future. Tombstone is still booming. Anyway, where do you see me fitting into your plans?"

"Britsco Mining and Smelting wants you to become a member of its management team and eventually to have an ownership position in the company. We would start out by having you examine a prospect up in Pinal County. An old sourdough by the name of B.J. (Billy Joe) Kimball supposedly owns it. He contacted us by way of a friend he has in Cornwall, who turned the information over to Sir Clarence. Our early interest was in the silver but if the ore is similar to what they've found in Morenci, we'd be very much interested. But this is only the beginning. We would want you to mount a broad-based exploration program for copper in all parts of the territory. I'm authorized to offer you a salary of $600 a month to join Britsco with the title of chief of

exploration. We'd cover all travel expenses, of course, and any inciden-
tals. We'd like you to get started as soon as possible. I will be going to
San Francisco next week to meet with some people who are interested
in building an east-west railroad through southern Arizona. We'd be
the party building and financing feeder lines to mine properties as they
develop. I'll probably be up there a month, then will come back here to
check on your progress with Mr. Kimball."

During the next couple of days, Konrad escorted Colin Barksdale
to the Ocotillo Mine and his gold placer operations. He also introduced
Colin to Barney Pryor, now general manager of both operations. The
livery stable owner had developed into an effective, loyal partner who
got along well with people and learned fast. Konrad also set up meetings with Barbara Casey, Ben Lawson, and banker Scoville in case the
Englishman decided to eventually set up an office in Ribera.

When Colin Barksdale boarded the stage for Tucson, Yuma, and
Virginia City, Nevada, he and Konrad shook hands, understanding that
they were now business partners. In the few days spent with Colin,
Konrad was confident he'd made the right decision to join Britsco Mining and Smelting. They were honorable people, had the capital to
invest in a large mining operation, and seemed intent on becoming a
major leader in copper mining. After a brief meeting with Barney, he
packed equipment for an extended stay up north and a visit with B.J.
Kimball. The new venture gave Konrad a sense of excitement that had
been missing since he bought out young Tom Hillenbrand and the
Bowie River gold mine.

CHAPTER 13

Sophie's Coach Ride

BARNEY PRYOR RUBBED HIS CALLOUSED hand over the several layers of new paint on his reconstructed Concord coach. Six months of meticulous labor had achieved nearly perfect results. The bright yellow spoked wheels gleamed in the sunlight and the new leather and dark burgundy body paint and detailed green trim filled him with pride in his work. The carrier was now ready for a test run.

He considered sending a message to Sophie but decided to walk up to the hotel and extend the invitation in person. He'd seen the lady on a couple of occasions since her visit to the livery stable but had the impression that she was either too busy to say hello or just not interested in seeing him again. It had taken a lot of courage to think of a way to get her attention. Nervously, Barney presented himself to the desk clerk at the hotel and asked to see Mrs. Kaminski.

After waiting in the hotel parlor for a half hour, he saw Sophie descending the stairs, looking like she was on her way to a ball. A form-fitting full-length blue gown complimented her deep blue eyes and light brown hair. Smiling broadly, she addressed Barney formally. "Good afternoon, Mr. Pryor. What is it I can help you with?" Barney was flustered by her tone and rubbed his chin while searching for a response. "Miss Sophie, some time ago I promised to take you for a ride in your coach when I finished restoring it. It's been fixed up right nice and if you can spare a few hours, I'll take you for a ride along the river and the Cimarron Cliffs. You'd get the best view of the country by sitting up with me in the shotgun seat. I know it's short notice, but it's a beautiful day and I guess you'd say I'm pretty proud of that wagon."

As Barney extended his invitation, Sophie finally recalled their last meeting. "Why, Mr. Pryor, I'd almost forgotten about that old wreck of a coach! And, we did discuss a ride in it after you'd finished working on it. I have so many things to do with the new show, but maybe it's time I took a break. I shouldn't but it's too nice a day to stay indoors. Let me get my hat and I'll be right with you. Barney, this sounds like fun."

So now it's Barney, the stable owner thought to himself.

The refitted coach had attracted a lot of attention from the citizens of Ribera. Tradesmen walked around it, admiring the workmanship and commenting on the newness of the vehicle; children danced and shouted, "I want a ride! Please give me a ride!" Sophie was taken aback by the attention of the small crowd but brightened when she saw the coach in the sunlight. "Barney, I can't believe what you've done with that old wreck. Why, it's beautiful." She eagerly climbed up into the coach and was quickly cradled next to the driver's seat, about ten feet above the ground. With a snap of the reins, the four mules pulled away from the hotel as spectators cheered loudly.

Barney drove the team north of town and crossed the Bowie River, gaining a spectacular view of Mount Cody, fifteen miles away near Growler Creek. Sophie began to relax and enjoy the natural beauty of the river, mountains, and foothills covered with scrub oak. Before long, she forgot about her business chores and planning the musical show. Her mind cleared as she took in the view of the town from a thousand feet above the river. It had been a long time since she had been able to appreciate the freedom of a leisurely ride in the country.

Slowing the mules to a halt, Barney pointed out the main buildings in town, including the Whitman Hotel and the construction site of the new hospital. Moving along the cliffs, he gave Sophie a condensed history of Ribera, including the shoot-out at the Bowie River dam site and Buzz Chatham's firefight with the Dresser gang. They re-crossed the river near the placer gold fields. As men noticed the coach, they paused, raised their picks and shovels, beat on their metal pans, and waved in appreciation of such a pretty sight.

"Sophie, it wasn't all that long ago that the miners and the River Bend Ranch were seriously feuding, right here. It all ended when Greg Newport and four other riders were killed when they assaulted the miner's dam. Eventually, with the help of Don Richmond, things settled down and the water was divvied up to each group's satisfaction. Now, over there is the main house of the River Bend Ranch, owned by the widow Garland Newport and her daughter Dolores. Her husband Don is a veterinarian but actually handles the cowhands. He's a real fine gent who has helped me with the horses and mules, especially when they're birthing. He's a real good farrier, too."

As the sun began to set in the west, Barney turned the mules back to town and finally, the Whitman Hotel. Helping Sophie down from the shotgun seat, he held her waist as she navigated the last step. Safely back on the ground, smiling, and with windblown cheeks, Sophie thought she'd just experienced one of the most exhilarating days of her life. Shaking Barney's hand, she couldn't restrain her enthusiasm. "Barney, this has been a wonderful day! I escaped from that jail cell of an office, got a grand tour of the town, and realized how much I've been missing holed up in my hotel. You've made me feel like a young girl again. I'd like to show you my appreciation. Would you join me for dinner in the hotel dining room, say at seven o'clock?"

With hat in hand and running fingers through his hair, Barney responded, "Sophie, that would suit me just fine."

Barney led the mule team down Main Street to the livery stable. He unhitched the coach, gave the animals some oats, and went to his room to clean up for dinner. After bathing, he shaved for the second time that day and searched his wardrobe for his best finery. He left the stable a little before seven, dressed in a white shirt, string tie, pressed dark suit and polished soft leather knee high boots. For once, he decided to leave his sidearm at home.

A few minutes after the hour, Sophie joined him in the dining room. She had changed her daytime outfit and looked stunning in a black velvet dress bordered with white lace. Her hair was tied with a bow of white ribbon.

Between the courses, the two chatted easily. "You know, Sophie, we haven't talked about your coach. I can't just let you give it to me for free." Sophie fixed her blue eyes on Pryor. "Barney, that was so long ago that I'd almost forgotten about it. And after all the work you've put into it; you're just going to have to accept the gift as I originally offered it. Maybe you'll let me borrow it for special occasions. The townspeople looked at that old coach as if it were a king's chariot. Please don't bring the subject up again, unless you want to offend me." All this was said with a warm smile that gave Barney hope for the future. Shyly, he rejoined with a mild "yes, ma'am."

Over desert and coffee, Sophie began telling Barney about her plans for the hotel and saloon. "Everything I read in the paper and hear in the hotel tells me that Ribera is destined to continue growing. Fort Gore is getting more soldiers, Tent City will continue to rely on us for food and supplies, and Bruner insists that there's enough gold to be panned for at least three more years. And best of all, we're on the main coach line between El Paso and Tucson. I've been in touch with a traveling musical variety show in Virginia City and I'm about to book them for a three-day stand here. I'm going to have to make some improvements to the saloon, but I'm pretty sure I can get it done in time. We're short of good carpenters, but with a little bit of luck, we should be able to build an elevated stage for the cast. Come on, let me show you what I have in mind."

Sophie led Barney to the saloon from a rear door. Several games of poker were in play and the bar was filled with an assortment of cowhands, miners, and drifters. It was a busy evening. Sophie walked to the front of the room and explained to Barney how the stage would be built four feet above the floor and with enough depth to accommodate eight to ten people at one time. Her eyes sparkled as she explained how the arrangement of tables and benches would serve for the less expensive seats. "I'm planning on being able to seat over a hundred patrons, plus space for a small band of musicians," Sophie said.

God, this lady sure has some big ideas, thought Barney.

As they turned away from the bar area, a burly miner grabbed Sophie's wrist, spinning her around toward him. Looking at her through bleary eyes, he burst out, "I remember you when you were in Tent City months back. Don't get fancy with me, honey. C'mere and give me a kiss."

Quickly interceding, Barney shoved the man away from Sophie. "You stay at the bar and be quiet mister, or you can leave." With teeth gritted, the miner pushed Barney into a table, shouting, "You stay outta this, whoever the hell you are. She ain't no lady, no matter what fancy clothes she's wearing. I seen her many times in Silverton; she's the madam runnin' a cat house there."

Sensing a fight, the onlookers moved away from the two men. The big man pulled a foot long blade from his boot and charged Pryor. Unarmed, the teamster grabbed a heavy bar stool and crashed it over the miner's head and shoulders before he could close in for the kill. As the man lay unconscious, Barney turned to Clancy Corrigan, the bar keep, and said, "Take this guy out into the street and when he wakes up, tell him he's not welcome back here ever again." Clancy nodded in agreement and assured Barney he would take care of things. In a matter of minutes, the drinking and poker playing resumed as if the altercation had never happened.

Recovering her composure, Sophie took Barney by the hand and led him back to the hotel sitting room, now unoccupied. "Barney, thank you for standing by me when that miner accosted me. I'm truly sorry for what happened in the saloon tonight; it ruined an otherwise perfect day. I won't lie to you. I have done some things in my life that I now regret. Yes, I did live in Colorado for a few years. I came to Ribera hoping to start a new life but I guess I'll never be able to hide my past. I don't know who that man was but there could be others who could identify me from my earlier days. Thank you again, Barney. I'll try my best to not embarrass you again." Her speech concluded, Sophie Kaminski turned sharply, ran up the stairs, leaving Barney Pryor dumbfounded. Sophie, it doesn't matter, he whispered to himself.

CHAPTER 14

A Visit to the Smelter

BARNEY PRYOR WAS BUSY SHOEING a horse at the livery stable when Don Richmond walked in. "Hey, Barney, what's this I hear about you defending the virtue of one of our fine citizens, and flattening some drunk from Tent City?" Barney looked up from his work and saw the smile on the rancher's face. "Well, I guess most of what you've heard is true, Don, but I sure wish people would stop talking about it. It ain't that big a deal. The guy was drunk and insulting Miss Sophie and I guess I let my temper get the best of me. I'd just as soon forget about the whole thing."

"I hope the miner feels the same way as you do," Don replied. "But I wouldn't be too sure. From what I hear from the hands, Burr Tilden's not the kind of guy who forgets this kind of thing. And I guess the miners are giving him a rough time over the licking you gave him. I'd keep an eye on that guy for a while. It's time for some coffee. Let's go over to the clinic where we can chat a bit."

The stable owner and Don Richmond entered Doc Lawson's office just as Kate Lawson was pouring a cup of coffee for her husband. She offered Don and Barney some and then took up the issue of Burr Tilden. "We've had a few patients in here this past week who told us that Tilden is a bad actor from way back. You'd best watch out for him, Barney, especially if he comes into town and starts drinking."

The attention being paid to his welfare was beginning to annoy Barney, no matter how well intentioned. "Okay, I get the message. Now let's talk about the hospital and how construction is progressing."

Doc Lawson took the hint to change the subject. "Things have slowed down since we finished the foundation. Ernie Borden has run out of two by fours, so he's working on doors and windows in the meantime. When his shipment comes in from Copper Flats, he'll be calling on us to get the second floor and stairwell built. We may have a problem about Copper Flats. Barbara Casey has had a few sick cows and I think they may have been poisoned by contaminated water coming down the Bowie River. She mentioned seeing dark, reddish brown streaks in the water where the herd was drinking. I've got to get up there this week to check things out before we run into something similar in the town's drinking water. I've also heard from Captain Steele, the regimental surgeon at Fort Gore. It seems that a smallpox epidemic has hit the Indian population on the San Carlos Reservation."

The mention of smallpox alarmed Kate Lawson. "Wait a minute, Ben. Do you want to get involved with smallpox on the reservation? The disease is highly infectious, plus many of the people are already fighting consumption. I hope you're not thinking of going up there. What about our children?"

Doc Lawson looked at his wife directly. "Kate, you know as well as I do that a medical doctor doesn't have much choice in the matter. Yes, the disease does have a high mortality rate but Captain Steele has asked me for my help and I've got to see what I can do. Maybe we'll be able to find out something that will prevent it from spreading down here."

The discussion over a disease he knew nothing about prompted Barney Pryor to ask, "Tell me, Ben, what exactly is smallpox?"

Kate, Barney, and Don looked in Doc Lawson's direction. "Well, if we go back far enough, it's believed to have been brought to the New World from Europe. Spanish explorers infected the native population in Mexico and the disease gradually spread north into Texas, New Mexico, and Arizona. Basically, it was introduced just like tuberculosis and syphilis into a culture that had no natural immunity. It's likely it was also introduced into Florida, where it spread throughout the entire eastern seaboard. Some say the introduction of horse travel into America allowed these diseases to be easily transmitted throughout the country. It devastated the Native American population."

"The virus has a two week incubation period of fever, skin blisters, and insufferable itching. By scratching the blisters, the patient breaks them, and creates new blisters. The scabs retain the smallpox virus for a few weeks, which adds to the potential for transmission to other, healthy people. Worst of all, we don't have a cure for the disease." His listeners looked at Doc Lawson in horror.

"Captain Steele has virtually quarantined the reservation but it's impossible to prevent white merchants who come in selling whiskey to the Indians or to stop some Indians who try to escape. There's simply too much territory for the army to cover and, at the same time, go after marauding Apaches. My priority is to get up to Copper Flats and see if Les Ventor, the manager of the ISC smelter, has any answers about the discolored water in the Bowie River."

Before leaving for Copper Flats, Ben Lawson decided to talk with Konrad Bruner and see if he could shed some light on the possible Bowie River contamination. He walked over to Konrad's office to find the German in conversation with Clyde Bond, who did appraisal work and chemical analyses for the mining community.

"Hello, Ben," said Konrad in greeting. "Have a seat. We're about wrapped up here; I'll be with you in a minute. But if you're looking for more hospital money, it could be a lot longer. Only kidding."

Alone in Konrad's office, Doc Lawson explained why he wanted to visit Copper Flats. Moving his hand to his forehead, Konrad responded, "Ben, I'd like to check on how we're disposing of gangue at the Ocotillo Silver Mine before I sit down with the ISC people. Carlos and Amelio have left town, so I wouldn't mind going up there with you. If the Bowie is being poisoned, we're going to have to do something about it, and fast."

The two men reached the silver mine the following morning. Konrad checked the mine operation and the disposal of waste material. The miners were still breaking ore from gangue with sledgehammers and handpicks, then putting the waste rock into a hollow containment area. There was no way anything from the mine could get into Growler Creek and from there into the Bowie River. Konrad expressed his satisfaction that his people were doing everything they could to protect the river and was totally confident that the mine was in the clear. He and the doctor then decided to see what the people at ISC were doing.

They reached Copper Flats in the late afternoon and took rooms at the local hotel. After an early breakfast, they inspected the smelter slag dump and liquid discharge culvert that emptied into the Bowie River. Both men were upset to see rusted steel drums and puddles of dirty water containing some mysterious sediment. Carefully, Konrad took samples of the water and the solids for later analysis. He didn't like the look of the situation at all.

Les Ventor was not his usual friendly self when Lawson and Bruner entered his office. He had more important things on his mind, like a broken down furnace that was hurting plant output. The brickwork lining for the smelting unit was going slower than expected and hitting profits hard. Konrad began the discussion. "Les, consider this to be an official visit from the Ribera Water Board Association. We've got a few ailing cows at the Volunteer Ranch. But more important, we're concerned about drinking water quality for the residents of our town. We'll start by asking you if you've had any complaints about water from the residents of Copper Flats."

"No, I can't say that we have," said the plant manager. "Of course, you know that the town is situated north of the plant. What are you getting at? Are you guys on a fishing expedition or do you have something concrete to talk about?"

"Okay, Les, we'll put our cards on the table. We have a complaint of sick cows from Barbara Casey that appears to be related to contaminated water. It seems the cows drink from a small pond fed by the Bowie. In checking, it looks like the contaminant might be the residue from sulfide ores that have been smelted, producing a low-grade sulfuric acid. Unfortunately, Barbara flushed the ponds before we could take samples. We've checked out the Ocotillo Mine and are confident that the miners are not causing any problems. Besides, we don't use any chemicals in our processing; ore concentrates are shipped to ISC for smelting."

Ventor listened quietly as Konrad finished. "Well, as far as I know, we're dumping all our slag inland, away from the river. But let me check with Paul Grabonik, who's in charge of the furnace room." In a few minutes, Grabonik came into Ventor's office, visibly upset with the interruption of his work on the furnace. "Paul, please tell these gentlemen how we dispose of our slag and any other refuse from our operation."

Grabonik began haltingly, wondering what the questioning was all about. "Our slags vary depending on what type of ore is being processed and the smelting practice used. All slags are tested to ensure we're getting the maximum metal recovery. Then they're sent to the dump up the canyon, about five hundred yards from here. That's about it, I guess."

Ben Lawson looked straight into Grabonik's eyes. "Are you dumping any material, directly or indirectly into the Bowie River?" he asked. Sensing a trap, the big foreman answered, "Only on rare occasions."

The room fell silent as Ventor, Bruner, and Lawson waited for a further explanation.

"We had a pretty good run of copper ore a couple of weeks ago that was all sulfide. It also contained a lot of pyrite, which is iron sulfide. We generated a lot of slag and, in a rush, dumped some into a ditch that eventually runs from the main dump to the river. We installed a twelve-inch pipe in the ditch to get rid of the liquid stuff as quickly as possible. I didn't think it would hurt anything."

Les Ventor looked as if this were news to him but responded quickly. "Look men, we're not going to intentionally foul the river. I wasn't aware of what happened but trust me, it will never happen again. Paul, I'll see you in the furnace room later."

Konrad and Ben Lawson were unsure that the dumping of slag and fluids was a one time event or standard procedure. They were certain of one thing, however. They had to protect their supply of potable water.

"Les, we're not happy to find out that your people are dumping stuff into the river," Konrad stated. "Mrs. Casey's sick cows should be a warning to all of us that we have to protect our river. The Bowie is one of the few rivers that flow year round and a lot of people rely on it for crops and drinking water. We're relying on you to follow up with Paul Grabonik and all your employees to prevent any further mishaps. In that we're talking to you as members of the Ribera Water Board, an official, written warning will be sent to you, with a copy of the letter going to Sheriff Buzz Chatham. I hope you understand the seriousness of the situation."

Ventor let a few minutes pass as he thought about a response. Finally, he said, "Okay, I hear you, but it seems to me to be a stretch saying we fouled the river drinking water for cows located fifteen miles from here. But we'll comply with your wishes. Now gentlemen, I've got work to do, so please excuse me."

Konrad wasn't finished making his point. "Les, if you have trouble believing our instructions, just walk your own slag disposal system and look at the pipe that feeds into the river."

After his visitors had departed for Ribera, Les Ventor placed his elbows on his desk, face in his hands. God, I don't have enough problems making a profit in the smelter, he thought. Now I've got to contend with two nosy guys looking over my shoulders. And they're good friends with the sheriff.

CHAPTER 15

Carlos Leaves for New York

THE PREVIOUS EVENING'S DINNER HAD been superb: a split beef barbecued on the patio, a mariachi band, and fond farewells from friends that Carlos Rodriguez Bruner had grown up with. There were many gifts and speeches. A package from his father contained an affectionate paternal note along with several mining books in English and a kit of prospecting equipment. He wasn't sure how to take some of the vaquero comments: an encyclopedia of advice on manhood, fast women, and life in the big city. Amelio Rodriguez had been surprisingly subdued most of the evening. Florina's toast had been touching and thankfully brief.

At breakfast the next morning, Amelio gave some last words of advice to Carlos and Lumberto Villegas, who would accompany the young man on his trip East. "Carlos, you are leaving Mexico and your home for the first time," the elder Rodriguez began. "The trip from here to New York, by way of Tampico and Perth Amboy, New Jersey, is one I have no experience of. Lumberto, while uninformed of America's eastern coast, has served your father and I well over the years. Therefore, I insist that he accompany you to New York and help get you settled there. He has been a trusted member of our inner family for over twenty years and has never failed to act with good judgment. There will come a time when both of you will agree that it is time for him to return to Mexico. In the meantime, please listen to his advice and respect what he says. I won't burden you with best wishes; you had enough last night. I expect you to write to me at least once a month or I will send soldiers after you! Be well and enjoy your trip to New York."

Carlos hugged his grandfather and Florina and joined Lumberto in the passenger cab of the stagecoach. As they crossed the Continental Divide later in the day, Carlos began to grasp the extent of the poverty that gripped most of Mexico. In village after village he observed tiny farms growing corn, beans, and squash; ancient irrigation systems and weathered adobe homes that were in various stages of disrepair. Most of all, he could read the sense of hopelessness in the faces of the peasant children. It reminded him of his good fortune being a member of the Rodriguez family dynasty.

Company headquarters in Tampico looked like a militarized fort rather than an office building. High, barbed wire fencing and uniformed, armed guards secured the silver ingots stockpiled and stacked on pallets. About a mile up a hillside overlooking the harbor, the company maintained a residence for family members and visiting guests. The view of downtown Tampico and the seaport was magnificent. Orlando and Juanita Ramirez, who maintained the property for the patron, joyously welcomed Carlos and Lumberto. The visitors were shown to their rooms where they bathed and relaxed on the veranda where they observed harbor activities below. The harbor was busy with fishing boats, tramp steamers, and runabouts scurrying between the boats and the piers along the shore. Sipping an estate-bottled wine, Carlos leaned over to Lumberto and asked, "Lumberto, you have worn the pistol since we left the ranch. Do you ever take it off?"

The companion looked up at his young charge and allowed a few seconds to lapse before responding. Clearing his throat, Lumberto replied, "The short answer is yes; I do remove the weapon when I wash up and sleep, but let me assure you, it is never very far from me. For this trip, I will stow the handgun and shotgun and use a small pistol that fits in a shoulder holster. I think the New York police will frown on anyone carrying a sawed off shotgun. However, I will have a derringer that I can slide into my boot and a knife for self-protection. My job is to get you to New York and safely settled. Understand this, Carlos: I take my job seriously, having worked for your grandfather for most of my life. Someday, I will tell you the story of how I first met Senor Rodriguez who has placed the utmost trust in me for your safekeeping."

That evening, the two men enjoyed a meal of Gulf shrimp grilled over charcoal and served on a bed of wild rice, peppers, onions, and herbs.

The following morning, Carlos and Lumberto rode to the Rodriguez dock and introduced themselves to the captain of the ship that would take them to Perth Amboy. "Welcome, gentlemen. We will begin loading our cargo around noon and are scheduled to leave with high tide around four o'clock. Feel free to relax or come up to the bridge. And don't hesitate to ask for coffee, a cold drink, or food. Our mess is well stocked to take care of any of your needs. Now, please excuse me while we get ready for our trip."

While touring the ship, Carlos and Lumberto watched the unloading of a large shrimp boat. "Your grandfather's nephews run the shrimp operations in the Gulf of Mexico," Lumberto explained. "They've done a good job with their inheritance and built up a fleet of maybe thirty boats over the years. They served the Senor well and have been generously rewarded."

The loading of the *Durango*, a coal-fired freighter, was well organized and tightly controlled. The wagons of silver ingots entered the loading dock under heavy, armed guard. Each load pallet was marked with the weight stenciled on it and recorded by the ship's purser. It soon became apparent that several million dollars worth of silver was being transported to the United States in this single cargo. Finally, the purser nodded to the boatswain, the hatches were secured, and the ship slipped away from the dockside.

Carlos and Lumberto were quite comfortable in their new surroundings. Each stateroom had a desk and a bunk bed. They met Senor Batista, the head of security, and dined with him at the captain's table. Batista and his eight policemen would accompany the vessel to New Jersey where it would be unloaded. Then the dockworkers would reload the ship with equipment and supplies destined for the mines in Zacatecas. The shipment would include British heavy pumps purchased to dewater one of the flooded mines owned by Senor Rodriguez.

The *Durango* was scheduled to arrive on the East coast in about eight days, assuming decent weather in the straits between Florida and Cuba. The weather was pleasant and the ship made a steady seven knots. Carlos took the opportunity to read his newly acquired mining books while Lumberto kept busy chatting with the crew. One night, after being asked for the third time, Lumberto agreed to reveal how he had first met the patron.

"I was one of three children, born to parents who had no money and few, if any, prospects. My mother was a good woman but was unable to deal with my father's drinking and failure to provide for his family. By the age of twelve I was on my own, doing whatever jobs I could get. My older brother and sister had already left home. I worked on local ranches and became a skilled horseman and roper. Still, I could never find a permanent job. Our village was a few miles from the

Rodriguez estate, which was an island of prosperity even back then. From time to time, I would see the patron and his wife in the village as they visited the padre or on their way to Zacatecas."

"One day, as they rode through the village, their carriage horses were spooked by a flock of pigeons. The lead horses reared up and the other two struggled in their harnesses as the Senor lost control of the reins. In an instant, the horses began twisting and turning, while dragging the carriage to the left and right. I was sitting by the fountain and saw all of this transpire. Your grandmother was screaming and the Senor was trying to regain control of the horses. Without thinking, I raced to the two front horses, placed my hands over the eyes of one of them, and shouted "whoa!" He stopped abruptly and in an instant, the other horses followed. Senora Rodriguez was badly shaken so I suggested that the Senor ride with her in the carriage while I took the reins and drove them back to their hacienda. When we got there, servants took over and I was given a few pesos for my trouble and told to move on. I even had to walk back to town, expecting nothing more from my intervention."

"About a week later, Father Petrillo instructed me to report to the Rodriguez ranch and ask for the patron, as he wanted to see me. When I arrived at the hacienda, the same groom escorted me inside the house where I met Senor Rodriguez. Of course, I was very nervous being in such a beautiful home. He looked me over and told me he had asked Father Petrillo about me. Then he invited me to tell him all about myself. I told him my life story in a matter of minutes but I could tell he was listening intently. The result of our meeting was that he gave me a job as an apprentice vaquero. I guess I did well enough because a year or so later I was invited for another visit with the Senor. This time, a little girl was crawling around on the floor of his office."

"That visit changed the course of my life," Lumberto continued. "The Senor thanked me for helping him and his wife the year before and congratulated me on my advancement as a rider and roper on his ranch. Then he offered to do something for me beyond my wildest expectations. He made arrangements for me to join the corps of cadets at Guadalajara Military Academy to receive military training and an education."

"I really didn't understand the immense gift being given to me but I had the sense to recognize the opportunity of a lifetime. The next thing I knew I was at GMA, attending a special summer course to prepare for the next semester. Most of the other cadets were home for the summer. A professor and several older students tutored me for long hours. Mathematics was the most difficult, as it was almost entirely new to me. In the fall, I entered the first year of military training, which was even more demanding."

"We were divided into squads of twelve students; three squads made up a platoon. A professional military officer commanded each platoon. We quickly learned to watch out for the platoon sergeant, who was a third year cadet. He was a disciplinarian and harassed us from dawn to dusk. We polished shoes, cleaned rifles, and made up beds so tight a coin could bounce off the top blanket, that sort of stuff. Within three months we became a decent group of soldiers, especially on the parade ground. During this time, I took extra courses in math and learned to speak, read, and write English. We were indoctrinated to believe that the gringos to the north were our enemies since they had stolen our land."

"Near the end of my first year, we were trained in swordsmanship and how to shoot both pistol and rifle. When the training was over, I was awarded the plebe medal for marksmanship. My skill with the sword was mediocre, however. As most cadets were packing to go home for the summer, I was summoned to the commandant's office. He gave me a commendation and told me that I was in the top five percent of my class. I looked forward to returning to GMA as I was now confident I could do the work required to be an infantry officer."

"I returned to the Rodriguez estate in full uniform; they were the only clothes I had that fit me. The food and exercise at the academy had helped me grow to six feet tall and 190 pounds. A few of the ranch hands were jealous of my year away but most were genuinely happy to see how well I had progressed. The Senor was proud of my accomplishments and told me so."

"During the summer, it became evident to me that a neighboring rancher—a supposed friend—was stealing our cattle. We eventually caught up with him but the patron was seriously wounded in a gun battle. I took charge of the men and routed the poachers. When September came around, the Senor was in no condition to lead his men, so I resigned from the academy and became his right hand man and personal bodyguard. By Christmas, the Senor was back on his feet but threats to the success of the ranch demanded I stay on. That was twenty years ago Carlos, and I have no regrets. Your grandfather has been very good to me. I owe him everything."

Both men were quiet and allowed the silence to command the moment. Then a lookout interrupted with a shout of "land ho!" Three hours later, the *Durango* was met in New York Bay by a pilot cruiser. He took over the helm and guided the freighter to a wharf owned by Handy and Harman, one of the world's largest silver dealers. Stevedores worked all night to unload the cargo. Bills of lading were signed and the Mexican ship left Perth Amboy at dawn to pick up machinery at a pier in Brooklyn. Docking in New York, the captain gave half the crew liberty for twenty-four hours. At this point, Carlos and Lumberto gathered their luggage, hailed a horse-drawn cab, and made their way to a hotel near Columbia University. After being shown to their rooms, the two walked to the university where they received a brief tour while it was still light. Carlos was deeply impressed by the campus and buildings; they were grander than he expected. "I think I'm going to like it here, Lumberto. This is a new beginning."

CHAPTER 16

Konrad Surveys the Kimball Prospect

AS HE PREPARED FOR THE trip north to find Billy Joe Kimball, Konrad thought a little more seriously about employment with Britsco Mining and Smelting. He'd been his own boss for over five years, successfully developing the Ocotillo Silver Mine and the Tent City placer gold deposits. Both operations were doing well; he had a substantial net worth and his newly constructed office and home gave him roots in a community he liked very much. Reconnecting with Sir Clarence Bingham had been a pleasant surprise; it also gave him the opportunity to repay the gentleman for the help he provided many years ago. His biggest concern was Colin Barksdale and working with him as the representative of the syndicate. Barksdale annoyed Konrad in a personal way, too. Barbara Casey seemed to enjoy the man's company and often dined with him or rode with him at the Volunteer Ranch. It never really dawned on Konrad that the attractive, wealthy widow might even have a casual interest in other male companionship. Konrad loved Barbara Casey but his mining opportunities seemed to take precedence in their relations.

He was comfortable working for Sir Clarence but reporting to the directors through Barksdale bothered him. Konrad rationalized his decision to become an employee by realizing that all new copper mining properties required financial resources he simply didn't have. Was it jealousy over Barbara that bothered him, or the Englishman's personality? What resonated the most however, was the simple fact that he had agreed to work for Britsco and that he would live up to the agreement.

Konrad had mapped out his journey to the Globe Mining District by following the San Pedro River basin to the San Carlos Indian Reservation. Clearly, the trip was risky. Apaches were still attacking remote settlements, prospectors, and U.S. Army troopers. After establishing that the more direct route would save over fifty miles, he conferred with Barney Pryor to get his advice. At first, Barney advised Konrad to use existing stagecoach lines; it would take a little more time but was safer. Konrad rejected that idea on the basis that he wanted to examine the geology of the land as he approached Globe, an area that was completely new to him. But he respected Barney's concerns and hired Half Moon, an Indian scout, and Andy Corsica to travel with him. Corsica was a placer miner who was weapons savvy and interested in getting back to hard rock mining. And the possibility of success with a new company appealed to the man. He also liked and respected Konrad Bruner for the way he dealt with people and his technical knowledge.

It took six days for Bruner, Half Moon, and Andy Corsica to reach Globe. Konrad insisted that they make frequent stops so he could examine rock outcrops and geologic structures. Their two pack mules, loaded down with provisions and equipment, also needed to rest during the arduous journey. Arriving in Globe, Bruner and Corsica took rooms at the General Crook Hotel while Half Moon rode on to the San Carlos Indian Reservation to find his brother and sister whom he hadn't seen in many years.

Over breakfast the next day, Corsica reported on his search for B.J. Kimball. Between sips of coffee, he related his visit to the assay office, livery stable, and a couple of saloons. The assayer provided a general direction to Kimball's place but warned that the old man was extremely protective of his property. Any trespasser was regarded as a thief trying to jump his claims and risked being shot. The people in the saloons who knew him were less kindly. They thought he was a broken down prospector who was either eccentric or insane, depending on the time of day, the weather, or his reaction to the people around him. Not one person believed Kimball had anything resembling the beginning of a metal mine. Corsica then visited the general store to find out what Kimball usually bought to survive in an extremely rugged and remote area. Beans, flour, bacon, sugar, salt, and coffee seemed to be all that the storekeeper could recall. He did remember one thing, though: The old sourdough always paid in gold dust.

"Mr. Bruner, we can reach Kimball's camp in a day, but it'll be a rough go," Corsica reported. "We should take provisions for a few days and an order of stuff the old guy normally buys at the general store. We'll need some kind of a story when we do find him so he doesn't get all riled up and do something crazy." Undisturbed, Konrad responded, "Don't worry, I think we'll be fine.

"I've also got my hands on a few topographic maps of the Globe area," Corsica continued. "I don't know how good they are, but I figured you'd want to look at them. They were expensive but I took the chance, not knowing when we'd be back. Globe is a very busy town, Mr. Bruner. Those gents over there are from Silver City; the rumor is they are looking at a silver prospect north of here. I've got everything we'll need for the trip. Just give me the word and I'll get a hostler to load up the animals."

The following morning, Corsica and Bruner left Globe to search for the old prospector who might have "something" for an international syndicate wanting to invest in the American Southwest. The pair followed Corsica's hand drawn map that led them to a checkpoint, then north through a narrow canyon where they stopped to water the horses and mules. As they saddled up to continue, a loud voice called out, "Just hold it right there, gents. Don't make a move. You can't see me but I can see you clearly down the sight of my .30-.30 Winchester. Now, just turn around real slow and git goin' the same way you came in and nobody'll get hurt."

Konrad removed his Stetson and shouted back, "Hold it, old timer. We have food and supplies from the general store in Globe and we're here because Jeremy Windham said you were the guy to contact. You sent him a letter a while back that he passed on to some people we work with. Does Jeremy Windham mean anything to you?"

"I know a Jeremy Windham of Truro, England. Is that the person you're talking about?"

"Yes, Mr. Kimball, that's the guy."

"I knew a Jeremy Windham but I haven't seen him in years," Kimball answered back. "If this is some kind of trick, you won't get away with it. Now prop that rifle against that wall over yonder and drop your pistols close by. Face the wall and don't make another move until I tell you."

Konrad and Corsica did as they were told. Neither one heard the miner approach until he poked Konrad in the back with his rifle. Slowly turning, they came face-to-face with a wiry, bearded man dressed in a Mexican sombrero, buckskin shirt and trousers, and moccasins. His gnarled hands gripped the rifle tightly. From his appearance, it was clear that B.J. Kimball had been living in the wild for some time.

Spitting tobacco juice freely, Kimball told his visitors to sit down and tell their story one more time, reminding them that he was ready to shoot them dead if they made a false move. After an intense hour of questioning, the prospector began to believe Konrad's story. The letter from Sir Clarence in which he mentioned Jeremy Windham clinched Konrad's case. The fact that Kimball could read and understand the letter encouraged Konrad.

Convinced that Konrad and Corsica were telling the truth, Kimball led them back to his cabin. The three men hiked through two constricted rock masses until they reached a breach in the canyon, then climbed upward to reach a small, secluded meadow and the campsite. Kimball's home was far less rustic than they anticipated. He had two bunk beds, a stove, a table and chairs, and solid plank flooring. Once the animals were taken care of and corralled, the trio sat down to enjoy a whiskey while B.J. fixed dinner. While simple, the roasted antelope, beans, and greens were excellent fare. Coffee and a dessert of apples and hard candy completed the meal.

"You gents take the bunk beds; I've got a loft I can take for the night. I know you're tired, so let's call it a night. I'll give you a complete rundown in the morning."

The men were up at first light and were soon downing coffee and pancakes. As they sat around Kimball's table, the prospector told him his story. "I met Jeremy Windham while we were prospecting in the gold fields of La Paz. He came over from England to strike it rich, like hundreds of others. We placered together for a few months then decided on hard rock prospecting. Hell, we even tramped the Superstition Mountains looking for the Lost Dutchman. Actually, we did well enough in our travels to allow Jeremy to return home with enough money to live comfortably for the rest of his life. But he got restless again and went back to work in the Cornwall tin mines. Then I lost track of him."

"I decided to prospect my way over to Morenci with the thought of eventually settling down in Silver City. That was maybe two or three years ago. Now, the Superstitions are pretty rough country, but nothin' compared to nosin' around Pinal Creek. All this time I might add, the Apaches are leaving me alone. Can't tell you why. Anyway, I stopped near here before going into Globe. The area intrigued me: steep canyons, narrow, dry washes, and isolated. You've probably noticed the rock discoloration; I could also see outcroppings that looked interesting. The dark greens and blues looked like copper mineralization to me. That's probably enough for now; we can take a closer look when you gents are ready."

Leading his tamed burro, B.J. showed Konrad and Corsica the way down a hillside and then hiked a mile or so to where they noticed a series of stone monuments on the side of a gently sloping mountain. The stones located a series of claims. Actually, several pits had been dug along an exposed vein about four feet wide and two hundred feet long.

"This here metal is a mixture of native silver, argentite, and galena. It seems to widen with depth," explained B.J. "The mineral identification was done by the Mittenger Brothers, assayers in Silver City, New Mexico. I've got the papers stashed near the cabin. I don't think we're looking at another Tombstone but I could make a decent living just high grading what you see here. Look around all you like and take some samples. Don't be in a hurry. Old Bessie's got a shovel, pick, and sample bags on her back if you get real ambitious."

For the rest of the day, Konrad, with the help of Andy Corsica, examined the outcrop of silver ore and generally confirmed B.J.'s description. It would require a lot more development work to determine the extent of the ore body but the key question remained: How would they get the ore to the smelter? Konrad also doubted that Britsco would be interested in the silver reef on a stand-alone basis. The copper mineralization did get him thinking, though.

The next day, Kimball took his visitors on a wide sweep away from the silver outcrop, periodically stopping to look at half a dozen pits where copper minerals were exposed. Before the day was over, the men had hiked over ten miles of rugged, rock-strewn terrain. Konrad and Andy were exhausted when they reached camp but Kimball seemed energized by the trip. After pouring his guests whiskey and water and inviting them to bathe in an adjacent spring, the prospector went off to hunt for dinner. He came back a few hours later with two rabbits that went into the stew pot. Before the sun was down, Konrad and Corsica were wrapped in their blankets and enjoying the fire Kimball had prepared for them.

The men breakfasted on the rest of the rabbit stew and fresh biscuits served up with strong, black coffee. It was obvious their host knew his way around a kitchen and was an equally competent hunter and gatherer. Konrad had no idea where the sweet and juicy berries came from. As he yawned and stretched, he noted that Kimball was spreading several maps on the table. He then motioned to Konrad to come over to the table and look at his drawings. One map, drawn roughly to scale, showed key topographic features, the location of the cabin, and the silver ledge. It also established the individual test pits that showed heavy copper mineralization.

"Take a look at this mineralization, Konrad. This is what prompted me to write to Jeremy Windham in England. This here map covers an area about two miles wide and three miles deep. You can see the silver outcrop here, but look at the pattern of pits where I dug for copper. I dug them over the past year and a half and only recently put them on the map."

"Then I took samples, split them, and sent half to Silver City and half to Copper Flats, down your way. All the assay reports are in my secret vault that you can look at later. But I can tell you this for certain: All the samples run from eight percent to over fifteen percent copper. What that suggests to me is that the mountain we're sitting on is full of the red metal. Who knows how deep, but that's what got me to write to Jeremy. I figure it's at least a mile wide and possibly two miles long. Now, I ain't no engineer but that sounds to me like a big discovery. It's also a breakthrough way beyond my means. Why, I can see the mine, smelter, company town, and railroad to the main line out there someday. Tell me if I'm nuts or drinking too much whiskey."

Andy didn't know what to make of B.J.'s comments and Konrad continued to peer over the map spread out on the table. At long last, Konrad looked at the old miner and cautiously offered, "It sure looks like a find to me, B.J. A lot of work will be involved, but what do you want to do next?"

Kimball was obviously prepared for such a question. "So far, I've kept everything you've seen in the past few days a secret. Your visit here might set off an alarm, but I don't think so. This place is just too damn hard to get to and all my assay work was done out of town. The first thing I'd like to see done is complete staking of the claims, so that we're owners of one great piece of property. If we turn to the job now we could get it done in a couple of days, then go to town and complete the recording. Once that's done, we can dig another twenty pits or so, take samples, and add to the information we already have. At that point, we'd have a pretty well defined field package. I'd like to leave the actual mining, concentrating, and smelting to the money boys. The same with a railroad connection to Bowie. I'd like to maintain an interest in the property, but that can be worked out after we get the go ahead from the investors. So, Mr. Bruner, that's my story and my proposition to Britsco. If you agree, we'll get started tomorrow."

As he tried to fall asleep that night, Konrad knew that he'd over-stepped his bounds as chief of exploration and did not have home office approval. But he also believed that Kimball had a project of interest to Britsco. He wasn't sure how Colin Barksdale would react to his decision, but was confident that he was acting in the best interests of the company.

At the crack of dawn, the three men drove corner stakes, measured claims, and built monuments to create a map of contiguous ownership of the newly formed mining company. Four days later, they rode into Globe, recorded their claims, and celebrated their success over dinner at the General Crook Hotel. Konrad decided to have Andy Corsica return with B.J. to the cabin while he contacted Colin Barksdale and told him of Britsco's first mining venture in Arizona.

He telegraphed the Englishman in San Francisco, only to learn that he was about to return to Ribera. With that information, Konrad took the stagecoach to Florence, Tucson, and then on to Ribera. He was optimistic as he reconstructed the map of the Pinal Creek area containing the Copper Mountain Mining Company. This prospect had all the indications of a massive copper mineralized mountain that hopefully would be of interest to his employer.

CHAPTER 17

Valley Water Problems

"DON, I APPRECIATE YOUR COMING back here to help us make some sense out of our farming, or I should say, irrigation difficulties. Tonight's meeting of the growers was just another example of the futility of getting a hundred farmers to agree on anything. Dan Perkins is a good example of what we're up against. He's got hundreds of acres of good ground with direct access to the Salt River and is making money hand over fist. As I see it, he's not about to join any water company."

Don Richmond tapped the spent tobacco from his pipe before responding to Henry Dempsey. "Henry, I don't think we're approaching the problem the way we should. Just look east of here where the Mormons have established themselves and are thriving. Sure, they have their religion to unite them, but it's more than that. They see the benefits of a co-op and have the strong leadership to allocate the water properly, for everyone's benefit. What if we were able to structure a water company headed up by a president and have an elected board to counter the potential excess of power of his office? Swelling did something like this back in the late 1860s along the Hassayampa River. Maybe we should investigate what he was able to accomplish and see how he kept out the speculators whose only interest was buying up water rights for resale. The speculators pose a serious problem to agriculture in this valley and we're going to have to deal with them. Otherwise, we'll have inflated prices and chaos. What would you think of approaching Dan Perkins directly and see what he thinks?"

"After what he had to say at our last meeting, I'd be surprised if he even agreed to meet with us," Dempsey responded. "He's in the driver's seat and doesn't need anyone's help. Organizing the valley farmers just isn't part of his thinking."

A week later Henry Dempsey and Don Richmond were surprised when Dan Perkins agreed to meet with them. The three men met in Dan's office that overlooked an expanse of four hundred acres of cultivated farmland. The main canal, which flowed through the middle of his property, was supplemented by a series of tributary ditches. It was early March and any more frost was unlikely. The men sat on an elevated porch sipping lemonade and watched as a small army of Mexican laborers seeded plots of wheat, barley, melons, and beans.

Lawyer Henry Dempsey opened the discussion. "Dan, we're here to get your thoughts on a proposition we hope you'll be interested in. We decided to approach you first, as you're one of the largest growers in the valley. After eighteen months of open meetings, we've determined that getting twenty or thirty farmers to agree on anything is just not workable. Eventually, we see eight to ten water companies covering farms on the north shore of the Salt River and on the south side. We'll stay clear of the Verde and Gila rivers for the moment. After the establishment of the water companies, the property owners would receive a water allocation based on acreage, farm location, and the existing canals and watercourses. These entities would allow us to address the periodic problems of drought and flooding. Our studies show that Phoenix has about 70,000 acres under cultivation today; we believe this could eventually be expanded to 120,000 acres if properly managed. We further estimate that this could all happen by 1900 if we learn to cooperate with each other. I will assist you and others in drawing up the legal documents and Don will work with the legislature to educate them on our plans and get their support. This is critical, as down the road, we see the need for federal money to build a system of dams that will store water to be used in periods of drought and to control flooding when we receive too much moisture. Don is also in the process of studying the 1872 flood that severely damaged our irrigation network. We need details of this because, unfortunately, it could happen again."

As Dan Perkins brooded over what had just been presented to him, Dempsey and Don Richmond remained silent. "Well, gentlemen, I can easily agree that our democratic process for making decisions hasn't been fruitful. We seem to enjoy fighting with one another far too much. But I've got to think long and hard on the other point you made. I'm already in a very strong position, so why would I want to change? Before you comment, Henry, let me finish. I can visualize a water company covering several thousand acres if Adolph Steinmark would agree to be part of your scheme. Then we might have something to talk about. That would cover maybe six to eight thousand contiguous acres and be a force to reckon with. Tell you what, men: You get that old German to join up and I think you'll have a deal. How's that for a challenge?"

When Don Richmond and Henry Dempsey climbed into their carriage, the lawyer was exuberant, while Richmond pondered in silence. "Good lord, man, we just got Perkins to agree to a deal and you're sweating over something that I can't figure out," Dempsey exclaimed. Staring straight ahead, Don replied, "Henry, I see two problems. Getting Adolph Steinmark to partner with Perkins is problem number one. Assuming he agrees to the deal, we then have to face problem number two. And that question, my friend, is going to be, who is going to be president of this water company? Even though he has less land and canal mileage than Perkins, that old Prussian is going to want to be the boss. Any comments?"

The meeting with Steinmark did not get off to a good start. Adolph insisted that his son be in on the discussion during which Eric Steinmark constantly interrupted Dempsey with irrelevant questions. His father finally saved the day by telling his son to supervise plantings that were underway a mile from the house. "Gentlemen, please accept my apology. I'm not well and eventually Eric will have to take over the family holdings. I'd hoped he would conduct himself with maturity but, as you can see, he hasn't. I will have to deal with that problem later. Now please, tell me your proposal again."

After a complete review of the problems of irrigation control in the valley, Dempsey told Adolph of Dan Perkins' interest in a solution and the hope that Mr. Steinmark would also agree to participate in the venture. "You are to be commended for developing this proposal," Adolph began. "I'm sure you have spent many hours surveying the valley's agricultural prospects. Sunshine and warm weather have favored this land; and if water can be provided on a timely, controlled basis, we will grow and prosper. You have also identified the risk of political dissension. If we continue to fight among ourselves we will surely fail our children and grandchildren. Creating an organization as you have outlined is crucial to the future of Phoenix and someday, the state of Arizona. At the same time, I have personal considerations I must work on. As I mentioned, I am a sick man; Dr. Carter has suggested that I have a year to a year and a half to live. My son Eric is incapable of taking over the family farm, at least at this time. Madi, my eighteen-year-old daughter, is educated and exercises good judgment. Unfortunately, I don't think she would be accepted by the farm community if I made her manager of my estate. Take notes, Mr. Dempsey; I'd like this conversation to be documented and witnessed."

"Eric has natural brain power, but is immature," Steinmark continued. "I intend to send him away to Chicago or the East coast to study engineering or perhaps the law. This period should help him grow up and learn to control his impetuous nature. It will also give him time to think about the family holdings and his future ownership. In the meantime, my wife Helga—the most capable person in the family—will run things. We will hire an outside general manager to run day-to-day operations and I already have two excellent young men in mind for the job. Eric and Madi will each own 40 percent of our holdings, which includes a ranch north of Globe. Helga will own 20 percent, so with Madi, will have a majority control. I'm hopeful that they will act sensibly but there are no guarantees. I've been very hard on my son, gentlemen, and perhaps when he is out from under my wing, he will take on the responsibilities he has avoided so far. Finally, I accept your proposal but with one condition: I will be president of the water company for the first two years, knowing that I will not live out the term. As vice-president, Mr. Perkins will automatically succeed me, for a minimum term of three years. To be honest, he is not one of my favorite neighbors but has my respect as a professional farmer, family man, and as someone who will act in the best interests of the community. Draw up the documents so we can get this organization going. You may share this conversation with Mr. Perkins, but only in confidence. And now, I must get some rest; it's been a very long day."

Indeed, it had been a very long day. The surprising visit with Adolph Steinmark gave Henry Dempsey and Don Richmond much to be pleased about. It also meant that the lawyer had a ton of legal documents to prepare. With Dempsey tied up for at least two weeks, Don Richmond decided to board the stage for Prescott, the former capital of the Arizona Territory.

Located about 100 miles north and west of Phoenix, Prescott lies in the tall timber mountains at an elevation of 5,000 feet. Richmond was impressed with the changes in the landscape as the stagecoach climbed out of the Salt River Valley. Cactus, creosote, and palm trees gave way to scrub oak and juniper bushes, then to white pine and ponderosa pine that stood 80 to 100 feet tall. Annual rainfall was at least double that of Phoenix, contributing to a four season climate. Don stayed a few nights close to Courthouse Square and Whiskey Row, where miners, cowboys, and townspeople mingled, drank, and gambled the nights away. His visit with Judge Palmerton confirmed that Washington was in no mood to rush legislation making Arizona a state. In fact, Congress was considering combining Arizona and New Mexico into one; a move that neither territory approved of. The judge advised that it was best to develop the Phoenix area and defer statehood for several years. He strongly agreed with the concept of regional irrigation, the development of the capital city, and being patient.

Don Richmond then moved on to Flagstaff, a town on the northern transcontinental railroad. Traveling by horseback, he took a week to ride the hundred miles through some of the most spectacular red rock country in the territory. He enjoyed every minute of the trip, except for the afternoon thunderstorms and lightning that spooked both horse and rider. On a hilltop about fifty miles south of Flagstaff, he stopped in awe to view the San Francisco peaks, ancient remains of prehistoric volcanic activity. The snowcapped mountains soared majestically to 12,653 feet, the highest point in the territory.

In the 1890s, Flagstaff was a boisterous railroad town, also supported by logging, trading with the Navajo Nation, and sheepherding. In the saloon at the Woodstock Hotel, he learned that the Riordan family, who felled, cut, and processed lumber to be shipped to the East and West coasts, owned the dominant forestry company. At 7,000 feet, Flagstaff enjoyed cool summers but harsh winters, sometimes receiving over 150 inches of snow in a season. The great ponderosa pine trees were clear cut and milled into railroad ties, framing and siding for houses, and timbers for mining operations in Jerome and elsewhere.

With an unusual mixture of cattlemen, loggers, sheepherders and Indians, Flagstaff was a rip-roaring town virtually isolated from the rest of the territory. Prosperity beckoned to any newcomer with brains who was willing to work hard. It also attracted its share of card sharks, gunslingers, heavy drinkers, and loose women. Richmond rode through and around Flagstaff several times, observing the legal and illegal activities of the town. He wondered how his own son Dale might grow and possibly thrive in such an environment.

After a week of scouting the area and recognizing that statehood was not a major priority for the citizens of Flagstaff, Don Richmond changed into business clothes and left for Phoenix and the irrigation problems he'd left behind three weeks ago. A letter from Dolores, delivered to Henry Dempsey's office, told him that all was well in Ribera. Dale was finally settling down and thinking about college. Elizabeth was seeing a lot of Tom Lawson, home from school in Chicago, where he was studying to be a lawyer. In between the lines, he sensed that his wife was wondering if this might develop into a serious romance.

With Dan Perkins and Adolph Steinmark agreeing to merge their interests into a water canal company, it wasn't very long before they had a group of farmers in the fold. Before leaving for Tucson and home, Don Richmond called on Adolph Steinmark. The older man appeared rested and happy to see him. He was especially pleased to report that his son Eric had decided to study engineering and was on his way to Yale University in Connecticut. After a brief introduction to Helga and Madi Steinmark, the two men adjourned to the farmhouse porch for further conversation.

"Mr. Richmond, I again want to congratulate you in helping us to establish our canal company. I understand that you've become active in politics and that is good. In ten or twenty years, Arizona should be a thriving state, productive in ranching, farming, mining, and perhaps, even forest products. Were I a man of your age and capabilities, I would look carefully at the Globe area. It's first-class cattle country with serious copper mining underway. If you ever get over that way, be sure to get in touch with Dewey Unger, my ranch manager at the Steinmark spread. It's about twenty-five miles north of Globe in some of the finest ranching country I've ever seen. I've enjoyed meeting you and now feel comfortable that my affairs are in order. I thank you and wish you a safe trip home."

Adolph's remarks gave Don pause. "Ranching north of Globe. Now that could be an idea worth exploring," he thought. He wondered what the old man was thinking.

CHAPTER 18

Booker Traps Aguijador

SERGEANT PORTER AND A TROOPER, as ordered by Lieu-
tenant Booker, escorted the old Indian woman and Soleado into Ribera.
They were not happy with the assignment but orders were orders.
They were much more interested in chasing after Aguijador and his followers than playing nursemaid. They were guided to the sheriff's office
where Sam Bellows, looking at the scraggly Indian woman and the
white child with blonde hair, decided to have them looked over by a
doctor.

Ben Lawson was at the Ocotillo Mine, so Doc Gilroy handled the
chores. He examined both newcomers. "Sam, they don't seem to have
anything seriously wrong that a good bath wouldn't cure," he told Bellows. "I'd suggest you get the old woman cleaned up first, then have her
sent to the Reservation. She's probably got kin up there."

Just then, Kate Lawson and Barbara Casey came into the clinic
looking for some medicine. When questioned about the child and
Indian woman, Doc Gilroy explained, "These two were deposited with
Sheriff Bellows this morning. An Apache raider group that was being
attacked by army cavalry abandoned them. Two soldiers brought them
here on orders by a Lieutenant Vince Booker, who is leading a force
against one of the Apache chieftains. Neither one has said much of anything; I'd guess the girl to be six or seven years old. I'm having the
Indian woman sent to the reservation; I'm gonna try and find temporary housing for the youngster until we can get an identification on her.
Sam's working on that now. Say, would you help getting these two
cleaned up and dressed in some clean clothes? It'd be a big help."

Barbara Casey looked closely at the young girl, nodded and agreed. "Let me take her to the store and get her some clothes. I'll let Kate rummage around for the old woman. After a bath and some clothes, I'll take her out to the ranch where she can get some rest. Maybe some Ortiz food will get her started on becoming a white child again. It would be nice to know how she got hooked up with the Apaches; but that'll have to wait until we hear from the soldiers."

While medics tended to several slightly wounded troopers, a detail dug a grave near the base of the mountain for the Indian scout. Booker considered his next move. He was pleased the way the platoon had conducted itself during the attack and knew the battle experience would encourage the men to continue the assault. As Spotted Pony's body, wrapped in a blanket, was lowered to its final resting place, Booker decided that the platoon would pursue the Indian contingent.

The lieutenant believed the war party, now burdened with women and children, would only be able to move slowly and would leave clear signs of their travel. If he were real lucky, they would be concentrating on getting the women and children to a safe place and not expecting the cavalry troop to follow up and exploit their victory. Booker sent his best trackers to shadow the Indian survivors, but none materialized. As dawn broke, it became apparent that the Indians were still withdrawing, seemingly unwilling to fight. This maneuver bothered Booker; he expected Apaches to always fight rather than run.

During breakfast, the trackers returned to camp and reported that they had followed the Indians to a large cave, about five miles away. Corporal Tully reported, "Sir, it was pretty easy to follow them; they've got wounded to deal with and the women and kids are tired. The trail is rough country, but they seemed to know where they were going. Eventually the trail narrowed, then sort of wrapped around the mountain to where this huge cave is. When they got there, they went about making fires, cooking food and getting the children settled. We had good cover to within 200 yards of the cave opening, and then used our field glasses. All in all, they're one tired bunch and seem to feel that they'd reached a safe destination. Only a couple of guards were posted, that we could see. It would be a tough place to get to, but to me, it looks like they ain't going any further. Kinda like this is going to be their last stand."

"How many did you see in the cave, corporal?" Booker asked.

"I'd say about sixty or seventy, but half of them are women and children, sir."

Vince Booker didn't like the idea of attacking women and children. But he also realized he had Aguijador bottled up in a cave, and his orders were to capture or kill the tribal leader. When he remembered the brutal massacre of Soleado's parents and brother, he made his decision. Booker summoned his squad leaders together and told them they were to continue the attack. They would ride close to the Indian camp that afternoon, make camp nearby, and be ready to strike shortly after dawn.

In the early afternoon, Booker led his troop to within a half-mile of the cave. Accompanied by Corporal Tully he made a personal reconnaissance of the hideout, confirming the trackers' earlier report. It appeared that the Indian men were building a low, rock wall at the mouth of the cave, while the women cooked and the children played quietly. It was hard to believe but it appeared as if the chieftain was setting up a permanent camp. Shaking his head, Booker returned to the bivouac area. "See that the horses are taken well back from here, where they can be guarded by just a few men. Issue orders that there will be no fires; remain quiet, and be ready to move out at 0400 hours."

As light began to barely indicate dawn, the platoon silently worked its way to the Indian cave. By the time the sun was up, they were positioned behind good cover, only fifty yards from the cave opening. Rifles were loaded and locked, and then Booker shouted to Aguijador to surrender and come out of the cave. A hail of arrows that hit nothing but tree trunks and large boulders met his invitation. After the lieutenant shouted out a second request, several braves stood up on the wall yelling they would never surrender. They fired into the air, screaming epithets to the soldiers.

Upon Booker's order to "fire at will," the troopers moved into new positions and fired directly into the cave. As bullets ricocheted off the cave walls and ceiling, cries from the women and children could be heard. Then, on orders of "cease fire," Booker again pleaded for surrender and had one of his men, who spoke Apache well, repeat the request. In response, four Indian warriors armed with lances and hatchets scaled the rock wall and charged the troopers. They were quickly cut down in a fusillade of bullets as the lieutenant gave orders to fire away at will.

Aguijador's position was futile and he knew it. He also knew that he would never surrender, even if it meant the loss of his tribe. Crowding the women and children into the deep recesses of the cave, he gathered his warriors for a final charge against the blue coats. Barely outside the mouth of the cave, the Indians were met by the firepower of twenty

Winchester '73 rifles. One by one, the warriors were shot down and killed in the suicide attack. When a final "cease fire" was sounded, the battle scene fell silent. Only the smell of gunpowder and the cries of the Indian women and children broke the morning quiet. Aguijador's body was identified among the casualties. He would fight no more.

When Booker reached the mouth of the cave, he was shocked to see the number of wounded women and children. After deciding that most of the wounds were minor, he ordered Tully to get back to camp and return with wagons to transport the captives to the San Carlos Indian Reservation. The troopers buried the slain warriors in one mass grave before leaving the battle site to return to Fort Gore.

On their way back to the fort, Booker detoured to Ribera for provisions and medical care for the wounded. Sam Bellows and the townsfolk were startled to see three wagons filled with Indians as they entered town. The lieutenant had them disembark and rest while he went for medical help and food supplies. Doctors Gilroy and Lawson patched up the wounded, as the townspeople gawked at the Indians. Most were surprised to see Booker pay so much attention to the captives, especially the wounded. Murmurs of "Why in hell is he helping those people?" rippled through the crowd.

Barbara Casey was not one of those people. She watched Booker handle his prisoners and thought him a man of uncommon decency. Sam Bellows approached, followed by the lieutenant.

"Barbara, this is Lieutenant Vince Booker from Fort Gore. He's taking these Indians to the San Carlos Reservation but before he leaves he wants to know what happened to the little girl he left here a few weeks ago."

"Mr. Booker, it's a pleasure to meet you," Barbara Casey responded. "Soleado is with me at my ranch. She's very quiet and doesn't say much but is putting on some weight. If you have the time, I'd be happy to take you there and you can see for yourself. Is she related to you?"

"No, ma'am, she's not. But I was the soldier who found her dead family after the Apaches attacked their farm and burned the place down several years ago. I think she was saved because of her blond hair and feistiness. She's been living with an Apache tribe for some years."

With Sheriff Bellows agreeing to look after the Indian prisoners, Booker and Barbara Casey took a carriage ride to the Volunteer Ranch. "May I ask you a question?" Booker began. "I was an enlisted man a few years ago in a platoon commanded by a Lieutenant Casey. We got into a big ruckus up north with some Apaches and he was killed. Was he any relation to you?" Startled by the directness of his question, Barbara

Casey pulled the team to a halt. "Mr. Booker, Lieutenant John Casey was my husband."

Embarrassed, Booker took a gulp but could only reply with a lame compliment. "I'm sorry, Mrs. Casey. The lieutenant was a fine man and a brave officer." Barbara Casey looked at her visitor, smiled gently, and responded, "Don't feel bad, Mr. Booker. That was over seven years ago. Yes, he was a fine man and I loved him very much."

Booker was impressed by the size of the Volunteer Ranch, its ample water supply, and the good looking horses in the corral. Barbara Casey told him a little bit of the history of the ranch and how she periodically sold horses to the army. It was her luck to have the best in breeding stock and almost unlimited pastureland. All that and the Bowie River to provide water made the ranch unique in southern Arizona. The fact that the owner was an attractive widow also piqued Booker's interest.

That afternoon the lieutenant enjoyed coffee and spice cakes in the Casey kitchen. He was also introduced to Soleado. The girl smiled shyly and shook his hand when it was offered. Then she sat on the floor, legs crossed, Indian style. Vince returned her smile. "It's good to see you getting well, Soleado. I guess you like staying here with Mrs. Casey and Mrs. Ortiz. Is there anything I can do for you?"

The young girl shook her head, replied "no, sir," and then stood up and walked over to Barbara Casey's side. The widow held Soleado close to her and looked over at Lieutenant Booker. "A lot has happened to me in the past few weeks, Mr. Booker. I have come to love this beautiful child as if she were my own. I would like to adopt Soleado and raise her as my daughter. Can you clear it with the fort commander and see what paperwork might be required?"

On the ride back into town, Barbara Casey and Booker chatted about Soleado, the ranch, and Barbara's late husband. The conversation was light and easy even though they had just met. Before saying goodbye, Barbara invited Booker to come and visit with her and Soleado at the ranch. As she watched him lead the wagon train and platoon out of town, Barbara Casey knew she would see Vince Booker again.

CHAPTER 19

An Epidemic Strikes the Reservation

THE ROOM WHERE CALEB BENSON did his mixing was heavily padlocked. The post trader made certain he was in sole possession of the key at all times. Unlocking the thick oaken door, Caleb placed the candle on a shelf, while mice scurried into holes between the flooring and baseboards. Otherwise, it was dark and quiet as he lifted the lid on a large barrel of river water. Working methodically, he followed the recipe notes tacked to the wall of the secret chamber. Two gallons of raw alcohol, three plugs of tobacco, five bars of soap, a half a pound of red pepper and a few handfuls of sagebrush completed the concoction. He then stirred the mix and using cheesecloth, strained the liquid into a second, holding barrel. With a tin funnel and ladle, he transferred the rotgut into empty bottles that he would sell or trade with the Indians. He smiled to himself, pleased that he no longer had to buy whiskey from the traveling purveyors of the elixir. Sometimes he added an ounce or two of strychnine, "the greatest stimulant in the world," to the liquid.

Getting sick after a two-day binge on Benson's whiskey verified to the buyer that the booze was the real thing. The post executive officer, Major Garrison, suspected Caleb of exceeding their normal split on the sale of stolen blankets and hand tools, but was totally unaware of the trader's new business of manufacturing whiskey. Actually, all had gone pretty well over the past three months for the trader despite the epidemic of sickness and death to the Indians. It seemed as if he had an unlimited number of customers willing to buy or trade the liquor as fast as he could produce it. Isaac Brinkerman was unhappy over his lost customers, but Caleb didn't worry a wit about the traveling salesman.

Benson's illegal activities did not go unnoticed. Reverend Hugh Packard, a Methodist minister enlisted by the Grant administration to oversee government policies on the San Carlos Reservation, knew the post trader was involved in the sale of whiskey to the Indians but had been unable to prove Caleb was the culprit. The base commander, Colonel Burlingame, would not start a formal investigation despite the fact that Indian men were dying of liquor poisoning. And the severity of the smallpox outbreak had him almost totally focused on the dread disease. The minister's report to Colonel Burlingame on the status of the epidemic was not encouraging.

"Colonel, I'm not a medic but I know that smallpox spreads rapidly and easily. We also know that we are virtually helpless in the treatment of the disease. We suspect that the Indians are more susceptible to smallpox than either the Mexican or the white man. Just why, we don't know. My records for the past three months show that the mortality rate for Indian men, women, and children is about eighty percent once the disease is contracted."

"Well, Hugh," replied Burlingame. "We know we have a problem; what can we do about it?"

Packard reached into his breast pocket to retrieve a small pad. Reading from his notes, he suggested three things that could be done immediately. First, persons who contract smallpox should be quickly isolated from healthy persons and kept in quarantine. Second, clothing and blankets used by smallpox victims should be boiled in water for at least half an hour or, better yet, destroyed by burning.

"I know this sounds wasteful, sir, but taking clothing and blankets from infected patients and using them again is unsanitary. Finally, we are woefully understaffed and should enlist the aid of the civilian population, both doctors and nurses." Packard knew the colonel couldn't order a civilian doctor to help but was hopeful that a message to the outside might get a few volunteers.

"Hugh, I'll appeal to the doctors in Ribera with a letter; maybe if you deliver it to them personally, we'll get some kind of response."

Before leaving Colonel Burlingame's office, Packard decided to bring up the conduct of Caleb Benson. "Off the record, sir, I want you to know that I believe Caleb Benson is shortchanging the Indians on rations and is selling them whiskey. I'm never in one place long enough to come up with any proof but I believe this to be true. Too many Indians that I trust have approached me with this complaint. I'm convinced Benson is not only stealing food, but selling whiskey, and worse, reselling dirty blankets from smallpox victims."

"Reverend, these are serious accusations. Benson has been on the frontier for quite a few years with the Army and has a lot of friends in the territory. I don't have the people to conduct an investigation nor would I without hard proof. Do what you can to collect some more proof and I'll alert Major Garrison to be on the lookout. In the meantime, let me see your notes so I can issue an order to do what you suggest. Now, back to a trip to Ribera. Leave as soon as you can to see if you can get some help from those folks."

Colonel Burlingame's conversation with his executive officer only served to warn his second in command that Caleb Benson was under suspicion. Major Garrison informed his partner of the news.

"I don't care what that scrawny little preacher says to the Colonel, but if he persists we'll just have to take care of him," Benson confided to Garrison. "I ain't gonna let some Philadelphia city boy upset our apple cart. If you can't keep him quiet, you can bet your boots they'll find him with an arrow or bullet in his back."

Garrison was shaken by Caleb's reaction and realized that similar circumstances might have lead to the mysterious death of Limping Bear, the Indian scout. Why, he wondered, did he choose to become involved with this guy?

Reverend Hugh Packard wasted no time in deciding what to do after leaving the post commander's office. He told Sergeant Major Purdy he needed horses and protection for his trip to Ribera, and he wanted to leave within the hour.

With two cavalry soldiers and a scout to accompany him, Packard was soon riding steadily to the river town. The men pushed their mounts until early evening, and bedded down after a cold meal. Rising at dawn to complete the journey, the party reached Ribera before noon. They went immediately to the clinic in search of Doctor Lawson. Kate Lawson was not happy when she heard what the minister had in mind.

"Mr. Packard, the Grant administration has torn this territory apart with its broken promises. The most recent debacle of crowding people on to poor farmland and expecting them to live decently is outrageous. Then this epidemic of smallpox breaks out and you expect us to come to your rescue. Reverend, you're sure not short on nerve! You know how easily smallpox can spread and you know we don't have a cure for it. Why, you could be a carrier yourself."

Calming herself, Kate poured Packard a cup of coffee. They were talking about the problem when Doc Gilroy and Ben Lawson entered the room. After introductions, Kate excused herself as Ben and Doc Gilroy listened to Packard explain the purpose of his visit.

"Gentlemen, I'm here because we need your help. Your wife has heard my story and I can appreciate her concerns, but people are dying and if we don't do something right now, many hundreds more will surely perish. I've never seen anything like this in my life. Please, will you help us? At the moment, the disease seems to be confined to the San Carlos Reservation, but I'm afraid it could easily spread maybe even to Ribera."

As Packard went into further details, the doctors concluded that they had to help. Finally, Doc Gilroy announced, "You're right, Hugh. We do have to help you out. I don't know how much good we can do, but we sure have to try. Ben, you've got Amy McPherson ready to give birth and that kid run over by a horse is gonna need your tending for a few days. So, it looks like I'm your man, Hugh. Maybe I can get one of the Bartlett girls to come along with me."

Doc Gilroy glanced in the direction of Ben Lawson and sensed his objections. "Now, Ben, let's not have any debate on who should go. We can't leave the town without a doctor, you've got a family and I don't, so it's a closed case. Mr. Packard, give me an hour or two to get my gear together, round up a nursing assistant, and we can be on our way. I'll get Barney to pack up one of his horses with medical equipment."

Despite his protestations, Ben knew that Doc Gilroy had made his mind up. Kate helped gather bandages and other supplies, quietly heaving a sigh of relief. She knew her husband would feel guilty over not going, but he'd get over it.

The group rode well into the night. Early the second day, they reached Fort Gore and finally, the San Carlos Reservation. Doc Gilroy was shocked then maddened, to see the horrible conditions of the camp. On his first tour of examining patients, he noted that the sick were mingling with the healthy and had complete freedom to roam about. A European medical book suggested vaccination, which Doc mulled over as he surveyed the situation, now out of control. Dead bodies were lying about while some patients huddled in blankets, scratching themselves furiously.

He ordered Nellie Bartlett to supervise the setting up of a large tent. Then he instructed her to sanitize the flooring. Once the tent was ready, the doctor moved a large group into the shelter and posted a big red cross on the canvas flap, a sign that the place was in quarantine with no visitors allowed. Blankets were removed from the dead and burned. The dead were then gathered and taken to a place out of sight of the populace, doused with kerosene, and cremated. Then, Gilroy set up inoculation procedures.

He made a scratch on the arm of a healthy child and matter from a smallpox blister was rubbed into the superficial wound. Usually, the child developed a mild case of the disease, but also immunity from future outbreaks. The tactics of separating the sick from the healthy, vaccinations, strict boiling of drinking water, and the rapid disposal of the dead and their clothing and blankets began to show results. Fewer Indians were dying. Doc Gilroy, Reverend Packard, and Nellie Bartlett worked unceasingly for over a week, tending to the sick and dying. But the constant exposure to the disease and an unfortunate pricking by an infected needle finally felled the doctor. Several days after contracting smallpox, Doctor Gilroy died. Reverend Packard presided over the funeral as Doc's friends and many Indians mourned his fate. When the minister told the story of Doc Gilroy's heroism to Major Garrison, the executive officer could only murmur grudgingly, "Well, it sounds like the old guy did some good, even if it was with some Indians."

Nellie Bartlett carried the news of Doc Gilroy's death to the town of Ribera. As the townspeople mourned the loss of their dedicated doctor, they also realized that they were back to having only one physician. Ben Lawson was already in touch with several medical schools but decided to hold off on any announcement until he had a firm commitment from a new doctor who was willing to relocate to Ribera.

During the memorial service, which coincided with the completion of the town's new hospital, the board of directors announced they had unanimously agreed to name the new facility the Doctor Henry J. Gilroy Medical Center. The crowd cheered their approval of the fallen hero.

CHAPTER 20

A Pittsburgh Rendezvous

RACHEL LAWSON, DAUGHTER OF DOCTOR Ben and Kate Lawson, entered the University of Michigan at the age of seventeen. Formal medical studies, especially for women, were still new; many viewed doctoring as an art as much as a science. Rachel fell in love with the Ann Arbor campus and enjoyed most of her classmates who ranged in age from seventeen to forty-one. While all the professors were male, the female students lived in a large, stately house managed by a house-mother who directed the cooks and servers. The students attended classes Monday through Friday and a half a day on Saturday. It wasn't long before Margaret Halliday, the oldest of the women students, became the class leader. She had hospital experience as a nurse in Cleveland and was intelligent, friendly, and helpful to her classmates. Between Margaret, the housemother, and the dean of the medical school, the semester moved along without any major problems for the young women.

By Christmas however, two girls elected to withdraw from school and enjoy the holidays at home with their families. They were not convinced that doctoring was what they wanted to do for the rest of their lives. Most of the other women stayed on at Med House, as it was known, over Christmas recess, either to catch up with their studies or rest for the next semester. Rachel thought about taking the train to New York City to see Carlos, but since she hadn't heard from him in over six months, decided to remain in Ann Arbor. She reasoned he was probably too busy with his studies to write. Or maybe he had another girlfriend who was occupying his time and why not. He was a very attractive young man.

The day after Christmas, Rachel received a package from home with news of local happenings and a box of homemade cookies. The package also contained a thick letter to her in Arizona, marked with the words "Please forward." As snow began to fall on the campus, Rachel settled into a comfortable chair in front of a warm, crackling fire. Then she opened the letter from Carlos and began to read:

Dear Rachel,

I apologize for not writing sooner. I can't believe that I've been here for four months. The trip from Tampico was long but interesting. At first, I resented being chaperoned by Lumberto Villegas, but he has been a good guide and a new friend. Columbia sits by itself in the northern part of the city. I share a dormitory room with Arn Gustafson, a student from Minnesota. His father runs an iron ore mine on the Mesabi Range. I guess Arn plans on doing the same thing when he graduates. We're not the closest of friends but we study together and it has paid off. We are both doing well in our engineering courses. Most of the students come from the coal country in Pennsylvania or the steel mill towns of western Pennsylvania and Ohio. We haven't been anywhere close to a mine or mill since I've been here; the professors insist that we build a solid understanding of math and science first.

I haven't seen much of the city and only visit Lumberto on Sundays, when we have dinner together. He spends most of his time across the river in Perth Amboy, New Jersey learning the process of alloying silver for manufacturing knives, forks, and spoons. On a November holiday, we went downtown to enjoy a Thanksgiving dinner at a seaport tavern. The food was very good and we hired a small boat that took us completely around the island of Manhattan. It was a cold day to be on the water but I really enjoyed the outing.

The most startling thing about New York City is the diversity of the people. There are the descendants of the original Dutch and British settlers but also Irish, German, and Scandinavian immigrants. Then there are the Italians who seem to be arriving by the shipload. Then Jews mainly from Russia who some say are escaping from the terrors of the czar's army. As I mentioned, my studies are going well, especially in courses that Arn and I attend together. By comparing notes and discussing the more difficult problems, we are both getting good grades. The university requires a semester at a steel mill, mine, or textile factory and a paper describing the experience before a degree in engineering is awarded. Maybe I will be able to sign on with someone near Ann Arbor so I can come and visit you.

I love the excitement of the big city but I also miss Mexico and the short visit I had with you at Mrs. Casey's Volunteer Ranch. Please write to me and tell me how you are doing at medical school.

With love,
Carlos

There were a few details that young Carlos left out of his letter to Rachel. Visiting the docks area one Sunday night, he and Lumberto dined at a restaurant near where the ships disgorged and loaded cargo. The food was good but the neighborhood was unsavory, particularly at night. When they left the establishment, they had difficulty locating a carriage and decided to walk to a street where they knew cabs waited for passengers. Before they could reach this safe zone, four thugs brandishing clubs and knives accosted them. The crooks demanded their money, watches, and jewelry but were met by Lumberto's flying fists. As he flattened the lead man with a crushing blow to the jaw, Lumberto yelled for Carlos to run for his life. But the young man stood his ground. He elbowed another assailant in the stomach while Lumberto slugged another one of the thugs. With three of the attackers dispatched, the fourth man turned and ran just as a policeman came on the scene.

"We were ambushed, officer. But everything is all right," Carlos explained. Once the policeman left, Lumberto addressed Carlos in a serious tone of voice. "We were lucky tonight, Carlos, and you conducted yourself well. But in the future, when I tell you to run, I want you to do just that, without hesitation. Understand?"

"Yes, Lumberto, I hear you. But I would never leave you behind in a fight."

During the next few weeks, Carlos met with a Chinese man who taught him various defensive positions, judo holds, and other means of protecting himself. After weeks of practice, the young student became skilled in the art of self-defense. When his instructor told Lumberto that Carlos was more than qualified to handle himself in a fight, the Mexican was satisfied. "He's strong and fast and has learned his lessons well. You won't have to worry about him if someone decides to pick a fight with him."

On another occasion, Lumberto invited Carlos out to dinner and then a Broadway musical. Two very attractive women accompanied them: Rita, a woman in her early forties and Karen, a brunette, in her twenties. Dinner was excellent and the champagne flowed. The musical show consisted of several acts of singing, a chorus line of statuesque girls and a few vaudeville acts. The foursome had a private box curtained on all sides except the one facing the stage. It was the kind of arrangement where a gentleman could entertain his mistress without being seen by a friend, business associate, or the prying press who were always alert to a potential scandal.

After the performance, Lumberto and Rita excused themselves. After several glasses of champagne, it was easy for Karen to lead Carlos to a nearby hotel. Removing a key from her purse, she unlocked the door and invited the young man to join her for a nightcap. The spacious room had a large double bed, chaise lounge, a private bathroom, and a bottle of champagne cooling in a bucket of ice. Removing her coat, Karen glided into the bathroom after giving Carlos a brief but sensuous kiss. Smiling, she invited her young guest to make himself comfortable.

Aroused but apprehensive, Carlos removed his overcoat and suit coat and sat on the bed as he removed his shoes. Any misgivings gave way as soon as Karen approached him in a black, silk negligee trimmed with white lace. She then lit a candle, poured two glasses of champagne, and slowly removed Carlos's tie, shirt, and trousers. Turning down the bed cover, she turned to Carlos and kissed him hungrily, rubbing her body in a slow grind to meet his manhood. They entwined briefly and settled into an exploratory embrace. They made fierce, untamed love for several hours before drifting off to sleep.

Awakening at mid-morning, Carlos stared at the ceiling and smiled as he recalled his night with the beautiful, enticing Karen. As the sun streamed through the bedroom window, he glanced over to the chaise lounge where his clothes were neatly arranged. The candle and champagne were gone. A note next to the bed read, "Carlos, thank you for a wonderful evening. My love always, Karen."

He didn't see Lumberto for several weeks after that evening. Carlos turned back to his books in preparation for semester exams. When his friend appeared, it was to announce that he was returning to Mexico on the next company ship leaving from Brooklyn. On the day of departure, Carlos and Lumberto hugged and wished each other well.

The night at the theater was never mentioned.

Rachel Lawson reread the letter from Carlos and inserted the note back into its envelope. The letter affected her deeply; she hadn't realized that she was in love with Carlos and missed him terribly. But she didn't know how to deal with the distance that separated them or if Carlos really loved her. Casting aside what others might think of her forward behavior, she decided to write to Carlos and suggest they meet. She had no misgivings when she posted the letter.

A week later, a telegram from New York arrived at the Med House. Rachel tipped the messenger a nickel and rushed to her room to read the message in private:

Dear Rachel—Wonderful to hear from you. Will be in Pittsburgh for four days in February to interview for a job in a steel mill. Wire me the days you can get away and I will reserve rooms for us at the Pittsburgher Hotel. Love, Carlos.

That afternoon, Rachel sent the first telegram of her life. In it, she gave Carlos the preferred dates for a rendezvous in the steel city. It was less than three weeks away! Rachel's heart beat faster in anticipation of the trip.

CHAPTER 21

The Whitman Hotel Fire

THE REMODELING OF THE WHITMAN Hotel was complete. The first floor had a front desk, parlor, kitchen, and dining room. Stairs led to a second floor that housed the owner's suite and eight guest rooms. A fresh coat of white paint with dark green trim gave the appearance of a new exterior. Expansion of the attached saloon was unfinished but well underway.

"Mr. Carmody, we've got a theater group coming here for a three-day visit over the Fourth of July. Are you going to be ready?" asked Sophie Kaminski.

"Well, Miss Sophie, we've had timber shipment delays and we're short of skilled carpenters, but with a little luck, we should have the work completed," Carmody replied. "We'll be starting on the stage area this week; that's the big job. Your change of thinking about building four box seats probably makes sense to you but it's an addition that we hadn't anticipated. As we stand here today, we'll complete our original contract, but I'm 50-50 on the box seats. I've got a couple of young Mexican woodworkers putting benches together and they're doing real good work. They'll have the benches done a week ahead of time."

Keeping the saloon open and running to generate cash while the theater was being built had caused a few problems but most customers didn't seem to mind. Sophie had to shift poker tables around but the card players hadn't missed a beat. She knew that most townspeople were aware of the fracas settled by Barney Pryor but gossip had quieted down to almost nothing. Sophie had little contact with the women folk of Ribera, excepting Barbara Casey and to a lesser degree, Kate Lawson. Several of the men, including a few of the town pillars, had given her leading glances but she ignored them and went about her business. She appreciated the fact that the miner who had accosted her in the saloon had not been seen or heard of again. She had plenty to do working on the hotel and didn't want to see Barney beat up or involved in a shoot out. While Sophie enjoyed his company, she feared that her past was too much baggage for him to overlook. Secretly though, she wanted to expand her relationship with Barney but was reluctant to make the first move. She hadn't seen him in several weeks; perhaps it was for the better.

As it turned out, Barney Pryor was at the Ocotillo Silver Mine working on an exploratory tunnel to enlarge the proven reserves of the property. He thought of Sophie constantly and wondered how he could re-establish their friendship. And regardless of her Silverton past, he thought Sophie Kaminski was the finest lady he'd ever met. He just had to figure out a way to get the romance started.

While Sophie immersed herself in the rehabilitation of the hotel and expansion of the saloon, one miner, now a saloonkeeper in Tent City, brooded over the embarrassment of a beating administered by the owner of Ribera's livery stable. Several of his patrons continued to remind him of the humiliation and Burr Tilden was sick of it. He'd let his beard grow to cover up the scars and figured it might be a good disguise for what he had in mind. Riding into Ribera on a quiet Sunday afternoon, Tilden smiled as he rode past the newly painted hotel and expanded saloon. It was early and only a few souls were out and about. A sign heralding a Fourth of July show, "Direct from Virginia City, Nevada," caught his attention. "Now wouldn't it be damn shame if that troupe arrived to find nothin' but charred ruins where they expected to perform," he mused. Wheeling his horse around for home, Burr Tilden decided he had the perfect answer for Sophie and her protector. By the time he got back to Tent City he had a plan.

For the next week, Tilden worked short hours on his claim while stealing small amounts of kerosene from scattered locations around Tent City. He filled three, one-gallon jugs previously used for whiskey and kept the containers hidden in his tent. On the night of July third, he unhitched his horse and quietly left for Ribera. Reaching town shortly after midnight, he tied his horse on the cliff side of the river and carried the three jugs of kerosene to the saloon construction site. There, he made a number of small piles of wood shavings and kindling, doused them with kerosene, and lit the fires one by one.

As flames enveloped the saloon they were followed by ignitions in the hotel. Soon, the buildings were engulfed in a fiery blaze as screams of "Fire, Fire!" rang out. Crunched down by the bridge, Tilden could see it was the Chinese cook alerting the town. It was shocking to see the speed with which the flames became a fiery blaze. As Tilden climbed on his horse he could see figures fleeing the hotel, which was rapidly being consumed by the inferno. "Now we're even, honey," he said to himself.

The fire at the Whitman Hotel was out of control before a bucket brigade could be organized to fight the blaze. The following morning all that remained was a collapsed roof and charred wreckage. With tears in her eyes, Sophie Kaminski surveyed the damage and recognized that her dream was ruined. That she had escaped the inferno on Ho-Ching's warning shouts wasn't enough for her to feel grateful. It never occurred to Sophie that the fire was not accidental.

By nine o'clock the townspeople were crowding around the smoking ruins, speculating over an early alarm that had saved the owner but had not awakened one guest, who perished in the fire. Ho-Ching's shouts had saved the general store and other town structures. He was now in Ben Lawson's clinic, recovering from severe burns on his arms and legs.

Sheriff Bellows recovered the body of the visiting cattle buyer for the U.S. Army after sifting through the debris. Talking briefly with deputy Marty Rollins after the inspection, Bellows remarked, "I don't think there's any question that we have a case of arson and murder on our hands. Ho-Ching hasn't been able to say too much but we'll get some answers to this mess after he feels better. I don't think there's any link to the cattle buyer, so that leaves Miss Kaminski as the target of the crime. I can't figure why at the moment but it seems to me she was minding her own business and not offending anyone. Here the place is burned to the ground and all she's frettin' about is some minstrel show that's due in town today. And she's already been down to visit the Chinaman to see how he's doing. I'm going to cordon off the area. When things cool off some, we can take another look and see if we can come up with something that will give us a clue."

When Barney Pryor heard about the hotel fire, he left the mine immediately and arrived in Ribera by mid-day. When he found Sophie she was with Barbara Casey, discussing the possibility of an open-air performance of the minstrel show on Main Street in the middle of town. Sophie had recovered from the shock of losing the hotel and saloon and was struggling to salvage her commitment to the troupe from Virginia City. A total loss could be avoided if she could hold the show outdoors. Over the next few hours, Sophie and volunteers scrounged enough timber and planking from the fiery ruins to fashion a stage. They found enough saloon benches, still intact, to provide seating for at least sixty people. Barbara Casey loaned out the back room of the general store for use as changing rooms for the troupe. Chairs were borrowed for the musicians and kerosene lamps provided the lighting. All afternoon, men worked on building the stage while many townspeople offered rooms to the visitors. After hearing about the fire, Mrs. Strickland, manager of the touring group, accepted the conditions and exclaimed, "We're here to do a show, so let's get on with it!"

Shortly before dusk, brass trumpets, trombones, and a drum roll announced the start of the program. It was the first community-wide Fourth of July celebration ever held in Ribera. The show consisted of a small chorus line, some slapstick comedy routines, and lots of loud and lusty singing that included audience participation. Before the night was over, the happy crowd was singing and dancing in the streets, shouting for encores. As the musicians, dancers, and citizens mingled, all agreed this was the best Fourth of July ever.

Before leaving the festive scene with Barbara Casey, Sophie had a few quiet moments with Barney. "The fire has been a disaster and one person is dead. I don't know how it happened; I'll leave that to Sam Bellows and Marty Rollins to figure out. But I do know this town has a heart. They passed the hat several times during the show and I've got more money, after paying Mrs. Strickland, that I thought possible; maybe eight hundred dollars. The way people pitched in to save the day has been unbelievable. I'm overwhelmed."

Barney looked into Sophie's eyes, now brimming with tears. "Sophie, you need some rest; it's been a long day and night for you. You're in good hands with Barbara Casey. Sleep well; we can talk some more tomorrow." With a brief hug and kiss to her forehead, Barney Pryor said goodnight.

The next day Barney joined the two lawmen in poking through the rubble of the fire but found very little to salvage except some heavy pots and pans from the kitchen. The remnants of a few whiskey jugs and a couple of boards that smelled of kerosene puzzled Bellows. The speed of the fire and the death of the cattle buyer gnawed at the sheriff. He knew he had an arson case on his hands but decided to hold off any speculation until he had talked with Ho-Ching.

Later that week, Sam Bellows visited the cook at the clinic. "You take your time answering my questions, Ho-Ching. I'm not in any hurry. Tell me, what did you see the night of the fire?"

The Chinaman rubbed his bandaged hands together before responding. "Velly quiet night. I wake up to snorting of horse. See man carry stuff to saloon, then pour something in saloon and hotel. Then I see flash and fire start. Same thing near hotel. Then man run away toward river. I run out, beat fire with rug but fire too much. I yell 'Fire, Fire.' Missy Sophie comes down stairs, we leave place quick."

"Did you know who the man was? Have you ever seen him before?" Bellows continued.

"No, Mist Sheriff, no ever see before. He only man I see."

Sam Bellows thanked Ho-Ching for the interview but was disappointed the he couldn't identify the person who had killed a man, hurt another pretty badly, and destroyed a person's life savings.

"Get well, Ho-Ching. If you recall anything else of that night, be sure to get hold of me."

Burr Tilden was in the audience during the theatrical group's performance. He even made a generous donation when the hat was passed. Smiling, he thought, "Go ahead, Miss Sophie. Build another place. I'll be happy to burn that one, too." Leaving the crowd, he walked to the livery stable where he had his horse tied up. Barney Pryor was talking to someone and did not recognize the bearded Tilden.

In the weeks that followed, Barney called on Sophie but she refused to take a coach ride with him. The loss of the hotel and saloon and the promise of a new life weighed on her. Over coffee and a sweet roll at the boarding house where Sophie was staying, Barney tried to take a positive approach to the disaster.

"Sophie, you could have been killed in that fire, just like the cattle buyer. Be thankful you're alive and well and can get started again. Just listen to what I have to say. You still own the land where the buildings stood. Bellows has finished his investigation so we can remove the rubble. I have three big ore wagons from the mine you can use. I also have mules and teamsters to haul the debris away. Once that's done, I think you should build a saloon to replace the old one, but leave the theater addition for later. You know as well as I that liquor and gambling will always be with us, so let's get started before someone else comes to that conclusion. I figure you can put the last one to shame for about four thousand dollars. You might lose a few lady friends but business is business and life's gotta go on. Come on, what do you say?"

Sophie was quiet as she considered Barney's proposition. "Barney, the idea of starting with just the saloon makes sense, but I don't know if banker Scoville will lend me the money. You've got a good idea but it's only a dream for me."

Not discouraged, Barney continued his sales pitch. "Sophie, don't give up so easily. Scoville might surprise you; you've got nothing to lose by asking."

Over a drink that evening, Pryor told Brad Scoville the story and asked the banker, "Look Brad, Sophie's a very capable business woman. She won't take money from me but I think she'll be coming to you for a loan shortly. Go through your normal routine, but in the end, give her the loan, up to four thousand dollars. I'll guarantee it, but for God's sake don't let on that I'm backing her. It's to be a secret between us and us alone. If she found out that I cosigned the note, she'd have a fit. So, remember—it's confidential to you and me, period."

The banker looked at Barney and secretly wanted to advise against getting involved financially with a woman, but decided the business deal was too good to pass up. "Sure, Barney, I'll take care of it just as you say."

And just as Barney Pryor had predicted, Sophie applied for a loan, got it approved, and began building a new saloon ten days later.

CHAPTER 22

Bruner and Barksdale Disagree

DINNER STARTED OFF WELL. COLIN Barksdale described his trip to San Francisco and meeting with Leland Stanford's top officers. "They're the kind of people we want to be associated with. They've already connected San Francisco with a railroad to Los Angeles and San Diego and are now laying track eastward into Arizona. They don't seem to know very much about mining activity in the Territory, but are interested just the same in building up traffic for the main line. And I sure like the way they conduct business. We must have been out on the town every night I was there. I had the best oysters I've ever eaten, delicious crabmeat and steaks, champagne, and the friendliest ladies to spend the night with. I'll tell you Konrad, I didn't want to leave the place."

It wasn't Bruner's style but he listened politely, wondering how much company money had been squandered, and if there was any resulting agreement. Well, he wasn't an investor or owner at this point, so he nodded and waited patiently to review B.J. Kimball's claim and his visit to Globe. When Konrad felt it was time to deliver his report, Colin suddenly stood up, looked at the German, and ventured, "I hear Madame Colette runs a fairly decent bawdy house here in town. Why don't we defer business until tomorrow and sneak down the street for an evening's pleasure?"

Konrad looked at Barksdale with barely a smile. "Colin, I'm not interested in visiting Madame Colette's tonight or any other night; why don't you go ahead without me. I'll have coffee and strudel set up for us here in the morning."

"Well, if you're going to be such a prude, I think I will go there by myself," the Englishman responded. "I don't expect I'll have any trouble finding the place in this metropolis."

It was ten o'clock in the morning before Barksdale showed himself at Konrad's office reeking of cheap liquor and barely able to navigate. "Jesus, Bruner, get me some ice water and coffee before I fall on my face. You missed quite a night. Why, I had no idea these girls could provide that much fun in one evening. Unshaven, bleary-eyed and disheveled, Barksdale collapsed on Konrad's sofa until he could put his hands around a mug of thick, black coffee. When Konrad added a finger of whiskey, the Englishman began to show signs of recovery.

A half hour passed and finally, Colin looked at Bruner and asked, "Well, Mr. expert geologist, what did you find out for me about this Kimball person?"

Konrad was a little surprised with the tone of Colin's question, but decided to overlook the sarcasm. "All in all, we spent over two weeks getting there, examining the prospect, and taking the Tucson stage to get back here. I've got several reconnaissance maps and detailed exploration pit maps and should have a compilation of assay reports within the week. Let me just say that based on what we saw, I expect the assay data to show a minimum of 15 percent copper, plus some gold and silver. Andy Corsica, the miner I hired, stayed up north to help B.J. continue the work and protect our interests."

Barksdale suddenly straightened up. "Wait a minute. What do you mean you hired a man? And what do you mean by 'protecting our interests'? Don't tell me you've made a commitment for Britsco without my approval. Just what the hell have you been up to while I was away?"

Now Konrad was really annoyed with Colin's line of questioning but did his best to control his temper.

"Colin, I hired Andy Corsica to help me with my equipment and to have a companion for the trip. We went through territory that the army still considers hostile, and Andy is not only a good, reliable miner, but also handy with a pistol and rifle. I also hired Half Moon, an Indian scout from Fort Gore, who knows the country well, to lead us. And it paid off; we got to Globe without any problems. When we got there, we checked out the town, which is bustling with activity. There are lots of prospectors and ranchers raising cattle."

Colin looked at Bruner skeptically. "I don't know how much you're paying these people, but we'll get into that later. Go on."

"We ended up staying with Kimball for about a week. His cabin, which is six to eight miles outside Globe, is in pretty rugged country and not easy to find, but it's surprisingly comfortable. When he saw the letter from Sir Clarence referring to Jeremy Windham, he warmed up and showed us his claims, outcrops of silver, and copper prospect pits. We crisscrossed a sizeable chunk of land, did some additional staking, and recorded everything in town. Most people smiled at us; a few even laughed, but I don't think they will be laughing five years from now."

In no mood to take any more insults from Colin, Konrad went on. "To answer your original question, Mr. Barksdale: Yes, I hired Andy Corsica and he's currently in our, or my employ. Half Moon was with us for the trip to Globe and is now probably in the San Carlos Reservation looking for lost relatives."

"On the basis of the information we received from Kimball, and an examination of his maps and a personal look at the property, I committed Britsco to a certain amount of development work, improvement of the campsite, and partnering with B.J. Kimball. I did so because I believe his property deserves serious investigation and because I believe he is an honest man. And finally, I thought that was the reason I was hired by Britsco in the first place."

Fully sobered up, Barksdale was about to launch into an attack but Konrad held up his hand to stop the Englishman's interruption. "You should also understand that this part of Arizona is being looked at by other investors. A property in the Clifton-Morenci area is under development by people from Silver City. We have secured a preferred position with Mr. Kimball because of his relationship with Jeremy Windham and the fact that he trusts me. If you don't understand that proposition, then we have a problem."

Colin Barksdale bristled. Employees simply didn't talk to their superiors in this manner. "Well, Mr. Bruner, we in Britsco don't do business in this fashion. We expect detailed geologic reports from competent professionals before we even consider entering into negotiations with some backwoods sourdough. I haven't met Kimball. How do I know he's legitimate? And further, decisions of this magnitude require board approval. Just what did you commit to, Mr. Bruner?"

By now Konrad could feel the blood pounding in his temples. "I have a signed paper that gives B.J. Kimball 25 percent ownership in the Copper Mountain Mining Company, providing we meet two conditions within sixty days: Britsco would hold 75 percent ownership in the new company, but first, we would pay Kimball $25,000 for his discovery and exploratory work on CMMC, as it presently stands. Second, we will spend a minimum of $100,000 in the next twelve months to drill,

study, and map the property. Our hope, of course, is to be able to delin-
eate an ore body of sufficient size to justify a private or public offering.
If we don't meet these conditions by the end of sixty days, B.J. retains
total ownership of the property, including the work that I've done in my
last visit up north."

"Bruner, your proposal is preposterous," Colin replied. "You're
telling me that we are going to give Kimball $25,000 for a hole in the
ground I've never seen? There's no way I can go along with the commitment you've made, without my permission, I might add. You will
have to negotiate a delay so that I can examine the situation and satisfy
myself that an imposter is not hoodwinking us. I suggest you revisit
Globe, tell your miner friend we need more time, and get us a three-
month delay."

Very slowly and with a careful choice of words, Konrad responded,
"Mr. Barksdale, for the sake of clarity and the prevention of any further
misunderstanding, let me repeat my proposal." After going over the
details of the Kimball proposition one more time, Konrad concluded,
"Sir, you have insulted my character and integrity and suggested I don't
know much about mining geology. Well, you have the agreement
signed by Mr. Kimball. I intend to honor that agreement with or without your company. You have a week to wire your Britsco principals and
decide whether you want me to be your representative and approve the
document I've shown you, or cancel our association. The choice is
yours."

A week later, Konrad searched Ribera for the Englishman only to
find him chatting with Barbara Casey outside the general store. As
Bruner approached, Barksdale looked up and remarked, "I'll be with
you in a minute." Then turning his attention to Konrad, he smiled and
reported, "The board of directors has accepted my recommendation
not to enter into an agreement with Mr. Kimball. And further, as of this
moment, your services are terminated."

The turn of events did not surprise Konrad but he decided to question the Englishman anyway. "I'm curious Colin, but was their vote
unanimous?"

"No, one person was in favor of going ahead. But he was outvoted
three to one."

After hearing Barksdale's answer, Konrad presented him with a
detailed report of his expenses incurred over the past two months,
including his salary.

Glaring at the German, Barksdale hissed, "There must be some mistake, Mr. Bruner. You are fired. There is no way I'm giving you one farthing for all the trouble you've caused me and Britsco."

And with that, he wheeled around and sauntered into the Ribera general store.

CHAPTER 23

Richmond Takes on a Project

DON RICHMOND TRAVELED TO PHOENIX as fast as he could as soon as he got the news that massive flooding had devastated the Salt River Valley. The combination of a heavy snowfall the previous winter, an early spring thaw, and an unusual amount of rainfall had elevated the river to fifteen feet above flood stage. The Salt was dangerous due to tributary flash flooding and the rising of the Gila River, now over a mile in width. When he finally reached Tempe, he learned that all bridges into Phoenix had been swept away by the turbulent, debris-filled Salt. Crossing into town was impossible.

While waiting for the floodwaters to recede, Richmond accepted the hospitality of Adolph Steinmark and his family. Their home was located on a rise above the valley and had a spectacular view of the rampaging waters. Don conceded that never before had he seen such destruction inflicted by Mother Nature.

The raging torrent gouged out the river bottom and forced the Salt to overflow its banks, ruining crops and tearing through the existing network of canals. In low-lying areas, it deposited rich accumulations of silt. A few settlements east of where the Verde River joined the Salt were miraculously spared.

A week after the rain stopped falling and the floodwaters had receded, Don and Henry Dempsey explored the area to assess the damage. The lawyer was optimistic that a community-wide effort to rebuild the bridges, repair the canal system, and plant new crops would probably take six months.

"Don, the community has been dealt a nasty blow, but we'll survive and rebuild what's necessary to get back to farming. More important, we have to publicize the crisis we're in and take steps to prevent such devastation from hitting us again. I think people will understand that we can't do it alone and need federal financial support. The disaster should also tell Washington that such help is more than justified. But first, we've got to develop an overall plan that we can take to Washington while the problem is still fresh in their minds. If Congress is set on developing the West, the legislators are going to have to support flood control projects like the kind we need in the Salt River Valley. We have to sell them the idea that a dam system here would pay for itself by generating and selling electricity in the Territory. It may take us five years to get a bill passed, but we've got to do it. Other states and territories have similar projects in mind; we not only have to be first with our proposal but it's got to be convincing."

Don listened intently to Dempsey's comments. "I believe everything you've said, Henry, but I don't see a political structure in place that has the necessary leadership. I can see the canals being rebuilt and crops planted again but I'm afraid we'll just go back to business as usual, hoping we won't have another flood for another ten years or more."

"Don, you're absolutely right, which is why we have to set up a formal organization now while people can still see the suffering caused by the flood. We also have to remind them that it wasn't all that long ago that we were in the midst of a drought. The twenty-year history of floods and drought should convince all the skeptics that a concerted effort is needed to petition Congress for help. Most of the big canal guys who control the Maricopa, Grand, Arizona, and Consolidated and Highland are solidly behind us. They understand the benefits of a unified approach to irrigation and water storage problems. I want to establish a valley-wide organization that will enable us to go after federal money. I've even got the person in mind to head up the program. He's a strong believer in statehood for the Territory, is trusted by the farmers, and has the energy to see this thing through. Don, I believe that person is you."

The lawyer's proposal caught Richmond by surprise. "Whoa, Henry! I'm a rancher and sometime veterinarian and live over hundred and fifty miles from here. I'm not a farmer and I have a wife and children to look after. Besides, I'm not much of a politician. I'd be happy to help you and your friends in this endeavor, but I'm not the guy to be lead dog."

Henry Dempsey was not put off by his friend's reaction and continued his appeal. "Don, please give it some serious thought before you turn us down. I've worked with Adolph Steinmark, the Mormon colony, Dan Perkins, Jock Slinger, Hank Barker, and Len Antonio on this and they're all very supportive of you becoming director of what we're calling the Salt River Project or SRP. Despite his declining health, Adolph has been very active and vocal in his support of you. We believe the crucial element in our plan is a series of storage dams, the biggest of which would be where the Tonto Creek joins the Salt River, about 65 miles from here as the crow flies. We've got a lot of work to do of course: topographic mapping, more data on past floods and droughts, and most important, how such a system would help populate and develop the Phoenix area and eventually, the state of Arizona. I understand that you and Eric Steinmark are heading out tomorrow to visit the Circle S ranch outside of Globe. Think about our proposition, Don. We can talk some more when you get back here."

"Henry, you've been a good friend, but please don't push me. Your SRP job could take years and require considerable effort to convince our own legislators, let alone the federal government that we have a valid demand. And where's the money going to come from that we'll need to run newspaper ads, staff an office, and travel back and forth to Washington?"

There was a slight chill in the air when the two men parted company.

Eric Steinmark turned out to be a good travel companion. He knew what he was talking about when it came to ranching and knew the rough terrain as well. As they made their way to Globe, they chatted about running a ranch and the hostility between sheepherders and cattlemen. Eric believed there was plenty of grazing room for both animals but he also recognized that beef ranchers had an emotional disdain for sheep, as they believed they carried a disease harmful to cattle. In fact, the two animals were known to graze alongside one another without any problems.

The two men stayed north of Globe and camped out near a clump of juniper bushes and a stream. Eric was an excellent cook and they both enjoyed a restful evening under the stars. The next morning, after a breakfast of bacon, beans, and sourdough biscuits, they left for Eric's ranch. Steinmark asked Don about the relative merits of Hereford, Angus, and Longhorn cattle, and which was best suited for country like the Sierra Ancha Mountains with its varied elevations, vegetation, and adequate water.

Not wanting to give any misinformation, Don deferred, "I've got to know more about the animals before I give you a decent answer, Eric. My guess is that Longhorns are more popular for desert country and can better handle sparse vegetation and the heat." The question prompted Don to ask Eric about his decision to study engineering over ranching, which seemed to hold great interest for him.

"Don, I don't want to upset my father about his long-range plans. I'm sure he told you about his poor health. Wherever I go to college, I'll study basic science and math courses that lead into engineering. I figure it won't hurt me much if I decide to do something else. You're right, though; my first love is ranching. I'm not at all concerned about the valley farm. My mother and sister are capable enough to run the place. And a good, experienced general foreman could front for them in dealing with the farm operations. And the irrigation project, if needed."

The Circle S Ranch was a three-hour ride from Globe. Dewey Unger, the ranch foreman, gave Eric a report on recent happenings on the spread. "We've fenced in 22,000 acres, dug three more ponds like you wanted, and have recorded about 200 births so far. They were evenly split between Hereford and Angus. We're keeping the Longhorns near the horse corrals, tightly controlled, like you wanted. All the herds are healthy and gaining weight, better than expected."

After a day and a half of inspecting the facilities, animals, and field management, Don volunteered his opinion. "Eric and Dewey, you've got a first class operation going on here. The animals are healthy, the herds are growing, and there's plenty of grassland. And you've got a market for your beef. You're to be complemented on what you've been able to do here in less than five years. I have one question, though: Where do you stand in the range war I keep hearing about?"

Eric nodded to Dewey for the answer. "Don, that's a good question. Things heated up here just about the time we started up. Some sheepherders were moving down from Flagstaff, grazing from time to time along the way. I'm not exactly sure where they were going but anyway, one rancher didn't like it when they crossed his unmarked spread. There were about 30,000 sheep I'm told, and it wasn't easy for them to change course. At any rate, they didn't move fast enough for the rancher, so he opened fire on one of the herders and killed him. Two days later, the rest of the sheepherders, usually a quiet bunch, took revenge and killed two cattlemen. Then they moved on. Well, stories get twisted in the telling and it wasn't long before Pleasant Valley became a battleground between the Grahams and the Tewksburys. They've been fighting now for over five years; I'm told that at least twenty gunslingers and a few innocents have been shot and killed. We were never close to the real action and have done our best to avoid being placed in either camp or labeled as sympathizers for either group. Things have pretty much cooled down for now, maybe for good, I hope. This is one of the best places in the world to punch cows, and with copper production cranking up, this area could become a very prosperous, growing community. All we're really missing is a decent rail connection to one of the main lines and we'll be off and running, big time."

Dewey Unger's brief analysis of the Globe and Mogollon Rim region impressed Don greatly. While Ribera was growing and becoming somewhat civilized, Phoenix, Globe, and the north central country were on the verge of exploding. People were streaming in to take advantage of the territory's mineral wealth, pleasant climate, and opportunities in ranching and farming.

On their return to Phoenix, Eric and Don learned that Adolph Steinmark had died while supervising some repair work on one of the canal irrigation gates. "I think Dad would have preferred that to a long, lingering illness like the one he was trying to live with." Mrs. Steinmark and Madi agreed. Adolph's body was embalmed and stored in an icehouse in preparation for final burial in a small cemetery on the family's property. A short ceremony, attended by many of his farmer friends, brought some solace to the immediate family.

After the funeral, Don accepted Henry Dempsey's offer to join him for a beer in the attorney's office. They were barely seated when Henry opened the conversation.

"How was your trip with Eric Steinmark?"

"Henry, I learned all over again not to jump to conclusions about a person until you spend some time with him. I assumed Eric was self-centered and spoiled and wouldn't or couldn't grow up. His father helped give me that idea. But the young man surprised me. He's thoughtful and serious and will probably do quite well in this world. I'm not sure that engineering will be his life's work, but he sure knows his beans about ranching and cattle. The family Circle S Ranch is one of the finest spreads I've ever seen. We had a great time together and I gained a new appreciation for the potential of this Territory."

"Now about the Salt River Project. If the job is still open, I'm interested. However, I don't know how this is going to sit with my wife and the kids. But I'm confident we'll be able to work something out."

Henry Dempsey let out a whoop of joy and stood up, waving several sheets of paper in his hand. "Don, there are over fifty signatures on this petition to hire you as our director. They'll be as thrilled as I am to know that you're going to be our lead man. I know you're anxious to get home but as soon as you can get away, we want you up here, full-time."

Don Richmond had mixed feelings as he left Dempsey's law office. He wanted the job but realized that he had serious family obligations in Ribera. What would Dolores think of his new undertaking?

CHAPTER 24

Booker and Benson Clash

LIEUTENANT VINCE BOOKER REPORTED TO Major Brad Garrison, executive officer of the 27th Cavalry Regiment, as ordered. He'd just released the Apache women and children to the Reverend Hugh Packard. They were in excellent physical condition despite the lengthy wagon ride from south of Fort Gore. In talking with Packard, the lieutenant learned of the devastating smallpox epidemic and the probable death of at least three hundred men, women, and children.

"Many of the deaths could have been prevented if basic hygiene had been employed," the reverend asserted. "I know that contaminated blankets were reissued to the Indians and I'm sure that rations were stolen and sold to ranchers and miners in the area. And the problem with liquor is worse than when you left. When you get settled, come over for dinner and I'll tell you what I know about liquor sales and Caleb Benson. I'm convinced that he's got protection from someone senior to be able to get away with what he does."

Major Garrison was all business as he invited Lieutenant Booker to take a chair. "I've read reports on the chase and destruction of Aguijador and his warriors. You're to be commended, Booker. What I don't understand is why you didn't finish the job and kill the wounded women and children. Perhaps you've forgotten that the Indians are our enemies. Furthermore, you've wasted food and medicine on a group of animals that will only die here anyway. What is your explanation, lieutenant?"

Vince Booker was surprised and shocked at the major's line of questioning but decided to speak the truth, at least as he saw it. "Major, you have my service jacket, so I won't bore you with my record of combat experience in the war and my tours of duty here in the Arizona Territory. What we have done to the Arizona Indian is nothing short of an attempt to exterminate a nation. It's criminal and someday history will document the atrocities. Just look at conditions here on the reservation. There are severe food shortages, disease, contaminated water, and corruption. Plus, the sale of liquor is clearly against the law."

Booker knew he had crossed the line but decided that he could no longer follow orders that approved the killing of innocent women and children.

Major Garrison jumped to his feet, almost knocking over his desk. Ink spilled on the floor, lamps were overturned, and papers flew in every direction. "Lieutenant, you'll stand at attention while I answer those charges." Focusing steely eyes on the regimental executive officer, Booker came to attention, responding, "Yes, sir." With his chin up, his eyes zeroed in on the regimental coat of arms hanging on the wall behind the major.

Regaining some composure, Garrison spoke in a measured tone. "I have never favored the commissioning of enlisted men, regardless of their heroics on the battlefield. They don't have the education and cultural background to conduct themselves as an officer and a gentleman. And I will not permit bending orders, insolence, or insubordination. We are under strict orders to contain the Indians at the lowest possible cost in men and materials. We're here to protect the settlers, ranchers, and miners. Your attitude of pacifying the enemy is despicable and cowardly. If you don't have the guts to eradicate these vermin, perhaps you should consider leaving the army and go live with them. What do you think of that, Mr. Booker?"

"Major Garrison, sir, I will take your suggestion under consideration. Is that all, sir?"

The major replied in anger, "No, Booker, it isn't. You play by my rules from now on. You will stay away from the trading post and work with the Reverend Packard on a new containment pond and digging irrigation ditches. That should help you in your zeal to baby these savages. They will learn our ways to farm or they will starve. You're dismissed, lieutenant."

Vince Booker saluted the major, did a sharp about face and returned to his quarters. Calmly removing his boots, he stretched out on his bunk and stared at the ceiling, considering his next move. With twenty-three years in the army, he was eligible for retirement but that would mean caving in to an officer who he believed was lining his pockets with illegal profits made by Caleb Benson. He quickly decided he wasn't going to be intimidated by the executive officer. But he also knew he had to avoid a direct confrontation with the West Pointer. Booker left the fort the next morning, telling Sergeant Major Dixon he was going to the reservation to visit Hugh Packard.

"Have the men clean their clothing and gear and oil their weapons. I don't think we're going anywhere for a while, so you can give the men some time off once they've cleaned up. I should be back in a couple of days. If you have any problems, take them to the major."

"Lieutenant, we won't have any problems that I can't take care of, sir."

Having served with Dixon in several campaigns, Booker had little doubt that there would be any need to contact the executive officer. The troops were in good hands.

When Lieutenant Booker located the reverend, he was working alongside a group of Indians, digging an irrigation ditch. As the soldier dismounted, Packard removed his hat, mopped his brow, and gestured to a shady spot under a cottonwood tree. "Vince, the past two months have been terrible with the smallpox epidemic, the shortened rations, and the general overall abuse of the Indians. If I hadn't seen the treatment myself, I don't think I would have believed it, especially if I was a U.S. senator reading a report while fanning myself in Washington. My plea through church channels has gone for naught; they're not interested in an intervention that might shut off funding for these people. I'm about convinced that the whole bunch just want the Indian problem to go away and disappear by itself."

"However, maybe I have some information that might be useful to you. A peddler who comes through here regularly has lost a lot of whiskey sales. Through his own detective work, he has figured out that Caleb Benson is producing his own brand and selling it directly to his customers, in this case, the Indians. I haven't personally seen him making a sale, but I'm told that he is out here a couple of nights a week when he visits one of his female friends. It's kind of a big, open secret: Benson delivers and sells the whiskey, the Indians get drunk, and the trader sleeps with one of the girls."

"It's a disgusting story on all counts, lieutenant, but I'm afraid it's true. I'm pretty sure that Major Garrison doesn't know about this. Something is going to pop, though. The tribal leaders are upset over this brazen move. I have to believe Benson is concocting his whiskey somewhere in that trading post but I don't know exactly where."

The officer took all this in and assured the reverend that he would look into it.

It was time for Caleb Benson's weekly visit to the reservation. With the aid of his helper, Joe Palumbo, Benson loaded whiskey on to two mules and started out as darkness set in. It was pitch black when they arrived at the rendezvous point to start selling the rotgut. As Benson went looking for his female partner for the next hour, Palumbo sold the whiskey and collected money or goods in exchange from the Indians. Once the bootleg liquor was sold, Palumbo relaxed and took a few swigs from a jug of corn whiskey. A blow to the side of the head that knocked him unconscious and sent him sprawling interrupted his drinking. His attacker tied Palumbo hand and foot, stuffed a rag in his mouth, and stowed him next to the mules. On his return, an "Apache" asking for whiskey approached Benson. Before he could reply, the trader received a powerful punch to the stomach followed by several blows to the head. As Benson lay helpless on the ground, the attacker stomped on both his hands, breaking bones and crushing flesh. He then tied the trader to one mule and the still unconscious Joe Palumbo to the other. The assailant then whacked both mules on the hind end, sending them back to the fort.

Shortly after dawn the following morning, loud shouting from pickets alerted the gate sentries to a pair of mules carrying two men. Palumbo was able to stand when untied but Benson had to be carried to the infirmary where an army doctor examined him.

"You've taken a pretty good beating, Caleb. It'll take a while for these hands to heal and when they do, they won't be the same. You also have a couple of broken ribs and I'll have to put a few stitches in your scalp. You'd better take it easy for at least a week. By the way, here's a note I found in your shirt pocket. It says 'Don't ever come back if you know what's good for you.' Maybe that makes sense to you, but it sure doesn't to me."

During his recovery from the attack, Caleb Benson concluded that it had to be a white man who had beaten him so severely. He figured the minister might want to do him wrong but his religious beliefs would prevent that. Besides, Packard was no physical match for the taller, heavier Benson. It couldn't have been the peddler, either. He was too small, but maybe he hired someone. Gradually, Benson bracketed the army enlisted ranks and decided that no one fit the bill.

After much contemplation, he fixed on the Sergeant Major and Lieutenant Booker as prime suspects. The more he ruminated over the situation, the more he believed that Booker was the most likely candidate. He was an Indian lover, was immune to bribery, and was big enough and strong enough to deliver a beating like the kind Benson had endured. The trader didn't want to take the problem to Major Garrison but after two weeks of healing and the need to resume liquor sales, he decided to do just that. And when Benson told his story to his accomplice, the major was visibly shaken.

CHAPTER 25

Barney Invests in Tent City

WITH HIS TWO EMPLOYEES BUSY with customers, Barney Pryor decided to deliver a load of hay and tack to Tent City himself. Besides, he wanted to talk with Tim Royster about a livery stable start up and see what was going on in the town these days. It had been at least a year since he'd visited the "temporary" mining town, now six years old. Although Tent City and Ribera were only three miles apart and had about the same number of people, they were distinctly different in appearance and governance. Due mainly to its diversity and population of families, Ribera had all the qualities of an established town. It had wooden houses; some two stories high, wooden sidewalks, a school, a church, a general store, a bank, a newspaper, and a new hospital. It was also a stagecoach stop where travelers brought in news from the outside world. Tent City was beginning to show signs of permanence, especially since the fire at the Whitman Hotel. Burr Tilden's saloon had expanded from an oversized tent with wooden planks set on empty whiskey barrels for a bar to a wooden structure complete with planked flooring, chairs and tables, and a large mirror over a well-stocked mahogany bar. And business was booming.

The cause of the Whitman Hotel fire had been clearly determined by Sheriff Sam Bellows but no one was under serious suspicion, let alone in custody. The only description that Bellows had to go on was the one provided by Ho-Ching who saw a big man near the hotel and saloon the night of the fire. Sam pictured a man perhaps six feet tall and weighing about two hundred pounds. A broken piece of whiskey jug completed the sparse inventory of evidence. Both Sam and Barney

Pryor thought about a vengeful Burr Tilden as the culprit but decided that the miner had stayed close to Tent City after being thrown out of the Whitman saloon. "He just doesn't fit the profile of an arsonist," said the sheriff. In reality, Bellows felt strongly that Tilden was their man but wanted the saloonkeeper to feel comfortable and above suspicion. He also didn't want Barney taking the law into his hands.

Tim Royster had settled his livery operation near the river on the south side of town. Handy with frontier tools, he'd built several corrals and a roofed enclosure to protect his hay bales, grain, saddles, and blankets from the weather. In an adjacent tent, he kept his personal equipment, bedding, and cooking gear. Tim had started with nothing but the clothes on his back but had prospered with a lot of hard work and credit extended by Barney. Barney's philosophy of investing with people of sound character prompted him to offer Tim a business idea.

"Tim, I believe that Tent City will continue to be home to a couple of thousand or more placer miners. In fact, my partner Konrad Bruner believes he's got at least three more years of reserves on the river. Those miners who have been here for a while wouldn't mind having a boarding house available to them with winter coming on. They'd be willing to pay for a warm house and decent food. I've bought land west of the River Bend Ranch that is heavily timbered. We could cut down some of the trees for a building site and use the wood for our boarding house. I'd be inclined to construct a place for thirty or forty miners at first and see how we make out. The upper story would be a dormitory for sleeping; the bottom floor would have a kitchen, dining room, and maybe a sitting room. I'd build a separate place for storage and quarters for the cooks. I've already talked to Mrs. Colchester about running the place and once Ho-Ching is well, he can do the cooking. I don't think Miss Sophie will mind, and the Chinaman needs a job. I want you to supervise the construction and when the job is completed, become the general manager. I'd be willing to give you a twenty percent ownership instead of a salary after the first year. At the end of each year, we'd look at the books and each take our proportionate share of the business. How does that sound to you?"

Tim was speechless at first, but soon warmed to the proposition. "It sounds good to me, partner," he replied. In the following weeks, Royster organized a work party. He hired three miners who were former woodsmen and were happy to take a break from sifting gravel in the river. They felled trees and sawed the logs into planking that they stacked for drying. As the ground cleared, Tim followed rough plans for a foundation and two-storied building. As word got out that a boarding house for miners was being built, he had all the help he needed to get the building up before winter set in.

A week after windows and doors were installed, Mrs. Colchester took control of the kitchen and dining room and Ho-Ching began serving meals. Within a month, the Tent City boarding house was completely rented and in full operation. Royster and Pryor were even planning on building a second house.

Tim had a visitor shortly after the grand opening. Burr Tilden, owner and operator of Tent City's only saloon, had several questions and wasn't very polite in the way he went about asking them.

"Royster, I don't want any competition from the likes of you or anybody else for that matter. As long as you and the widow Colchester stick to running a boarding house, we'll get along just fine. You start selling beer and whiskey and you'll be looking at big trouble. Understand?"

Though shorter and lighter in build than Tilden, Royster was not accustomed to being intimidated and stood his ground.

"Mr. Tilden, the last time I checked this was still a free country. We'll run our business lawfully and as we see fit. It's not very likely we'll want to start selling whiskey but I ain't making any promises. Now, if you'll excuse me, I've got chores to take care of."

Eyes burning with hatred, Burr reached to grab Tim by the collar but the alert and wiry young man shoved the hand away as Mrs. Colchester and Ho-Ching looked on. Backing away and shaking his fist at Royster, Tilden wheezed, "You better pay mind to what I said. Remember the Whitman Hotel fire?"

As Tilden turned to go back to his saloon, Ho-Ching remarked to Tim, "He big man. Maybe same man who start fire at hotel." Tim looked at Ho-Ching and Mrs. Colchester but said nothing.

CHAPTER 26

Carlos and Rachel Meet in Pittsburgh

SPRING WAS AT LEAST TWO months away when Carlos and Rachel Lawson left their respective college cities to meet in Pittsburgh. Both realized the impetuous nature of their decision, both were apprehensive and nervous, yet excited about their first meeting in over a year.

Rachel was the first to arrive at the Pittsburgher Hotel. She'd taken a horse-drawn car from the train station, bypassing the inexpensive trolley because of her cumbersome suitcases. Arriving at the modern, massive hotel, Rachel checked in and a bellhop took her upstairs to her room on the eighth floor. Snow was falling as she opened the window to look at the downtown area and surrounding hills. She was able to see where the Allegheny and Monongahela joined to form the Ohio River. This "point" was a famous Pittsburgh landmark. She quickly closed the window when cold air, coal dust, and soot from the steel mills blew into the room. The industrial activity was unlike anything she'd seen before. Barges moved up and down the rivers and gigantic smokestacks spewed grit and dust into the blackened sky. Railroad and trolley cars criss-crossed the metropolis.

Rachel changed from her heavy, woolen winter clothing into a lighter garment and lay down to rest, waiting for Carlos. Soon she was sound asleep. When she awoke, the room was dark. Looking at her watch, she realized that Carlos had probably been delayed and decided to order some food from room service. After finishing her meal, she began to worry that something serious had happened to the young man. Her fears increased until she heard a light tapping on the door to her room. Without opening the door, she asked, "Who's there?" Laughing, Carlos replied, "It's me, your Mexican caballero."

Rachel unlocked the safety chain and slowly opened the door. Carlos pushed the door open, crossed the threshold, and embraced Rachel with a hug that left the girl breathless. He then held her at arms' length and looked deep into her eyes. "Rachel, Rachel, my God, you're more beautiful than I even remember." He then pulled her close, crushing her in several lengthy kisses. The young lady responded fiercely, then whispered, "Please, Carlos, close the door." The spell was momentarily broken as Carlos turned and closed the door. They silently looked at each other with expressive, knowing admiration. As excited as she felt about seeing Carlos, Rachel knew that unless she held back they would end up in bed together, something she was not prepared to do, not now anyway.

"Carlos dear, please sit down and tell me about your trip and all about New York City," she demanded. Feeling slightly rebuffed, Carlos found a chair opposite Rachel and told her about his first year at Columbia and what it was like to live in the big city. She sat quietly, gazing at the young man as he spun out the story of his planned visit to Pittsburgh. She knew she was in love with him but was not so sure that Carlos felt the same way about her.

"The dean of the college of mines and metallurgy has arranged for me to work in one of Mr. Carnegie's steel plants. I'll have a day's orientation to visit the furnace operations, rolling mills, and fabrication facilities, and hopefully, I'll be able to decide which part of the factory I want to work in. My roommate Arn will visit coal mines and a limestone quarry next week as part of his thesis project. I'm due to talk to a Mr. Grundig tomorrow, at steel company headquarters."

Both young people were tired from the their long journeys, especially Carlos who was delayed due to a train wreck outside Harrisburg. As they stood up to say goodnight, Carlos pressed Rachel close to him and kissed her once more. Their mutual physical attraction almost overcame them before Rachel broke free and pushed Carlos into the hallway. "Goodnight, darling. I'll see you at breakfast around 7:30," she said, closing the door.

Mr. Grundig was a German immigrant who had started out in the open-hearth department and progressed to become general superintendent of the massive steel-making complex. He was pleased to learn that Carlos's father was also German but somewhat surprised to learn that Herr Bruner had ended up on the western frontier. Grundig believed the frontier was a violent place where Indians killed and scalped white people. Carlos smiled and assured Grundig that the Indian stories were greatly exaggerated and that the U.S. Army had subdued most of the Apache renegades.

Carlos spent the full day touring the plant facilities with Felix Altman, Grundig's assistant, as his tour guide. Of German heritage, Altman had been born in the United States and educated as an engineer at Lehigh University in Bethlehem, Pennsylvania. He had joined the steel company about ten years ago.

"Carlos, let me get you a felt hat, goggles, and some work clothes so you don't have to wear an expensive business suit on our tour. Otherwise, the dust and sparks will damage the goods, as they say." After donning his new uniform and work shoes, Carlos followed Felix to the raw material yard where giant cranes were systematically feeding buckets of iron ore, coke, coal, and limestone into an inclined tramway that fed two huge blast furnaces. "The iron ore comes from the Mesabi Range in Minnesota, where the company owns the open pit mines. It's then transported by lake steamer to Cleveland or Conneut, Ohio, and loaded into rail cars for delivery to Pittsburgh. We have our own coal properties in West Virginia and Pennsylvania, where it is mined and shipped here by rail to make coke. The limestone comes from company quarries not far from Pittsburgh. The raw materials are mixed into batches and fed into the blast furnaces to produce pig iron. Stay close to me when we get inside. It's noisy and look out for overhead cranes moving ladles of hot metal. It can be dangerous at times."

Their timing was excellent. When they entered the blast furnace department, the workers were tapping a furnace. Carlos and Felix watched molten pig iron splash down a sand-encased runner into a huge ladle. Some of the molten iron was cast into "pigs" for sale to foundries, but most of the hot metal went to the open-hearth shop where it was poured into rectangular furnaces for further refining. The open-hearth building consisted of a dozen such units, each furnace capable of treating about seventy tons of melt per "heat." The pig iron was treated with fluxes, ferromanganese, and other alloying material, depending on the ultimate end use of the steel. On completion, the furnace was tapped and the finished steel poured into ladles and transported to a building where cast iron ingot molds stood on flat cars. The steel was then decanted into the molds and allowed to cool.

After lunch, during which Felix answered a few questions posed by his visitor, the two men moved to the processing facilities. "We first strip the ingot mold from the cooled ingot, reheat it, and take it to the primary, or blooming mill. We'll look at this from upstairs where it's safer and where we can get a better view. There will be plenty of sparks, Carlos, so keep your collar tight around your neck. Some of the ingots are rolled back and forth into slabs, then sent to inventory in a yard outside the plant. Others are rolled, sliced, and formed into rails and structural steel. Sometimes, ingots are forged into various shapes; some are pierced and drawn into gun barrels or heavy tubing. We also have a separate unit where we cut and rivet steel into shapes for bridges and the like. We're not going to see the rail mill; it's getting late in the day. Come out for lunch tomorrow and we can answer any questions you might have, and you can tell us where you think you might want to work."

After a complete scrub down in the assistant superintendent's bath facility, Carlos changed into his street clothes, said goodbye to Felix, and returned to the hotel for a late dinner with Rachel.

Rachel's day had been equally exciting. By pre-arrangement, she visited a hospital that had a specialized pediatric unit and a new orthopedic unit. She was able to witness several complicated procedures including the repair of a compound fracture of a lower leg and an operation to mend a child's smashed elbow. It was all very impressive to Rachel but how it might relate to her father's clinic in Ribera, Arizona, didn't make sense to her at the time. The doctors and nurses were friendly and notably, two of the surgeons were women.

The hospital visit helped Rachel take her mind off the previous night and Carlos. She loved him with all her heart and even though their mutual physical attraction disturbed her, she realized that people in love were bound to experience some erotic feelings. As she walked through the lobby Rachel smiled in anticipation. "What will be, will be," she thought to herself.

Both Rachel and Carlos were in a festive mood as they dined at the Paragon Restaurant, a supper club recommended by Felix. They feasted on raw oysters, lamb chops over wild rice, and strawberries in brandy, all to the background music of a string quartet. Chatting animatedly, they held hands under the table from time to time. Returning to the hotel, they capped the evening with a bottle of French champagne, ordered previously by Carlos. As Rachel stood to go to her room, Carlos reached around her waist. "Rachel, I love you," he whispered as he kissed her neck and ear. Flushing, she turned to him and responded, "Carlos, I love you too."

Hugging and kissing passionately, they undressed each other. Rachel lay down on the bed, now a sea of fresh white cotton sheets and neatly placed a large bath towel beneath her. Carlos came to her side, caressed her gently and moved his body on top of hers. Penetration required more patience than he thought he had but finally, they moved in unison. Their coupling was brief; one experiencing some pain, but both enjoying the interlude.

Resting, Rachel and Carlos gently kissed and expressed their love.

"Carlos, you are my first and only love. I don't know how I will be able to go back to Michigan and be separated from you for months at a time. I could become pregnant, and I don't want that problem hanging over us."

"Rachel, don't be afraid. I love you now and I will love you forever. Whatever comes along, we will deal with it. I want you to be my wife. Will you marry me?" Glowing, Rachel smiled and said yes. Between breakfast and packing, for Rachel had to take the afternoon train, they made love again, this time in a more leisurely fashion. As Rachel dressed and put on her outer clothes, Carlos noted that she had washed several dried bloodstains from her bath towel, hanging the wet cloth over a radiator to dry.

As she boarded the train for Detroit, Rachel looked lovingly into Carlos's eyes. "Until we have figured out how we're going to marry I don't plan on telling my parents of our engagement. Do you agree to do the same?" she asked. "Of course, my darling, anything you say," Carlos replied.

But keeping their engagement a secret left Carlos a bit confused. He wanted to announce his happiness to the world.

The luncheon meeting with Felix and Mr. Grundig took place in a downtown men's club that catered to Pittsburgh's business tycoons and executive steelmakers. Surrounded by polished hardwood panels and dark hues of green and burgundy, the two men were in a jovial mood.

"Felix and I have enjoyed your visit to our plant, Carlos. You've had a short tour of our facilities; is there any part of the exploration that you particularly enjoyed?"

"Mr. Grundig, if I'm able to come to Pittsburgh for six months, I think I'd like to work in the blast furnace department or the open-hearth shop. There's something about hot metal that intrigues me. Seeing molten steel being tapped is pretty exciting." Grundig and Felix looked at one another and smiled. "That's wonderful. That's exactly what we were hoping you'd say," Grundig exclaimed. "We will have an opening in the open-hearth shop when you are ready to get started. We will be testing a new piece of equipment called a Bessemer converter. It could be an excellent thesis project for you. And maybe you can help us."

With their agreement in place, the trio enjoyed a final Pittsburgh boilermaker: a shot of whiskey, chased by a glass of cold beer.

CHAPTER 27

Two Young Men Leave Town

DALE RICHMOND HAD BEEN WORKING on his grandmother's River Bend Ranch ever since his home schooling had stopped. He was tall and strong and handled his chores well, but his interest in the ranch had waned in the past few months. He considered further schooling, joining the military, or working in Barney Pryor's livery stable, but not seriously. Conversations with his parents did little to help and led him to think about leaving Ribera. He wasn't unhappy but he was not thrilled the way things were going.

Tom Lawson had attended boarding school in California for a year, but couldn't decide on college let alone what course of work to consider. He knew it wasn't medicine; watching the number of hours his father worked buried that idea. Besides, he never did like biology and chemistry, and felt he didn't have the brains or discipline that Rachel had. And after laboring for three months at the Ocotillo Silver Mine, he knew hard rock mining wasn't his cup of tea.

The two young men bumped into one another at Burr Tilden's saloon in Tent City. Tom waved to Dale as he entered the bar room for a beer. It was a Saturday afternoon and a noisy crowd was forming, so the two stepped outside where they could hear each other speak. "Gosh, Dale, I haven't seen you in quite a while; what've you been up to?" Dale Richmond confessed his frustration and Tom reciprocated by describing his boredom. As the afternoon wore on, Dale and Tom agreed that perhaps it was time to leave their respective nests and strike out on their own. Several beers later, the two had reached a decision to move on to greener pastures. Leaving the bedlam of the saloon behind, they staggered to their horses, shook hands, and rode upriver toward home.

Don Richmond heard his son enter the house, bump into chairs, and grope his way to the stairs and up to his room. He breathed a sigh of relief when he heard the thump of boots dropping to the floor and his son crawling into bed. "Well, I guess Dale has had his fill of beer and liquor, but this is not the time to make a case out of it," he thought to himself. Dolores Richmond slept through her son's homecoming without a murmur.

The following morning, Don waited patiently for his son to join him in the kitchen. Allowing Dale to pour coffee and sit down, he finally broke the morning stillness. "Son, I think it's time we had a talk," Don began. Through bleary eyes and a splitting headache, Dale looked at his father and replied, "You're right, it is time we had a talk. I learned last night that beer and whiskey don't mix too well, but otherwise, we didn't get into any trouble. I'm not happy here and I'm sure you and Mom are worried about me doing something worthwhile like going to college or learning a trade. Well, I met up with Tom Lawson last night and found out that both of us are in the same boat. We decided that we might do better to just leave town and strike out on our own."

Don gulped a mouthful of hot coffee, put the mug down and asked, "Just what do you have in mind, son?" As Dolores walked in and joined them at the table, Dale went on. "We really don't have any solid plans but most likely we'll look at Prescott and Flagstaff. If we can't come up with something there, we'll move on to San Diego. I've got school friends there who might be able to help us find work. Each of us has about a hundred dollars in savings that should keep us going for a couple of months until we find jobs."

Before Dale Richmond could speak further to his father, Dolores cut into the conversation. "I'm not sure you're making the right decision, Dale, but you're old enough to make that choice. The ranch will miss you, you're grandmother will be heartbroken, and I'll hurt but if that's what you want to do you have our blessing. And if things don't work out for you in your new adventure, remember this will always be your home." With tears welling in her eyes, Dolores turned, walked to the sink and began washing dishes. Later that evening, Don looked at his wife with puzzlement. "You know, you butted in today and almost encouraged Dale to leave here. I'm trying to figure out why you would do such a thing without first talking to me. Why did you do that?"

"Because you're a softie, Don, and would try to talk him out of it. I "butted in" as you say because I love him and it's the right thing for him

to do. He's a grown man and it's time he decided what he wants to do."
She then broke down in a flood of tears.

Dr. Lawson was out of town on a medical emergency when Tom
spoke to his mother. "Mom, you left Tennessee when you were a young
girl so I hope you'll understand when I tell you I'm leaving town next
week with Dale Richmond. More education is not for me; I've had
enough of the Ocotillo Silver Mine, and I don't see myself working in
a general store." Kate Lawson had gone through a sleepless night, worrying that her son was getting beat up in a bar fight, in a brothel, or
both. Even with Tom home safely from the previous night's excursion,
the idea of him leaving home frightened her. "Your sister is in Michigan
studying to be a doctor and now you tell me you're bored with life here
and want to be an explorer. The thought of two of my children being
away from home is not a pleasant one. Why can't you see the opportunities that exist right here in Ribera?"

Before Tom could answer, his father entered the room and sat down
in a chair, exhausted. He immediately knew there was a problem.
"Tom's decided to leave home," Kate Lawson cried out. Before his
mother could continue her lament, Tom blurted out, "Dad, I just
explained why Dale Richmond and I are leaving town to find work up
north. If we aren't successful there, we'll move on to California. We're
not doing any good here, so we've decided on fresh scenery. It has
nothing to do with either of our folks. We know they're the best."

The two young men did not waver in their decision. A week later,
as the Richmonds and Lawsons waved their goodbyes, Dale Richmond
and Tom Lawson turned in their saddles, returned the gesture, and
rode out of town.

They decided to bypass Tucson—"too many Mexicans"—and
headed for Phoenix. They spent a few weeks in town and to their disappointment learned that the only jobs available were in farming.
They rode on to Prescott. The mile high town was more to their liking, especially Whiskey Row with its nightlife and loose women.
Within two days Tom and Dale were robbed of their wallets, the victims of drinks laced with sleeping potion. Waking up in an alley next
to a hotel, the young men looked at each other in humiliation. "We're
a real couple of rubes," they admitted to themselves. A ten-dollar bill
hidden in Dale's boot was all the money they had for the rest of their
trip.

Autumn was turning into winter as they headed toward Flagstaff. A
light snow was beginning to fall as they made camp and built a fire.
Reaching higher elevation they soon realized that it was getting much

colder. When Tom and Dale awoke in the morning, their blanket rolls were covered with a foot of snow.

The sun was shining in a clear blue sky as they rode into Flagstaff. They devoured a huge breakfast, depleting their resources by another two dollars. By the end of the week, they were dead broke with no prospect of work in sight. They froze at night, sleeping in alleyways or under bridges and stole food when the opportunity presented itself. Bartenders spotted them eating bar food without buying a beer or whiskey and told the young men to "get out and stay out." They sold one horse, then the other, and their saddles. On a rumor of possible work, they hiked eight miles west of town to a lumber camp only to learn it was moving to a new location. Carl Dexter, the burly foreman in charge, looked the two up and down. "Get some food, help us make the move and maybe I'll be able to find something for you. If you had some experience cutting wood or logging, I could almost guarantee you a job as we always lose a few men when we move to a new campsite. I can't pay you, but you'll have grub and a place to sleep under cover."

They worked from dawn to dusk as buildings were torn down and sledded to a new location deeper in the forest. As the weather grew colder, Tom and Dale realized they wouldn't make it through the winter without heavy work boots, woolen shirts and jackets, and warm gloves. They gave serious thought to returning home and warmer weather but couldn't face the embarrassment of failure.

The new camp, about twelve miles outside of Flagstaff was constructed in the middle of a ponderosa pine forest. The majestic trees, eighty to a hundred feet in height, would provide a sawmill with an almost unlimited supply of raw material. When the camp set up and woodcutters filled the bunkhouse, Carl Dexter called Tom and Dale into his office. "Boys, you've done well these past few days and I'm grateful. Unfortunately, I only have one job opening as a helper in the kitchen. But I guess I owe you something. I'll hire Dale at twenty dollars per month, but set up a tent for two. Tom, you can stay here and I'll feed you but I don't have a job for you. Maybe something will turn up. We'll have to see." With winter closing in, the young men were grateful for anything.

As the temperature dropped into single digits, Carl Dexter got two strong helpers in the kitchen for the price of one. He smiled to himself at the thought of saving at least eighty dollars over the winter.

With the arrival of spring, the melting ice and snow turned the logging camp into a quagmire. Company management decided to close down for two weeks or until the ground hardened to allow cutting and dragging logs. In a matter of hours, the woodsmen shaved, cleaned up, changed their clothing, and climbed on wagons for the trip into town.

On the way into Flagstaff, Togar Lindstrom, an old logger, confided in Tom and Dale. "You fellas worked real hard this winter. Without your help, the kitchen would have been in trouble. I don't like being a snitch, but I don't like to see that conniving Carl Dexter cheating you boys either. I've seen him pull the same trick before."

"What do you mean, Togar?" questioned Dale.

"Well, he hires one guy and tells the other that there's no job, but being a nice guy, he lets the second guy stay in camp. Most times, the second guy pitches in without pay. A job never comes up, so ole Dexter gets the work of two and only pays for one. He comes on as a helping friend but he's really just a cheatin' skunk. The money he saves on the second guy goes right into his pocket. I've seen him do it a couple of times."

Seeing the look of disbelief on Dale and Tom's faces, the old man cautioned, "Now don't get any ideas of gettin' even. Dexter's got too many friends in town and you'll end up in big trouble. Take it as a learnin' experience and let it go at that."

Stunned, Tom and Dale looked at each other and could only shake their heads. If they quit now, Dexter wouldn't have to pay anything to Dale. Wanting to kick themselves, they acknowledged the wisdom of the old Swede's remarks. But it sure didn't help the hurt go away.

A month later, Dale received eighty dollars for his pay, less twenty dollars spent on winter clothing for the two. When offered two positions in the cook shack, Dale refused and told Dexter he and Tom would try their luck elsewhere. They hitched a wagon ride into town and headed for the Lodge Pole Saloon for a drink. Sipping a beer, Tom looked at a nearby poker table where four men were playing cards. After a few minutes of watching the cards being dealt, it was clear to Tom that the dealer was palming cards and raking in a pile of winnings. This went on for several more hands with the same results. In exasperation, two of the players threw their cards down on the table. "This game's too tough for me," one player muttered as he stood up in disgust. The dealer looked at Tom and Dale and asked, "Care to join us, gents?"

In a joking voice, Tom answered, "Are you serious, the way you're dealing the cards?" The dealer moved his chair back slightly as the other player looked on. Incensed with the remark, Mitch Lawlor stared at Tom.

"You looking for trouble, sonny? Just what did you say?"

"I said I'm not interested in playing poker with anyone who wins every hand by palming cards. They run people out of town for that kind of thievery."

As Lawlor reached inside his vest, he growled, "You best apologize young man or be ready to draw." Guessing the man was about to reach for a concealed weapon, Tom bolted for the table and tipped it over. Just at that moment, the sound of a small pistol going off filled the room. As he fell on top of the gambler, a second round was fired. Then it was still.

When the sheriff arrived moments later, he found Dale Richmond badly wounded and Mitch Lawlor shot dead with a bullet hole in his head. Witnesses charged Tom with the crime in spite of the fact that he was unarmed. The sheriff obliged by taking him into custody.

Two weeks went by. Dale Richmond was still hospitalized with a serious wound that kept him from participating in Tom's trial. The testimony of Boots Yarnell, the gambler's accomplice and the key witness in the case, resulted in Tom's conviction for manslaughter and his sentencing to five years in the Yuma Territorial Prison. Most folks were pleased with the proceedings, although a belligerent minority was hoping for a public hanging.

CHAPTER 28

Konrad Bruner Takes Control

KONRAD BRUNER HAD DELAYED HIS trip to Globe far too long; it was time he decided his next move and explained his position to B.J. Kimball. "Gott in himmel, what have I gotten myself into?" he asked himself. It was one thing to invest in an operating mine or placer that was producing metal. The Kimball property was a big time crapshoot. Questions raced through his mind. Would the ore grade hold and to what depth? Were the skeptics right? How the devil were they going to get the concentrates to the smelter? When he arrived in Globe, he still hadn't made up his mind.

He reviewed the exploratory work done several times and was confident that they really had something, but when it came to estimating time and money requirements to develop the mountain he was not as sure as he'd like to be. And what about B.J.? Konrad had made a commitment to him only to be fired for overreaching his position. What was his obligation to the man? The combination of belief in the property, respect for Kimball, and an intense dislike for Barksdale and Britsco led him to smile to himself and muse, "Bruner, this could be the challenge of a lifetime. Don't pass it up. It's risky, there are many questions at this point, but the possibility of building a world-class copper mine is too great to disregard. You're going ahead."

Konrad sat down with B.J. and Andy Corsica and shared his experience with Colin Barksdale. "Gentlemen, Britsco is no longer our partner and Colin Barksdale is on his way back to England." Andy looked at Bruner expecting the worst. "It doesn't change the immediate future but long term financing of the project does not exist today. B.J. and I are going to be partners with the understanding that I will bankroll the continuing exploration phase, knowing full well that we will run out of money in a year or year and a half. By that time, we should have an investment package that will attract the big money for development, or we could end up losing everything. That's about as clear as I can be."

"Konrad, I was worried a bit when you were late showing up, but Andy here had no doubt that things would work out," B.J. offered. "I'll confess, I never did like the sound of Barksdale even if I never met him. And don't go any further. I agree to whatever you're putting on the table. We'll have to come up with a new name for our deal but in the meantime, let me tell you about some of the changes we've made while you were away. We built new, larger corrals and hogged out a cave for storing supplies. We also expanded the cabin with bunks for four people and started building a house for miners down the hillside where we plan to start the decline shaft."

The dinner that night was a celebration. The men feasted on steaks, fresh cornbread, newly dug potatoes, and a dessert of deep-dish apple pie followed by coffee and brandy.

"B.J., I'm going into town tomorrow to deposit your check for $25,000. It's yours whether we succeed or not," Konrad announced. I will also deposit $100,000 that will be our working capital for the next year. We'll draw on that to pay for labor, food, and supplies. I should be back tomorrow; then we'll get this place going full speed ahead."

When banker Stoddard asked for the name of the new company, Bruner smiled and replied, "Let's call it Copper Hill Mining Company, Konrad Bruner, President."

CHAPTER 29

Booker's Retirement

"MAJOR, I HAVEN'T SOLD ANY whiskey in over two months and that damn Brinkerman is making a fortune," Caleb Benson fumed. "I'm heated up enough to start brewing our stuff again; all you have to do is kick Brinkerman off the reservation and keep Lieutenant Booker tied up on the irrigation ditches and them ponds. Just so you know, I got him pinpointed as the guy who worked me over. I'll take good care of him in my own way, in due time. You'll see."

"Caleb, you stick to mixing and selling whiskey and stay away from the women," Garrison replied. "And keep clear of Booker; he's nothing but trouble for us. Colonel Burlingame thinks highly of the lieutenant; they served together on several campaigns. I'll keep him busy away from the trading post so he doesn't interfere with your whiskey making. And I'll rig up something to keep Brinkerman off the reservation; just give me a week before you start selling again."

Actually, Lieutenant Booker did Major Garrison a favor. After a sweltering day supervising the excavation of a containment pond, Booker stumbled on Brinkerman selling whiskey to several reservation braves. When the officer drew his pistol, the Indians bolted and ran into the brush to escape. Brinkerman then made his second mistake of the day by offering the soldier a bribe. "Lieutenant Booker, I know you ain't getting rich chasing Indians. Why don't I just give you a hundred dollars and we can forget what happened here this afternoon. You get the money, I get to keep my whiskey, and everybody's happy. You can divvy up the cash any way you see fit, just so the corporal there doesn't remember me."

"Isaac, you've made your last whiskey sale on the San Carlos Reservation," Booker answered. "Corporal Willett, this man is under arrest. Handcuff him and take him to the officer of the day for internment. I'll follow up later with a full report to Major Garrison."

Recognizing the trouble he was in, Isaac Brinkerman pleaded with the lieutenant. "Don't be a fool, Booker. Caleb Benson and Major Garrison are the culprits you should be putting in jail. Caleb's been making the whiskey right in a secret room in the trading post and the major's been protecting him. If you really want to stop the flow of whiskey, you're gonna' have to deal with the major and probably Colonel Burlingame."

"Isaac, you'll have provide me with rock solid proof before spouting off about the major and the post commander. You can start by telling me where Caleb Benson is making his whiskey."

The salesman drew in his breath and began his story. "Benson's been making his whiskey in a room that looks like a closet. It's behind the counter in the trading post. It's padlocked; he'll tell you it's where he keeps his valuables but behind the door is a short hallway to a room where he does his mixing. He's got a rear door that's camouflaged with tools that are actually nailed to the exterior surface of the door. I saw it a couple of weeks ago when one of his spies put me wise. I gotta' hand it to old Caleb, he's a pretty slick customer. The rear door doesn't open like a regular door; it slides on rollers for a quick open and close if necessary. He does most of his work at night, all alone, when it's quiet and the sentries are more concerned with other things."

As Corporal Willett led Isaac Brinkerman to horses that would take them to the officer of the day, Booker mulled over his next move. First, he had to document catching Brinkerman selling whiskey to the Indians. With Willett as a witness, Isaac was in serious trouble and would likely end up in jail, probably in the Yuma Territorial Prison. Unfortunately, he didn't have any evidence on Benson or Major Garrison to be able to bust the whiskey business. Even with Brinkerman's testimony, it would be very hard to accuse the major of wrongdoing. The Army did a pretty good job of protecting its officers, particularly it they were West Pointers. He finally decided to concentrate his efforts on closing down Caleb Benson's whiskey factory.

Several nights later, Booker crept up to the rear of the trading post and approached the back wall. It was exactly as described by Brinkerman, studded with hand tools, shovels, and rakes. He'd blackened his hands and face with soot to match his dark shirt and trousers. Peering through a crack between two boards, he saw Caleb

Benson busily pouring liquids into a wooden barrel. Candlelight also revealed boxes and jars of powders, probably used in making the whiskey. A shelf full of empty bottles was nearby. As he took in the scene, he was suddenly prodded from the rear by a rifle-bearing sentry. "Just hold still, whoever you are. I'd rather not shoot you but I will if I have to." Minutes later, Lieutenant Vince Booker was facing Major Garrison in his office.

"Mr. Booker, you have disobeyed a direct order from me to stay away from Caleb Benson and the trading post. Consider yourself under house arrest, pending court martial proceedings. Corporal of the guard, escort this officer to his quarters immediately."

As soon as Booker and the escort left his office, the major hurried over to the trading post to confront Caleb Benson. "Caleb, the party's over. If that sentry hadn't caught Booker in the act of meddling in our affairs, we'd be in deep trouble. Booker could have gotten us for sure. Now, you leave the lieutenant to me but get rid of everything that looks or smells or tastes like whiskey. And I mean all of it, just in case the colonel orders an investigation. And take that sliding door down, remove the rollers, and nail back the wall shut. It's got to look like permanent siding of a building. I want it done by sunup."

Benson looked at the officer as if to question the order but decided it was neither the time nor place to argue with the major.

Two days later, on orders from Major Garrison, the duty officer inspected the trading post, especially the rear wall, and reported no evidence of Lieutenant Booker's accusation. Observing from a slight distance, Caleb Benson smiled and thought that maybe the major knew what he was doing after all.

Booker was resting quietly and reading when he heard a knock on the door of his room. Opening the door, he was greeted by Colonel David Burlingame standing on his porch. "May I come in, lieutenant?" Booker invited the colonel inside and offered him a chair.

"Lieutenant Booker, I've known you for a long time," the colonel began. "Your record as an enlisted man, NCO, and as a commissioned officer is something you can be proud of. The charges filed by Major Garrison have created a situation that I'm very uncomfortable with. He is unwavering in pressing these charges. Something is amiss here but the major is unforgiving and has insisted on a general court martial. You know the army rules and regulations on disobedience as well as I do. The trading post has been inspected and found to be clean, refuting your allegation that it was a place for making whiskey. Caleb Benson has denied any wrongdoing and I have no evidence that he has been making whiskey and selling it to the Indians. I'm afraid that time is running out on us, Mr. Booker. The trial is scheduled for the first of the month."

"Both of us know what a dishonorable discharge means. Unfortunately, it appears that the major has an ironclad case, one that you will probably lose. It could also mean prison time, reduction in rank, and forfeiture of your pension. That's what we're confronted with. As I said earlier, something is amiss here but time is running out. I don't want to see this court martial, but I have no choice in the matter. The deck is stacked against you."

"Which brings me to the reason for my visit. Under the circumstances, I believe it would be best for you to retire from the army before the court martial begins. If you do, you can avoid a trial and probable conviction and your record remains clean. You will also protect your pension and current rank. That I can see to. And I promise, I will pursue this case and prove your innocence. I can't say anything more, Mr. Booker, except to tell you that I trust you and believe that the true culprits will eventually be brought to trial."

Vince Booker's announcement of his retirement after twenty-three years of service shocked his fellow officers. Major Garrison was unhappy that the lieutenant had slipped through his noose but knew he could not continue to accuse a civilian and make the accusations stick. He had plenty to worry about, though. Caleb Benson was back to making whiskey and fornicating with Indian women.

On a warm, sunny Friday afternoon, Lieutenant Vince Booker, uniformed in dress blues, retired from the United States Army. Tears filled his eyes as the troopers passed in review. Thoughts of what his new life as a civilian might hold raced through his mind. Major Howard Garrison knew that he'd dodged a bullet; Colonel Burlingame swore an oath of retribution for a frontier warrior done wrong.

CHAPTER 30

A Bombing Is Foiled

BRAD SCOVILLE KICKED THE MUD from his boots as he stomped into the livery stable. It wasn't his first visit to Barney Pryor's place and he never knocked to announce his arrival.

"Hey, there you are Barney." Without so much as a good morning, the banker continued, "I thought we were good friends. I leave town for a few days and come back to find you've withdrawn $80,000 from my bank. What'd you do that for?"

"Well Brad, I've been thinking about it for some time. I don't like having all my eggs in one basket and I have relationships outside Ribera. We do a lot of business with ISC in Copper Flats, so I decided to put some of my money there. Then, we have accounts in Tucson. Besides, Bedloe gives me a better interest rate than yours. And you're still operating your bank out of an old building with an ancient, beat-up safe that should have been retired years ago. You should be building a new bank with a modern vault. By the way, I understand that Sophie is going ahead on the hotel construction. Has she been in to see you?"

"Oh, so that's the game you're playing. I thought we had a deal. If and when she wants a loan, you cosign it and I'll give her the money. You get sweet on some woman of dubious character and then decide to go shopping for her. Well, I doubt like hell that any of your friends in Copper Flats or Tucson will give her a loan unless you cosign the note. As I've told you several times, depositors don't cotton to banks loaning money to a woman unless her husband or other relative cosigns the deal. And it's doubly difficult with a person of Miss Sophie's character."

"I don't like your remarks about Sophie Kaminski's character, Brad, and whether a hotel and saloon is a good investment. I'll tell you one more time: When she comes in for a loan, give it to her and I'll cosign for the repayment. Just be damn sure you keep my name out of it."

When the two men parted company both were upset. God, what a way to do business, Barney thought to himself.

Sophie was not in the best of moods. Sheriff Sam Bellows had told her that the hotel fire was not an accident, but a case of arson and murder. No matter what Barney said, he couldn't cheer her up. Dinner and a ride in the fancy coach didn't interest her either.

"You know, maybe you're looking at this rebuild the wrong way, Sophie. Just consider this idea. Why not expand the saloon first, open it up for business and start making money right away? I'll bet Scoville might listen to that idea. You could design it in separate units: the saloon on the ground floor, then the hotel rooms on the second floor, and add another floor when business demands. You could pay off the loan as you go along."

Sophie brightened as she considered Barney's idea. "You're right, Barney. Why didn't I think of that? No mind, it's an excellent approach and maybe one day that old skinflint will buy into it. I'll go see him in the morning." As Barney left Sophie to return home, he could hear her singing a gospel song. Barney wanted to sing, too, but thought better of it.

The following morning, after protracted negotiations with Brad Scoville, $6,000 was deposited in Sophie Kaminski's account. She thanked the banker profusely and almost skipped out of his office. With money to spend, Sophie hired carpenters and ordered framing lumber, flooring, and nails. She then led two empty wagons to Tucson to buy bar equipment, second-hand furniture, and a supply of beer and whiskey. Within ten days, the Whitman Saloon was filled with Ribera customers, happy again to have a watering spot of their very own. At a formal opening, the first fifty customers received a free drink. The fifty-first, in the person of Barney Pryor, bought a second round for the imbibers. For the first time in months, Sophie smiled, glanced at the teamster, and raised a glass to him.

It didn't take Burr Tilden long to notice that he was losing customers. Even the offering of free drinks from time to time didn't help business. The miners, he learned, liked Sophie's feminine charms, hospitality, and better whiskey even if they had to ride three miles upriver. It was worth it to them. Burr thought better of a second fire, but he knew he had to do something; he was losing too much money. He decided to hire Bink Zeller, onetime cattle rustler and gunslinger to do the dirty work for him.

"Bink, I want you to discourage Madame Kaminski in Ribera with a stick of dynamite. Go up there after the Saturday night crowd has gone home and blow up the front part of her saloon. Use a fairly long fuse, so's you can leave quietly and get back here without any trouble. Another warning like this and she just might decide it's time to leave town."

The Saturday night crowd at the Whitman Saloon had drifted away shortly after midnight. Bink Zeller watched the barkeep rearrange the chairs, sweep the floor, and close up. By then, it was two in the morning and Main Street was quiet. A black cat, on the prowl for mice, patrolled the alleyway. Across the river, coyotes howled. Zeller approached the saloon, placing one stick of explosive in front of the locked door. As he struck a match, he heard someone call out, "Drop that match and get your hands up." Bink couldn't see where the voice was coming from, but in a panic, lit the fuse and dashed into the alleyway next to the saloon. Sheriff Bellows reacted instantly, jerking the sputtering fuse from the stick, then took off after the bomber. Entering the alley, he caught the shadow of a man running toward the back of the general store. "Pardner, you better freeze and get your hands up before I shoot." Realizing it was Sheriff Bellows talking, Zeller knew the peace officer would shoot if he didn't give himself up.

Sam marched his prisoner back to the Ribera jail and handcuffed him to a heavy chair. Then he made a pot of coffee. As he sipped the fresh brew, he looked at the man who attempted to blow up the Whitman Saloon.

"I don't know who you are, but you should know you're in a pack of trouble. Come morning, you're gonna' be charged with attempted murder, 'cause the night watchman sleeps in the rear of the saloon. With the story I can testify to, I'll bet you're good for at least twenty years at the Yuma Territorial Prison. And just in case you're not familiar with the place, escapes never happen and half the prisoners die before completing their sentence. And you can bet I'll check my posters in the morning to see if you're wanted someplace else. If you got something to say, you'd best get to it."

The prospect of twenty years in Yuma shook Bink Zeller to the core. "Sheriff, you gotta' give me a break. I didn't know there was anyone in that saloon. I didn't mean to hurt anybody."

Bellows listened intently and urged his prisoner to continue. "Well, Bink, if that's your real name, it's time to come clean if you want any help from me." The sheriff poured Zeller a cup of coffee.

"I was hired by Burr Tilden, who'd lost a lot of customers to that woman who owns the saloon. He said he didn't want to set another fire 'cause it was too dangerous. He decided on a small charge of dynamite to scare the Madame, as he called her."

By the time Bink Zeller finished his coffee, he had implicated Tilden in the hotel fire that killed a man and badly injured Ho-Ching. Just before dawn, Sam Bellows had a detailed, signed confession that would enable him to arrest Burr Tilden and take him to jail.

Tilden had slept poorly. He knew something was wrong since he hadn't heard an explosion and Bink had not returned to collect the second half of the money he was owed. It was barely light when he dressed, buckled a pistoled holster to his hip and made his way to his saloon. Sam Bellows was waiting for him. "Burr, come here with your hands up. I want to talk to you."

Certain he was in trouble, Tilden reached for his gun. Before he could get a shot off, Bellows fired a bullet that hit Tilden in the shoulder, dropping him to the ground. Grabbing his bleeding shoulder, Tilden cried out for Bellows not to shoot. The sheriff dismounted, hastily bandaged the criminal, and tied him to the saddle for the ride back to Ribera.

Judge Parker held court about a month later, ironically in the Whitman Saloon. Burr Tilden was convicted of arson and murder and sentenced to death by hanging. Bink Zeller was convicted of attempted murder and received a sentence of twenty years in the Yuma Territorial Prison. Sheriff Sam Bellows tried his best to get Zeller a reduced sentence but the judge would not agree to the plea. And, as a handful of townsfolk looked on, Burr Tilden was hanged until dead.

CHAPTER 31

Tom Lawson Enters Prison

THE PRISONER, SHACKLED HAND AND foot, shuffled slowly to the waiting stagecoach that would take him to Tucson and the train ride to Yuma. One of the local guards called out, "Enjoy your vacation in the sunshine" as Tom Lawson was turned over to Rex Bodine, his official escort for the trip. Bodine, a six-foot bruiser of a man, enjoyed transporting prisoners to their destination. When he wasn't involved in prisoner transfer, he was hunting escaped prisoners for a bounty. He did his work well and had never lost a prisoner. But he did kill one recently during an attempted escape.

Tom bid goodbye to Flagstaff as he was helped into the coach. He had received scant information on the condition of Dale Richmond but had heard that he was still in the hospital, recovering from a bullet wound.

As the stage began the long descent to Phoenix and Tucson, Bodine leaned over the young man and remarked, "You're nothin' but a number to me, sonny, so don't make a false move and keep your mouth shut unless I ask you something or tell you to do something. This ain't no joy ride as you'll find out soon enough." Grimacing through broken teeth, Bodine then drew up his fist and smashed Tom hard across the face. Nose bleeding and with a split lip, Tom said nothing but curled closer to the corner of the stage. "Now, that's exactly what I want you to do; I don't want to deliver you to the warden all busted up." Four days later, after administering several more beatings—all body blows—Bodine delivered his prisoner to the main gate of the Yuma Territorial Prison. The guard at the gate signed Tom in, took him inside, and removed his shackles. He was then taken to the office of Thomas Gates, warden of the infamous penal institution.

The Yuma Territorial Prison opened in 1876 and remained in operation for thirty-three years. It was situated on seven acres of land adjacent to the Colorado River, the natural border between California and Arizona. Individual cells, carved from solid sandstone, measured seven feet by nine feet and normally housed four to six inmates. Summer temperatures sometimes reached 120 degrees; winter nights could fall below freezing. Up to 120 men and women were held at one time.

Tom was surprised when he met warden Thomas Gates. He was of average height, wore glasses, and spoke like a schoolmaster. "Mr. Lawson, you will spend the next five years of your life here. Adhere to our basic rules and your stay will be tolerable. Stay away from gangs and do what the guards tell you to do. You may have the opportunity to work on our farm that supplies the prison with vegetables. But we'll let you get acclimated first. Don't be tempted to escape. Most who do end up drowning in the river or die trying to cross the desert. Prisoner insubordination will not be tolerated. Minor infractions will get you on the rock pile, breaking stone. Several infractions will land you in what the prisoners call "the hellhole." The guards and assistant warden will review your status here. Be careful whom you associate with, son. Good luck to you."

His interview over, Tom Lawson, better know as #805, was photographed and his height, weight, and eye color noted on his prison file. It was also noted that he had no apparent addictions to opium or tobacco. After being logged in, the prisoner's head was shaved and he was issued clothing, bedding, shoes, and a wide brimmed hat. Levi Strauss of San Francisco, California, manufactured the striped uniforms. He was then led to a cell, already occupied by three prisoners. Peter was a Mormon from Snowflake sentenced to three years for polygamy. He was a model prisoner and worked steady in the vegetable garden. Sanchez was a Mexican national who had been convicted of armed robbery and was serving ten years. Luis was a hulk of a man who was in for manslaughter. He and Sanchez worked in the prison kitchen. They had little to say as Tom placed his straw mattress on a lower, empty bunk. He minded his own business over the next few days, keeping quiet and doing everything he was told to do.

One morning, returning from breakfast, Tom saw his cellmates standing outside the cell while guards carried out an inspection. Methodically, the guards picked up each mattress and shook it. Underneath Tom's pad, one of the guards found a steel shank fashioned into a knife. He was quizzed about the weapon and replied that he knew nothing about it or how it got there. But Tom knew that it was the handiwork of Luis. He dared not snitch; stool pigeons didn't survive long in Yuma. The guards, needing a victim, were satisfied that Tom Lawson would be the one to spend two weeks in "the hellhole."

"The hellhole" was a steel box that barely confined a man to a sitting position. Murderously hot in the daytime, it was bitter cold at night. The prisoner was allowed one half hour per day to walk and stretch outside the container and was fed bread and water three times a day. Between the meager rations, terrible heat and cold, and lack of exercise, Tom shed fifteen pounds in the course of his confinement. When released and returned to a new cell, he practically collapsed into the bed. After several days of decent food and exercise, he felt himself fit again and met his two new cellmates. Rafael was in for five years for assault and battery. Harry was a former banker convicted of embezzlement with two years remaining on his eight-year sentence. The banker took a liking to Tom, especially after getting word that Luis had issued orders to his gang members and others that prisoner #805 had paid his dues by protecting the Mexican during the knife episode.

Soon after completing his first year in prison, Tom received a letter from Dale Richmond postmarked from Flagstaff. In the letter, Dale thanked Tom for saving his life and explained how he had recovered from his wounds and married a local girl whose father owned and operated a lumber mill. He also went on to tell Tom that he'd written his parents about the events in the north country, including Tom's manslaughter conviction and sentencing to Yuma for five years. He reasoned that both sets of parents would eventually find out and he wanted them to be sure they heard the truth.

A month later, Tom was taken to the assistant warden's office where he was surprised to see his parents waiting for him. They had taken the train from Tucson to visit him. Tom and his father embraced but Kate Lawson nearly fainted when she saw her oldest son in prison clothing, thin and with a shaven head. While a guard and the assistant warden looked on, the family chatted for the next two hours. Tom learned that his father had hired a highly regarded attorney to review Tom's conviction. After examining the circumstances, the lawyer decided that the best they could hope for was a reduced sentence for good behavior. Tearfully, Kate and Ben Lawson concluded their visit and departed for the trip home.

Meanwhile, Tom made a friend of Harry Cox, his new cellmate. Harry detected above average intelligence in the young man and decided to become his mentor. His small but excellent library became the vehicle for Tom's continuing education. The two men started with reading the classics and followed with discussions of Greek and Roman history. Tom also learned to read, write, and speak Spanish and practiced the language with several inmates. The banker also drilled Tom in the intricacies of accounting and finance. They discussed balance sheets, income statements, and problems that could bedevil companies such as inadequate cash flow, too fast growth, and lack of customer care. The best part of Tom's education involved solving problems created by Harry to test the young man's analytic powers.

"Tom, I've taught you everything I know about financial analysis," Harry declared. "You've worked hard and even though you don't know it, you've received more training in these subjects than a professional accountant would get in college working for a degree. Someday, when the time for your release arrives, you'll be ready to begin a new career. Coupled with what you've learned about human nature in this place, you'll be able to take on the world."

Tom agreed to do as Harry advised but wondered who would hire an accountant with a prison record and an embezzler as a tutor.

CHAPTER 32

The Death of Grandfather

THE TRAIN RIDE FROM NEW York to Pittsburgh gave Carlos Rodriguez Bruner and Arn Gustafson time to discuss their respective internships with Carnegie Steel Company. Arn had learned that he would begin his tour on the Mesabi iron ore range in Minnesota and finish at a limestone quarry in Pennsylvania. He was looking forward to the steamship ride to Duluth and was due to board ship in a week. Carlos was scheduled to report to a steel works in Braddock, Pennsylvania, where Felix Altman would introduce him to the superintendent of the open-hearth shop. He would also spend time in the new experimental Bessemer facility where steel was being produced at much lower cost. Andrew Carnegie, after seeing the equipment in England, had purchased two units and had them brought to Pittsburgh. As the two young men parted company at the Pittsburgh train station, Arn waved and shouted, "I'll see you back in New York, Carlos."

Arriving at the Edgar Thomson works in Braddock, Carlos was surprised at the size of the steel plant. The open-hearth shop alone had at least a dozen operating furnaces, each producing sixty tons of steel every six hours, tap to tap. Scotty Ferguson took him on a tour of the plant where several hundred men worked around the clock. "Carlos, we receive molten pig iron from the blast furnaces, pour it into open hearths, and cook it to remove impurities. We then add manganese and other alloys to meet customer specifications. It's getting more complicated all the time but a good melter with a sharp eye for furnace conditions is still a valuable person."

The tour of the Bessemer plant was very exciting. Here, molten iron was poured into a steel vessel shaped like a pear and refined by blowing air into the metal through bottom tuyeres. The Englishman Henry Bessemer invented the process in 1855. By the turn of the century, the use of the invention was widespread in the United States.

In the early weeks of his internship, Carlos worked in both plants, studying the chemistry of each process and learning the metallurgical practices used by the operators. As his knowledge increased, he began to see that for certain types of steel, the Bessemer process was clearly lower cost than the older, open-hearth method. It was also a thrill to watch the "blows" in the dark as carbon and silicon were burned out of the melt, sending sparks flying into the night.

When he was called into Scotty Ferguson's office, Carlos knew that something was wrong. "Carlos, the front office has just received a telegram from New York City. It says that your grandfather is very ill and it's best if you left for home immediately. It was signed by Lumberto Villegas."

Carlos reacted swiftly to the news. He raced back to his hotel and quickly packed a suitcase. The Carnegie Steel Company traffic department got him train reservations to Mexico by the fastest possible route and sent a man and a car to drive him to the train station for the evening passenger express to Chicago. Delivered to the first class compartment, Carlos was able to bathe and change his clothes as the train sped westward. He prayed that he would reach the ranch before his grandfather died. Two and a half days later, he stepped off the Mexican National Railway car to be greeted by Lumberto.

"Try to relax, Carlos," Lumberto advised. "Your grandfather is hanging on and doing better than we had hoped. It will be best to let him sleep tonight. I'm sure you wouldn't mind a good rest yourself. The doctor is staying at the ranch; if we have an emergency during the night, I'll wake you up." Exhausted, Carlos fell asleep as Lumberto directed the team and buggy to the hacienda.

Senor Rodriguez was smiling when his grandson entered the patron's bedroom suite. "Ah, my dear boy, it is wonderful that you got here. I don't have too much time left and I wanted to explain what I have spelled out in my will. Lumberto, stay here please while I talk to Carlos." Waving the doctor and maid to leave the room, the elder Rodriguez began.

"Everything I am about to tell you is covered in my last will and testament which you can read after I'm gone. And don't be afraid of my dying; I've had a good life and have been blessed with an heir who will carry on our bloodline. Now help me to sit up and we will share a glass of good red wine."

"To Lumberto, my trusted compadre, I leave one million pesos in gold and 25,000 hectares of ranch land on the northeast border of my holdings. You're still young, Lumberto, perhaps this will enable you to start a family of your own. I also want you to oversee the silver mines, the factories in Mexico City, and my interests in Tampico until Carlos graduates from the university."

The old man breathed heavily, sipped some wine, and went on.

"Carlos, I'm leaving you many responsibilities early in your life but I am confident that you are up to the challenge. I had hoped for a few more years but that is not to be. I have willed the shrimp fishing operations in the Sea of Cortez to my brother and his family. He has been a good brother and worked hard all these years to build a fleet of over fifty boats, a shipyard, and processing plants. He and his sons have started to farm the irrigated land along the coast of Sonora; this should pay big dividends for his family in the future. My will gives you the details on what you will inherit; I've only covered the major things. One thing about the silver mines, Carlos. Your father spent three years here and built my mines into one of the largest silver producing operations in the world. Many times, they supplied the money to invest in what I now own here, in Mexico City, in Tampico, and what I've given my brother. And as I hope you have or will find out, Konrad Bruner is a very good person. Get to know him."

"Things are changing rapidly. I have decided to support the construction of a telegraph line from the ranch to Tampico; it will enable us to contact customers and suppliers from around the world. I've left the connection from Zacatecas to Mexico City up to the federal government, such as it is. When service is established between Zacatecas and the capital, you should build the connection to here. My contacts in Mexico City tell me that should happen within the year."

"Carlos, this hour has exhausted me. With the grace of God, we shall enjoy lunch together. In the meantime, I will take a morning siesta."

As he finished the sentence, Senor Rodriguez dozed off to sleep. Before Carlos left the room, Lumberto suggested they meet on the patio for coffee and sweets. As the morning sun illuminated the bright red and purple bougainvillea, the two men sat down to talk.

"The patron has been very generous in leaving me land. I never expected that he would do such a thing, but that is not the reason I wanted to talk with you, Carlos. It is something I wanted to discuss with the senor, but I held off because of his failing health. Now, it will be your responsibility to approve my investigation."

"In general, the estate is in good shape. However, there is one exception and it's the silver mining operations. I suspect that something is amiss with Carlos Ortega. Your grandfather believed he was a loyal, excellent business manager but over the past month I've learned that he is drinking too much and carrying on with a mistress in Zacatecas. His wife Carlita is too refined and proud to tolerate this stupidity for very long and I fear the breakup of his family. While his personal life is none of my business, it is if our mining operations are not performing well. I've done some checking and have found that production is falling off and we have labor problems. In fact, we had a one-day strike about two weeks ago. I apologize for this; I should have been more alert to the situation."

"Don't worry about that now, Lumberto," Carlos replied. "What do you think I should do?"

"I would bring in a professional accounting firm from Mexico City to audit the books and follow the activity stream from the mines to the smelters and eventually to shipping the ingots," Lumberto advised. "It will be expensive but I feel it must be done. I know this will upset Ernesto Cardenas, our controller, but so be it. We haven't had an outside examination of our records in over five years."

Nodding his approval, Carlos thanked Lumberto for his observation and described his plan of action. "So, I have about a year before I complete my mining studies at the university; law school will have to wait. My place is here to run the family business to the best of my ability. Let's go ahead with hiring the Mexico City accountants. I ask you to keep me advised on their progress. Once the telegraph line is installed from the ranch to Tampico, we will be able to stay in close contact with each other without too much trouble. I'll open a small office near campus and will hire a secretary to keep track of things. I've lost some time in the past week but should be able to get back on track by double shifting at the steel mill. In the meantime, use the Columbia University telegraph line to contact me in an emergency."

The conversation between Lumberto and Carlos was interrupted by the screams of a maid. "The patron is dead, the patron is dead!" Racing upstairs they found Doctor Vasquez pulling a sheet over the face of Amelio Rodriguez. "He died in his sleep, gentlemen."

Carlos assumed the role of patron immediately. He welcomed local and state officials and friends and relatives to the funeral service conducted by Bishop Bellinegro. Flowers adorned the walls and every corner of the room where the body of Amelio Rodriguez lay in an open casket. The funeral mass was followed by a lavish meal of food, wine, and beer served on the patio of the main house. Carlos began to realize just how important the patron was to the community. Hundreds of ranch hands, miners, farmers and their families depended on the Rodriguez estate for their livelihood.

Two days later, Carlos shook hands with Lumberto and began his journey back to Pittsburgh. Before setting out, he decided to make a quick stop in Michigan to see Rachel. Arriving in Ann Arbor, he learned that Rachel was at the university hospital and wasn't expected at the Med House until later in the day. Mrs. Purdy offered Carlos a seat in a cushioned leather chair facing a gently burning fire and he readily accepted. Weary from the trip, he dozed off immediately only to be awakened by a kiss.

"What a wonderful surprise, darling," Rachel gushed. The young man groggily stood up and embraced his fiancée. "God, how I've missed you," he replied. "I was on my way back to Pittsburgh after attending my grandfather's funeral in Mexico and being close to Detroit, decided to stop and see you. I hope it's all right."

Over dinner that evening in a quiet restaurant, Carlos explained his emergency trip, his grandfather's death, and his new responsibilities. Rachel listened attentively and began to understand Carlos's close connection to Mexico, his homeland. The reality of this connection unsettled her. The prospect of living in Mexico, on a ranch, even as a rich landowner's wife, did not mesh with her plans for the future. And they'd never had a serious discussion about their religious beliefs and how religion might influence the raising of their children. Mexico was a deeply traditional Catholic country and the thought of her children being raised in that culture gave Rachel a chill.

After dinner, the couple relaxed by a crackling fire. Despite the joy of their reunion, Carlos sensed Rachel's unease. It was something new to him. Holding his hand, Rachel looked at Carlos and asked, "What plans do you have when your studies at Columbia are completed?"

The young man thought for a moment and then responded, "I guess I'd like to see us married in Ribera, then move to the hacienda in Zacatecas." When he saw the color drain from Rachel's face, he knew it was not the answer she expected or perhaps hoped for.

Now it was Rachel's turn to share some of her concerns. "Carlos, if I agreed to what you propose I will have spent almost three years in medical training only to start a practice in some Mexican mining town. I planned to work in Phoenix but more likely in San Diego or Los

Angeles where they have hospitals and nursing staffs. I just never antic-ipated that you intended to be the head man of a big company."

Rachel's honesty took Carlos aback. "Well, Rachel, I suppose my grandfather didn't plan on dying either, at least not now. You talk about Mexico as if it were a second-class country unworthy of your medical skill. It's unfair, especially since you've never seen the ranch."

Both were becoming upset over the tone of the conversation and decided to leave the restaurant. Reaching Med House, Rachel sug-gested they meet for an early breakfast. Lightly kissing Rachel on the forehead, Carlos left her at the door, fearing that the evening could deteriorate further if they continued their conversation. Neither slept well that night; what should have been an intimate, loving reunion had turned into the beginning of a serious disagreement. Carlos couldn't understand Rachel's concerns. Did she plan on being a full-time doc-tor? What about marriage and children? What about their life together?

The discussion didn't improve at breakfast. Choking back tears, Rachel looked at Carlos and tried to explain her feelings. "Both of us have put ourselves under a great deal of pressure; you with the death of your grandfather and new role as head of his businesses; me trying to decide on plans for my medical career after graduation. Maybe we're not ready for marriage. I love you, Carlos, but I'm confused and think we should let things cool down some."

Heart sinking, Carlos shrugged his shoulders and tried to appear calm. "If you are saying we should break off our unofficial engagement, then I'll have to go along with you."

His response only served to upset Rachel even more. "Fine, you may consider yourself disengaged." Her face flushed with emotion, Rachel stood up and left the table while Carlos sat frozen in silence.

Shaken by Rachel's words and sudden departure, Carlos paid the bill, returned to his lodgings, and was soon on his way back to Pitts-burgh. On the train ride from Detroit to the steel city, he pondered how he could salvage his relationship with the girl he loved. Digging inside his vest pocket, he pulled out a small, square velvet box. Inside was a flawless two-carat diamond ring, the one he had intended to place on Rachel's finger to seal their engagement. Gazing at the ring, he won-dered how things had gone so wrong. How was he going to regain Rachel's love and respect?

CHAPTER 33

Richmond Takes the Job

ON HIS RETURN TO THE River Bend Ranch, Don Richmond approached his wife warily. He was not sure how she would react to his decision to take on a full time job in Phoenix. Periodic trips to the capital were one thing, but taking up residence there to head up a project that could easily require five years was far more serious. He needn't have been concerned.

"Don, I've watched your interest and involvement in Phoenix grow for the past two years and knew something like this was bound to happen. For someone who professes to not being a politician, you seem to get along pretty well with people of different interests and problems. Your work with the water board here is a good example of what you're capable of doing. It wouldn't have made any difference, but I only wish you had discussed it with me before you made a decision. I suggest you rent or buy a house in Phoenix so I can visit you from time to time. Why, this could be the excuse I was looking for to visit Dale and Abby in Flagstaff and meet the daughter-in-law I've heard so much about."

Their conversation ended amicably as Dolores Richmond thought more about a trip to the north country.

When Don was unable to find Henry Dempsey, he went to the Steinmark farm in hopes of finding Eric. Helga Steinmark informed him that Eric and Madi were in the fields looking over a new crop of corn and probably wouldn't be back until lunchtime. She insisted Don spend the night with them and stay as long as he liked. Over a huge lunch of bratwurst, cabbage, and dumplings, the friends talked abut the lack of rain and the pending drought. They agreed that the problem only reinforced the need for reservoirs and an interlocking series of canals to provide water to the farmers when the rains didn't arrive. Don agreed to spend the night with the understanding that he would leave before breakfast to meet with Harry Dempsey. After dinner, Don and Eric talked about the Circle S Ranch. "Don, there's plenty of good ranch land there but it won't last forever. Don't put off a purchase for too long if you're seriously interested," cautioned the young man. As he moved to retire for the night, Madi looked at Don and winking, wished him a goodnight. What was that all about? he wondered.

Shortly after sunset, Don Richmond removed his clothes, got into bed, and soon fell asleep. Sometime after midnight, as if in a dream, he felt a warm, naked body slide into bed alongside him. Startled, he awoke to feel Madi embracing him. Whispering "Quiet, we don't want to wake up the house," she groped for his privates and kissed him on the lips feverishly. As he stiffened, the girl rolled on top of him and gently moved up and down in ecstatic rhythm. Shortly after a muffled groan, she pushed harder until Don erupted. Before he could collect his thoughts, Madi slid out of bed, kissed Don again, and retreated from the room. Don lay dumbstruck looking at the ceiling, wondering if it had all been a dream. He hoped it was but knew that the brief sexual encounter was authentic. What really distressed him was that he had enjoyed every minute of it. Sleep was now impossible. At daybreak, Don Richmond dressed quickly and quietly and left the Steinmark house. He hoped he would forget his encounter with Madi, but knew it would be nearly impossible. As he rode away from the house, Madi Steinmark looked on from her bedroom window and said a silent good-bye.

As usual, Henry Dempsey was upbeat and smiling when Don entered the lawyer's office. "I'm fearful of a drought coming on, Don. That's all the more reason we should be pushing our project. I've got a house rented for you that has a kitchen, three bedrooms, and a sitting room we can fix up for an office. We can display our topographic maps that show the rivers and potential dam sites and reservoirs. I think we can agree that the big dam we have in mind is going to need federal money, so we've got to complete our plans and present them to the boys in Washington. We've heard that at least two and maybe three other states and territories have big irrigation projects in mind. With the work we've already done, I think we're ahead of them, but Washington politics can be very unpredictable. The recent USGS survey that locates water storage reservoirs should help us a lot."

For the next two weeks, Henry Dempsey and Don Richmond rode up and down the Salt and Verde rivers, examined water storage sites, compiled weather data, and talked with all the important growers. Virtually all agreed that if dams and reservoirs could be built, water would enable the valley farmers to establish a major agricultural region in the West. The federal government would surely want cost information on the project and how it might be financed. A partial answer arrived when an engineer with the USGS mentioned electric power sales to offset a good part of the project cost.

Don Richmond arrived in Washington after a train ride of three days that took him from Phoenix through New Orleans, Atlanta, and Richmond. He was impressed with the Mississippi delta, the rebuilding of Atlanta and Richmond, and the white marble brilliance of the nation's capital. The Arizona Territorial delegation was housed in a building about a block from the White House. It was not the best time to be visiting Washington; the nation was still recovering from the panic of 1893 when British investors, sensing weakness in the American economy, unloaded securities, most of them railroad. In addition, Hawaii had just been annexed in 1898, and labor unrest had received national attention with strikes at Homestead, Pennsylvania, and the Pullman work stoppage. The Arizona delegation was able to arrange visits with Secretary of the Interior Adlai Stevenson and Vice President Grover Cleveland.

"Mr. Richmond, we're very appreciative of your efforts to develop the Arizona Territory," explained Mr. Stevenson. "I personally like your plan to build dams and water storage lakes. We're here to help you, but please understand that we have many high priority projects that demand our attention. I like the work you and your associates have done, so don't be discouraged by our delay in making up our minds. Keep up what you're doing."

The head of the Arizona Territory delegation in Washington was satisfied with the meeting. "Don, I think we've done as well as we could expect from your visit. They know where the Salt River is now and what the results would be when a dam is built east of Phoenix. And I know we got their attention when we mentioned the sale of electric power. Electrification is a big buzzword here in Washington. We're also pushing for statehood, and think we've got a good chance in a few years or so. Wouldn't that be something if we got the two of them at the same time?"

Arriving back in Phoenix after a grueling train ride, Don was advised by Henry Dempsey that efforts to raise private money for the project had failed. Local farmers and bankers simply did not have the resources to take on such a huge job. Once more, Dempsey and Richmond recognized that federal financial support was necessary if the project was going to move forward.

Don was confident that ultimately federal money would be granted. With that thought in mind, he bought the house he had been renting and purchased furniture, rugs, and kitchen equipment. Heeding Eric Steinmark's advice, he also decided to buy a ranch near the Circle S Ranch north of Globe. Eric helped Don finalize the deal. While momentarily enticed to see Madi Steinmark again, Don knew he loved his wife and was going to bring her to Phoenix as soon as possible. Any further infidelity would be far too costly.

CHAPTER 34

Bruner Refuses an Offer

KONRAD BRUNER GOT WORD OF the death of Amelio Rodriguez in a letter from Lumberto Villegas. Also included in the letter was a note from his son Carlos. Bruner admired the Mexican and was sorry to read the news of his passing. Even at the age of seventy-seven, the death of the patron was unexpected. Lumberto also explained that Carlos was now the sole owner of the old man's holdings, and as a result, was a multi-millionaire and the owner of one of the world's largest silver mining operations. The letter also mentioned that Carlos was returning to Columbia University to complete his mining and metallurgical studies, and was expected to be back in Zacatecas in about a year. Konrad smiled as he thought about the wealth and responsibility suddenly heaped on young Carlos; he remembered him as a friendly, easygoing person who loved ranch life, and not as a landowner and patron to hundreds of employees and their families. Momentarily, Konrad considered asking his son for investment grade money but quickly dispensed with the idea. He would raise the capital for the mine on his own.

As Konrad entered Globe, he noted many new buildings under construction and more people hustling about. When he mentioned this to his banker James McNulty, he agreed that the town was growing rapidly with money coming in from ranching and mining. "A new school is in the works as well as a hospital, church, and many new stores. I'll take care of setting up an account for B.J. Kimball with the $25,000 deposit; that should make the old man happy. By the way, Bern Heinzelman, who represents the Goldsmith brothers of Silver City, has been asking about you. He's staying at the Highland Hotel and would like to meet up with you. They're the people who are developing the mine over in Clifton, and from what I understand, are doing quite well. Last I heard, they were talking about building a smelter to process their ore locally, rather than shipping concentrates to New Mexico. I'd be happy to host a lunch if you'd like to meet the man."

Konrad thanked the banker for his help but declined the offer. "I'll meet up with Mr. Heinzelman shortly; I plan on being in town for a few days."

A day later, the two men met for dinner in the dining room of the Highland Hotel. Bern Heinzelman, originally from Vienna, Austria, was a rotund, balding man who wore glasses and a thin mustache and goatee. He spoke excellent English with a slight Viennese accent. "Mr. Bruner, we've little information about your activities in the field but know you've been busy establishing Copper Hill Mining Company. That's a pretty important sounding name. Do you really have an ore body that well defined? Do you have something now, or is it something more promotional in nature? And before you answer, let me say that we know who you are, your reputation, and successes in Mexico and Ribera. Please, don't take my remarks adversely; I intend no offense. We also know about your fallout with Mr. Barksdale and Britsco; it's simply our way of investigating a possible business opportunity."

Konrad listened patiently to the Austrian but simmered with resentment under his controlled exterior.

"Mr. Heinzelman, this kind of questioning may be the way you do business but I find it disagreeable. However, let me be equally candid. You are correct regarding Britsco. Colin Barksdale and I disagreed. I have no regrets in that regard except that I now find myself in the unfamiliar world of high finance. In earlier adventures, I've been a hired hand working as a technologist; now I must learn the ins and outs of accounting, finance, and dealing with people like you. Believe me, I will learn this business of financing a mine and its development. No doubt you have some information about our discovery, or we wouldn't be sitting here. How you got this information is immaterial. On a very preliminary basis, I believe we have a mountain of copper with some gold, silver, and molybdenum. The deposit will eventually justify the building of a railroad and smelter. In the next year, I intend to complete a survey of our claims that will attract investors. While digging exploratory pits, we'll bring out some high-grade ore and a few concentrates to sell and generate cash. Until we have completed this work, I have no intention of partnering or selling out prematurely."

"Well said, Mr. Bruner. You have an excellent plan. All you have to do now is to execute your plan and hope that copper prices hold or get better. Keep in mind that starting up a copper mine usually requires a management team of technical people, mine and mill operators, and lots of money. On top of that, the Pinal Creek has been known for terrible flash flooding, and we've had a lot of snow in the mountains this past winter. My point is this, Mr. Bruner: While we respect your capabilities, projects of this size are hard to handle, especially when one goes it alone. If you ever run into problems that seem insurmountable, please let me know. And if you ever decide to take on a partner or sell out your interest, please keep us in mind."

When Heinzelman and Bruner departed the restaurant, Konrad went to his room and jotted down a few key points of their conversation. As he climbed into bed, he had second thoughts about his meeting with the Goldsmith contact man. He shivered in the cool night air as he wondered if he was truly ready for his next challenge. Did he have enough money to see the first phase through, or would he be begging the likes of Heinzelman for help?

In spite of these misgivings, Konrad woke up in high spirits. He went over to Gelber's General Store to buy clothing, boots, heavy gloves, and blankets and had them wrapped in a bundle he could tie to his saddle. He then went to the assay office where he ordered mapping paper, a plane table, drafting pens and pencils, and ink. He then spoke with Norm Dickson about prices for volume assay work and record keeping.

"Mr. Bruner, if you require confidentiality on your samples you have my word that your specimens will be examined and the results kept secret. I've never been asked to sign a confidentiality agreement but if that's what you want, I'll oblige."

Konrad looked around the office and then at Norm Dickson. "No Norm, that won't be necessary. Your word is good enough for me."

After flashing signals with a mirror and getting the required response, Konrad rode into camp with his supplies and reported on his activities to B.J. Kimball and Andy Corsica. "I've deposited $25,000 in the Pinal County Bank and have set up accounts at the hotel, assay office, and Gelber's General Store. All you have to do B.J. is sign the bill that I'll cover when I go into town. If you think of anything else we need, let me know. Tomorrow, I'd like to get started on getting our second cabin built so we can store samples and maybe pile up ore from our exploration work. The important thing is to mark each place we sample to correspond with the sample bag or we'll have poor data to support our results. I'll start marking places by the end of the week."

As the trio left their main camp, they walked downhill to the streambed. It was here that Konrad determined that the streambed was actually a fault line with sedimentary rock on one side and a granitic igneous mass on the other side. After deciding where their second cabin was to be built, the geologist walked back to the streambed to take a closer look at the contact zone between the sandstone, limestone, and granite. Sensing the intrusion and subsequent fracturing as typical of porphyry copper deposits, Konrad had renewed hope that his Copper Hill deposit was a major find. He smiled to himself as he tramped back up the hill.

CHAPTER 35

The Railroad Comes to Arizona

THE CIVIL WAR BARELY AFFECTED the Arizona Territory, but the conflict interrupted the Butterfield Overland Mail leaving the area without commercial transportation. Shortly after the war ended, the Southern Overland U.S. Mail and Express linked Tucson with Mesilla, New Mexico Territory, and points east. In 1870, stagecoach travel between San Diego and Tucson started up, and southern Arizona began to attract settlers and miners. A very profitable line was established linking Tucson with Tombstone, then the most populous town in the territory.

The major economic event of the late 1800s was the arrival of the railroad. Federal surveys had been conducted in the 1850s, but nothing came of the efforts until the end of the Civil War. In the postwar period, the government offered huge incentives to build a transcontinental railroad. The Atlantic and Pacific Railroad was the first to receive a charter, and the line was constructed from Springfield, Missouri, to Albuquerque, New Mexico, and then west along the 35th parallel to the Pacific Coast. The railroad made little headway however, and collapsed during the financial panic of 1873.

A second concession was awarded to the Texas and Pacific Railroad that was designed to run from Marshall, Texas, along the 32nd parallel to San Diego, California. At the time of the 1873 panic the line had reached Dallas, Texas. As both lines floundered, the "Big Four" railroad financiers of California—Mark Hopkins, Collis P. Huntington, Leland

Stanford, and Charles Crocker—began construction of a line to connect San Francisco with San Diego. They called it the Southern Pacific Railroad.

Spur lines were laid eastward to Needles, California, and Yuma, Arizona, assuring the rail barons of a dominant competitive position in the Southwest. With strong lobbying efforts successful in Washington, D.C. and the cooperation of the Arizona legislature, the Big Four had track laid to Tucson by 1880, eventually connecting with the Texas and Pacific at Sierra Blanca, a small town ninety miles east of El Paso.

Meanwhile, the Santa Fe (Atchison, Topeka and Santa Fe) was laying track from Kansas to New Mexico. Under the leadership of Cyrus K. Holliday, the Santa Fe acquired the Atlantic and Pacific Railroad and began building a line through northern Arizona, establishing towns at Winslow, Holbrook, Flagstaff, Williams, Ash Fork, Seligman, and Kingman. By 1885, the Santa Fe had reached an agreement with the Southern Pacific to acquire the Needles-Mohave line and connect with rights to San Diego. With this transaction, a second transcontinental railroad was completed.

As the two rail lines crossed the Arizona Territory, towns came into existence to house the families of the Irish, Chinese, and other immigrant groups who did the hard work of laying track and blasting through mountain passes. Merchants, gamblers, saloonkeepers, and prostitutes swarmed into these communities, then moved on, following the track that moved ahead of them.

As the mining towns of Bisbee, Jerome, and Clifton-Morenci boomed, railroad feeder lines were built to connect with the main lines. In some cases, it was the arrival of the railroad that established the economic viability of the newly discovered mineral deposits. By the early 1900s, every major town in the Arizona Territory enjoyed the benefits of rail service.

CHAPTER 36

Booker Meets an Old Friend

LIEUTENANT VINCENT CYRUS BOOKER LEFT the San Carlos Indian Reservation as Vince Booker, civilian. He was alternately mad with himself, upset with the army, and confused about his future. He was particularly disturbed when he thought about Major Garrison and Caleb Benson's whiskey business. The army had rules and regulations, and he felt helpless in fighting his recent departure from the service after twenty-three years. Disgraced, Booker felt like a ship lost at sea.

Most of his old friends were army friends, stationed east of the Mississippi River. While he had several hundred dollars in mustering-out pay, he had no idea what he was going to do or where he might get a fresh start. At age forty-five, he was washed up. When a freighter offered him a ride to Tucson, Booker readily accepted.

Arriving in the Old Pueblo, he was surprised to see how much the town had grown and how heavily it was populated with Indians and Mexicans. He got along well with the Mexicans as he spoke fluent Spanish, and could hold his own with the Pimas using a mixture of sign language and some expressions he had picked up during his army service. Booker felt uncomfortable however, as he had difficulty explaining who he was and how he'd gotten to Tucson. Keeping his army background a secret after a lifetime of service was not easy. From time to time, he would mingle with troopers from Fort Huachuca, on leave or in the process of picking up supplies for the fort. Thankfully, most were youngsters who did not recognize him.

The Saguaro Cantina was the wrong place to be one Saturday night. Corporal Stan Robbins, on a weekend pass, saddled up to the bar and ordered tequila for him and two other soldiers. As he bumped into the retired veteran, he looked at Booker through glazed eyes, exclaiming, "Well, I'll be damned, look who's here!" As the troopers downed more liquor, Robbins became belligerent. "Don't try pulling any rank on me, Booker. You're nothing but a broken down pony soldier who quit the army before you were booted out with a dishonorable discharge. You and your damn regulations got me into more trouble and cost me more promotions than I want to remember."

The cantina crowd grew silent as the two men glared at each other. "Robbins, you always were a troublemaker. Now stay away from me or I'll tear you apart." Not one to back away from a challenge, Robbins, with the aid of two trooper friends, charged Booker who landed a crushing fist to the corporal's chin. As the two troopers pummeled him, Booker steadily hit Robbins in his midsection, but was no match for two men wielding heavy oaken chairs. The three men gained control of the fight and slugged Booker to the floor, kicking him into submission. Realizing the trouble they'd created, Robbins shouted, "Come on men, let's get outta' here before the sheriff shows up."

When Booker woke up, he was slumped over in an alleyway, his money and boots missing. He also had sore ribs, a large lump on the back of his head, skinned knuckles, and a black eye. As a stray dog licked the bottom of his feet, the ex-soldier recalled the night's events. Corporal Robbins, a poor excuse for a two-striper soldier, who along with two buddies had given him a pretty good thrashing, had identified him. Shoeless, with torn clothes and no money, Booker decided that going back to the Saguaro was not a good idea. He felt in his shirt where two gold coins had been attached to the fabric, and thanked a fellow traveler for once suggesting drilling a hole in a coin so it could be fastened and hidden. He pulled the two coins from his shirt and slowly drifted up the street to a large, rectangular watering trough. He wanted to climb in to cleanse his whole body but only plunged his face and hands into the warm water. As he pulled his head from the trough, he sensed someone looking at him. He opened his eyes and was confronted by Mrs. Barbara Casey of the Volunteer Ranch. Greatly embarrassed, Vince Booker turned away but it was too late.

"Lieutenant Booker, don't you dare walk away from me," Barbara Casey called out. As he turned again to face the lady, Barbara pointed to a loaded wagon. "You're just the man I need to get that cargo back to Ribera. I don't know what happened to you, and I honestly don't care, but I need help with the supply wagon. Enrique can sit with the provisions and you can ride up front with me." While Booker was not accustomed to taking orders from a woman, he readily complied with the ranch owner's request. "There's a pistol and an army rifle in the box behind me, Mr. Booker. Get them out and make like you know how to use them." Now smiling, Barbara Casey went on, "We'll stop at the general store near the edge of town to buy you a pair of boots and a straw hat so you don't fry in the sun."

Over a campfire that evening, Barbara Casey explained that she'd been on the lookout for the lieutenant. "The story of your retirement from the army filtered down from the post from soldiers passing through town. At first, I just listened to people talking about you in the store. Then I started asking questions. It didn't take me long to find out that you were forced into leaving the army under very cloudy circumstances. I just couldn't believe that you were involved in selling whiskey to the Indians. And I'm not questioning you; I just don't believe those stories." The ex-trooper wasn't a man to show much emotion but he came close to tears as he listened to Barbara's words. "Mrs. Casey, thank you for the endorsement. It really helps a lot."

When they arrived at the Volunteer Ranch, Booker helped unload the wagon and started to make his way to the bunkhouse. Before he was halfway there, Barbara Casey stopped him. "Vince, you're my guest, and you'll have a private room in the main house. You can be as alone as you want to be. Take some time to rest and enjoy the cooking of Betty Ortiz." She looked at Booker directly, smiling, "I want you to feel at home here. Give yourself time to get your health back. You may think you're okay but a good look in the mirror will tell you that black eye has to heal. I'll get some clothes for you; I've got a trunk of my husband's stuff that I never got rid of. They'll fit pretty well; he was just about your size." And just about the same disposition, too, she murmured under her breath.

Gradually, Vince Booker adjusted to the routine of the Volunteer Ranch. He usually enjoyed breakfast with Betty Ortiz and her husband while Sam explained the workings of the place. As his basic interest in horses re-emerged, Vince worked with the foreman and also took solo rides around the ranch. It wasn't long before he realized that the widow Casey was a very wealthy lady. It made him uneasy.

As a rule, Barbara and Vince dined together in the evening. She did the cooking even after a full day's work at the store. Sometimes, Soleado joined them, and soon the young girl became comfortable with the former officer. After a month or so of Barbara's hospitality, Booker concluded that their relationship was getting complicated and he decided to move on. To where, he couldn't say. After a dessert of rice pudding, Vince explained his intentions. "Barbara, you, Betty, and Sam have made me whole again with your kindness. But it's time for this old soldier to pack his bags and move on. I could still be rotting in a Tucson alley if it weren't for you. You're the finest lady I've ever met. I just hope someday I'll be able to return the favor. And the memory of a disgraced army officer isn't fair for you to have to live with, here or in town."

Barbara Casey sat and listened to Booker's words calmly at first but with growing impatience. "Well, Mr. Booker, I don't care what anybody has to say about your staying here. I respect your thoughts, but I'm not going to let foolish pride lead you to making a bad decision. Vince, sometimes I think you must be blind. I don't pity you. I love you. Can't you see that? The store and ranch mean nothing to me if you're not here to enjoy them with me. I knew you were the man for me when I saw you deal with the Indian women and children when you passed through here after the battle with Aguijador. You were kind and compassionate and treated the Indians the way they should be treated, regardless of what the army said."

Now it was Booker's turn to be truthful. "Barbara, I'm not good with words but you have to know I have real feelings for you. I just figured an old pony soldier like me never had a chance of courting you." Shaking her head slowly from side to side but smiling as tears rolled down her cheeks, Barbara Casey looked over at her soldier and replied, "That's enough said, Vince. Come over here and kiss me."

CHAPTER 37

Barney and Sophie Argue

THE EXECUTION OF BURR TILDEN and delivery of Bink Zeller to the Yuma Territorial Prison were but mild interruptions to the reconstruction of the Whitman Saloon. As carpenters sawed and hammered, a makeshift bar opened and Sophie Kaminski was back in business. The closing of Tilden's establishment in Tent City also helped Sophie's business off to a fresh, resounding success. Miners and cowhands quaffed beer and whiskey to celebrate the grand opening. Ho-Ching's return to the kitchen also helped to reestablish the saloon as Ribera's major attraction. And passing the hat at the July 4th celebration was an unexpected bonus.

Less than two months after opening, Sophie decided to pay down her original loan and visited Brad Scoville. The banker was never comfortable with smart, attractive, and sometimes demanding women like Sophie. "Mr. Scoville, I'm here to pay off my outstanding loan and look into a construction loan for the hotel. Receipts have been much better than my original plan, and I believe I'm ready to move ahead with the new hotel. What will I have to provide you with to get started? I want to hang on to my crew before they start leaving town for work elsewhere. I've roughed out plans for a two-storied structure, a bill of materials, and a labor estimate that comes to $10,500.

Without thinking, Scoville chuckled and replied, "Miss Kaminski, you can have the money anytime you need it, just get Barney Pryor to cosign the loan like we did before." When he saw the look of complete surprise on Sophie's face he realized that Barney had never revealed the secret financing deal they'd put together for the Whitman Saloon.

Sophie was shocked but quickly recovered her poise. "Mr. Scoville, let me be sure I heard you correctly. Are you telling me that I got the loan from you only because Barney Pryor agreed to cosign the note?"

Scoville was now clearly distressed but knew it was time to tell the truth. "Yes, Miss Sophie, that was the deal we put together. Without Barney's support, I would have never loaned you the money to build a saloon. Why, the men in this town would be up in arms if they ever found out that I'd loaned money to a woman."

"Why, that's just plain nonsense, Mr. Scoville, and you know it," Sophie responded angrily. "If I didn't rebuild the saloon and hotel, somebody else would have. You know as well as I do that whiskey, good food, and women are universal in towns like Ribera. So, you get Barney Pryor to back me, I pay nine percent on the loan, and life is beautiful for you. In the meantime, loans are available in Copper City at eight percent. That sounds like unfair treatment to me, and you make believe like you're doing me a big favor."

"Now, see here, Miss Sophie. Women don't generally get bank loans without the approval of their husband. The extra one percent in your case is more than justified, I feel." When Sophie heard that, she stood up, turned, and stormed out of the banker's office slamming the door behind her. Wiping his brow, Scoville knew Barney would be in an unforgiving mood when the news broke.

Barney Pryor knew something was out of kilter when Sophie entered his office without knocking. Before he could utter a hello, the irate beauty poured forth her rage. "Barney, going behind my back to cosign a bank loan without telling me is just plain wrong. Wrong! I just made a complete fool of myself with that stuffed shirt banker. Here I'm trying to borrow money to build a hotel and he's sitting back with a toothy grin telling me to check with you. I can't believe you would do something like this without telling me."

Now Barney was clearly upset. "When you're finished with taking my head off, how about sitting down for a minute and giving me a chance to explain. I'd like to wring Brad Scoville's neck, but what's done is done. I kept things quiet because I knew Scoville wouldn't loan you money without hard collateral, which you didn't have. I also knew that you had enough business savvy to make a success of whatever you put your mind to. And finally, you wouldn't let me loan you money because you think all I want from you is to get you into bed. With all your smarts, Sophie, you got this figured wrong."

"Just so we don't get crossed again, here's my offer. Pay off the loan to Scoville and tell him to go straight to hell. Then I'll loan you what you need for the hotel plus interest at eight percent to be paid back within a year. I'll have lawyer Selwig draw up the papers with a clause that says if the loan isn't paid within a year, I own the saloon and the hotel. That way, you bypass the bank and Scoville, get a better interest rate, and you won't have to see me for a year. You'll have the paperwork in a few days. Now, if you'll excuse me, I'm going to get me a cup of coffee." His speech over, Barney jammed his hat on his head and walked out of the office.

Left alone in the livery office, Sophie began to realize that she'd hurt the best friend she had in Ribera. But she was also a practical businesswoman who knew that if she wanted to build the hotel she'd have to accept Barney's offer. Somehow, when the hotel was finished, she'd make it up to him.

When Fred Selwig delivered the contact to her, Sophie signed the documents with confidence. When the money was deposited in her account at the Mercantile Bank, the teller thanked her without any comment. At the same time, he wondered what the real deal was between Sophie Kaminski and Barney Pryor, but he didn't venture to ask any questions.

The construction of the hotel began as soon as work on the saloon was finished. Word soon filtered back to Barney that Sophie was pushing the project with ten to twelve hour workdays. When Barney and Sophie passed each other on the street, he stared straight ahead without uttering a single word. The carpenters groused about the sixty-hour workweek but continued to labor at breakneck speed. The boss lady was demanding but fair, paid top wages, and was present at the worksite every day working alongside the men from dawn until dusk. With her hair tucked under a wide brimmed hat, it was only a bright red bandanna that differentiated Sophie from the work crew.

Tim Royster's boarding house in Tent City was doing well. Tim reported to Barney that revenues were better than originally expected and profits double their plan. The partners were now thinking of an extension that would include a bathhouse and laundry.

In a visit to his business partner, Barney also paid a visit to Mrs. Colchester. "I hated to see Ho-Ching go back to the Whitman Hotel but Duk Cho and his brother have taken up the slack. I honestly think our boarders are happier with them and their sweet rolls they bake every morning. They think nothing of getting up at 3:30 every morning to start cooking; they're hard workers."

Barney wanted to avoid Sophie and spent little time in Ribera. He visited Tent City monthly, left the running of the stables to Juan, and mostly lived at the Ocotillo Mine. Ore production was steady at $400 per ton and the experienced workers kept costs under control. When work slowed at the 300-foot level, Barney decided to give the delay personal attention. He rode down in the man cage with Whitey Caulfield, one of the new men hired only recently. As they walked the tunnel, a loaded ore car unexpectedly came thundering down the tracks, striking both men. Drillers from the stope dashed to the scene to discover the severely injured men. The battered bodies were rushed to the surface while first aid was administered. Compresses were applied to the wounds to stop the bleeding, but it was clear that professional help was needed if the men were to survive. Barney and Whitey were bundled into a flat bed wagon and driven to Ribera and Doctor Ben Lawson.

Surprised at dinner, Lawson and his wife Kate surveyed the patients and decided that Caulfield, with two broken legs and a lacerated arm, would survive. Barney Pryor, still bleeding from a head wound, was the more serious challenge. Lawson feared internal injuries and decided to operate. The surgery lasted for over two hours as the doctor discovered broken ribs, a punctured lung, and torn tissues. After wiring the broken ribs and stitching the damaged lung with horsehair the doctor decided that with luck, Barney Pryor would survive. He was also thankful for the new equipment and operating room of the Doc Gilroy Hospital. Leaving the patient with Mrs. Wallace, a trained nurse, Ben and Kate cleaned up the operating room and finally turned in for a short night's rest. They were confident that barring infection, Barney would make it, but only after a lengthy convalescence.

The following morning, Sophie Kaminski, already exhausted from the summer heat, collapsed when she heard the news of the mine accident and Barney's injuries. Revived, she rushed to the hospital to find Barney still unconscious. Ben Lawson explained the situation. "Sophie, I think Barney will survive but he's banged up pretty bad. It's best if we give him a day or two before he sees any visitors. He needs rest. I'll let you know as soon as he wakes up and is able to see you."

For the first time in her life, Sophie Kaminski stumbled to a chair and sat down, praying for Barney's recovery. "Please God, let him live. He's all I've got in the world."

CHAPTER 38

Early Release

WEEDING, HOEING, AND WATERING VEGETABLES in the prison garden was hot, tedious, and boring work but it allowed Tom Lawson, prisoner #805, to be outside most of the day. With water taken from the Colorado River, the prison garden—almost five acres in size—provided the inmates with an ample supply of corn, beans, melons, and other staples. When he was inside the prison walls, Tom borrowed and read every book he could lay his hands on and practiced his Spanish. When Harry Cox, the former banker, was due to be released he gave Tom his complete library.

"Tom, you're as sharp a young man as I've ever met and you've been a good student. I'm giving you these books so you can continue your studies, especially the chapters on auditing a business. It's something that could be very useful to you when you leave this place. I expect I'll be going to Phoenix to find work. I have a sister there who has agreed to take me in. She recently married a man by the name of Randolph Dugan who does something in the grain business. When you leave this fancy palace, look me up. I'll do what I can to help you get settled. Good luck, son."

When Tom was ushered into the warden's office, he was surprised when warden Gates invited him to sit down. "Tom, you've become the kind of prisoner we always like to see. You've learned from your first serious mistake, have applied yourself educationally, and done well working in our vegetable farm. I don't want you to get overly optimistic but a Mr. Stan Cochrane, mayor of Flagstaff, has applied to the board of appeals for your early release. Is Cochrane a relative or friend of yours or your family?"

"Mr. Gates, I don't recognize the name. Maybe he's connected to my father in some way." Then remembering a letter he received from Dale Richmond announcing the birth of a son named Stanley, he offered that the mayor could be Dale's father-in-law. "Sir, I've never met the man but my friend married his daughter a year or so ago."

"Well, Tom, Mr. Cochrane apparently submitted some new testimony to the court that might help you. But that's not why I invited you up here." Tom was apprehensive as the warden clasped his hands together on his desk. "My wife and I live outside the prison compound with two boys aged eight and six. Our sons have gone to a local school and have had some home schooling that simply is not working for us. When Harry Cox was released from here a few weeks ago, he mentioned you as a possible tutor for the boys. He said you could be completely trusted. Believe it or not, I knew Harry when he was a banker in Silver City, New Mexico, before he moved to Tucson. How he ever got mixed up in bank fraud is beyond me, but that's neither here nor there. I'd like you to work with my boys two or three afternoons a week to improve their math skills and knowledge of history. They don't have a clue as to how this country got started or who George Washington and Thomas Jefferson are. I'll get you some books to teach with. The schooling will be held at our home and you'd be returned to your cellblock in the evening. What do you think, Tom?"

"Sir, I'd be honored to help your boys. It would also give me the opportunity to brush up on American history and mathematics. When do you want me to start?"

And so Tom Lawson became tutor to Everett and Matthew Gates. Three days a week, he was escorted to the warden's home where he worked with the boys on U.S. history and mathematics. The youngsters immediately liked Tom and were quick learners. In a short while, Tom was teaching them geography and helping them read newspapers from San Diego and Phoenix. Mr. and Mrs. Gates were thrilled with the progress of their sons' education. In the process, Tom was able to get a good picture of what was going on in both cities.

One afternoon, Everett and Matthew asked Tom if he would take them fishing on the Colorado River. Half serious, Tom replied, "If your mother agrees, I'll take you to the river." The boys scampered off from the covered patio to find their mother. A few minutes later, practically dragging Mrs. Gates to where Tom was sitting, they shouted, "Tom, Tom, Mom says it's okay."

"Tom, the boys are all fired up about fishing, but I'm having second thoughts. Neither of them swims well, and the river current can be dangerous at times. I can't say no to them but please be careful." Tom wasn't sure how to respond but before he could say anything, Everett piped up, "Don't worry, Mom, we'll be careful." He then grabbed his brother and ran off to gather fishing poles they'd made the day before in their father's workshop, along with hooks, lines, and bobbers.

The boys led Tom down a path about a hundred yards to the river. The two placed their equipment on a sandbar, anxious to test the water now moving at a moderate pace. "Hold on, boys. I want to try something," Tom called out. "Everett, strip to your underwear. I want to see how well you can swim." Wanting to get on with fishing, the older boy took off his clothes and stepped into the river. Soon, the water was up to his knees, then his waist. He then began to swim away from the sandbar. "Just go out about ten yards, then swim up river, and then come back," Tom ordered. Following Tom's instructions, Everett paddled out a few yards, then swam up river, turned, and floated back to the sandbar. "Okay, Matt, now you give it a try the same way as your brother did." Matt paddled out easily but had trouble bucking the current and had to return to land. "It looks like we have some work to do, Matt. You've got to learn how to swim if you're going to fish on this river. Now, put a worm on your hooks, cast your line up river, and let it drift down with the current. When you see the bobber drop quickly, you've got a strike. Let it be for a few seconds, then pull the pole up to set the hook. You'll get the hang of it. Now let's give it a try."

On his third cast, Everett hooked a fourteen-inch trout and pulled it to the sandbar. Tom showed him how to remove the barbless hook and tossed the fish back into the river. "Keep fishing, Everett. We want something bigger for your dinner." At first, Matthew wasn't as lucky but it wasn't long before he cast the line out about twenty feet. This time, he didn't lose the worm and the bobber settled easily on the water's surface. In an instant, the bobber was pulled beneath the surface and the bamboo rod bent into an inverted "U" shape. The fish ran down river and quickly turned to swim upstream to find deeper water. With only twenty-five feet of line, the fish pulled Matt into the water as the line became taut.

"Let him go, Matt," Tom shouted, but Matt's hands were clamped to the pole as if welded to a steel pipe. Suddenly offshore over his head, the boy's head bobbed up and down as he held on to the pole. Seeing the emergency, Tom dove into the water, swam to Matt, grabbed him from behind and returned to the shore. The fish, still secured to the end of the line, flopped on the beach trying to escape to the freedom of the river. As he peeled off his wet clothing, Tom exclaimed, "I think you've got a keeper, Matt. Now let's get back to the house and some dry clothes before we get into any more trouble." Much as Tom would have liked the afternoon's expedition kept a secret, the boys couldn't help but give their parents a detailed description of how Matt and Tom horsed in a twenty-five inch whopper of a fish. That evening, prisoner #805 joined the Gates family for a fish dinner complete with garden potatoes and yellow and green squash, followed by a dessert of deep-dish apple pie.

Over the next several weeks, Matt became a strong swimmer and both boys became ardent fishermen. When word arrived of Tom Lawson's early release based on new evidence, Everett and Matthew Gates were crushed. They had learned to love Tom as a teacher, fishing guide, swim coach, and all around friend. The Gates household would never be the same even though Tom promised to stay in touch with the boys.

With ten dollars in his pocket, a new pair of jeans, a shirt, and new boots, Tom Lawson said his goodbyes and boarded the train for Tucson. With a well-worn carpetbag filled with all his books, the new civilian, now a much wiser person, was ready to face a world he'd left just four years ago.

CHAPTER 39

Copper Mining

WHILE COPPER IS ABUNDANT IN the earth's crust, there are relatively few concentrations of the element above 0.5 percent, what most mining geologists feel is the minimum to be commercially exploited. Copper ores can be divided into the sulfide variety such as chalcopyrite, or as oxides, the most important of which are chrysocolla and cuprite.

Ores originate from underground magmas and are deposited in cracks and fissures of the host rock. Where mineralized, rocks are at the earth's surface; sulfide minerals may be oxidized by air, groundwater, and heat. In many ores, such as what we see in the western United States and Mexico, the minerals are dispersed like raisins in a loaf of bread. These ores are called porphyry copper deposits and sometimes contain economic amounts of gold, silver, and molybdenum.

In the early 1900s, porphyry copper mine operations commonly utilized massive steam shovels to dig thousands of tons of ore per day. After crushing, the ore was placed in a box-like container where the copper was separated from waste material by floatation. The concentrated material was then fed into a smelting furnace to produce blister copper. The blister copper was then refined further to produce 99.9 percent pure copper.

The history and growth of copper production is the story of American industrialization, the development of a rail infrastructure in the West, and the fulfilled ambitions of a small group of businessmen who took major risks to eventually become wealthy copper barons. As this story unfolds, mining towns like Bisbee, Clifton-Morenci, Jerome, Miami, and Ray sprang up like wildflowers after a heavy rain.

Michael Faraday discovered electromagnetism in 1831, and Sir Joseph Swan invented the electric lamp in 1860. These two developments stimulated a tremendous demand for electric generators, power cables, and motors for the electrical engineering industry. Companies like General Electric and Westinghouse led the way in devising methods to distribute electric power. The World's Columbian Exposition in Chicago in 1893 with its 265-foot Ferris wheel, the fair's signature emblem, personified this march of progress. Between 1890 and 1905, the output of electric power in the United States increased a hundred fold.

Many copper discoveries remained isolated and uneconomic until they could be reached by railroad. As transcontinental tracks cut across northern and southern Arizona, mine development became a reality as feeder lines reached Bisbee, Jerome, and others. This development of low cost transportation played a major role in the birth of the Arizona copper industry.

The third element in the founding of Arizona's copper industry was the commitment of several individuals who led the way in technological change and had the foresight to recognize that copper was key to industrial development. Daniel Cowan Jackling was the father of open cut mining and proved that low-grade ores could be produced economically. Jackling began his work at Bingham Canyon, Utah, by organizing the Utah Copper Company in 1903. Jackling pioneered surface mining using massive equipment and engineered new crushing and metallurgical processes. His contribution to copper mining and metallurgy earned him the title of "father of porphyry copper mining."

The Guggenheim brothers and James Douglas also rank among the industry founders as they invested in and built the Arizona copper industry in the form of American Smelting and Refining, Kennecott Copper, and the Phelps Dodge Corporation. Under different names and ownership, many of these operations continue today.

CHAPTER 40

The Project Turns Sour

BERN HEINZELMAN'S COMMENTS ABOUT MANAGING a project like the Copper Hill Mining Company continued to ring in Konrad Bruner's ears. His search for a junior geologist had come up empty, so he decided to train Andy Corsica in sampling techniques and accurate recording of field data. Andy had already supervised the building of Camp 2 down the mountain a mile or so from headquarters. The difference in elevation of 800 feet made for a difficult descent and an even more precarious return up the hillside. In time, Camp 2 became fully operational and housed Andy, Ron Calder, and six laborers.

Konrad had decided to dig a declining tunnel through a zone of oxidized ore that was exposed on the surface. He hoped it would give him more information on the depth of the ore body before he committed to a vertical shaft that would dissect the deposit. He was confronted with the problem of working with inexperienced miners who required close supervision. One Mexican miner, Orlando, was handy with drilling and explosives, but the others were only capable of removing the ore at this stage. Language problems also complicated matters. As the declining tunnel was under construction, high-grade ore was stacked near Camp 2. As yet, Konrad did not have a plan for getting the stockpile to the smelter, over nine miles away. While close by, the streambed had almost vertical walls that precluded the utilization of conventional freight wagons. Bruner worried that the ore stockpile couldn't be converted to much needed cash to meet his payroll and buy rapidly dwindling supplies.

The man hired by Konrad said he was an engineer but had not been able to convince the owner that he had solid field experience. Ron Calder had worked in the underground Missouri lead/zinc mines but so far had not come up with an idea to get ore from Camp 2 to the checkpoint. He'd mentioned the possibility of an aerial tramway but Bruner had offered little encouragement for the concept. Meanwhile, mule pack was the only way they could traverse the narrow, twisting canyon streambed.

As the German crisscrossed the property, the problems of manpower, cash reserves, and the prospect of finding an investor kept his attention. Everything seemed to take longer and cost more money than anticipated. Where was the project going? Was it in jeopardy? Samples given to Norm Dickson continued to show excellent copper content but now even he was pressing to get paid.

Without Konrad's knowledge, heavy rain had been falling for several days north of Globe, raising the level of streams that fed into Pinal Creek. One evening, after Corsica, Calder, and the miners had turned in for the night, Camp 2 was inundated by a wall of water about fifteen feet above the normal streambed. The rampaging water, sand, silt, and debris slammed into the camp without warning and washed men, equipment, and mules several miles downstream. Aside from the roar of rushing water, the catastrophe went unnoticed in the company's main camp.

The next morning, B.J. Kimball and Konrad inspected the camp and discovered not a living soul or any sign that anyone had survived. It was impossible to walk the streambed as it was still filled with mud and debris over four feet deep. They backtracked over the hillside to the checkpoint only to find more mud, a boot, a frying pan, bits of clothing, and scattered pieces of ore. Walking carefully downstream, they discovered the partially buried body of Ron Calder but no others. Konrad and B.J. stared at the scene in numb disbelief.

"I guess we should have built Camp 2 further up the hill," muttered B.J. "I should have known better; I've seen flash floods before but nothing like this. I guess we've got water in the tunnel, but the real loss is Andy and Ron. I don't know where we're gonna' get replacements for them, particularly Andy."

The flash flood did extensive damage along the streambed into Globe and beyond. Several buildings in town were swept away when the rushing water eroded their foundations.

Konrad went into town to replace equipment and mules and take a break from the devastation. The townspeople were sympathetic but could do little to help. Most were concerned with their own losses and the challenge of rebuilding. When he met Bern Heinzelman in the hotel dining room, the Austrian told Konrad he was sorry for his misfortune but there was nothing the Goldsmith brothers could do to help. They had similar problems themselves.

His stay in Globe did not go well. He was only able to buy three mules at double the regular price when he wanted to purchase six. Prices for food had also skyrocketed but he bit his lip and paid the price. Bruner had plenty of time to feel sorry for himself as he led his mule train back to base camp. The trip was difficult, as he had to maneuver on ground that was well above the still-impassable streambed. For the first time, Konrad considered walking away from Copper Hill and going back to Ribera. There, he could be a big fish in a small pond.

While Konrad was in town replenishing supplies, B.J. Kimball had hiked the terrain above the streambed, keeping clear of the muck and silt that was as deadly as quick sand. Not finding anything, he said to himself, "I wouldn't be surprised if those bodies ended up five miles downstream from here. Most likely, we'll never be able to recover those poor fellas."

The decline tunnel was in surprisingly good shape with only three feet of water in the face of the digging. On his return to the cabin, B.J. met Konrad, who gave him news of more financial problems in the form of greedy merchants raising prices in a time of crisis. "Konrad, don't get yourself down. Somehow, we'll make it. Things will get better, you'll see."

Konrad was not so optimistic. "B.J., our worst loss was Andy and Orlando. Calder may have done some good down the road but the aerial tramway didn't make sense to me. Anyway, Camp 2 is gone, the miners are most likely dead, and there's no help I can see in Globe. I'm going to have to go to Phoenix and see if I can rustle up some people there, and I don't know when I'll be back. It could be several weeks before I can find some mining talent. Take good care of the mules, partner; they're about all we got left."

It took Konrad almost a week of hard riding to reach Phoenix. It looked like the heavy rain had hit parts of central Arizona hard. Arriving in Phoenix, Konrad sought out lawyer Henry Dempsey who he knew through Don Richmond. "Mr. Dempsey, I'm a Ribera friend of Don Richmond. We worked together on the water board problems a few years ago. I have a mine property east of here that I'm trying to develop. A flash flood has wiped out my labor force and equipment, and to put it plainly, I desperately need a good, all-around exploration man and an experienced miner who can handle drilling and explosives. Anyone able and willing to muck ore out of a tunnel will fill the bill for the other three people I want. Can you help me, or do you know someone who can?"

"Mr. Bruner, I don't know that much about mining, at least at the present time. However, any friend of Don Richmond is surely welcome here. Let me check around town and see who I can come up with. By the way, Don is in town right now; maybe he knows someone who can help you."

When Konrad called on the lawyer a few days later, he was given two names; one recommended by Don Richmond. The first one never showed up for the interview; the second candidate was an ex-convict who had no mining experience but knew accounting and finance and spoke and wrote Spanish fluently. Tom Lawson admitted his prison time and promised to learn mining as fast as he could, just as he'd learned Spanish and finance in Yuma.

"Mr. Bruner, I can learn mining with your help and work as hard as anybody. I need a new start, and I promise you'll never regret it." Konrad was impressed by the young man's candor, family background, and enterprising spirit. His directness, enthusiasm, and personal fire got Tom Lawson the opportunity he wanted and needed.

CHAPTER 41

Cardenas Confesses

A BITTER COLD, SNOWY WINTER kept Carlos Rodriguez Bruner inside his dormitory or cloistered in a small rented office two blocks from Columbia University. He'd leased the office on his return from Mexico to keep in contact with Lumberto at the hacienda. Installing a private telegraph connection, he hired Frieda Glockner to file reports, take dictation, and handle messages that began to flow to him as owner of his grandfather's estate. His studies were winding down and in two months he would be graduating, leaving New York City, and returning to Zacatecas.

Carlos and his father had gotten into a routine of exchanging monthly letters. He enjoyed Konrad's mail describing the Copper Hill mine development but was disturbed when he learned of the devastating flood and the serious financial setback. He wanted to help his father but couldn't decide how to provide assistance. As a result, he procrastinated and did nothing, hoping his father would overcome his problems on his own.

Mail from Rachel in Ann Arbor wasn't as regular and left Carlos feeling frustrated. In her last note, Rachel told him she would be graduating from medical school soon and planned to spend all her free time in a local clinic as an emergency physician. She described in detail how some broken and bleeding patients would refuse treatment until a male doctor could come to their aid. But she felt she was making gradual progress in overcoming the prejudices toward female physicians. Her greatest success had been with very young patients who cared nothing about her gender. Her training at Michigan had been excellent and there were good opportunities for further research at Johns Hopkins in Baltimore and a Boston hospital. She was also mulling over the idea of returning to Arizona for a year to work with her father. Was this a hint at some kind of reconciliation with Carlos? It seemed Rachel was avoiding any comment on their relationship, especially the tension of their last meeting. He was particularly annoyed with Rachel's signature, "with love," as if she was corresponding with her brother. Was she being stubborn, or was she comfortable with the idea that they would never be together again? But Carlos's letters to Rachel were equally non-committal. He wrote about university life, the weather, and his dealings with his estate. Never once did he write to tell her how he really felt about her. Carlos didn't know where he stood with Rachel and he wasn't going to ask her.

Rachel had learned of Carlos's plans in one of his typical, fact-filled letters. On graduation, he was going to close the office—managed by "the German girl"—and return to Mexico. Frieda Glockner had proven to be a very capable secretary who handled communications between Carlos and Lumberto efficiently and effectively. Rachel had her suspicions about the relationship but kept her thoughts to herself. While she didn't know it, Rachel's intuition was right. On many a cold, dark afternoon, Carlos would brave the elements to go to his office to check his mail and ended up making love to his willing secretary.

Even if Carlos was having an affair with his secretary, Rachel recognized that they were no longer engaged and that she was free to form new relationships. She'd considered some of the advances from the male doctors but couldn't break away from her love for Carlos. At times, the double standard of male and female relationships brought her to tears.

After careful study of her options, Rachel decided to postpone taking a permanent position and chose instead to spend some time in Arizona working with her father. After writing personal letters to Baltimore and Boston, the freshly minted doctor left Michigan for the lengthy train ride to Bowie, Arizona, where her parents, Kate and Ben Lawson, met her. On the way to Ribera, Kate and Rachel never stopped talking while Ben kept his eyes on the horses and trail. Rachel was surprised to see the new Doctor Gilroy Hospital and the Lawson's new home. In the three years since she left Ribera, the town had taken on a new persona.

Tom's imprisonment bothered her, but she was happy to hear about his early release and employment with Konrad Bruner's Copper Hill Mining Company. She knew that Tom was very smart and hoped someday he would complete college. She also heard good things about Bruner and thought he would be a good influence on her brother. Rachel adjusted easily to her childhood environment and enjoyed meeting with Sophie Kaminski for lunch at her new hotel. The two soon became close friends as the hotel owner unburdened her worries about Barney Pryor and how she had hurt him. In turn, Rachel lamented her break up with Carlos and the futility of a lost love.

There was little talk of her leaving Ribera as she pitched in to help in her father's practice. Rachel mainly treated children who came to her father's office with broken bones or childhood diseases. Ben Lawson also learned new approaches to pediatric surgery from his daughter. It was obvious that Rachel liked what she was doing and was very good at it. Ben Lawson was proud of his daughter's accomplishments and what medical school had taught her.

The relationship with Carlos continued to disturb her. Over lunch one day, Rachel broke her silence. "Mom, we had something wonderful together and suddenly it simply unraveled. I have much to be thankful for here with you and Dad but I miss him terribly, and I don't know what to do about it. It's been almost a year and now we're not even writing." Tears flowed down Rachel's cheeks as she went on, "I believe he loves me but he won't make a move to apologize for our break up. I'm not going to go chasing him in Mexico either. In the meantime, I've got to decide on whether to stay here or go back East for advanced medical training."

Now it was time for Kate Lawson to deliver some advice to her daughter. "Rachel, you're young and talented and have much to look forward to. You don't have to rush into anything. Give Carlos some time. If you really love each other, he'll eventually come around. Keep in mind that his upbringing has been mostly in Mexico. He also has huge obligations to the estate left him by his grandfather. Many people depend on him now for their livelihoods; we have nothing like that in the States. Try to be patient with him."

At the end of their conversation, Rachel decided to stay in Ribera for another six months. She also determined that if nothing happened with Carlos during that period, she would move on without him.

Back home in Mexico, Carlos was rediscovering the pleasures of ranch life. While he thought about Rachel constantly, he was also deeply involved in learning about his new role as owner of a vast estate. The condition of the hacienda pleased him and he enjoyed the companionship of Lumberto Villegas immensely. The two men regularly toured the villages and hinterlands and were greeted warmly wherever they went. Carlos's contentment was spoiled however, when Lumberto brought up the subject of the silver mine operations. The audit, only recently completed, revealed the theft of millions of pesos stolen over the past several years. It appeared that Carlos Ortega, the general manager, and Ernesto Cardenas, the comptroller, headed up a small group that was falsifying scale tickets and removing ingots of silver somewhere between Zacatecas and Tampico. No authorities had been advised of the theft; Lumberto wanted to wait until Carlos was back home before taking action. While wary of the audit, Ortega and Cardenas showed little concern that their activities had been exposed. Carlos decided to personally interview each man separately, starting with the financial man. He carefully studied the documents, listened to the comptroller's answers, and decided to challenge him directly.

"Ernesto, as you know, we have concluded a detailed external audit over the past six months. I have reviewed the findings and concluded that you have been a participant in the theft of over one million pesos of company money. What do you have to say for yourself and your co-conspirators?"

Shocked, Ernesto answered, "There must be some mistake, Carlos. I've been a loyal servant of the company for over five years and I have never taken a peso from your grandfather." Carlos looked directly at Cardenas and shot back, "Listen carefully to what I have to say; I will not repeat myself. The auditing firm we hired is one of the most capable accounting firms in all of Mexico. We have evidence that will probably send you to jail for thirty years. Or you may cooperate, name your accomplices, make restitution, and move on to another profession, after you have been stripped of your accounting certification, of course. Consider yourself under house arrest. You will be placed under guard and confined to a room in this house until noon tomorrow. By that time if you do not confess and name your associates, I will turn you over to the local police who will detain you, pending formal trial, in "la cucaracha palacio," as the inmates call the place. Rest assured that you will receive no special consideration as you will have lost any protection from me, the patron."

After a sleepless night the accountant realized that he'd made a huge mistake and conceded to Carlos's demands. Begging the patron for mercy, he swore that all the silver had already been sold but agreed to partial restitution by surrendering his substantial bank account. He also signed a confession naming Carlos Ortega as the ringleader and resigned his certificate of accountancy. The confession was sealed and retained by Carlos as collateral just in case the thief broke any rules of the agreement.

Alerted by Carlos, the police captured Ortega as he was attempting to leave town with his mistress. Both culprits were in jail when Carlos arrived to interrogate Ortega. The patron was shocked when he entered the filthy cell, crawling with roaches, spiders, and rats. The written report of the auditors and the confession of the comptroller convinced Ortega he had little to defend himself with. He had squandered the stolen money on a mountain home and a Tampico bank account for his mistress. This time Carlos showed no mercy. Stubbornly defending himself without counsel, Carlos Ortega was convicted by jury and sentenced to thirty years in prison. After sentencing, his family was allowed to retain the company-owned house, and his wife received a modest monthly stipend until all the Ortega children reached the age of twenty-one.

The experience taught the young patron a lesson he would never forget: trust but verify. New financial controls were installed and an administrative assistant was hired to improve internal auditing procedures. With these changes, Lumberto announced his retirement and decision to work on his new ranch and lands. Feeling more secure with the management of his holdings, Carlos turned his attention to his father and reconnecting with Rachel Lawson.

CHAPTER 42

Kate Lawson Visits Tennessee

A TELEGRAM FROM HER BROTHER in Tennessee hit Kate Lawson like hail raining down on a field of wheat ready for harvest. Alarmed at first, Kate read the message from Joe Hurley a second time, and realized it wasn't news of an emergency. Joe and Kate's parents were getting on in years and wanted to see Kate and her family but couldn't muster the strength to journey over 1,700 miles. Knowing that Rachel and Tom Lawson were away from home, Joe suggested that perhaps Kate and her two youngest children could visit the family farm. Ben Lawson wasn't thrilled with the idea but gradually came around to the thought of being a bachelor for a couple of months. Hell, they didn't invite me anyway, he thought to himself.

Sam and Carol Lawson were excited about the trip and the prospect of train travel. When all the goodbyes were said, Kate and the two children boarded a train in Bowie, Arizona, that took them to El Paso, New Orleans, and finally to a stop near a landing on the Tennessee River. As they stepped down from the train, Kate exclaimed, "We're getting close, kids. We'll be able to take a flatboat down river to Peters Landing just like I did many years ago. That's where Uncle Joe will meet us and take us to the farm just outside Waynesboro."

Disembarking at Peters Landing, the Lawsons were excited to see Joe Hurley waiting with a large buggy and four beautiful horses. Kate warmly embraced her brother and introduced Sam and Carol. While Kate and Joe talked about the farm and their folks, Sam and Carol looked over the green, unfamiliar landscape. It was something they'd never seen before.

When Joe returned home from the Civil War he wasn't sure he wanted to be a farmer and stay in Wayne County. Still recuperating from wounds suffered at Shiloh, he'd met Corliss McBride, a local girl who'd been raised on a farm similar to the Hurley spread. They courted for six months and decided to get married when Dave Hurley deeded the farm to his son. Meeting Corliss and inheriting the farm convinced Joe that he had a future in Wayne County. Joe and his wife had two children, Bryan, a student of civil engineering at the University of Tennessee and Edith, who remained at home to help her parents and grandparents run the farm.

Kate and her mother wept when they were reunited; Dave Hurley hugged his daughter with a "welcome home, Kate; it's been too long." When the greetings and introductions were completed, the families retired to the parlor to share tea, cookies, and news. In time, trunks and suitcases were unloaded from the carriage and a hasty meal was prepared. Exhausted from their long trip, Kate and the children retired early for the night.

During the following weeks, Joe and his sister exchanged stories covering the past thirty odd years, from their schooling to Joe leaving for the Confederacy and their respective lives since then. Kate soon realized that she and her brother had spent their adult lives in two totally different environments. Arizona's territorial growth was a story of frontier justice, mining and cattle ranching, and the subjugation of the American Indian. Joe had spent his youth in a terrible war but had been lucky enough to return to a prosperous farm and marry a fine woman. Kate didn't regret leaving Tennessee as a young girl, but she also appreciated that Joe could be with their parents as they aged. Joe and Dave Hurley had been able to enlarge the farm to over 3,000 acres of land that included a sawmill and dairy operation. Their vegetable farm supplied produce to hotels and restaurants as far away as Memphis.

Joe Hurley took his sister into his confidence when explaining his plans for the future. "This place is bigger than I can handle on my own, Kate. Bryan seems to think he wants a career in architecture or civil engineering. That means moving to a city, which is understandable since he's never shown an interest in farming or animals. Edith likes the farm but I expect she'll marry a local man, stay here, or farm elsewhere with her husband. She's already got her eye on the Basford kid down the road. He doesn't know it yet, but will in due time. Dad's almost out of the day-to-day operation of the farm, so there's a good opportunity here, especially for a family member. Have your Sam take a look at the

University of Tennessee while he's here. They have a very good aggie school."

The University of Tennessee had a history dating back to 1794. Severely damaged during the Civil War, it was rebuilt after the war ended as a land grant agricultural and mechanical institution.

Bryan Hurley proved to be an enthusiastic tour guide and told Kate, Sam, and Carol about the school and extolled Knoxville as a great place to live. When it came to think about returning to Arizona, Sam Lawson decided to join his cousin at the university and study agriculture. Kate loved her youngest son dearly but knowing that he'd be close to her family eased her mind about his decision. It also brought back memories of her decision to leave her home and family many years ago. Carol had enjoyed her visit with the Hurley family but was ready to return with her mother to Arizona. The Bowie River, ranch life, and frontier living was too important a part of her life to leave behind. But the trip to Tennessee also helped her come to a decision about her future. Carol intended to become a teacher and enroll at the University of Arizona in Tucson.

En route from New Orleans, Carol shared some of her thoughts about the trip East with her mother. "It was a great visit, Mom, but I'll be happy to get home. I asked Edith how much different life has been since slavery was outlawed. She told me not much since the fighting didn't reach their area and their slaves were always treated pretty well. Jonah and Ezekial stayed on the Hurley farm after the war even though they were free to leave if they wanted to. It was probably too much of a challenge for them to start life over again, but Edith thinks their children will eventually move on. According to Edith, it'll take quite some time before the South digests its defeat in the war. I honestly don't know how the blacks will fare in the future; they've been slaves for many generations."

Kate looked at her daughter thoughtfully. "I think I agree with Edith. Jonah and Ezekial were never treated harshly, and your uncle Joe and I grew up with their children. But Daddy never accepted the Emancipation Proclamation; in his mind, his slaves were still slaves. It's a complicated story, Carol, and is one of the reasons why I decided to leave Tennessee."

"I'm bothered about something else, Mom," Carol responded. "Blacks in the South are legally free, and some are moving to other regions of the country and becoming property owners. Others are attending universities and starting their own businesses. Why then are we having so much trouble with the Indians? They were here before any of us. Why can't we treat them with respect? Why do we have them crowded onto reservations that are awful places of disease and famine? It's just terrible what's going on at the San Carlos Reservation."

"Carol, it all started when political leaders in Washington decided to push westward to California and the Pacific Ocean. They practically ignored New Mexico and Arizona until gold, silver, and copper were discovered. The Indians were pushed aside, killed, or captured and sent to reservations. Feeble attempts were made to negotiate fairly with the Indian tribes, but agreements were broken and the white man moved in to confiscate the best land, minerals, and water. A few tribal leaders recognized that the white man was destroying them and fought hard for survival. When the Civil War ended, the government was able to shift troops to Arizona and reestablish forts and continue the war of attrition. When Geronimo surrendered in 1888, it marked the final submission of the Apaches. The crowding of different tribes on to the San Carlos Reservation, with marginal land and limited water, has been unfair and illegal. Thousands of Indians have died on the reservation, the victims of disease and malnutrition. In my opinion, we've treated the Indians worse than slaves and created a whole nation of people who are now wards of the government. Washington must now provide them with food, clothing, education, and medical aid. It's not a good plan for the tribes and has already become expensive and a source of corruption. And no one knows how long this will go on. Your father and I have talked about the medical needs of the Indians many times. But the loss of Doc Gilroy has left us undermanned in Ribera. Also, many people resent giving any help to the Indians."

CHAPTER 43

Vince Booker and Barbara Casey Marry

THE REVEREND CLIVE TOWNSEND'S VOICE boomed over the congregation as he presided at the wedding of Barbara Casey and Vincent Booker, United States Army, retired. The bride was dressed in a pale blue, ankle length silk gown with a garland of spring wildflowers in her hair. The groom wore dark trousers and jacket, a starched white shirt with a black string tie, and polished, knee high boots. Kate and Dr. Ben Lawson stood up for the couple as they were joined in holy matrimony on a bright, sunny day. The church was packed with townspeople as Mrs. Emily Conroy sang some favorite hymns suggested by the couple. What started out as a simple, small ceremony turned into a town-wide celebration that ended at the Whitman Hotel. While Barney Pryor and Sophie Kaminski were both in attendance, they barely glanced at each other as dancers twirled to the music in the dining room.

After an hour of drinking and toasting, the newlyweds slipped out a side door where a driver was waiting to return them to the Volunteer Ranch. The couple had decided weeks ago to forego any lengthy honeymoon trip.

It was early evening when Barbara and Booker climbed the staircase to the privacy of their bedroom. Sam and Betty Ortiz had placed two small pieces of wedding cake on a table in the room, along with two glasses and a bucket of iced California champagne. The couple toasted each other with words of love as Vince examined the room in confused anticipation. Now, what am I supposed to do? he thought to himself.

Barbara confidently came to his rescue. She helped her husband out of his jacket and embraced him, and suggested he help her remove her clothing. As they undressed, their excitement increased as hands caressed and lips met in the fading light. Much later, lying quietly in each other's arms, they thanked each other for a wonderful wedding day.

Gradually, the Bookers worked out a routine for their life together that began at 5:30 a.m., followed by breakfast at 6:30. By 7:00, Barbara would leave for the general store that she opened an hour later. The store had expanded to four full-time employees; three took care of customers in the front while Enrique ran the warehouse and stockroom. At the ranch, Vince met with the general foreman each morning and spent most of the day riding the range, checking out fence lines, the herd of horses, and their biggest asset, the cattle.

While life was good for the couple, they were confronted with two problems. The general store put great demands on Barbara's time. She had to buy the merchandise and be present to service large, important customers. Her relationship with her vendors was just as important as they were in California, Mexico, and St. Louis, and provided her business with a major competitive edge. But she had long ago decided that she preferred ranch life, and her marriage to Vince only increased that desire. She thought about Batchelder, Moroni, and Gable and decided to see if the agreement that fell apart six years ago might be reopened. She felt Peter Hillenbrand had scuttled the deal but was never able to confirm this.

One evening, over dinner with her husband she presented the idea of selling the store. "Vince, I want to talk to you about selling the general store. I thought I'd contact the BM&G people in New York City and also ask Barney Pryor if he is interested. Sophie Kaminski and Kate Lawson also come to mind, but both are tied down with full-time commitments. Scoville is another possibility although he doesn't really fit the mold of a retail investor. And besides, I don't think the locals would favor the idea."

"Barbara, you know I have very limited business experience, and selling dry goods to the public is close to the last thing in the world I'd like to do. You've built the business and it's your decision to keep or sell it. I will say this: getting more than one prospect is a good idea, and maybe finding a new manager to run the place could make sense. Whatever you decide is fine with me; I must admit, having you here at the ranch all the time would be great."

And so, Barbara Booker sent a telegraph message to BM&G in New York City asking them if they would be interested in buying the Ribera General Store. Within a week, she received a response, "Pleased to hear from you. We are definitely interested in buying your store. Mr. Norman Stenton will contact you to schedule a meeting in Arizona within the month. Yours truly, Sam Batchelder, senior partner, BM&G."

She also visited Barney Pryor who was still recuperating from his injuries. "Let me apologize for not seeing you earlier, Barney. I'll get to the point: I'm putting my store up for sale and I've had some interest from a New York trading company who will be sending a man out here this month to look into establishing a business in the Territory. We've been through this before, but I think they might be serious this time. I prefer selling to a local but my choices are limited. I don't see Scoville in the picture, Sophie has the smarts but probably has her hands full with the hotel and saloon, and Bruner is a mining man with a set of problems of his own. That leaves you, my friend. I don't need an answer right now. Give it some thought and we can talk next week sometime."

The Bookers other problem was more difficult. Soleado had been living with Barbara for about a year and seemed to be adjusting to her new surroundings. But in the last few months her schoolwork had fallen off, and she seemed listless and uninterested in anything or anyone. At first, she was happy when Barbara and Vince married, but it wasn't long before she went back to being withdrawn, impassive, and bored.

Vince was concerned enough that he decided to meet with Soleado's teacher, Miss Collins. Anne Collins was an attractive young woman who had been educated in North Carolina before arriving in Ribera two years ago. She was liked by the townspeople and worked very hard with the children. She was not surprised when Booker called on her after the day session was over.

"Miss Collins, I was in charge of the attack on the Apache Indian camp when Soleado was discovered," Vince began. "I was also on the scene when we investigated the massacre of her parents and brother after she was kidnapped. She lived with an older Indian woman who might have been closely related to Aguijador, the Apache chieftain. Apaches have raised her for at least four or five years. I'm not sure how this relates to her present situation, except that she could be confused over her identity. She might be wondering if she's Indian or white."

" Since my marriage to Barbara Casey, Soleado has reverted to the behavior from her previous life, when I found her with the old Indian woman. She doesn't smile, shows no interest in her studies, and has to be told what to do repeatedly. I thought perhaps you could tell us what kind of student she is now, how well she gets along with her classmates, and if you have seen any changes in her manner in the past few months."

"I'm glad you decided to visit, Mr. Booker. I share your concern," Miss Collins replied. "Yes, there has been a change in her deportment, and she's fallen off in math and history. I'm not sure why, but let me go back a bit. When Soleado first arrived at school, she was not familiar with the habits of most school children, and her classmates weren't very kind to her. They pinched her, pulled her hair, and called her names. She rarely fought back and did her best to avoid trouble. But it also became apparent that she was very bright and the kids were jealous of her intelligence. I've tried to give her additional, more challenging lessons but she had not responded well. I believe she's one of the most intelligent students I've ever taught, and with her potential she is capable of becoming anything she wants to be: a doctor, lawyer, teacher. I suggest we be patient and see how her new assignments work out. She's endured a lot at a very young age."

Vince Booker thought a lot about Soleado on the ride back to the ranch. He shared his conversation with Miss Collins with his wife but was a little disappointed that they had not come up with answers. On a hunch, the retired trooper decided to visit the San Carlos Reservation and look up Two Willows, an elderly Navajo Booker had known for many years as an enlisted man. When he located the elder Indian, Two Willows greeted Booker warmly. "Sergeant Booker, It's good to see you. It's been a long time. I have nothing to offer you except the shade of my wikiup. I try to keep away from the main body of prisoners; there's too much disease and crime here."

After exchanging pleasantries, Booker told Two Willows the full story of Soleado and her adoption by Barbara Casey. "I guess my concern is that she probably doesn't know whether she's Apache or white." The Indian grunted, puffed on his pipe, and volunteered, "Her life as an Apache is still with her. She may miss the old woman. It's best that you and your wife encourage her to keep her Apache training while also adopting your ways."

The two men reminisced about their past association and the terrible situation at San Carlos. "I have decided to leave the reservation soon and return to sheepherding up north," Two Willows confided. "I need fresh air, open space, and the freedom of the desert. I will not let them stop me. I must see the red rocks of Navajo land again or die try-ing. It's that simple, my friend."

Vince Booker was appalled at the conditions he'd seen trying to locate Two Willows. Overcrowding, poor sanitation, and the broken spirit of the once proud Indians made him sick to his stomach. No one should have to live that way, he thought to himself as he turned his horse to Ribera.

After a long conversation with his wife, the Bookers decided to remove Soleado from the public school. With the help of Miss Collins, Barbara and Vince hired two women in town to tutor their daughter in English, French, history, math, and geography. Soleado responded well to the change, and her young teachers, newly arrived from their col-leges in the East, were delighted to be teaching such a bright girl. Gradually, Soleado's social skills improved and she began to emerge from her solitude.

Heeding the advice of Two Willows, Booker had Soleado choose one of the ranch's prized horses for her very own and allowed her to train and ride the animal Apache style. He also encouraged her to work in the kitchen with Betty Ortiz and share her knowledge of the Apache way of preparing and cooking small game. Finally, Vince and Barbara spent more time with Soleado to show her their love as parents and members of white society. They also listened attentively as Soleado related stories to them of her life among the Apaches.

Barney Pryor was itching to get down to business on buying the Ribera General Store. He did his homework counting customers, aver-aging out each purchase amount, and learning about fabrics, kitchen-ware, clothing, canned and dried food, and a myriad of specialty items. When he heard that Norman Stenton was in town to meet with Bar-bara, he knew that before long he'd know if he was going to be a store owner or not. He relished the thought of expanding his business inter-ests and the idea of growing with the town.

CHAPTER 44

The Richmonds Visit Flagstaff

"DOLORES, THIS IS AS GOOD a time as any to visit the north country. The ranch is doing just fine and we could be back in a month or so, sooner, if necessary. With summer coming on, you'll be able to appreciate the difference in climate in this great state of ours. Well, we'll be a state some day. It's funny, but Washington politicians picture us as a pile of sand and terrible heat yet few have ever been west of the Mississippi. The house in Phoenix is in decent condition, so I'm not taking no for an answer."

Dolores Richmond put her sewing aside and looked at her husband. "As long as you agree that we can see Dale, Abbie, and baby Stan in Flagstaff, I'll be happy to join you. Give me a day or two to get ready; I'll need some new clothes and I want to buy some gifts for Abbie and our grandson."

Don Richmond was one of the few Arizonans who had visited most of the major towns in the Territory. He knew the differences in climate, physiography, and vegetation. Nogales in the south was at 4,000 feet, the Phoenix basin was 1,500 feet above sea level, and Flagstaff reached 7,200 feet in elevation, creating vast differences in rainfall and cactus versus tall timber. With little prompting, Don was happy to start his travelogue as they headed north.

"Tucson is going to be a major city someday. When we get the university going it will help farmers and ranchers to grow the best crops and breed the most productive beef herds. They'll have to pay attention to water conservation, as most of it comes from wells, but it's going to be a great place to live. I don't think it will ever lose its old

196

Mexico character, however." Don and Dolores were only in Tucson for a couple of hours before transferring to the Phoenix stage. Rather than spend the night in Casa Grande, the driver changed horses and pushed on to the capital. They arrived in Phoenix shortly after dawn and headed to their newly purchased home. Dolores had to admit that her husband had chosen a very nice house that might become a comfortable home with certain modifications. She also decided that they needed a couple like Sam and Betty Ortiz to take care of the place when they were away. While Don visited Henry Dempsey, Dolores shopped in town to outfit the kitchen to her liking. She also wanted to investigate what people did to keep cool in the blistering summer heat. Maybe the town shuts down for a siesta like in Mexico, she mused.

Henry Dempsey and Don Richmond had finished looking at a USGS map that they felt would help sell their project in the nation's capital. "As more people come to Phoenix, the more we have to push Washington for help in developing this valley, Don. I hate to mention it, but I think we're going to have to go East again if we want to get a full hearing. We have to contend with competition from other areas in the West. One of the USGS men told me they had field men on the Gunnison River in Colorado and some place in Nevada. We have to face the fact that government isn't going to fund all of them and will likely take one and see how it works out before moving ahead on the others. You know as well as I do that we're talking big money and a lot of pushing and shoving behind closed doors. We've also heard that a war with Spain could be brewing over Cuba and the treatment of slaves, as if we don't have enough to worry about. It's a potential distraction at this point but an issue that could take center stage.

Visibly disturbed, Richmond complained, "Why the hell are we worrying about Cuba?"

"The U.S. is beginning to think globally, Don, and the government wants a navy fueling station in the Pacific. Spain controls the Philippines and Washington is eyeing Manila Bay as a fuel stop, or at least that's what I hear."

"So, we want a place in the Pacific to supply our ships and Cuba is the excuse to squeeze the Spanish into making a concession," responded Don.

"Some members of Congress seem to be willing to go to war if the Spanish don't cooperate," added Dempsey. Richmond didn't like his friend's remarks but understood that going to war with Spain could mean a serious delay or even a cancellation of the Salt River Project.

Renting horses, the Richmonds toured the Phoenix valley, enjoying the scenery and camping out under the stars. Staring into a campfire and listening to the howls of coyotes, the couple came to appreciate their family again and their personal relationship. They spent the better part of a week covering the valley farms and realizing the agricultural potential of the area. The farmers needed a system of dams, containment lakes, and canals to realize this potential, however. The scope of her husband's work finally made sense to Dolores. "Don, now I have a better understanding of what you, Henry, and the others are trying to do here. It's fantastic."

They also visited the Steinmark farm and witnessed some of the experimental work going on to develop better methods of growing cotton. They also enjoyed a sumptuous mid-day meal provided by Mrs. Steinmark in old German fashion. Dolores could not but notice unexpected familiarity between Madi Steinmark and her husband. It bothered her, but she decided to let it pass. She reluctantly had to admit that any man with blood in his veins would find the blonde, blue-eyed young woman attractive. Eric Steinmark wanted to take Don and Dolores to the Tonto Basin to show them his ranch, but the Richmonds begged off, citing project work that had to be attended to. After his brief conversation with Dolores on ranching, breeding cows, and growing grain, he knew that she would support her husband's decision to buy land near his spread.

As the stagecoach left Phoenix, Don continued his description of Arizona topography. "You've seen the Valley and how hot it can get during the day. Now, we're going to start climbing to cooler air. You'll begin to see live oak, juniper, and eventually ponderosa pine that can grow up to 100 feet in height. I wish we could have visited the old capital at Prescott but it would have delayed our trip, and I know you're anxious to see your grandson."

Nearing Camp Verde, Dolores was astonished to see the snow-covered summit of Mt. Humphreys, the tallest peak in the Territory at over 12,000 feet. She was equally surprised when told that the extinct volcanoes of the San Francisco peaks were over 50 miles away. She felt like a pioneer woman who had climbed through a mountain pass to discover a new, beautiful land on the other side. Don had not exaggerated the varied splendor of the Territory after all.

Weary from their trip from Phoenix, the Richmonds checked into the Lodge Pole Hotel. After bathing and a brief nap, they sent a note to the Cochranes announcing their arrival in Flagstaff. Within the hour, they received an invitation for dinner signed by Mayor Stanley and Lonnie Cochrane.

A carriage driver met the Richmonds at six o'clock and drove them several miles north of town to an estate entrance of two stout ponderosa pine beams supporting a horizontal bar. A carved sign hung from the top beam announcing Aspen Grove. A mile past the entrance, the driver deposited the Richmonds at the house entrance where Mayor Cochrane greeted them. The mayor escorted his guests into a huge log home and showed them into a sunken great room dominated by a native stone fireplace where a warm fire burned brightly. Dale Richmond was waiting for his parents there. As introductions progressed, a laughing, curly-headed young boy ran into the room. Delighted, Dolores lifted him to her bosom. "This must be Stanley Richmond, our grandson," she exclaimed. "Yes, Mom, this is Stanley in one of his more friendly moods. Come here and meet my wife Abbie." In a few minutes, the Richmonds met the mayor, his wife Lonnie, their sons and the two other Cochrane children, Roberta, age sixteen and Grace, age thirteen.

The mayor took immediate charge of the evening's proceedings. "Forgive me for being so forward but I've sent my helper Santoro and his wife to your hotel to pick up your belongings and bring them here where you'll be staying as long as you're in Flagstaff. We have a guesthouse that I'm sure you'll find comfortable. That way, you'll be able to spend more time with young Stan and his parents. Don, I thought you might enjoy a tour of the area tomorrow and get an idea of what Dale's been up to the past couple of years."

The Cochrane family treated the Richmonds royally. Homemade corn bread and butter accompanied a dinner of lamb, potatoes, corn, and squash. The excellent red wine was from California. Looking at Dolores, Lonnie commented, "My husband's hospitality can be overwhelming sometimes but he means well. I know you're tired from the trip so we can call it a night whenever you choose. We'll have plenty of time to chat tomorrow when the men go off on their tour. Perhaps we can go into town for lunch. I'd like to show you some of the native silver jewelry and hand-woven Navajo rugs and blankets that we're becoming famous for. The prices are very good; there's no trader middleman."

Don and Dolores slept soundly, past their usual waking hour. "I guess we were more tired than we thought," offered Don. The Cochranes were sipping coffee when the Richmonds joined them in their kitchen. A Navajo woman quickly provided the visitors with fresh coffee and grainy muffins. Don looked at his wife and smiled. "I think I could get used to this mountain style of living."

Mayor Cochrane and Don rode for several hours before reaching the sawmill, overseen by Dale Richmond. "I wasn't too sure about your son when he asked for Abbie's hand but he's proven to be a fine young man and solid business partner. He doesn't realize it, but he runs our logging and mill operations better than I ever did. And you can see that Abbie thinks the world of him. We're pleased to have him as our son-in-law."

The logging operations consisted of a base camp housing thirty to forty lumberjacks and a Chinese cooking crew. Sections of pine forest were clear-cut and the logs dragged to the mill by teamsters and oxen. The mill had a dozen men involved in cutting the logs into railroad ties, framing lumber, and siding for commercial buildings. While Stanley Cochrane conversed with the kitchen crew, Dale and his father spoke in private.

"Dad, I think you can see why I like it here. Abbie is a wonderful wife and mother; in fact, we're expecting another child in six months. I love the four seasons of the north country, and the business is growing steadily. The mayor can get a little windy at times but he's an honorable man and has been very good to me. He's never held the murder case against me and even helped Tom Lawson get an early release from prison. I guess what I'm saying is that I plan on staying here for good. I don't know how that hits you, but I thought it best to tell you."

"Son, your mother and I always hoped that you'd come home to Ribera, but after spending a week here, we can understand your decision. You know that you'll always be welcome if you decide to change your mind."

Later that week, the Richmonds said goodbye to the mayor, his wife, and their son and daughter-in-law and boarded the stage for Phoenix. The only other passenger was a special agent Pinkerton police officer employed by Wells Fargo. The fact that the agent was armed did not cause them undue concern; men commonly carried side arms in plain sight.

The stage was about twenty miles south of Flagstaff when the gang of robbers struck. A rifle shot rang out, striking and killing the stage guard who fell into the trail from his seat next to the driver. A large tree had been felled to block the trail, preventing any attempt by the driver to out run the four assailants. Braking to a sudden, jarring halt, the driver threw up his hands in surrender. The unexpected stop jostled the passengers, and in the melee that followed, the Pinkerton agent shot

into the midst of the thieves, killing one and wounding another. Leaning into the interior of the coach from his horse, the gang leader fired both barrels of his shotgun, killing the police officer outright and severely wounding Don Richmond. He then wrenched open the door of the coach, grabbed Dolores by the arm and threw her to the ground.
"

"Okay, driver, I'll give you five seconds before I drill you and the lady. Where's the Wells Fargo chest?" At the count of two, the driver screamed, "It's under the seat where the Pinkerton man was sitting. Please don't shoot me. I've got a wife and three kids to support."

"Too bad, buster, you picked the wrong trip this time." And with that snarling comment, the gang leader fired two shots into the chest of the driver, killing him instantly.

Meanwhile, Dolores picked herself up and rushed to her husband's side. Screaming at the gang leader, she reached for the Pinkerton's weapon only to be pistol whipped into unconsciousness. Two men then ransacked the coach to find the bank chest containing over $20,000 in gold dust and bullion. They split the loot into three parts and put it into thick leather saddlebags. Each rider took a bag; the third sack was tied to a horse for the escape south. Before leaving the scene, Clancy Rupert looked at his wounded accomplice who was stretched out at the base of a tree. "Sorry, Joe, I hate like hell to do this, but you'll only slow us down." He then leveled his gun at the man and fired a fatal shot into his chest. He then coolly remarked to his companion, "Let's cut dirt. We've got some heavy riding to do."

The robbery wasn't discovered until late that evening when the stage failed to arrive in Phoenix. Telegraph messages buzzed back and forth between the two towns and finally, a posse from Flagstaff reached the scene of the crime to find four dead men and a woman who was still alive but barely coherent. The only words Dolores could utter were "Where is my husband? What's happened to Don?" An all points bulletin was fired off to sheriffs in the Territory and to the gray militia, or Arizona Rangers, who were training in Prescott. A group of these riders caught up with Clancy Rupert and his companion in Skull Valley. Both robbers were killed in a brief gun battle; the full shipment of gold was returned to Wells Fargo.

Don Richmond never recovered from his wounds. The Cochranes and her son, Dale, took Dolores to a hospital in Flagstaff where she was tended. She was kept under heavy sedation for several days then moved to Aspen Grove where nurses looked after her around the clock. Two weeks passed before she was able to get out of bed and begin her recovery. Rupert's gun barrel slug to the head fractured her skull and caused a brain concussion. At first, Dolores had no memory of the holdup but gradually began to recall the horrific experience. Evening walks with her son and playing with young Stanley helped speed her recovery.

"Dale, the Cochranes have been wonderful to me, and young Stan has done more for me than you can imagine. But life goes on, even after the robbery and the death of your father. Ribera will always be my home, and I want to take Don back there for burial. Another week here with you and Abbie should give me the strength to go back to the River Bend Ranch."

Accompanied by her son and his family, Dolores Richmond returned to Ribera to complete her husband's internment. Townspeople joined territorial officials and farmers to mark the occasion. Henry Dempsey spoke eloquently of his close friend and business associate whose life had come to a shocking and premature end. "This tragedy will be felt by the entire Territory of Arizona for a long time to come. Don Richmond, may you rest in peace."

CHAPTER 45

More Trouble at Copper Hill

MONTHS AFTER THE FLASH FLOOD that destroyed Camp 2 of the Copper Hill Mining Company, reminders of the devastation continued to emerge. Bits of clothing, a pick, a ruined Bible, and a body were discovered as the heavy mush of sand and silt dried out. Sadly, Konrad decided that the body of Andy Corsica was buried somewhere along a stretch of several miles and would never be found. While accepting the catastrophe as an act of God, he saw a ray of hope in Tom Lawson.

Conversant in Spanish, Tom was able to recruit Mexican laborers and help train them to become miners. He also studied geology and mining textbooks and peppered Konrad with questions. In a few short weeks, he learned how to use a Brunton compass, map, and how to record discovery pits and accurately handle sampling. While it sometimes annoyed the German, Tom's incessant questioning soon made him a valuable assistant. When Konrad decided to open the books to the young man, he was amazed to see how much accounting Tom had learned in prison. He was also shocked when Tom told him, "Konrad, your records are terrible. But I can tell you this, you're burning cash beyond what I see you're capable of earning. Unless you have a secret bank account somewhere, we're headed for trouble and soon. The flood probably cost you $4,000 in stores and equipment. And while I can't quantify how much high-grade ore you lost, it has to be a big number. We've got a dozen men on the payroll digging the decline tunnel and exploration pits and we provide room and board. And Renaldo isn't working out as your drilling and blasting expert. He needs more training, or maybe you should train me to do the job so we can tunnel faster. It would also help if we figured out a way to ship some ore to the smelter. We've got to start generating some cash."

Konrad Bruner flared up at the young man's remarks but had to accept that what Tom said was generally correct. He also wondered how the young man had picked up on things so fast. Konrad also decided that Tom should be included in his financial outlook. "Tom, I've got money to pay off the bills at the general store, hotel, and Norm Dixon and continue for about three to four months at our present rate of spending. I might squeeze a little more out of my silver mine in Ribera, but unless I sold it outright, it really wouldn't help us here. As far as getting ore to the smelter, maybe we should look at Calder's idea of a tramway. It might make some sense but where in God's name would we get the money to build it?"

The possibility of getting help from his son Carlos never entered Konrad's mind. The conversation with Tom left him upset and discouraged about the future of the mine. The burden of inadequate income to finance operations was a heavy weight on Konrad's shoulders. His sleep was frequently interrupted and headaches began to plague him. He desperately needed a break.

"Tom, I'm going into town this afternoon for a few days. I'll take the time to see what can be done about reducing our expenses and extending our credit. When I get back, we can talk some more. By the way, I appreciate all the work you're doing for me. Thank you."

When Bruner checked into the hotel, a telegram from his son Carlos was waiting for him. In it the young man reported that his studies at Columbia were completed and that he would be in Arizona in a week or so. At that time, he planned to visit Bruner at the mine. The news gave Konrad some hope; maybe things were beginning to turn for the better. But it wasn't long before the fear of running out of money returned. He thought about contacting Bern Heinzelman but decided he would quit the mine before dealing with the promoter. As he rode out of town to return to Copper Hill, Konrad learned that copper prices had declined another four cents per pound. The news only added to his uncertainty about the future.

By now the streambed had dried out completely and was passable by horse and rider. Tom was anxious to test a ride to the smelter with a string of four mules and a wagon loaded with ore. When he made his way down the fault line the wagon wheels cut through the brittle crust of soil slowing the trip considerably. After three days, Tom finally made it to the smelter to sell 4,000 pounds of rich ore he'd accumulated.

When he was given $155 for the load, he realized mule haulage was not going to solve their transport problems. Maybe a combination tramway and railroad was the answer but that would require outside financing. His frustration grew as he realized he and Konrad were beginning to run out of time.

"Well, Tom, at least we know that wagon haulage is out," Konrad commented on his return to the camp. "I think I agree that a tramline and railroad is the answer and should be included in our investment package." Tom and Konrad studied their topographic maps, searching for the most direct route to the main line. When an answer was not obvious, they decided to map a route of their own with Tom doing the reconnaissance. Taking a young Mexican miner with him to help carry equipment and rations, Tom climbed, hiked, and explored an estimated ten-mile connection and finally came up with a plan. The first section would consist of a tramline, which would connect to a rail line that required two tunnels and three bridges. Tom was unable to estimate a cost but both he and Konrad knew it would require new, big money. The present challenge was to hang on until an outside investor could help the project survive.

Time was running out on Copper Hill and they both knew it. Tom estimated they had at least 50 million tons of good ore and probably a lot more but were stymied by terrain that prevented them from reaching the smelter on an economic basis. There has to be answer, Tom dreamed.

The visit by Carlos Rodriguez Bruner provided his father with a refreshing but temporary diversion. "Father, you seem worried. What's going on here? Is there anything I can do to help?" Before giving Carlos an answer, Konrad led him on a tour of the property and explained the transportation problem to the newly minted engineer. Building a smelter on site was out of the question, at least until the mine was in full production.

Carlos respected the size of his father's undertaking. "I'm still grappling with the details but this venture is enormous. You're looking at millions of dollars for a railroad that, as Tom suggested, appears to be the answer. For a man with little formal education, Tom seems to have picked up a lot of knowledge from you. It has gotten me thinking about a man from the Missouri School of Mines who is working in a mine up in Utah. His name is Daniel Jackling and he's been able to get financing by using open pit mining methods where large tonnages of ore are processed using steam shovels and rail equipment inside the mine. I intend to follow up on his work when I get home since we know there are similar low-grade copper deposits in Sonora. Tom has told me about your financial problems. I want you to know that while I am unable to be the big investor you're looking for, I can help you stay alive for another six months. That might just give you enough time to find an investor. I believe you have something here that could be the lead operation in a major mining district. Keep up the exploration work, be patient, and someone will come through with the money." Through misty eyes, Konrad nodded and replied, "Thank you, son."

After Carlos's departure, Konrad sat down with B.J. Kimball for a quiet drink of whiskey. Before he could open the conversation, the old prospector looked at his partner and offered, "Konrad, I know Copper Hill is giving you fits. I just want you to know that I still have $18,000 in my bank account and that it's yours when you need it. And I'll also tell you that I wrote my buddy in England last month and told him how that guy Barksdale did you dirt. I knew you wouldn't like me to mouth off like that but I just didn't like what that scoundrel did to you."

"Well, B.J., I wouldn't have complained about Colin Barksdale but what's done is done. And thanks for the offer of the money; I may need it before this thing is over." The small celebration was confirmed with a second drink of whiskey.

When two miners asked Tom for time off, Konrad was unhappy and ready to fire them. But Tom persuaded Konrad not to take action. "Konrad, they want to see their families, and if we don't give them time off, we could lose the whole group. Maybe a break will do us all some good. I thought I'd go to Phoenix to see if I can find Harry Cox, an old friend of mine who has a banking background."

Harry Cox proved easy to find. He was living in Tempe and working in real estate development. The former banker greeted Tom warmly. "Tom, you're really a sight for sore eyes even if you look like you've been in the sun too long. Just what have you been up to?"

When Tom explained his activities over the past six months, the older man commented, "Sounds like you have a tiger by the tail, Tom. Just think, this town is about to explode in population and people are going to want houses to live in. We've got a new flourmill and the normal school has already got over two hundred students. Why, in five years I expect Tempe will have over 3,000 people. You could start selling lots and houses with me and you'll be a rich man before you're thirty."

"I appreciate the offer, Harry, but I can't leave Mr. Bruner. He's got his life savings tied up in Copper Hill and frankly, I like the idea of mining copper. I don't know if Copper Hill is going to make it but I want to do everything I can before we declare bankruptcy."

"Tom, I've watched many a man break his pick over discovering an outcrop that he believes is the next bonanza. They're dedicated, hard-working men but get all wrapped up in technology, ignoring the business side of the equation. This guy Bruner sounds like the typical mining expert with the best of intentions but no plan for capital requirements. In your case, you can have the richest ore in the world but unless you can get it to the smelter at a profit, you'll never succeed. Ajo's a good example of what I'm talking about."

"My advice to you is twofold: First, take all the maps and data and calculate what the proven reserves are. Then add in what you can back up with something on what we call inferred reserves. The combination number is what will attract investors, especially if you have a good transportation plan. Second, focus on return on investment. You'll have to estimate ore grade, mining costs, and transportation for a delivered cost to the smelter. And don't overlook the cost of money over a time frame that's consistent with completion of the tramway and railroad. Then, put all this stuff in a package that will convince some flinty-eyed banker or foreign investor that the risk is manageable and that the project has an attractive pay back. You've got to think like an investor and forget what you think you see on that damn mountain. Now that's enough advice for the day. Let's go get some good food and wine so I can talk you into staying here."

Tom and Harry Cox had an enjoyable dinner, swapping stories of their tour at the Yuma Territorial Prison. They parted with Harry having the last word, "Tom, remember what I said about Tempe and its growth. There's money to be made here and we'd make good partners."

Riding back to camp, Tom Lawson digested some of Harry's advice. He realized that if he and Bruner were going to attract a substantial investment they'd have to start thinking like bankers. He wondered what Konrad might think about that idea.

CHAPTER 46

Bryan and Sam Start a Business

IN LESS THAN TWO MONTHS, Bryan Hurley and Sam Lawson tired of dormitory life and moved off campus. They rented a small cottage and hired Sadie Williams, a former slave, to clean and cook for them. Sadie, a widow whose husband died in the Civil War, also tended a small garden and periodically provided the two young men with motherly advice whether it was asked for or not. They grew into good friends beyond the normal boss, employee relationship.

Bryan was a top engineering student but only in those subjects that involved practical, hands-on solutions to everyday problems. Anything involving mechanics, fixing equipment, land surveying, and construction kept his attention; history, English, and other required courses simply didn't appeal to him. As his third year approached, Bryan neglected his formal college courses in favor of repairing farm equipment, improving manufacturing processes, and land surveying. The money he earned from farmers, gin operations, and land developers convinced him that completing college was a waste of time.

"Sam, I'm staying in Knoxville for a while to see if I can parlay my engineering work into getting a parcel of land. I might even barter my services into a minority ownership in a cotton gin. Most of these operators don't know a wrench from a screw driver and breakdowns are costly to them."

Sam Lawson didn't have Bryan's native intelligence but attended all his classes and studied hard. He especially liked working with the employees of the University Farm Extension Service who assisted local growers in establishing practices to increase crop yields. The work involved tilling procedures, the use of fertilizers, water conservation, crop rotation, and perfecting new strains of cotton, the largest planting in the South. From his work with these agents, Sam learned that the most productive area for cotton was along the Mississippi River where Arkansas, Mississippi, and Tennessee joined. Sadie Williams scoffed at Sam's newfound knowledge. "You sho' don't need college to know that, Sam. If you'd just asked, I coulda' told you that."

Eli Whitney had invented the cotton gin in 1793, but because of a loophole in United States patent law, never succeeded in profiting from his invention. Farmers in Georgia, where Whitney installed his first gin, rebelled against his conversion fee and circumvented his patent by making modest, homemade changes to the original design. With these changes, farmers built their own ginning equipment. In the mid-1890s, word of these modified machines eventually reached Knoxville and Bryan Hurley. He soon found himself repairing machinery and enlarging individual plants. It wasn't long before Bryan gained the reputation as the best cotton gin engineer in the state. True to his aspiration, he became a landowner and generated the profits necessary to consider farming as his next investment.

In the interim, Sam Lawson was building a reputation as an expert in growing tobacco, sugar beets, and cotton. He wasn't making much money as a graduate assistant in the Farm Extension Service but had the respect of his associates and the people he served. On a rare weekend when both young men were home, their conversation drifted to Sam's graduation and Bryan's engineering business. Bryan volunteered that he was tired of making rich men out of the gin owners; Sam offered that his job working for the Farm Extension Service was a dead end. Before the evening was over, the two decided to visit the Hurley family farm and talk things over with Joe and grandfather Dave.

Both Hurleys were happy to see Bryan and Sam. At the same time, Joe wasn't too sure that their return to the farm was a good idea; he'd recently hired a couple of hands and the Basford kid was about to marry his daughter Edith. Basford was a successful grain broker who had prospered in commodities and would be a valuable addition to the farm business. Joe also thought that despite the boys' intelligence, enthusiasm, and charm, they were unsettled and unpredictable. Unlike Joe, Dave Hurley was anxious to keep the boys on the farm. "Hell, Joe, we can make room for Bryan and Sam. We'll just let the new hands go. There's plenty of work in the county for them."

Joe Hurley swallowed hard, then looking at his father, said, "Dad, those new hires have been with us for over a year now while the boys have been in Knoxville. They're trained and responsible men and have families to care for. It wouldn't speak well for the farm and us if we dumped them because Bryan and Sam want a job. Besides, they haven't said a word about what they're up to."

Before Joe and his father could get into an argument, Bryan spoke up. "Sam and I have decided to move to Memphis and beyond if necessary. We have an idea that we want to run by you and see what you think. For the past year, I've been studying and working part-time as a mechanic fixing cotton gin equipment. My work has gone well enough that I'm through with the university. I've had enough of that theory stuff, and I think I know enough about cotton gins to fix, design, or build ones better than what I've seen in operation. I've decided to build one of my own based on what I've learned in the past year."

"Sam hasn't been asleep either. He's worked with the farmers and professors enough to get a good idea of how to grow cotton, sugar beets, and tobacco. With his know-how in raising cotton and my experience in ginning, we think we have a good combination of talents to make a living. We plan to visit the northwest area of Mississippi where land is cheap and where cotton grows best. We'll start with a small gin to attract growers then integrate backwards to a plant."

Sensing the inevitable request for start-up money, Joe interrupted, "Sounds like a good idea, son, but just where are you going to get the money to get this thing off the ground?"

Now it was Sam's turn to speak up. "Bryan has most of the money and we've saved about $1,500 between us. We figure we can buy 300 acres of land with an option to buy more and plant our first crop next year. Bryan will hang out a shingle as a cotton gin repairman and I'll see what I can do to assist growers with problems. Our first goal is to get relocated and establish credit locally."

Joe Hurley was breathing a sigh of relief that his son wasn't going to ask for money but Bryan was far from finished. "Dad, that's not the whole story. Our plan will get us started but to speed things up we'd like to buy or lease more land—about 4,000 acres—that would supply enough cotton for the gin I want to build. Once we're established, we'll use the gin as a demonstration unit to attract customers. Planters are a crafty lot, but once they see our farm and cotton gin they'll recognize a low-cost operation and will want to join with us."

At this point, Dave Hurley removed his hat, slapped it against his thigh and shouted, "Gol' darn it if we ain't gonna' be in the cotton business." Joe Hurley knew he couldn't argue with his father but added,

"You two meet your original plan for the first year and we'll be interested in loaning you money for expansion. But we need two commitments: Any money advanced to you will be a formal loan with a competitive interest rate. We also expect a monthly report on your progress so we stay informed."

Bryan and Sam nodded in unison and announced their agreement. "That's a fair deal; let's get going!" Dave Hurley was pleased but Joe was skeptical and said to his father, "Well, maybe they do have a good idea but let them spend their money before we bank their growth. We have lots of places where we can invest right here."

CHAPTER 47

Carlos and Rachel Reunite

AFTER SEVERAL DAYS OF BUMPY, dusty stagecoach travel, Carlos Rodriguez Bruner arrived in Ribera and settled in at the Whitman Hotel for a week. He washed up and went to the Lawson household only to discover that Rachel Lawson was in Tent City tending to a miner with a broken leg.

It was Rachel's first visit to Tent City. While setting the miner's leg, word filtered out that a doctor was in town. Soon, Dr. Lawson had an afternoon of tending to patients. The treatments varied from minor cuts and bruises to pneumonia and a tooth extraction. In the process of helping the sick, she also had the chance to meet Tim Royster, Barney Pryor's friend and business partner.

"Mr. Royster, I had no idea we had a boarding house of this size in Tent City. Judging from the number of patients we had today, we may want to consider an afternoon call once a week in the future."

Rachel didn't add that a new physician mightily welcomed patients willing to pay for services in gold dust. But she was careful to point out that serious cases could still be referred to her father's hospital in Ribera.

Openly admiring the young doctor, Tim agreed that it was a good idea for her to come to Tent City once a week to help the tenants of his boarding house. When his glance turned into a stare Rachel realized he was looking for more than medical assistance. Tim Royster was good looking and seemed to be running a successful business, Rachel thought to herself. And bachelors were scarce in Ribera, a fact that she could not deny. She smiled at the young man.

Emboldened by the doctor's attention, Tim blurted out, "There's a community dance Saturday night; would you like to join me?" Half joking, Rachel replied, "Why Tim, we haven't even been properly introduced but I'd love to join you. Of course, if there's a medical emergency, I'll have to take a rain check."

When the doctor climbed into her buggy and wheeled out of town, Tim jumped up and clicked his heels in midair. Mrs. Colchester, who loved Tim as her own son, reflected that it was about time he showed a smile or two. And it looked to her like the female doctor was the cause of his elevated spirits.

Carlos was discouraged by Rachel's reaction to his visit. Kate Lawson could see there was something awkward in the behavior of the two young people. "It looks like you've had another busy day, Rachel. Sit down and relax with a cup of tea. I want to pick up a few things at the general store; visit with Carlos while I'm gone. I should be back in an hour." And with that Kate withdrew.

As Rachel sat down at the table, Carlos reached over and covered her hands tightly with his own. "Rachel, I'm sorry I dropped in like this but I got involved with my father's problems up north and wasn't sure when I'd be able to leave until a few days ago. I'll get better at keeping in touch; please forgive me."

Rachel removed her hands from Carlos's grip and joined them in her lap. Looking directly at the young man she once passionately loved, Rachel burst out, "You take me for granted, Carlos, and I'm sick and tired of it! For goodness sake, it's 1898. We have regular mail service and the telegraph so there's no excuse for not keeping in touch. You're one of the most inconsiderate persons I've ever met."

Carlos had never seen Rachel like this and was tongue-tied. Regaining her composure, Rachel stopped crying as her mother came through the door. "I'm sorry Carlos; I didn't mean for this to happen after not seeing you for a year." She then got up and walked out of the kitchen leaving Carlos to help Kate Lawson unload several bags and boxes of groceries. Sensing his embarrassment, Kate suggested to the young man to give things a rest. "We have a community dance tomorrow night, Carlos. Perhaps it will give you both the opportunity to see each other under neutral conditions. Will you be able to join us?" Carlos agreed to join the Lawsons at the dance and excused himself. Returning to his hotel room, he was surprised to find a bottle of premium whiskey and glasses on a table. A card with "compliments of the house" written on it was signed by Sophie Kaminski, the proprietor. For a frontier town, this sure was a nice touch, thought Carlos.

To pass the time the next morning, Carlos rented a horse from Barney Pryor's stable and rode out to the Volunteer Ranch to visit Barbara Casey and her new husband, Vince Booker, a retired cavalry officer. "Vince is out riding with Soleado, who is now our legal daughter. Vince has become a real father to her, and she's made great progress in her schooling. She's a wonderful child; you'll see major changes in her when they get back."

Over lunch, Carlos and Vince talked about ranching but were interrupted by Soleado who rushed in with news. "I think we're going to war with Cuba, and an Arizona militia is being formed to take part in the invasion!" When Vince questioned her about the source of this information, the girl cited the local newspaper and the social studies class taught by Miss Grover, one of the tutors hired by the Bookers. With an intense look in Vince's direction, Barbara queried, "Maybe that explains why you decided to go into town with Major Keating rather than have lunch here last week."

Vince Booker licked his lips and stroked his chin before answering. "Barbara, the major is an old friend of mine who is recruiting teamsters and mule skinners to volunteer for possible service in the army in case we go to war with Spain. He knew from the beginning that I wasn't going to be one of his recruits. I told him I'm too old to be running off to anywhere outside Arizona, and my recent experience with the army has convinced me to remain a civilian. Plus, I'm really happy being here with you and Soleado. I didn't say anything to you because I didn't want you worrying over something that wasn't gonna' happen. Honey, I ain't going anywhere."

The community dance was held in a large room that was used as an auditorium in the schoolhouse. Tables were set up at one end of the room with cider and baked goods for the dancers. Local musicians played guitars, violins, drums, and an accordion. Barney Pryor, partially recovered from his mine accident injuries and Clyde Bond split the chores of calling square dances. An occasional waltz allowed the dancers to catch their breath and rest between sets.

By eight o'clock the festivities were in full force. On entering the hall, Carlos scanned the room looking for Rachel. When he saw her dancing with Tim Royster and clearly enjoying herself, he raised his hand in a brief wave as a twinge of jealously hit him in the heart. Who could that be dancing with Rachel? he wondered. Turning to the other side of the room, he walked over and asked Sophie Kaminski for the next waltz. "Mrs. Kaminski, that was very nice of you to leave a bottle of good Tennessee sipping whiskey in my room. I surely appreciated it.

Do you do that for all your guests?" Sophie, outfitted in a dark blue sateen dress, replied politely, "No Carlos, only when I know my guest is a wealthy rancher or owner of a silver mine, and you happen to be both." The two laughed as they twirled around the floor with the other dancers. Carlos also danced with Barbara Casey and Soleado before he realized that the evening was almost over. When he located Rachel talking with Tim Royster, he quickly walked across the room and asked her to dance.

"It's nice of you to ask, Carlos, but Tim has me tied up for the last two dances." Seething with rage, Carlos wheeled abruptly from the couple and excused himself with a terse "good evening." When Tim asked the identity of the man, Rachel bowed her head slightly and replied, "Just an old friend, Tim."

Carlos fled the scene of his rejection and practically ran back to the hotel. The clerk handed him an envelope that contained an invitation to dinner at the home of Dr. and Mrs. Ben Lawson. It had been written before the dance. Thank you, thank you, Mrs. Lawson, Carlos repeated to himself as he prepared to retire for the night.

The next evening, Carlos washed and dressed in his best suit for the dinner party. He then visited Mrs. Cauley's flower garden where he cut a bunch of daisies, carnations, and wildflowers. When he presented the bouquet to Kate he knew at least one member of the Lawson family was pleased to see him. Kate showed Carlos into the parlor where Ben Lawson was waiting to ask him about his son Tom who was working for Konrad Bruner.

"Sir, Tom is doing fine and has become a vital part of my father's plans for developing the copper mine. While at 'Yuma University' as he calls it, he learned a lot about accounting and finance. And by working alongside my father, he's becoming an accomplished geologist and mining engineer. I have never met a person of his background who has learned the details of a copper mining start up like he has. My father is a first-rate mining technologist but doesn't have the understanding or interest in the business side of a plan. He's very fortunate that Tom came along when he did."

Ben and Kate were pleased to hear how well their son was doing and showed their guest into the dining room to enjoy a hearty meal prepared and served by Rachel. After dessert and coffee, Kate urged the two young people to walk out and enjoy the sunset as she and Ben cleaned up.

Standing near the railing of the porch, Carlos put his arms around Rachel's waist and kissed her longingly. "Please, don't say a word," he whispered. "I want you to know that whatever I've done to offend you, I'm deeply sorry. You are my first and only love and I love you with all my heart."

With tears in her eyes, Rachel buried her face in Carlos's chest and hugged him closely. "I love you, too, and I've missed you so much. Now, please let's get back inside before we do something that would embarrass my parents." With considerable difficulty, Carlos released Rachel from his embrace, wished her parents a good night, and slowly walked back to the hotel, a much happier man than when he arrived.

CHAPTER 48

The Board Meeting

SIR CLARENCE BINGHAM NERVOUSLY PACED the floor, report in hand, as sleet hit the window of his office. An early dusk had fallen on Glasgow, but an emergency meeting of Britsco had been called at his insistence to face up to a serious investment blunder involving his nephew. As Bingham poured himself a whiskey, Geoffrey Gibbons, Clyde Hawkins, and Clifton Barnes filed into the oak paneled room. The foursome had been together for more than twenty-five years as investors and as friends. As the men helped themselves to the refreshments at the bar, Sir Clarence folded the report and placed it in the inside pocket of his suit jacket. He'd read the report several times, hoping the conclusions were somehow inaccurate, but detective Wesley Ferguson had built his case on solid evidence. It was now time to explain to the board how his nephew, Colin Barksdale, had defrauded the company. Bingham's sister pleaded with her brother for clemency and a second chance for her son, but Sir Clarence refused and decided that termination of Colin was the only option open to him. He had trusted the young man but Colin had stolen company funds and probably cost the firm an excellent business opportunity.

"Gentlemen, before I get started on new business, I want to review our situation in Cornwall. I think I've talked to each of you over the past few months regarding the closure of our tin operations. The formal report that you will receive provides a timetable for mine and mill closings in the Redruth area. It will involve a layoff of 2,500 miners, a devastating event for the economy of the region. However, we have no alternative since we've been losing money there for the last six months.

Terminations will be staggered over the next few months but we will be out of the tin mining business by the end of the year. But that is not the reason for this meeting."

"A few months ago, Mr. Jeremy Windham, one of our retired miners, received a letter from a fellow miner and friend in the United States. The letter made some serious accusations against one of our employees. He was uncertain about what to do with the letter and did nothing for several weeks. He finally decided to contact London management. I knew Windham from my days as a new engineer, so our solicitor forwarded the message to me. Now normally I wouldn't pay any attention to a charge like this but Windham's action required an investigation on my part. You see, it pointed to wrongdoing by my nephew, Colin Barksdale."

"Colin was selected to go to the United States, hire a qualified exploration man, and investigate a copper prospect discovered by Mr. B.J. Kimball. Windham and Kimball go way back when they worked together as underground mine foremen. Bear with me; I don't mean to make it this complicated. On my recommendation, we hired a Mr. Konrad Bruner, a mining technologist with first-rate qualifications, who lives in Arizona. Bruner went up to northern Arizona to meet Kimball and made a preliminary evaluation of the property. He decided to commit the company to a full examination of the claims, which would take about a year. Our total exposure amounted to about $125,000."

At this point, Clyde Hawkins interrupted. "Did we have a written contract with Mr. Bruner to make such an agreement?"

"No, we did not," Bingham replied. "Windham has reported that Bruner noted the transaction in his field notebook in explaining the agreement to Mr. Kimball. When Barksdale came back from his California visit, Bruner told him what he'd done and Colin promptly fired the man and refused to pay any salary and expenses. Bruner then went back to Globe to meet with Kimball and ended up taking over the exploration commitment on his own. He is now a majority owner of Copper Hill Mining Company. Before you ask, I believe Bruner's intentions are honorable and not a scheme to cut Britsco out of a good investment opportunity for his own selfish interest."

"None of this information has been given to Colin Barksdale; he's now in Cornwall assisting in the mine closures. I received Ferguson's report yesterday, and unfortunately, Colin's expensive travel tastes are well documented. He spent heavily in San Francisco and has been reimbursed for expenses in Arizona that were never incurred. In firing

Konrad Bruner, he reported expenses that he put in his own pocket. Why my nephew thought his actions would never come to light is beyond me. At any rate, Mr. Barksdale will be terminated for cause, owing the company about $8,000. When this 'loan' is paid back to Britsco, his slate will be clean and he can move on as he sees fit."

"My main reason for the emergency meeting is not to discuss the activities of my nephew. I'm concerned that we may be missing a significant opportunity in the States. Arizona already has copper mining operations in Clifton-Morenci, Bisbee, and Jerome, and the Kimball property might be the next one. My proposal to you, gentlemen, is that we try to salvage our original interest with Mr. Bruner and see if we can participate in his venture. I am prepared to personally make this trip provided one of you joins me. You know as well as I do that electrification is the wave of the future and copper is the key to its development. You are also aware that our tin business is essentially dead. If we plan on staying in the mining business with all its risks, we should look into this U.S. investment opportunity. Are there any comments or questions?"

Clyde Hawkins spoke up. "I'm sorry about your nephew, Clarence, and I hope he'll learn from his mistake. But I believe you have acted decisively and fairly. I suggest we contact Mr. Bruner immediately to see if we can reopen negotiations with him and Mr. Kimball. You know the man, so it's important that you take the lead. I also recommend that Geoffrey make the trip with you since he's our most experienced partner in mining and finance and has contacts in New York that might be helpful. Do you gentlemen agree with my proposal?" The board of directors of Britsco Mining Company agreed unanimously.

CHAPTER 49

Barney Pryor's Recovery

BARNEY PRYOR CHAFED AS DR. Ben Lawson insisted that he remain at the Doc Gilroy Hospital for at least a week before being released. "Just because you call a few squares at a dance doesn't mean you're fully recovered, Barney. Another week won't kill your business; from what I hear, the livery stable is doing just fine." Pryor had to admit that sometimes breathing was hard especially when he tried to bend over, but he was anxious to get back to the mine and check things out at the 300-foot level. Whitey Caulfield had already been released from the hospital but was confined to a wheelchair as his legs healed. Doctor Lawson had told both men to stay away from the mine for at least a month. That suited Whitey but Barney had other ideas. He planned on returning to Growler Creek when he damn well felt like it but he didn't say that to the doctor.

Later that week, Sophie Kaminski managed to complicate Barney's life further. "Barney, the hotel construction is just about completed, including a second floor suite that has a sitting room and two bedrooms. You might have trouble getting up and down the stairs, but you'd have privacy and get on with mending your ribs. You're looking pretty good, at least on the outside. The doctor did a good job on your scalp wound; the scar will be hardly noticeable when your hair grows back. Ben has told me you should go easy for the next few weeks, so moving in to the hotel makes sense."

"Thanks Sophie, but no thanks. I'm able to take care of myself, and I'm getting pretty damn tired of Lawson and now you trying to run my life. And make no mistake, I sure don't need your pity." Barney was still

smarting over the secret bank loan to Sophie that had been exposed by
Brad Scoville's forgetful comments. He was in love with Sophie but
didn't want her to feel obligated to him. Sophie's feeling of inferiority
further complicated their relationship. At best, she might be his friend
someday.

When Doc Lawson lightly pressed his hand into Barney's rib cage,
the patient winced and gasped perceptibly. "Barney, I know about
Sophie's offer. Wake up, man! You need a place to rest up and have
someone look after you. Half the men in town would give their right
arm for such an offer; the other half would lust in silence. Seriously, I'd
feel a lot better if someone like Sophie was taking care of things."

Barney gave Lawson a quizzical look. "Okay, Ben. I'll go along with
what you say." A few days later, a pair of heavy leather suitcases were
carried upstairs to the owner's suite of the Whitman Hotel. Barney followed, climbing the stairs laboriously. He took over the larger of the
two bedrooms, which contained a large double bed, a galvanized iron
sink, and a dresser with four drawers. Standing proudly on top of the
dresser was a bottle of whiskey and a bowl of apples, dried fruit, and
nuts. Picking up his only suit from the bed, he hung it in a closet and
placed his hat on the eye-high shelf. Geez, I'd better be careful; I might
get to like this place, he thought.

Sophie tapped lightly on the open door and entered the room.
Smiling widely, she commented, "I hope you find our hotel friendly and
comfortable, Mr. Pryor. If we've overlooked anything, please let us
know and we'll do our best to take care of the problem. We only ask
that you remove your boots before getting into bed." As Barney smiled
at the little jab, Sophie moved toward him, getting close enough for
him to smell the lilac water she was wearing. "Barney, why don't you
take a rest before lunch. Ho-Ching has prepared venison stew with
dumplings that I'm sure you'll enjoy. We can serve it up here and save
you the trouble of going up and down the stairs. I'll wake you in an
hour or two."

Barney was tired from the morning's activities and accepted the
suggestion of a rest before lunch. As he lay on his back staring at the
ceiling, the pleasant aroma of lilacs reminded him of where he was. As
he drifted off to sleep a vision of a beautiful brown-haired woman
danced before his eyes.

Barney was roused from a deep, restful sleep by a knock on the door
and the voice of Ho-Ching. The cook placed a tray of steaming hot
food on the table. The stew and dumplings were excellent, just as
Sophie had promised.

For the first week in his new quarters, Barney saw little of his hostess. Sophie didn't want to appear like a mother hen but kept track of him through the eyes of Berto, her handyman and servant. She also supervised the final carpentry detail work in the hotel and spent time in the saloon, keeping tabs on important customers and the poker table. Revenues from the saloon were getting better each week and the hotel dining room was now open with a full-service kitchen and boxed food for stagecoach passengers. Telegraph service would soon link the hotel with Tucson and the rest of the world.

When Ben Lawson came by to visit his patient, Sophie accompanied the doctor upstairs to Barney's room where the stable owner was sitting and reading a book. The doctor asked Barney to remove his shirt. "I want to look at those ribs again," he said. As Sophie looked on, Lawson removed the bandage wrapped around Barney's chest and carefully pushed and probed the rib cage. When Barney accepted the moves without showing discomfort, the doctor smiled and announced, "It looks to me that life at the Whitman Hotel has been good for you. Go easy for another week and I think you'll be fine. Walk as much as you want; it'll help you regain your strength. But don't get on a horse just yet. I'll see you in a week."

The relaxed atmosphere of the hotel had given Barney ample time to think about the Ocotillo Mine and the accident that happened 300 feet below the surface. He was certain of one thing: First aid equipment had to be available where men were working and housed in an enclosure to protect it from dust and dirt. Foreman also had to get some sort of emergency medical training and a bell system installed to announce any mishap.

While he was the junior partner in the mine, Barney felt the need for a professional survey of the property to determine confirmed and inferred reserves. Konrad Bruner was the man to do the job but he was in Globe and not expected back in town soon. Barney wanted to know how much collateral he had so he could diversify his investments. It would also help in negotiations for the general store if he decided to buy it.

Barney and Sophie began seeing one another for a drink of whiskey or a glass of wine at the end of the day. Sometimes they enjoyed dinner together in the hotel dining room. His health much improved, Barney was able to relax and enjoy Sophie's company. They shared stories of their younger days before Ribera, although Sophie avoided details of her experiences in Silverton, Colorado. "Those were very rough days for me, Barney. It cost me my self-respect but also gave me the wherewithal to start a new life here." Reaching across the table to touch Barney's hand, she sighed, "And I have you to thank for me being able to return to a normal life. You were there to protect me personally and to help me rebuild the hotel." Now blushing, she squeezed Barney's hand and murmured a soft "thank you." Barney reddened but said nothing.

Readying for bed as dusk began to fall, he recalled Sophie's comments. He knew he loved her. Barney's door was slightly ajar when he heard a soft tap. As the door slowly opened, he stood in silence as Sophie stepped into the room, a candle in her hand illuminating her face and chest. Her thin, filmy nightgown showed off her breasts and the curves of her thighs. She reached out her arms, wrapped them around his neck, and kissed him passionately. Responding to her advance, Barney helped Sophie remove her nightgown and hastily slipped out of his pajamas. Almost falling into bed, they made ravenous love. After a short rest, they made love again. Neither one uttered a word as they cuddled, kissed, explored each other's bodies, and succumbed to a third round of lovemaking. Exhausted but clinging to each other, Sophie and Barney pulled the covers over their bodies and fell into a profound sleep.

The following morning Barney awoke to a spectacular red, violet, and orange sunrise. Sophie entered the room with a tray of steaming coffee, fresh fruit, and warm pastries. As she set the tray down on the bed next to Barney, she leaned over and kissed him. "Good morning, my love. I hope you slept well. I think I can report to Doctor Lawson that you are completely healed and that all body parts are functioning well." Chuckling, Barney answered, "My recent nursing experience has certainly made me feel whole again." They both laughed rakishly as Sophie poured the breakfast coffee.

CHAPTER 50

Don Richmond's Work Goes On

"DOLORES, I'VE BEEN THINKING. IT'S been four months since Don's murder and you're still sorting things out at his office. In going through his papers you probably have learned as much about the Salt River irrigation project as anyone. We need someone like you to keep the project going and maintain good records. I think the threat of the Hudson Reservoir and Canal Company building a private dam is over; they've given up trying to raise three million dollars. But we'll see others attempt to control water to irrigate valley crops. It sure would help us if you were to take over as secretary of our association. You could keep all the maps and records at your house. It's a perfect way to honor Don's work."

Dolores Richmond liked and trusted Henry Dempsey and knew her late husband's work was important to the Territory. She agreed to Henry's request but only for a trial period of three months. "Understand Henry, this is only a test period for both of us to see how we get along. If, after three months, either one of us wants to quit, we part company without hard feelings." Henry readily accepted her terms.

The three-month probation period soon expanded into a permanent position, as Dolores became an invaluable partner in the quest for flood control and water storage in the Phoenix area. She attended meetings, met Territory officials, and gained an in-depth knowledge of the complex project. And the more she learned about the Valley's farms, canals, crops, and weather, the more committed she became to building a federally-financed dam where Tonto Creek joined the Salt River. Her collection of information clearly confirmed that the 1890s were terrible years for flooding and drought.

Riding with Arthur Davis of the United States Geological Survey (USGS), she was able to see the site where he believed the dam should be built. To Mr. Davis, an expert hydrologist, "nowhere else is there a more favorable dam site."

Henry Dempsey and Dolores Richmond worked well together and gradually realized their relationship was something more than that of business partners. When Henry, a bachelor for more than twenty-five years, asked Dolores to be his wife, she beamed and readily accepted. Her children were surprised at the news but offered their congratulations on the start of their mother's new life.

But the struggle to realize the irrigation project continued. Old-time farmers and settlers in the Valley continued to fight for private ownership or ownership by Maricopa County or the Territory. Gradually, they came to accept the fact that federal money was needed if the project was ever going to get off the ground. Bit by bit, little by little, the various factions united in an effort to acquire federal financial assistance. Railroads crossed the Territory, the Indian threat was eliminated, and farms and ranches dotted the landscape from Nogales to Flagstaff.

Copper mining began to add a new dimension to Arizona's economy. The journey to statehood however, was uneven and frustrating at times, and real progress didn't take place until the turn of the century. While Washington debated the issue, in the Arizona Territory, discussions and agreement on a constitution kept legislators bargaining back and forth.

CHAPTER 51

Mississippi Cotton Farming

"DON'T YOU BOYS WORRY NONE about me, I'll meet you here tomorrow, for sure." With that goodbye, Sadie Williams walked off to the colored section of Memphis, Tennessee, while Bryan Hurley and Sam Lawson signed in at the Hotel Peabody to spend the night before boarding the Missouri Queen the following morning. When they got to Friar's Point, they planned to hire a buckboard and travel to Clarksdale, Mississippi.

The trip downriver was a lazy, almost silent drift of 60 miles before the paddlewheel steamer touched the shoreline for disembarking passengers and freight. The only persons leaving the ship were two young men and Sadie Williams. The heat and humidity and the clammy, stagnant air told the group they were in cotton country. The movement of horses pulling the buggy created a mild breeze but otherwise the newcomers sweltered as they made their way to Clarksdale.

The town of Clarksdale was the center of cotton farming in northwestern Mississippi and offered little more than cotton fields, cotton gins, and the shacks of black field laborers. The hotel was nothing more than a run-down boarding house that provided twin beds and a washstand for the young guests. Sam and Bryan spent a miserable night swatting mosquitoes that buzzed incessantly. Dawn provided some relief while a breakfast of bacon and grits helped the two embrace the day.

Thorne Dumbarton, a local banker, showed Sam and Bryan around town and helped them decide on a small farm that needed attention. "Mrs. Wiley lost her husband a while back and hasn't been able to do much with the place. She's got two boys but they're too young to help out. They've got a cow, some pigs, and a vegetable garden but that's about it. No hired blacks, either. The house needs a new roof but she's got a good well and about 500 acres of land that hasn't seen a plow in over two years. Make her a decent offer and she'll be happy to sell and move on. I'll be happy to handle the paperwork; since it's a cash deal, you'll be able to take possession in less than a month."

The banker was as good as his word and three weeks later, Bryan and Sam moved in to their new home. They built a cook shack and room for Sadie—who agreed to cook, handle household chores, and grow a vegetable garden—next to the main house. "Boys, I just know we're gonna' be happy here," she called out as she sauntered to the garden to do some weeding.

Within six months, the partners had their first cotton crop planted with the help of Willis, a hired gang boss, and a dozen hands. A small dormitory and chow hall was built on the property, and as long as Willis kept track of his workers and Sadie dished out good vittles, the farm functioned smoothly.

Sam Lawson followed local custom on planting his first crop but decided to establish contact with the school of agriculture at Mississippi State University at Starkville. Leaving Clarksdale, he covered the trip in two days, stopping over in Grenada on the way. Using several Tennessee professors as references, he quickly assumed the role of a serious, scientific farmer who wanted to specialize in cotton growing. He also met Bonnie Stonehill, a graduate student who worked in the extension service while studying tobacco. She was attractive and unattached. They spent a lot of time together in the labs, over lunch and dinner, and any other free time. When Sam left to return to Clarksdale, they were more than good friends.

Meanwhile, Bryan's native curiosity encouraged him to survey local growers and processors. Not friendly at first, the farmers and gin operators soon learned that the newcomer was an experienced mechanic who knew how to repair farm and gin equipment. It wasn't long before he built a reputation as a stable serviceman who knew what he was doing. Bryan also recognized that most of the farms and cotton gins had aging equipment that often broke down. This opened the doors for improved machinery. With better maintenance and up-graded equipment, the owners also experienced improved productivity and more profit.

Bryan's next plan was to build a cotton gin that would process his and Sam's crop and others in the community. He was able to attract an

investor, Barton York, who owned thousands of acres of cotton and recognized the talents of the young man. Within a year, the York and Hurley Ginning Company was the largest, most profitable cotton gin in
Mississippi. It also enabled Bryan to meet Clementine York, his partner's daughter, and a southern belle of rare beauty. Clementine's
mother wasn't impressed with the young man from Tennessee and
hoped he would fade away like most of her daughter's previous beaus.

Bryan didn't fade away and his courtship of Clementine York
evolved into an affair. Chaperoned dances and dinners became less frequent while secret encounters increased. One evening while Mr. and
Mrs. York were in Jackson at a political convention, Bryan and Clementine consummated their love in the laundry room of the York mansion.
Six weeks later, Clementine's morning sickness confirmed that she was
with child. Sure that her mother would go mad over the news, she
approached her father in his office at the mill.

"What brings you down here, honey? I thought you and your
mother were going to the Tinsley's for lunch." Sitting close to her
father, Clementine nervously stroked her hair and confessed, "Daddy,
I'm pregnant." Clementine was shocked when her father shouted out,
"Why, that sum' bitch, I'll shoot him! After all I've done for that no
good tramp; just wait'll I get my hands on him." Appalled at her father's
outburst, the girl quickly decided to involve her mother. That evening
while seated in her father's den, Clementine repeated the story to her
mother as her father silently fumed. "I wish you had come to me right
away, but never mind; we'll find an answer," Mrs. York replied. Still ripping mad, Barton York looked at his wife and could only admire her
calmness in such a confounding situation. He didn't know that a housemaid had tipped the matron off about the secret meetings between
Clementine and Bryan.

Preparing for bed that evening, Dora York offered her husband a
plan." Barton, this isn't the first illegitimate baby born into either of our
families, and let's not dwell on how it happened. Bryan seems to be a
good businessman and should make a decent husband. Clementine has
made a mistake, but if we act quickly there will be little damage to her
reputation and ours. Bryan and Clementine will elope to Nashville
where we will find a neighborly preacher who will marry them and
backdate the marriage certificate. There will be some tongue wagging,
but you just leave any explaining to me."

Sam Lawson, normally a quiet, unassuming young man, didn't like
what he was hearing from his partner. "I don't understand, Bryan.
What do you mean you want to sell the farm and move into town to

join up with old man York? Where the hell does that leave me? We've got a good crop of long staple cotton in the ground, we're self sufficient in food, and we've got good help. Do you want me to throw all that away? I'm sorry but I won't do it."

"Sam, let me give you the full story and maybe then you'll understand. Clementine is pregnant and next week we'll be leaving town to get married in Nashville. When we get back, I'm moving into Fair Oaks with the Yorks to be with Clementine. I don't want to sell our place any more than you do, but I can't come up with an alternative unless you want to buy me out. I'd give you a fair price for the farm if you want to stay with the place. Think it over; I'm not in any hurry for an answer. I've got enough on my mind to keep me busy."

On his ride to Starkville, Sam thought long and hard about the circumstances suddenly dropped into his lap. Dissolving the partnership and giving up the farm forced him to see how important his relationship with Bonnie Stonehill had become. No matter what he decided to do, it had to include Bonnie. He realized he was in love with the girl.

Bonnie was in the greenhouse working on tobacco seedlings when Sam found her. Something clicked in her mind when she saw the young man. As they sat down on empty wooden crates, Sam took Bonnie's hand in his and leaned toward her. "I love you, Bonnie," he proclaimed. Pleasantly surprised, she blinked, smiled, and responded, "I believe I love you too, Sam." After several moments of silence, the girl looked at Sam and laughing, said, "This is supposed to happen over a candlelight dinner or on a moonlit riverboat cruise, Sam, not in a hot, musty greenhouse full of tobacco plants."

Sam had to smile in return. "I had to figure out a few things on the way down here and nothing made sense unless I was going to be with you. I'm asking you to marry me, Bonnie. Will you say yes?"

"Of course I will, Sam, but you better get my father's permission first. He's got some strong, old-fashioned ideas." The meeting with Professor Stonehill, who taught history at MSU, was brief and successful. However, Sam had one idea that would require his fiancée's approval. "I won't go into details now, Bonnie, but my cousin and partner wants to dissolve our business association. He's marrying into the York family in Clarksdale, a well-connected, wealthy clan with huge holdings in farming, cotton ginning, shipping, and real estate. He's going to be set for life so I sure can't blame him." Bonnie had to agree that it wasn't a bad way to get started.

Picnicking under a magnolia tree on the MSU campus, Sam explained a plan to Bonnie that involved moving westward. "Maybe it's the humidity or the partnership with Bryan falling apart, but I'd like to start over out West. I don't know exactly what I have in mind; I just believe a beginning in Ribera makes sense. My father and sister are doctors there and my mother and sister Elizabeth are also there. My brother Tom is in the mining business up north. I just see better opportunity there as the Territory grows. But I won't leave here unless you come with me."

"My father won't be overly thrilled, but his first love is the university and he'll get along without too much trouble. He likes you and thinks you'll take care of me and that's most important to him. I love you very much and will be happy to see what Arizona has in store for us." Kissing Bonnie goodbye, Sam Lawson made his way back to Clarksdale and the muddled events of the past few weeks.

Bryan Hurley was in an apologetic but optimistic mood when he and Sam met. "I admit I've made a mess of things, Sam, but Clementine and her folks seem to be happy with the way things worked out and Barton has accepted me as a son-in-law. I hate to see you leave, but if you and Bonnie decide to move to Arizona I'll figure out a way to buy you out. It's good land and Sadie and Willis have done a good job as farmers. Perhaps we can cut them in to run the place and we can split the profits. Sadie's a tough, smart lady and would welcome the news. Let's sit down with Thorne Dumbarton next week and see if we can put a deal together. And let's keep Barton out of the talks; it doesn't have to be any of his business."

By the end of the month, Sam Lawson and Bonnie Stonehill were married, had a contract with Bryan Hurley and Sadie Williams to run the cotton farm, and packed their belongings for their move to the Arizona Territory. Leaving the Mississippi Delta, they spent their honeymoon weekend in New Orleans, before entraining for the West. Bonnie was apprehensive but also excited and confident that their new beginning would be a good one.

CHAPTER 52

Konrad Bruner's Accident

KONRAD DIDN'T RELISH THE IDEA of meeting with Bern Heinzelman of the Goldsmith brothers but felt he had to do something to save Copper Hill Mining Company. They met on a cold winter's day at the Highland Hotel in Globe. Bern listened carefully to Konrad's story. "Mr. Bruner, we are quite familiar with everything you've said. Remember, we are also in the business." As he spoke, the Austrian twirled a cigar between his fingers, releasing a small cloud of smoke. "Copper mining is very risky, as you have found out. Yes, discovering a body of ore is exciting, but getting the rock crushed, concentrated, and delivered to the smelter is equally important and unfortunately, underestimated too many times."

Heinzelman's insinuation irritated Konrad but he managed to restrain himself. "Mr. Heinzelman, we didn't overlook the problem of finding a potential mine in a remote area; we were practically wiped out by a flash flood that killed six men and destroyed much of our equipment. A year ago, you were interested in our property, now you express no interest. What's changed?"

"Remember, Mr. Bruner, we're developing a mine near Morenci that has fallen behind schedule, and our investors are unhappy. Experienced miners are in short supply and now they're demanding more money. They've unionized and have planned slowdowns; they've even walked out once. Then the Mexicans among them wanted to be paid the same money as the Europeans. But, worst of all, the price of copper has dropped by ten percent in the past month, and the mills back East have cut their work forces. Demand for sheet, tubing, and wire has fallen off, so orders for raw copper have been curtailed. From what we hear, it's expected to get better in three or four months but in the meantime, we're stockpiling copper until things improve. Nothing personal, Mr. Bruner, but that's the situation as best as I can explain it."

"So, Bern, what you're telling me is that I can't expect any help from you and the Goldsmith brothers. You think you can sit back, watch us go broke, and then take us over for a song. Well, in spite of your strategy, we'll survive somehow and that goddamn mountain of copper will get to the market, with or without you."

Heinzelman sighed heavily and replied, "Bruner, things have changed in the past year. As I said before, when things improve we'll be happy to take another look at your place. But we've got to deal with our own problems right now. You'll have to excuse me; it's starting to snow and I've got to get on the road."

When Heinzelman left, Konrad went to his room and uncorked a bottle of whiskey. He poured himself a half glass, then walked to the window and stared outside at the falling snow. He wanted to believe Bern's story but really suspected the Goldsmiths of wanting to see him go under then come sniffing around for a bargain. It wouldn't be the first time the brothers waited out the prospector who thought he could develop a property on his own. Konrad poured himself a second glass of whiskey and decided to send a message to Barney Pryor telling him his ownership in the Ocotillo Mine was up for sale. That would give him enough working capital for another six months. By then something was bound to turn up.

He descended the stairs, entered the saloon, and ordered a double shot of whiskey. As he drained his glass, Hans Gelber, owner of the general store, approached. "Mr. Bruner, you've got an outstanding bill at my store that is now over $800. I've extended you credit for two months but I can't give you any more. When can I expect to be paid?"

His eyes glazed over and slurring his words, Bruner shouted back, "I've spent over $15,000 in your damn store over the past year and a half and you're worried about $800! You'll get your money when I start smelting ore and not a day before. In the meantime, I'll take my business elsewhere." The saloon grew quiet as the German staggered out of the barroom, looking for his hat and coat. Not realizing his outerwear was in his room, Konrad exited the bar and stepped off the board sidewalk into a heavy snow squall.

The driver of a wagon, almost blinded by the storm, never saw the pedestrian lurch into the street. The abrupt contact with a human body startled the four horses that panicked, bucked, and trampled the man who had stepped into their path. When the teamster finally gained control of his horses, he heard the moans of the victim coming from underneath the wagon. Unable to pull the drunken and shocked Konrad Bruner to safety, the driver called out to the saloon for help. Soon, helping hands were dragging his limp body to the bar. "Oh my gosh, it's Bruner!" the barkeep shouted in dismay.

Dr. Skillman did a quick examination of the unconscious man and decided to take him to the hospital. The doctor and some saloon regulars placed Bruner on a stretcher and carried him to the infirmary where Dr. Kortmann completed an extensive diagnosis. "He's got a nasty cut on the head and a likely brain concussion. We can take care of the broken arm and leg tonight; let's hope the horses didn't stomp in a couple of ribs. I'm most concerned about the head injury but I think he'll be okay. In any case, he's going to be here for a while. Does anybody know if he has friends or relatives in the area?"

Hans Gelber stepped forward. "I know the man, doctor. He's Konrad Bruner. He's working a mine site up the canyon. I'll get word to his friends as soon as the snow stops. I'm not sending anyone up that way while it's still storming; it's too dangerous. I'll stop by tomorrow to see how he's doing." Globe slept as snow fell for a night and a day.

While Globe dug itself out, Tom Lawson and B.J.Kimball worried about the inevitable melting and possible flooding. They also began to wonder what had happened to Konrad.

It took Tom and B.J. the better part of a day to hollow out a path to the privy and the barn so the mules and horses could be fed. They thought about the crew in Camp 2 and decided that they had food and shelter and could handle things on their own. On the third day after the storm, Tom strapped on a pair of snowshoes and set out for town. As he entered Main Street, he ran into Hubert Morton, a hotel employee who told him about Konrad's accident. "He was run down by a team of horses pulling a freight wagon and is in pretty bad shape, last I heard. He's at the hospital being tended to by Dr. Kortmann. Incidentally, there's a telegram for Mr. Bruner at the front desk."

Tom went to the hotel, tore open the telegram envelope and read, "We will arrive your location by mid-month to discuss possible interest in Copper Hill. Am looking forward to seeing you again. Sincerely, Clarence Bingham, Chairman, Britsco Mining Ltd." Allowing his imagination to run wild, Tom hoped this was the group with the money to keep Copper Hill going.

After checking in at the hotel, Tom got directions to the hospital and walked through snow piled as high as his six-foot frame. Meeting with Doctor Kortmann, he learned that Konrad's head wound had been stitched together but the patient was still unconscious. "It's fairly common in head injuries like this. The best we can do is to give Mr. Bruner complete rest. Wait a day or two before visiting him again."

Tom waited a day and a half and decided the telegram was too important not to share with Konrad. Ushered into his private room, Tom was stunned to see Bruner asleep, his head swathed in bandages and plaster casts on one arm and leg. Of greater concern was his gaunt appearance and pale, bearded face. As Tom stood close to the bedside, Konrad opened his eyes but showed no sign of recognition. "Who the hell are you?" he muttered. "And what are you doing in my room? If you work for Heinzelman, tell that bastard I don't want his money. We'll make it without his Morenci gang of thieves. Now get the hell out of here."

Tom was confused and hurt by Konrad's tirade but decided it was probably best if he left the room. "Don't take what he said personally, Mr. Lawson," a nurse consoled. "He's had a severe blow to the head that has left him a bit scrambled mentally. He's getting the best care from the doctor and I'm sure he'll be better; it just takes time." Tom thanked her and left the hospital.

He then walked to the general store to see Mr. Gelber and to thank him for getting the news of Konrad's accident to him. "When the telegram arrived, they decided to involve me since you folks generally visit the store when you're in town. I'm sorry about Konrad's injuries; I had no idea things were going so poorly at the mine. When I saw him in the saloon he was drinking some and wasn't himself. He got real upset when I asked him about the money he owed the store. When I look back, I wish I'd never brought it up. He's a good man and I hope he gets well again."

Tom decided to stay in Globe until he knew Konrad Bruner was going to be on his feet again. The sheriff had exonerated the wagon driver from any blame citing limited visibility and the fact that Konrad had walked into the path of the horses. Tom also talked with the assayer but concluded that the man was holding back information because he had a secret agreement with Konrad, was owed money, or both.

Bored in town, Tom stewed over the contents of the telegram from Sir Clarence Bingham of Britsco Mining. These are the people that B.J. mentioned. Was there some previous connection with Konrad? He checked the local library for information about Britsco but came up empty-handed.

Tom's second visit to the hospital was a little more productive. Konrad was beginning to take regular food but still looked thin and drawn. His long, stringy hair and unruly beard with strands of white didn't help any. He recognized Tom but was unable to recall the event that put him in the hospital. Tom decided not to tell Konrad about the snowstorm and the potential for flooding at the mine site; the man had enough to worry about. Heeding Dr. Kortmann's advice, he kept the conversation brief and mundane. As he left the hospital, Tom wondered what he would do if Bingham showed up before Konrad was well and out of bed and capable of joining a detailed conversation.

The snow had almost melted and the streets were beginning to dry out when the Britsco directors arrived in Globe. "Sir Clarence, I hope this trip hasn't been too uncomfortable for you; this is some of the roughest terrain I've ever seen," commented Geoffrey Gibbons, one of Sir Clarence's business partners.

"Well, Geoffrey, I'm not a youngster anymore and stagecoaches are not my preferred form of transportation but most mining operations are not in civilized places, as you know. A good bath, some hot food, and a dash of whiskey will help us a lot." The two visitors enjoyed a steak dinner in the Highland Hotel dining room and retired early, saving inquiries for the morning.

Tom Lawson ate his dinner in a small Mexican café two blocks from the hotel. He enjoyed the burritos, strong beer, and especially the teasing of Conchita, the serving girl. As she flashed a bright smile, he wondered if she was the daughter of the owner. He noticed she didn't have a wedding ring on and stirred a bit as she sashayed into the kitchen. Thank goodness the food was cheap; Tom was running out of money. Tom paid his bill and walked over to the hotel. As he stamped his muddy feet on the entryway rug, the hotel desk clerk called out, "Mr. Lawson, there's a message for you." Tom unfolded the note to read, "Please meet us for breakfast in the dining room at 8:00 am. Sir Clarence Bingham"

The clerk explained that two foreign gentlemen had first asked for Mr. Bruner but when told that he was in the hospital, asked for an associate. "That's when I told them about you, Mr. Lawson," the clerk said. "The other man with Mr. Bingham is Geoffrey Gibbons. They talk kinda' funny but were polite and nice enough."

Tom slept poorly and tried to prepare for questions that the Britsco people might ask him at breakfast. He finally decided to be straightforward and stick to the facts. The next morning, Tom washed, dressed, and walked downstairs to the dining room. The two visitors were easy to identify. They were dressed in dark, heavy woolen suits and wore starched collars and bow ties. He assumed the older, baldheaded man with glasses was Sir Clarence.

Both men stood up to shake Tom's hand when he introduced himself. They asked about Konrad and Tom assured them that he was on the mend but would not be available for lengthy conversations for some time. "He suffered a head injury in a wagon accident and the doctor has restricted visiting hours. But I'll take you over to see him this afternoon." Silently, Tom prayed that the German would recognize Sir Clarence. "In the meantime, let me give you an overview of the discovery. Then tomorrow we can visit the site. It's pretty rugged country so we'll have to use mules to take us to camp. You'll need heavy boots, gloves, and some warm clothing for the cool nights. Gelber's general store will outfit you. I suggest you check out of the hotel and plan on staying with us for two to three days. We've got bunks and blankets and you'll find out that B.J. Kimball is a pretty good cook. We may be short of whiskey, though."

Sir Clarence and Tom paid Konrad a visit while Geoffrey stayed behind to buy equipment for the trip. Konrad was cordial and the nurses had shaved his beard and cut his hair. Most important, he recognized his former employer and talked briefly about the Cornwall tin mines. The Scotsman was kind enough to keep the visit short and Konrad gave every appearance that he had his wits about him. Leaving the hospital however, Sir Clarence expressed concern for the man's health and complete recovery. "Tom, let's hope that Konrad is on his feet shortly. You can understand that without him on this project, our interest would be seriously impaired." Tom nodded but shuddered at Sir Clarence's remark.

For the next three days, Tom and B.J. Kimball led the Britsco men up and down and across the property, showing them the decline tunnel, sample holes, and exploratory work still underway. They studied Bruner's geologic maps that indicated a massive intrusion of granitic material into the host rock that was extensively fractured and faulted. The ore body cross-section indicated a huge blanket of mineralization, roughly parallel to the topography, extending to unknown depths. The tunnel, now over 300 feet in length, was still in rich ore of chalcopyrite and bornite. Bruner had also identified a major fault in the streambed and several smaller fractures that invaded the hillside. In the brief examination of the site, Sir Clarence and Geoffrey were overwhelmed with the potential of the project that up until now had been run by one man and a couple of assistants. It was Geoffrey who finally broached the subject of getting the ore to a smelter.

Tom then launched into a description of their plan. "Konrad had me map the terrain between here and the closest railway, about eight or nine miles away. In the beginning, I thought we'd build a road by cutting into the side of the hills and tunnel through two steep canyon walls. Just before Konrad's accident, we came up with another idea. The difference in elevation from the mine to the relatively level ground is 1,400 feet over the first two miles. We believe we could use an aerial tramway to move the ore over the roughest part of the roadway and stockpile the ore at the base of the tramway. Then we'd move the ore by wagon or eventually, by rail to the main line."

Noting skepticism on the faces of his guests, Tom ventured, "I know it may sound crazy, but there are several wire rope tramways in California that appear to be very successful. The articles were published in a recent engineering magazine that Konrad gets. If we could make it work here, we might be able to save a lot of money."

Further examination of the property convinced the Britsco men that B.J. Kimball had uncovered a huge copper deposit. But they were not sure that Copper Hill could be mined at a profit. While Tom Lawson's presentation was impressive, they noted that he did not have definitive answers about reserves, manpower requirements, and capital needs.

Meanwhile, Konrad Bruner's health was improving. His headaches had all but disappeared and he could stand without holding on to the bed. Tom Lawson was impressed with his friend's progress when he visited. "I hope you're feeling okay, Konrad. If you would prefer to delay the meeting with the Britsco people, I'm sure they'll understand."

"No, Tom. I'm certain they have many questions they want me to answer. I'm fine; have them come up."

Konrad was sitting by a window when Tom brought the visitors to his room. "Please don't get up, Konrad," Sir Clarence offered. "We know you've had a bad accident and should be resting."

"Thank you, Sir Clarence, but I've started walking again and the doctor tells me I should be nearly back to normal in a week or two. You've seen the property, so it will be easier for me to explain what we believe we have. Once we have the sample information compiled from the exploration holes, we should be able to come up with a fairly good number on reserves." As Konrad expanded on the subject, it became apparent to Tom and the Scotsmen that Bruner was very much in control of his faculties.

Over the next month, Tom escorted Geoffrey Gibbons over the tramway route, the possible sites of tunnels, and the location of a roadbed for the railroad that would connect with the main line. They discussed the possibility of a company-owned smelter, realizing that it was a project way off in the future. Geoffrey was an experienced field engineer, and Tom learned a lot about the complexity and cost of building a railroad by working with him. Konrad and Tom also learned that they had run through B.J.'s bank account and that Copper Hill Mining Company was essentially broke.

While compiling assay reports, Konrad knew that he had to tell Bingham that his company had collapsed financially. "To be direct, Sir Clarence, Copper Hill Mining Company is broke and will have to cease operations if there is no fresh injection of cash. I have a silver mine that I intend to sell but that will take some time before I can talk to my partner and secure a buyer. I hate to admit it, but this project has been a challenge far beyond anything I dreamed of. There's no question in my mind that there will be a mine here some day but I don't think it will have my name on the deed."

Sir Clarence studied Konrad's face intently. "Konrad, you are correct in your analysis of Copper Mountain. It is much larger than even we had anticipated. Geoffrey and I have spent quite a bit of time thinking how we might fit into the development of your mine. We've determined that it will take two to three years for Copper Hill to reach production on a scale that justifies the investment. We see the excavation of a vertical shaft, installing crushing and concentration facilities, and a floatation plant taking a year to a year and a half. The hard part will be the roadway, tramway, and railroad, which may have to come first so we can get supplies up the canyon. Frankly, it's a bigger undertaking than we've ever done and will require syndication to raise the money we think we'll need. But tin mining at home is about over, and we think we have a good chance of raising the capital."

"We're also banking on the idea that electrification is on the way and that copper demand will be huge ten years from now. With that time frame in mind, you can see that our partners must have patient money, as they say. Before proceeding, we will reimburse you for monies owed to you as promised by Mr. Barksdale. And before we can package a syndicate, the ownership and management issue will have to be resolved. Will you be willing to give up ownership and the management of the Copper Hill Mining Company? You should think this through carefully. We see you as our chief mining technologist, helping us to make decisions, but remaining in a subordinate role. After all you've put into the project, it won't be easy to give up control and become an employee and passive investor."

Konrad shared Sir Clarence's offer with Tom and B.J. over a rabbit stew at the main camp. "As I understand from Sir Clarence, Britsco would seek out partners in England and, if successful, buy us out. We'd end up with ten percent of the new company and have an employment contract for three years, or until the mine is producing a certain tonnage each day. He's made it plain that he wants us to be on the board but Britsco would run things and make the decisions. Assuming we have a ten percent ownership, I'd take seven percent and each of you would have one and half percent in the new company. Make no mistake, it could end up being worth nothing; if Copper Hill does succeed, it'll be at least five years before any payout."

B.J. Kimball listened to Konrad's explanation and was the first to jump in. "These fellas look like decent people and hell, what choice do we have anyway? Boys, let's get on with it."

Confident that the money could be raised, Britsco opened an account in Globe with a deposit of $50,000. Plans were made to start sinking a vertical shaft to at least 300 feet and a new survey to find the best route for transporting ore to the smelter. As part of the final agreement, Geoffrey Gibbons asked Tom Lawson to accompany him back to Scotland for home office training. In return, the Scots would send a pair of field engineers to Arizona to work on the tunnels, mineshaft, and transportation schemes. They would also transfer an accountant to the United States to set up necessary financial controls. The transfer of power was already underway. While Konrad's financial problems seemed to be behind him, he was nervous about the future but also relieved.

CHAPTER 53

Water Problems on the Rodriguez Estate

GETTING FROM RIBERA, ARIZONA TERRITORY, to Zacatecas, Mexico, had not been an easy trip for Carlos Rodriguez Bruner. In spite of stories that the newly constructed rail line from Juarez to Mexico City was up and running, his journey had been marred by inadequate water supplies and passenger stations that were non-existent. Instead of a comfortable overnight trip, he arrived thirsty, disheveled, and fourteen hours late. Good publicity, thought Carlos, but President Porfirio Diaz's plan to develop markets and unify the nation by building thousands of miles of railroad tracks had a long way to go. He hired a driver and buggy to take him to the ranch; on arrival, he went directly to his bedroom and collapsed into a deep sleep.

The next morning, his breakfast of chicory-flavored coffee and pastries was interrupted by the appearance of Lumberto Villegas. Carlos jumped up and embraced his old friend. "Lumberto, please sit down and have some coffee and enjoy this beautiful morning." Villegas declined the offer and launched into the reason for his visit.

"I would love to, Senor, but I have some news that you must be made aware of. Our cotton fields have been seriously infested with an insect that will damage the harvest. It's something the likes of which we've never seen before. But more important, a sickness has invaded our villages, causing severe health problems. It appears to be related to our water supply, and we have told people to boil their water. It has worked here in the main house, but our problem is getting the word out to our miners, ranchers, and farmers. We've lost five children to the disease already and many more are severely ill."

Startled by the grim news, Carlos instructed Lumberto to alert the key foreman to meet at the ranch after the siesta. He also decided to visit one of the affected villages to better understand the scope of the problem. The inspection revealed that over two hundred people in one village of fifteen hundred adults and children were ill with diarrhea and symptoms of flu. One area—somewhat remote from the village center—had escaped the onslaught, but the people were still relying on one well for their drinking, cooking, and washing needs. And they were not boiling the water.

The meeting with the ranch foreman did little to find the cause of the problem. The only immediate solution, prescribed by a doctor from Zacatecas, was to continue to boil all water for drinking and cooking. He ordered a shipment of iodine and instructed the people to add drops of the liquid to water vessels before drinking. Until the source of the contamination was discovered, ranch operations would have to be drastically reduced.

Strict rules were applied to potable water in the ranch house. Carlos also drank more beer and wine and coffee to stave off any water-related problems. As he pondered the blow to the community, he decided to seek counsel from Dr. Rachel Lawson. He wired his request for help and within a day received a message from Ribera that she was coming to Zacatecas, after a stop over in El Paso, Texas. Why is she stopping in Texas? he wondered. The problem was in Mexico and he wanted her help now. Carlos reluctantly boarded the Mexican Central Railroad and arrived in Juarez, state of Chihuahua, the next afternoon.

Lacking complete information as to the extent of the problem on the Rodriguez ranch, Rachel rushed to Bowie for the afternoon train. Arriving in El Paso, a grimy, dusty border town, she took a room at the Lone Star Hotel and went to bed, hoping to see Carlos the following morning. Several hours later, the Mexican Central Railroad rumbled into Juarez. Hurriedly grabbing his small leather suitcase, Carlos left the train and walked across the Rio Grande bridge to find the Lone Star Hotel. Learning that Rachel had left the hotel on an errand, Carlos decided to have breakfast. He enjoyed a hearty plate of steak and eggs and weak coffee. After starting to read the paper, he dozed off. Shaken awake by Rachel, Carlos groggily stood up and gave her a warm hug. "Carlos, you need a shave," she chided.

They went to Rachel's room overlooking the river boundary and Juarez, Mexico. Breaking away from his not so subtle advances, Rachel inquired, "Stop right there, Mr. Rodriguez Bruner. What's this all about? And it better be good." Hurt by Rachel's rebuff, Carlos told her about the situation at the ranch and asked for her help as a medical doctor and understanding friend. Rachel listened patiently as Carlos described in detail the extent of the disease and the lack of medical aid, as the ranch was fifteen miles away from Zacatecas. "We've got five wells in the villages and surrounding areas; one appears to be okay, but the other four are contaminated or look that way. We've ordered people to boil water, and most families are complying, but we haven't been able to locate the source of the problem. Five children have died from dehydration and diarrhea and a lot more will if I don't get help fast."

Rachel digested the information and realized she needed a microscope and other lab equipment to identify the bug causing the problem. "Carlos, I'll do whatever I can to help but I need to borrow some equipment. I'll meet you back here at two o'clock. That should give us plenty of time to catch the afternoon train out of Juarez. Try to get some sleep while I'm gone.

The first doctor recommended by the hotel manager did not have the equipment Rachel was looking for but his suggestion to contact Dr. Julio Gelvan paid off. Gelvan had a modern microscope and was also willing to loan her whatever she needed. "Dr. Lawson, use the equipment as long as you need it and feel free to wire me if I can be of any assistance. We've had dirty water problems here in the past, so I'm familiar with most sources of trouble. A few months ago, we had a flood that deposited animal waste in a lake that people were using for drinking water. We did the same thing you mentioned—boiling and iodine—and that took care of things before the water basically cleansed itself. But we have a staff who were trained in taking samples and that helped a lot."

Returning to the hotel well before two o'clock, Rachel entered the room to find Carlos sound asleep. Undressing, she stroked Carlos's clean- shaven face, leaned over and kissed him. As he opened his eyes, she kissed him again, this time more passionately. Responding, he removed his clothes and pulled her to him. The couple made spirited love and whispered loving words to each other. Later that afternoon, Rachel and Carlos dressed, packed the medical supplies, and bought food for the long trip to Mexico.

Lumberto met the couple at the train station the next day. Sadly, he reported that another child and an old woman had passed away while Carlos was in El Paso. After changing into riding clothes, Carlos and Rachel joined Lumberto and toured the villages, water wells, outlying reservoirs, and watershed. On their return, they visited a makeshift hospital that had twenty severe cases tended to by family members. Satisfied that the discipline of boiling water had been established and the use of iodine employed, the threesome retired to the hacienda to have dinner and discuss the results of their tour.

"Dr. Lawson, I cannot recall anything resembling this epidemic," Lumberto began. "I remember isolated cases of food poisoning and some diarrhea but nothing like this."

"Judging from what I've seen, my guess is that we have an infected water supply," Rachel replied. "The cause escapes me at this time but I will take samples of each well and examine them under a microscope as the first step. In the meantime, keep boiling water and adding a tincture of iodine. Moderate consumption of red wine is okay, too. At the hospital, patients should be kept in quarantine, and the caretakers should wash their hands frequently in hot water, borax, and lemon juice."

Since most of the villagers were unable to read or write, information on controlling the epidemic had to be spread by word of mouth. Gradually, the rate of incidence declined as boiled water was used not only for drinking but also for washing dishes, cleaning clothes, and in preparing food.

Looking at the water samples that evening, Dr. Lawson concluded that the pollution was being caused by animal waste penetrating the groundwater supply. But why were wells 1,2,3, and 4 contaminated and well number 5 and the hacienda not infected? She woke Carlos from his sleep to explain her findings. "Where is the animal waste coming from?" she asked.

Carlos sat up in bed rubbing his eyes. "We normally have several thousand head of cattle grazing up by the reservoir but they're not there now. We've been doing it that way as the seasons change for as long as I can remember. Is it possible that manure has percolated into the old riverbed and fouled the wells? That might make sense since well number 5 is in a different area. We can check that first thing in the morning."

With a brief kiss and a whispered good night, Rachel edged her way out of the room and returned to her work. She had to read up on waterborne diseases and how to treat them. She also had to reexamine the well samples and compare them to the pictures in her textbooks. The sun was rising when she finally went to bed with questions still swirling in her head. If the groundwater was contaminated by animal waste, how were they going to clean up the mess? What were they going to do for the hundreds of people who needed good, clean water? What were they going to do about removing waste from the villages and avoiding another epidemic?

It was noontime when a rap on the door awakened Rachel from a deep sleep. After breakfast, she changed into her riding clothes and left the hacienda. For the rest of the day, she reconnoitered the stockyards, pasturelands, and the reservoir and mountain lake, the main source of water for the estate. She also took samples from both bodies of water. Rachel was tired but in a hopeful mood when she returned to the hacienda.

Dining with Carlos and Lumberto that evening, she waited patiently until Carlos asked, "I haven't seen you for more than ten minutes in the last few days. Tell us what you've been up to." After describing her lab work and ride to the reservoir and lake, she looked at the two men and said, "Carlos and Lumberto, I believe you have a health problem that threatens most of the people in the villages. Something has to be done about it, and the answer isn't boiling water. That is only a temporary solution and inadequate for the long term."

"I don't know what's involved at the mines or how your cattle are moved around for pasturing. I'm guessing that the animal waste concentrated in the stockyards and adjacent pasturelands has caused the contamination in the underlying groundwater. It's the type of bacteria I've seen under the microscope. For the here and now, the villagers have to be strict about boiling and treating their water and the sick isolated and fed a diet of rice, bread, and bananas. And make sure those helping the sick use the disinfectant I prescribed."

Catching her breath, Rachel went on. "In the long term, you should clean out the present stockyard and move it away from the reservoir and pasture the cattle east of the villages. Over time, rainfall and releasing water from the lake should cleanse the groundwater. The lake and reservoir are free from bugs, so a gravity flow of water to a central location seems to be in order. Wells number 1,2,3, and 4 should be capped as soon as good water can be delivered from the reservoir to a water tower or cistern where it can be stored and made available to the villagers. The central water location will also allow someone to test the water regularly and add chlorine, if necessary. I would also consider shutting down the hacienda's well number 5 after the water station is built."

Frowning, Carlos responded, "My God, Rachel, that's a pretty tall order you're suggesting. I see canals or pipelines, pumping equipment, and a lot of money for your project." Annoyed with Carlos's comment, Rachel shot back, "It's not my project, Carlos. It's yours if you want your people and their families to be healthy. You asked me for my help in solving a problem that turned out to be dirty water. Getting the solution implemented and paying for it is your responsibility as the owner. Think about it, Mr. Engineer." Rachel then stood up, brushed her hair from her eyes, and said, "Gentlemen: It's been a long day, I'm exhausted, and I'm going to bed. Goodnight."

CHAPTER 54

Barney and Sophie Marry

BARNEY PRYOR AND SOPHIE KAMINSKI decided to accept the Bookers invitation to visit the Volunteer Ranch. They also decided to make the trip in style using the refurbished stagecoach that had been standing idle in the livery stable for over a year. Barney enjoyed washing it, polishing the brass fixtures, and massaging the leather with saddle soap. When Sophie Kaminski, dressed in a pink blouse, dark brown culottes, and polished high-heeled boots climbed aboard, a small crowd cheered and clapped their hands in delight. A bright, sunny day complemented the occasion.

Reining in the horses at the ranch, Barney and Sophie were met by Barbara, Vince, and their daughter Soleado with smiles of admiration. "Can I drive the coach?" the young girl shouted as she looked at Vince Booker for approval. The retired army man nodded and agreed. "It's okay with me as long as Mr. Pryor allows it." Soleado climbed up and seized the reins. Clucking "gee-haw," she snapped the reins and soon had the horses trotting in order in a large circle. Barney and Sophie looked on in surprise as the teamster observed, "That youngster sure knows her way with horses."

With Booker's marriage to Barbara Casey, the Volunteer Ranch had taken on a new dimension. Both cattle and horse herds had been expanded and augmented with new breeding stock from Europe and South America. A modest timber and sawmill operation had been started giving the ranch all the wood it needed and income from outside sales. While the ranch was expanding, Soleado was growing up and preparing for college. She had no young men in her life even though she was well spoken, intelligent, and pretty. Once in a while, some young man would make a leading comment to her at the general store but she paid little attention.

After a delicious meal, the Bookers gave Barney and Sophie a tour of the ranch, revealing their plans to build a bridge over the river and possibly develop the property. It was late afternoon when they clambered aboard Barney's coach for the ride back to Ribera and the Whitman Hotel. Relaxing in the suite formerly reserved for Barney, Sophie poured drinks. "Things have been pretty good for us," Pryor mused. "The Ocotillo Mine is doing fine, and Tent City looks better every day. The boarding house investment with Tim Royster is one of the best deals I've ever made."

Interpreting Barney's comments as a lead-in to bringing up the loan she owed him, Sophie responded, "Barney, I should be able to pay back all the money I owe you in another three months. I hope that will be satisfactory."

"Goodness no, Sophie. That's not what I meant. What I'm trying to say is that even with all my good luck in business something important is missing in my life. And I think I finally figured it out. It's you Sophie; you're missing from my life. I've loved you since the day you first set foot in this town. Will you marry me?"

Barney's proposal caught Sophie by surprise; she was certain it was business he wanted to talk about. Catching herself quickly, she realized he was sincere and meant what he said. The former madam from Silverton, Colorado, tough and hardboiled when needed, stammered "yes" and burst into tears. Drying her tears, Sophie looked at Barney and sobbed, "Barney, I think someone up there is looking out for me and for us. Let me explain. I visited Dr. Lawson this week, and he confirmed that I am two months pregnant. He insisted that I tell you right away but I wasn't sure what to do. I even thought about leaving town. I knew I wasn't going to railroad you into doing something you didn't want to do. I hope you'll be as happy as I feel about being a parent."

"Sophie, getting married and having a baby with you is beyond my wildest dreams. And who cares what gossipers in town might say." Embracing Sophie, he whispered, "You've made me the happiest guy on this great earth."

Within the week, Barney Pryor and Sophie Kaminski were married at the Bookers ranch as Doctor Ben Lawson and his wife Kate looked on. The newlyweds set up temporary housekeeping in the Whitman Hotel while Barney hustled an architect and builder to start work on their new house, the pride of Ribera.

CHAPTER 55

Sam and Bonnie Lawson Reach Ribera

THE ARRIVAL OF SAM LAWSON and his new wife, Bonnie, turned the doctor's home into mass confusion. Kate Lawson was delighted to meet her daughter-in-law and see her son again but she would have been a lot more congenial if the couple had given some sort of advance notice. Sometimes she thought her son's head was in the clouds. In spite of Bonnie's aversion to living with in-laws, she agreed with Kate that this was best for the short term, and they both got along easily.

Kate explained to Sam and Bonnie that Rachel Lawson was away in Mexico working on a water pollution problem at the estate of Carlos Rodriguez Bruner and they should take over her bedroom for the time being. Sam didn't mention what his plans were or how long he and his wife were going to stay in Ribera and Kate decided it best not to ask, at least not right now.

Hinting at the future, Kate talked about the new hospital, a second school for older children, and Barbara Casey Booker's general store. "She's looking for someone to manage the place until she decides what to do with it; her interest is now in the ranch. Then we have the Whitman Hotel rebuilt after the fire and new buildings in Tent City. We'll go out to the River Bend Ranch this afternoon and leave the Volunteer Ranch for tomorrow. It's about twenty miles out of town."

Mrs. Garland Newport greeted the three as Sam guided the buckboard to a halt in front of the house. With introductions completed, Garland invited the Lawsons into her kitchen for coffee and oatmeal cookies. Bonnie was dazzled by the lady's casual control of things. "Don't you believe I actually run this place; I've got some of the best wranglers and farmers in the Southwest working for me." Kate Lawson hadn't been to the ranch in years and was equally impressed with Garland. She was in her seventies and appeared to be as healthy as a horse. Kate loved horses and ranch life and wondered if Garland might be interested in selling the place or a portion of it now that her daughter Dolores had remarried and settled in Phoenix. But today was not the day to bring up the subject. On the way back home, Bonnie Lawson mentioned how much she would like to visit Garland Newport again, to talk about farming.

After a week of sightseeing, Sam grew restless and decided to visit Tucson and the recently established university. He met with Dr. Paul Trenton, acting dean of the college of agriculture and a specialist in growing citrus crops. He also spoke with a professor who was cultivating date palms imported from Haiti and an instructor who was involved in cotton production and the study of an insect that threatened to destroy local crops. The belief was that the boll weevil had come from Mexico and had worked its way north into Texas, New Mexico, and Arizona. Sam was interested in working at the university but was disappointed that there were too few students to justify the hiring of new teachers. Riding back to Ribera, he explored the idea of working in Phoenix or even returning to Mississippi, but the prospect of going back to Clarksdale or Starkville had no appeal. Perhaps he and Bonnie should strike out for California and the West Coast, he thought. By the time he arrived in Ribera, Sam was completely muddled. He decided to just relax and see what might develop in his hometown. At the same time, he knew he had no interest in running a general store even if he owned it.

Bonnie continued her exploration of Ribera and its surroundings, including the Volunteer Ranch and Tent City. She was shocked at living conditions in the gold mining settlement and doubly surprised that the community was now in its sixth year. When she asked Barbara Booker why there were so few permanent buildings, the storeowner replied, "Gold miners come and go, always looking for a new strike. When the Bowie River fails to give up even subsistence gold, the miners will pack up and move on to the next discovery or rumor of gold. They're not interested in building towns; all they want is the gold. Why, a good ten percent have left just in the past six months when they heard of a discovery in Prescott and the Hassayampa riverbed."

Bonnie and Sam's interest in agriculture helped them appreciate and understand the natural advantages of Ribera. A river with year-round flow, a moderate four-season climate, and established schools and churches led them to think seriously about settling in the community. When Garland Newport encouraged them to visit her at the ranch, Bonnie began to study the farming sector of the spread. The hay contract with Barney Pryor's livery stable provided a steady income and with a little luck, some plants could be double cropped. When she stretched her imagination, she wondered if apples, pears, and other fruit trees might do well in the foothills north of the river. When she mentioned this to Garland Newport, the older woman replied, "Bonnie, if anyone could grow trees around here it would be you." Laughing, she continued, "and I'll just bet that the deer would be a whole lot happier. Tell me what kind you want and I'll order them from back East. Figure on enough for an acre or two, at least."

Garland Newport enjoyed Bonnie's company. Her visits filled the void left by Dolores's absence. Widowed after the murder of her husband, Dolores was devoted to her new husband, Henry Dempsey, and her work on the irrigation project. Garland accepted her daughter's new life knowing it was unlikely she would return to Ribera. She'd had conversations with banker Brad Scoville about selling the ranch but held off doing anything. She loved the life of a rancher, didn't need the money, and always wanted to do something for the town.

Bonnie decided to confide in Kate Lawson. "Kate, don't ask me how or why I know, but I think Garland Newport might be interested in selling the River Bend Ranch or perhaps part of it. Would that be something you and Dr. Lawson might be interested in?" Kate was amazed at Bonnie's perception. "Girl, you must be reading my mind. That's a big piece of land and I have no idea what Garland would consider a fair price but we've nothing to lose by asking. Do you think you and Sam might be interested in staying here to help run the place? I'd love to get back to working with cattle and horses."

"Sam and I have talked about staying in Ribera," Bonnie replied. "But we haven't considered something like the River Bend Ranch; we just don't have the money. If we sold the 500 acres in Clarksdale we'd have a start."

Dr. Ben Lawson liked the idea of buying the River Bend Ranch, but he was skeptical that they could somehow strike a deal with Garland. But he knew it was his wife's dream to own a ranch, so he suggested that Kate, who knew Garland the best, broach the subject with her. The former cowgirl from Tennessee readily agreed.

Kate Lawson and Garland Newport were sharing morning coffee and watching the departure of several hundred horses being shipped to Fort Defiance and the army. "It's funny you ask, Kate, but I've been thinking about selling the place ever since Bonnie came over to talk to me about the farm. I just love that girl; she reminds me so much of Dolores when she was younger. I could get run over by a bull tomorrow so it's high time I made some plans. Let me tell you about the River Bend Ranch."

Over the next hour, Garland described the farmland and irrigation system, pastures, corrals, feedlots for the cattle, the huge area reserved for horses, timberland that was basically untouched, and the all-important property that bordered the Bowie River and the town of Ribera.

"Now, nobody in town knows about this, but I want to give Ribera enough land to build a park where folks can picnic, play with their kids, and ride horses. It would include a portion of the riverfront so that people would always have access to the river. I've even thought of building a bridge over the river so people could get to the Cimarron Trail. I'd name it in memory of my late son, Greg Newport. I've never forgotten that ill-fated day; it was a terrible thing to have happen."

That evening, Kate Lawson explained her conversation with Garland Newport to her husband, Ben. "I think there's a way we can make an offer to Garland that might benefit both parties. It would involve Sam and Bonnie pitching in to buy the vegetable, grain, and fruit section of the ranch; they would eventually have their own place on the land. We would own the ranch house but not move in until Garland died. She'll donate maybe 500 acres to the town to establish a park and we'd take over the cattle and horses and 50,000 acres of pastureland. Garland and her daughter Dolores would set up a foundation to protect about 300,000 acres of unfenced land, some of which is high country timberland. Sam and Bonnie would make a down payment on the farmland and split the profits over a five-year period to pay off the balance of what's owed. Garland and Bonnie have that all worked out."

Ben Lawson smiled at his wife's daring. He realized what Kate was proposing was a huge undertaking. It would also mean that his chief nurse was about to retire and he'd have to find a replacement. "If you think we can handle it, I'm with you, Kate. I don't have a clue as to where all this money is going to come from, but with Sam and Bonnie to help, it's too good to pass up."

Sam and Bonnie Lawson were already making plans to build a home between Garland's ranch house and the border of Ribera. With Bonnie already four months pregnant, they'd need space for a child and privacy for themselves.

CHAPTER 56

Tom Lawson in Scotland

TOM LAWSON'S TRIP OVERSEAS TURNED into an adventure. The cross-country train trip was an exciting discovery of the vastness and diversity of the United States. New York City, the port of embarkation, gave Tom his first exposure to a huge city with subway trains, horse drawn carriages, and motorized cars shuttling thousands of people up, down, and across town on a daily basis. Crossing the North Atlantic on the *H.M.S. Britania* taught him that the world was composed of more than landmasses. His appreciation of seamanship grew as the captain and crew guided the vessel through mountainous waves and bitter, icy weather. Landing in Southampton, England, on a snowy, cold morning, Tom Lawson was happy to step on to firm ground.

With the tin mining industry in steady decline, Sir Clarence Bingham and Geoffrey Gibbons decided to visit their mines in the Redruth district where mine closures were underway. While the two owners met with the directors of Cornwall Tin, Tom was given a tour of one of the mines, now 3,500 feet deep. He was surprised to see modern equipment, including dewatering pumps in the maze of the underground workings, even as a shutdown was underway. He was especially impressed with the quality of the workmanship in square set timbering and safety regulations. He took notes on the drilling machinery, ore handling equipment and the organization of the crews. He also recorded the names of several mine foremen; perhaps they could be transferred to the U.S. and Copper Hill for training purposes.

After the brief visit to Cornwall, the three men boarded a train for London where Sir Clarence was to meet with potential investors. Tom became a tourist and visited Trafalgar Square, Buckingham Palace, the British Museum, London Bridge, and numerous other attractions. He slept well on the overnight train to Glasgow, the ship building capital of the world. Near the downtown headquarters of Britsco, Tom registered at a small, stone building called the Hotel Kilbride and moved into a two-room suite. A coal-burning fireplace was the sole source of heat in the chilly rooms.

Tom saw very little of Sir Clarence as he was now working under Geoffrey Gibbons, the chief engineer. Gibbons became Tom's teacher, mentor, and eventually, good friend. Over the months, Tom learned that Geoffrey had worked for Britsco in the gold fields of South Africa, mercury deposits in Spain, and iron ore mines in Sweden. Under the close supervision of the Scot, Tom studied underground mapping, ventilation, dewatering techniques, and the calculation of mineral reserves. On weekends, he was given an engineering problem, provided with reference materials, and a membership card for the city's main library. It was this library, especially on cold days, where Tom studied and wrote reports to be given to Geoffrey each Monday morning.

One spring afternoon, Tom busied himself with accounting and finance books, working on a problem related to evaluating a mining property. As the day wore on, he became tired and dozed off, his face buried in the fold of a book. Receiving a gentle tap on the shoulder, Tom woke up to see the librarian standing next to him. "Sir, it's closing time. You'll have to turn in your books and leave." Tom begged to borrow the books over Sunday but the comely brunette advised, "I'm sorry, sir, but reference books cannot be taken from the library under any circumstances. Please, it's now five o'clock and you have to leave." As Tom hesitated, Shannon McGuire glanced toward a security officer waiting nearby. Pushing himself to a standing position, Tom murmured "I'm sorry, miss" and walked to a coat rack, donned his jacket and hat, and left the building.

While he continued to do his studies at the library, he was unable to strike up a conversation with the Irish lass. After several attempts, he waited outside the library one Saturday at closing time. As Shannon walked out of the front door, he tipped his hat and inquired, "Excuse me, miss, but I'd like to return this book." The librarian rushed past him as if she had a train to catch. "I'm sorry, but we're closed for the day; you'll have to return it on Monday." Then she recognized Tom Lawson. "Oh, it's you, Mr. Sleepy, who we always see on weekends." One word led to another and soon the couple was chatting over tea and biscuits at the River Clyde Tea Room.

Shannon McGuire guessed that Tom was an American, citing his freshness and easy way of speaking. After explaining what he was doing in Scotland, Tom asked Shannon how an Irish girl had ended up in Glasgow. "Many Irish emigrated to Scotland during the potato famine. My father knew boats as a fisherman and was able to get work at the shipyards here. When he got established, he sent for my mother, my sister, and me from County Cork. The schools are good here and I like books, so I studied to become a librarian." Glancing at her watch, she excused herself. "Goodness, it's getting late. I have to be on my way." As she got up to leave, Tom asked if he could see her again next Saturday. "Yes, Tom, I think I would like that."

As the spring days lengthened into summer, Tom and Shannon took walks together along the River Clyde and visited museums. His fondness for Shannon growing, Tom suggested they go out for dinner on their next meeting. "No, Tom, I think it best if you come home for dinner to meet my family before things proceed any further. I'm the oldest daughter in the house and my father has strict rules about meeting men, especially foreigners."

After locating the correct number on the sooty, brick row house, Tom rang the front doorbell, a bouquet of flowers for Shannon's mother in his hand. When the door opened, Tom came face to face with Shannon's father. Matt McGuire was a bull of a man at least six feet tall and weighing about 225 pounds. Thrusting a large calloused hand out, he said, "Come in, come in, Mr. Lawson. Welcome to our home." After dinner and dessert, Tom and the family moved into the parlor. Tom thought things were going well until the big Irishman broke the silence. Looking intently at Tom, Matt inquired, "And now, Mr. Lawson, just what are your intentions with our Shannon?"

Momentarily taken aback with the direct question, Tom paused and then answered, "Sir, my intentions are strictly honorable. We both enjoy books and learning and each other's company. I respect the wishes of Shannon's family and will never do anything that would offend you and Mrs. McGuire." Before Tom could continue, Mrs. McGuire entered the conversation. "We're pleased that Shannon has met a fine person like yourself, Mr. Lawson, and we hope we will be seeing you again." Later on, as she led Tom to the front door, Shannon gave him a light kiss on the cheek and smiling, said, "I'll see you next weekend, Tom. I think Mother and Dad are pleased with our association."

Well past his planned six months of training, Tom began to work on information trickling in from the copper property in the Arizona Territory. As assay reports were tabulated, hopes for a producing mine came closer to reality. It was also apparent that London investors were lining up to partner with Britsco to develop the property. Unfortunately, the main shaft sinking was behind schedule. Over tea one evening, Tom suggested to Geoffrey Gibbons that it was most likely due to inexperienced miners. "Geoffrey, you're furloughing good people in Cornwall; maybe you should send some of the men to the States to get the shaft excavation back on schedule and to train some of our best people." Pouring a second cup of tea, the engineer laughed and agreed that it was a great idea, and one that he should have thought of himself. Within the month, eight Cornish miners and their families were on their way to the American Southwest.

Sir Clarence and Geoffrey were pleased with the reports coming from Copper Hill and made progress on gaining new investors. The prospectus called the mine Britsco Copper Hill to publicize the fact that the Scottish corporation was the majority owner. "Bruner's work at the mine has been first rate but I don't think he's the man to be our general manager," Geoffrey Gibbons stated. Sir Clarence Bingham agreed with his chief engineer. "I've given it serious thought, Geoffrey, and believe we should take on that responsibility for a predetermined period. You are the most qualified person we have, and the stockholders would approve your appointment. I estimate a tour of about three years; then come home to become a company director. What do you think?"

Flattered, Gibbons thought a few minutes before answering the chairman. "I basically agree with everything you've said, Sir Clarence. Bruner must be retained; there's no doubt in my mind that he is the best man to handle technical efforts at Copper Hill. But he doesn't have the interest or skills to deal with financial and personnel matters. I think he would agree with our assessment. I'd be pleased to take on the job, assuming I can have Tom Lawson as my assistant. He has worked hard over the past year, has a strong work ethic, and is very intelligent. I would groom him for promotion, and send a strong message to the workers and locals that we intend to have an American managing things in a few years. He also knows the way we work and would be able to smooth out any problems with Bruner if he feels he's being pushed aside."

When Tom learned that Geoffrey Gibbons was going to be named general manager of Britsco Copper Hill and that he was going to be his assistant, he reacted with mixed emotions. He was excited about the position but leaving Glasgow and Shannon McGuire suddenly took on a new dimension. Considering the situation carefully, he decided to speak to Matt McGuire. Meeting at a pub near the shipyard, they sipped pints of ale before Tom opened the conversation.

"Mr. McGuire, I love Shannon and want your permission to marry her. Before you answer, you need to understand that I'd be taking her to America where I will have a new job in a western copper mine. I've been studying for the job for over a year and it's now come to pass. But leaving Glasgow and Shannon behind pains me. I've thought about waiting a year to get settled but I don't want to risk losing her. I'll be leaving with Mr. Geoffrey Gibbons next month and I want Shannon to come with me as Mrs. Tom Lawson. Also, understand that I haven't asked Shannon to be my wife; she knows nothing of this meeting."

The big, usually gruff Irishman looked at Tom and called out to the barkeep for two whiskies. "I've dreaded this day since you came to our home, but I knew that Shannon would be leaving us someday. I believe you're a good man, Tom Lawson, and will look after my girl." Raising his glass, he toasted, "And it's damn well better it's an American she'll be marrying and not some Englishman! You have my permission, son."

When Tom and Shannon met the next Saturday for tea, it was clear that Matt hadn't said a word to his daughter about their meeting. Shannon interrupted Tom's daydream of how he would propose. "Tom, you're off in another world. What is it that's bothering you?"

"Shannon, I got the word from Britsco this week that I'm being transferred back to the States. I want you to come with me."

"Tom, what do you mean? I should leave my family, quit my job at the library, and just pack up and follow you? Just what kind of woman do you think I am?"

"Shannon, I think you are the most beautiful girl in the world and I want to be with you for the rest of my life. I love you and I want you to be my wife. Will you marry me?"

Slamming down her cup into the saucer, Shannon McGuire burst into tears, crying, "Then why didn't you ask me in the first place! Of course, I'll marry you; that's if my father gives his consent." With a huge smile Tom took Shannon's hand in his. "I met with Matt this week and after a pint and a whiskey, he gave us his blessing. Now let's go tell your mother and sister the wonderful news."

CHAPTER 57

Rachel's Decision

AS THE DAYS TURNED INTO weeks, the sickness peaked then gradually relaxed its deadly hold on the villages comprising the Rodriguez estate. Isolated infrequent incidents were quickly associated with people who had relaxed their control and stopped boiling water. Most of the severe cases in the hospital had recovered and were discharged but the overall threat remained. Dr. Rachel Lawson knew that stringent water discipline had to be maintained or another, more widespread epidemic might occur. Providing a pure water supply for over 2,000 people was going to require a permanent solution and substantial investment. And she wasn't pleased with Carlos's reaction to building a waterworks.

After several weeks of study, Rachel was convinced that the contamination was confined to wells 1,2,3, and 4. All were relatively old, shallow wells in the path of the ancient streambed. The wells were originally dug by hand and lined with stones and mortar to prevent sand and dirt from collapsing into the water. She also learned that the water would sometimes turn cloudy and unsanitary after severe storms. Occasionally, cases of dysentery would appear but nothing like what had happened recently. The villagers usually took care of the problem by boiling water and adding herbs.

She and Carlos walked the old streambed from the wells to the reservoir and periodically took samples of the gravel down to a depth of three feet. Microscopic examination of the samples confirmed that the contaminant was cattle manure, most likely from an adjacent feedlot located between the reservoir and wells. Rachel was certain that the animal waste, deposited over many years, was the main problem. Moving the feedlots east, away from the dry wash, became project number one. Lumberto Villegas was given the job of supervising the undertaking.

Their work on the epidemic in the villages prompted Carlos to examine the mining community. "Rachel, I've been wondering why we don't have similar problems with the miners. I reviewed our underground maps and discovered that the silver deposit is centered on a fault. When I looked at the ground surface, I could trace the fault that almost runs north and south. On one side of the fault, we have limestone and sandstone; on the other, a granite intrusion that carries the ore solutions that deposit the silver minerals."

"Carlos, what you're telling me is that we have an entirely different set of conditions in the silver mining community. We should be grateful for that, but let's get back to the villages and wells 1,2,3, and 4. The wells are fouled and need to be flushed with clean water from the reservoir. Then the manure has to be removed and new pens constructed for the animals. I'd also suggest building berms around the feedlots so the containment ponds hold back water when it rains heavily. We've got to keep the dry wash free of cow manure."

Carlos agreed with Rachel's immediate plan but was still concerned about the future. "That makes sense, Rachel, but what do you have in mind for the long term? These people can't be boiling water forever."

Smiling in agreement, the doctor answered, "I thought I explained this a while back but let me go over the plan again. This is where it gets a little more complicated and a little more expensive. I believe you should build a canal or pipeline from the reservoir to a centrally located water tower or covered cistern where the water would be purified and tested on a regular basis, then delivered to several parts of the villages where it would be accessible to the people. Eventually, you should also build toilets for the villagers. These plans are only tentative, and I want to review them with Dr. Julio Gelvan in El Paso who I think has experience with municipal water and waste systems. I'm going north in a couple of days to visit my family and see how my father is getting along without me."

Carlos didn't want to see Rachel return to Arizona but knew it would be futile to argue with her. He decided to explore her staying at the ranch permanently. "Rachel, you've been here almost a month and have helped me tremendously. I want you to think about staying here with me as my wife."

"Carlos, I've thought a lot about things while being here with you. I have a much better understanding of your attachment to the estate and the people. I've also started to learn the language; that has helped me better understand the villagers' problems. And the recent epidemic has opened my eyes as to what can be accomplished here. I hope my trip to El Paso and home will give me a chance to sort things out. But understand that I will always love you." Rachel's remark hit Carlos squarely. What did she mean by that?

Carlos then produced a slightly worn, small velvet box from the inside pocket of his jacket. "You haven't told me no, so I'd like you to wear this ring I bought in Pittsburgh some time ago." He lifted the lid of the box and took out a brilliant cut two-carat diamond mounted on a thin gold band. He slid the ring on Rachel's finger and kissed her until a servant interrupted them with coffee and cookies straight from the oven.

The meeting with Dr. Julio Gelvan allowed Rachel to replace the lab equipment she had borrowed to take to Mexico. The doctor also invited her to visit a treatment plant that processed water for the city of El Paso. "You can see that most of our delivery systems are under-ground; I recommend that you do the same thing on the Rodriguez estate. Whether you use cast iron pipe or concrete is best decided by economics and availability; they both work satisfactorily."

"Rachel, your plans should work well on the estate. You're fortu-nate that you have fresh, mountain lake water to begin with. Gravity is an ancient and tried method when it comes to moving water over any distance. Just keep in mind that you will need several trained techni-cians to monitor the water supply. When you get started on a sewer sys-tem, we can talk further."

Kate Lawson spotted her daughter's engagement ring immediately and grilled Rachel with questions. "Does this mean you plan on living in Mexico and raising a family there? Are you sure about your feelings for Carlos? What about your medical career?"

"I don't know for certain, Mom, but it's something I want to talk to you and Dad about. It's a big decision."

Ben Lawson was happy to hear of his daughter's engagement and her work helping with the epidemic. He soothed any bad feelings she might have had about leaving him to work alone. "Rachel, forget about the disruption to my medical practice. I've already hired a young doc-tor from St. Louis who will be here in a few weeks. If you decide to stay here, that will be fine; there's plenty of work for three doctors. But I think you should think hard about your relationship with Carlos and what life in Mexico might mean for your medical career."

Rachel spent several days with her mother exploring the River Bend Ranch and visiting with her brother Sam and his wife Bonnie. She saw how happy they were in their marriage, the prospect of becoming parents, and their new venture into farming. After much thought, she decided that her life was not really fulfilled unless she was with Carlos, the man she truly loved. During dinner one evening, Rachel announced her decision to return to Mexico.

"More than anything, I love Carlos and know that his attachment to his grandfather's estate is profound. I want to be by his side as his wife and helper. From a professional standpoint, there's much important work to be done: building a hospital, developing a pure water supply, and constructing a sewage treatment plant, just to name a few. This work will never make headlines in Boston, but it sure is important to a few thousand Mexicans and to me, too. And I guess I can live pretty well as Senora Rodriguez Bruner."

CHAPTER 58

Tom and Shannon Arrive in Arizona

SHANNON LAWSON WAS OVERWHELMED BY the hospitality of Dr. Ben and Kate Lawson. Unfortunately, the rough ocean crossing and transcontinental train ride had left her feeling exhausted and unwell. Geoffrey Gibbons insisted that Tom take a month off before starting work at the newly named Britsco Copper Hill Mining Company, Ltd.

Geoffrey's words were music to Shannon's ears. "Tom, you've worked hard this past year and a half and the company wants you to take a break. You're newly married, have family in Arizona, and this is a good time to get away. Once you're on site, you'll be working long hours at least six days per week. Besides, it will also give me time to get reacquainted with Konrad Bruner and B.J.Kimball."

Ben Lawson and his wife quickly understood the reason for Shannon's fatigue and morning sickness. After a brief examination, Shannon learned she was eight weeks pregnant. While secretly pleased, she wasn't sure how her husband would react to the news. Discussing the surprise with Bonnie Lawson, now the mother of three children, she was happy to hear, "Shannon, forget about how it will affect Tom's work; he'll be delighted." And of course, her prediction was correct.

That night, when Tom asked how she was feeling, Shannon told him the news. "After seeing your father today, I learned that my exhaustion is not due to the trip from Scotland." A little confused, Tom answered, "I don't understand. What has this got to do with visiting my father?"

"Tom, it's nothing to do with your parents, except your father is a doctor, and his examination revealed that I'm pregnant. In about seven months, I'm going to have a baby. How does that sound?"

Stunned, Tom blurted, "Oh my God! I can't believe it, Shannon. How did it happen?" His display of happiness made Shannon laugh. "You ninny, you better know how it happened."

As Shannon began to feel better, Tom showed her around Ribera. She enjoyed meeting the Bookers and their daughter Soleado and dining with Barney and Sophie Pryor who was ready to give birth to their first child any day. The friendliness of the people helped her decide that she liked the American West. As the end of their vacation neared, Tom worried about Shannon living alone in Globe while he worked at the mine. With no family or friends close by, he thought it might be best if she stayed in Ribera for a few months until he found a decent house for them. Except for the hotel, Gelber's general store, the assay office, and a few Mexican cafes, Tom knew little about Globe.

"Shannon, I want to talk to you about Globe. It's much larger than Ribera but it's still a frontier town that I know very little about. The mine is a three- to four-hour ride by mule from town, and I don't know much about the housing situation. Until I get a better handle on things, I think it best if you stayed here with my folks until I can come up with something. I haven't talked to my parents yet, but I know they'd be more than happy to have you stay with them. And besides, they have the room."

The idea of being apart from her new husband did not please Shannon. "I love your parents but I want to be with you, Tom. You're my husband. It can't be all that bad in Globe." Torn between his concern for Shannon's health and the housing uncertainty, Tom finally convinced her to stay behind with his parents for a month or two while he scouted a house for them in Globe. Ben and Kate Lawson were enthused with Tom's "sensible" idea and, without wishing to meddle in the couple's personal life, had secretly hoped they would reach that conclusion.

Territorial roads were generally primitive and the two-hundred mile trip to Globe was a bruising, bumpy ride over rugged mountains and across washes sometimes filled with rushing water. Tom was fortunate and was able to complete the journey in just under forty hours. Main Street in Globe had been coated with loose gravel, and there were many new buildings, shops, and restaurants. But the pride and joy of the community was the new jail with room for twelve prisoners in separate cells. Britsco Copper occupied a small building two blocks from the hotel and housed home office communications and administrative activities. Chester Haig, a transplant from Glasgow, welcomed Tom to Globe. "It's good to see you; we've been expecting you. I've got a rig that will take you most of the way to the mine or you can make the trek by mule. I think you'll see major changes along the way but let me show you a map. Not that you'd get lost, of course."

Tom changed his clothes, selected a mule and was on his way. Halfway to Camp #1, he entered a tunnel that had been gouged out of hard rock. He realized that the burrowing had eliminated several narrow, twisting portions of the original trail. He also noted tall, steel stanchions that dotted the hillside that would eventually carry ore on the tramway to a collection point. Real progress had been made in his absence. Reaching mine headquarters, Tom was surprised to see a two-storied wooden building with a painted sign announcing, "Britsco Copper Hill Mining Company, Ltd." He wondered how Konrad Bruner and B.J.Kimball had cottoned to that change. Entering the building, he was greeted by Geoffrey Gibbons, B.J., and Konrad who were studying a sand table replication of the topography and location of the main shaft, decline, and Camp #2. A model of the tramway was being added to the scene plus the staging area where ore would be collected for rail delivery to the smelter. Tom was pleased with the grand scheme and the fact that some of his work had been incorporated in the changes.

"We're to the point where we're making ore shipments of forty to fifty tons per day," explained Geoffrey. "That is providing us with needed operating cash. The ore we're pulling out of the decline tunnel and main shaft is running fifteen percent copper, which is better than we'd hoped for. I'll give you the grand tour tomorrow, Tom. In the meantime, we've got a room for you upstairs, and dinner is served at 5:30."

Tom thanked Geoffrey and carried his bags upstairs to his room. A private room with windows overlooking the hillside was more than he expected.

The tour included a visit to the main shaft and descent to the 150-foot level. For several hundred feet, Tom and Geoffrey followed the tunnel that had been burrowed out of rich copper ore. "Konrad is telling us that at the present time, the ore body could be three hundred to four hundred feet deep and several thousand feet across. There's no doubt that this will be a major producer for many years to come. Our biggest problem for the future is our labor force and clashes between the miners from Eastern Europe and Mexico. The Romanians and Bulgarians are natural-born agitators and are intent on organizing. They look down on the Mexicans as second-class workers. We've had slow-downs and strikes and fights between the two groups and things are not getting any better. While I'm happy with the high grading going on, we've got to look to the future and lower grade stuff. That means we should be taking a look at what's going on up in Utah, both the mining operations and also the metallurgical practices. They're getting some gold along with their copper which sure helps in making some money."

At the end of the day, Tom admitted that Britsco knew what they were doing and on a scale that he was only beginning to appreciate. After dinner, B.J. asked to speak to Tom in private. "Son, you've seen enough today to know that this ain't any gopher hole operation. I have to respect what the Scots are doing, but I don't see myself in this picture. All this machinery, hordes of people running around, fighting and yelling at one another is far away from the life I've lived and want to live. Geoffrey's busy with things I don't understand and Konrad's wrapped up calculating how much ore we've got. Hell, I ain't gonna' be around ten years from now. I've stashed my salary for the past year so I've got enough to last me for the rest of my days. So, at the end of this week, I'm movin' on, doin' what I enjoy, like prospecting. Geoffrey and Konrad already know; both were nice about my going." Shaking Tom's hand, the old prospector said his farewell. "Goodbye, son. It's been good knowin' you. You've got the spine to make it big; I expect to be seeing your name in the papers before too long."

Tom was sorry to see B.J. go. "I guess I know how you feel, B.J. You started the whole thing. I reckon I'm a bit jealous, too. Where are you looking for your next bonanza?"

B.J.'s eyes glistened as he broke into a wide grin. "Tom, I hear good things about Colorado gold so I'll be going to a place called Cripple Creek. I understand there's some serious gold up thataway and I'm gonna' see if I have one more strike left in me. I'll miss you and Konrad. You take good care of yourself and that Irish lassie of yours. Sounds like you've got a winner there, too." By the end of the week, B.J. Kimball had risen early and quietly left the Britsco mining camp ready for his new adventure in the Rocky Mountains of Colorado.

Tom was disturbed by B.J.'s departure and buttonholed Konrad one day to share his concern. Talking outside the head frame of the main shaft, Bruner gave his view of the old man's decision. "Don't worry about B.J., Tom. He'll get along just fine. He was smart enough to realize that he likes discovery work more than the development of a big operation like the one we have here. It's a natural evolution of things. He made the discovery, and then engineers and financial people come in and take over. Outside money and founders rarely work well together. Geoffrey would have never fired B.J., but the oldster was getting bored and knew his days were numbered. It's got nothing to do with money; he's the kind of person who works best by his lonesome."

Tom Lawson soon plunged into the job of assistant general manager and took on the task of sorting out the labor situation as his first challenge. He began by talking to the Mexican workers he already knew at the mine and in the town. They complained to Tom about the two-tiered pay scale and disputes with the Bulgarians and Romanians. When he talked with the leaders of the Balkan group, he learned that housing and dislike of Mexicans were at the top of their list of grievances. Continued discussions didn't change things one bit, however. He finally concluded that they might never become close friends but could learn to respect one another. Extracting promises from both parties, Tom began construction of a dormitory and cookhouse and opened a company store where workers could buy denim clothing, boots, and sundries. He also promised family housing after the main shaft was sunk 300 feet and the tramway was in operation. Gradually, Britsco Copper Hill Mining Company began to develop as a self-contained unit and was no longer tethered to the town of Globe. On the personal side, Tom was able to promise Shannon that a house would be available for them in about six months.

Tom's next assignment was to visit Bingham Canyon, Utah, to study mining operations and the extraction plant. The mine was a huge operation, mining and processing over 50,000 tons of ore per day. The unique floatation techniques allowed for separating copper, gold, silver, and molybdenum from the low-grade ores. When he explained what he'd seen, both Konrad and Geoffrey agreed that this would open many more properties in Arizona, New Mexico, and Utah. The ability to mine ore containing two percent copper with some gold, silver, molybdenum and sometimes tungsten would enable the western United States to become a world-class producer. Even the normally conservative Geoffrey Gibbons was optimistic in his reports to the home office.

As B.J. Kimball's discovery ballooned into an operating mine, Konrad recognized that his specialized training made him an employee of Britsco but not a member of top management where key decisions were made. While as part owner he would receive healthy dividends one day, he was no longer a member of the inner circle that determined the direction of capital spending and other major issues. Geoffrey always kept him informed as to what was going on but usually after the decision had been made. It was also clear to him that Tom would eventually run the business. In spite of his liking for the young man, Konrad couldn't see himself reporting to someone twenty-five years younger than himself. The German decided that being a big fish in a small pond—like owning and running the Ocotillo Mine—was more to his liking. And the possibility of becoming a mining consultant had some appeal.

Konrad discussed his future with Geoffrey and Tom. "Both of you are to be congratulated on the progress of Britsco Copper Hill Mining Company. It's wonderful to see a dream come to fruition. There's no doubt in my mind that this mine will reward its shareholders handsomely in the future. At the same time, I don't have the interest in a big operation as I did with the original prospecting and exploring the geology of a new discovery. Why, it won't be long before we see families moving in, then schools, churches, and hospitals being built. Then there will be a smelter to add hundreds more to the population."

Sensing the departure of another friend and old colleague, Tom spoke up, "Wait a minute, Konrad. You're one of the original founders of this company. I sure hope you're not thinking of leaving us."

"Yes, Tom, that's exactly what I have in mind. I see my contribution as about over. The deposit is pretty well defined, we know there's enough ore in the ground for well over ten years, and that's without knowing how deep the high-grade stuff goes. The analytical, creative judgments have been replaced by more routine work that can be taken care of by Ted Braxton. Give me a couple of months to supervise and train him for the work I'm now doing and I'll give you my replacement at half the salary. He's got a good mind and the solid background to handle the job."

Geoffrey Gibbons entered the conversation to have the last word. "Konrad, ever since B.J. moved on, I've had the feeling you might get restless and come up with the same idea. I don't want to see you go, so please think it over for a week before making a final decision. Don't underestimate your importance to our success. We need your technical know-how."

CHAPTER 59

Konrad Resigns

A WEEK AFTER THE BRIEF conversation with Geoffrey Gibbons and Tom Lawson about his future, Konrad Bruner had made his decision. At peace with it, the German slept late, enjoyed his sundowner whiskey and water, and challenged Ted Braxton with more demanding assignments. "Tom, I've made my decision. I'll be leaving Britsco in another month or so and will formalize my decision with Geoffrey in the morning. I've given a lot of thought about the work and have decided to move on. I have no regrets. Just keep on doing what you're doing and get me some dividends," he said to his young protégée with a smile.

Tom Lawson was deeply disappointed but tried not to show it. "Konrad, I sure hate to see you leave; you've been like a father to me. Without your guidance and training, I'd never be where I am today. But I know you've thought long and hard about your decision and I respect that." Shaking the older man's hand, he added, "I wish you the very best of luck in whatever you decide to do. You're not going to retire to some old creaky rocking chair, are you?"

"Not a chance, Tom. Geoffrey plans on putting me on a consulting retainer, which means I'll still be involved with Britsco Copper Hill Mining. It's non-restrictive, so I might consult for other companies, particularly those in the exploratory stage. Otherwise, I'm not sure what I'll be doing. I read an article in a recent Phoenix newspaper about a new dam being built east of the city for flood control and irrigation. I think I'll take a look at it and do a little sightseeing along the way, then get down to Ribera and see how things are at the Ocotillo Mine. From there, I may go to Mexico to visit with my son Carlos. It's been a while since I've seen him and his estate. After the past hectic four years, I may even slow down a bit and smell the desert flowers."

Construction on the Salt River Dam #1, as it was originally known, began in 1903 at the confluence of the Salt River and Tonto Creek. Access to the construction site was provided by the Apache Trail that ran from Apache Junction to Miami, a distance of sixty miles. The portion of the dam to Miami was cut through rolling hills; the section from the dam to Apache Junction was a tortuous, narrow, twisting roadway with spectacular views. Over four hundred Pima and Apache Indians built it by chiseling a side cut path from solid rock. The trail enabled Phoenix merchants to participate in the economic boom created by the construction site.

Konrad rode horseback to the dam, leisurely taking in the flora and fauna of the area. From time to time, he spotted deer, javelina, and jack rabbits. Arriving at the engineering marvel, his trained eye carefully examined the narrow canyon and crush of workers excavating rock from adjacent quarries. Destined to be the largest masonry dam in the world at a height of 280 feet, the Salt River Dam would create a reservoir of over one million acre feet and generate 36,000 kilowatts of electricity. Konrad sat in wonder as hundreds of laborers scurried from the quarry to deliver rock to the masons building the dam.

Sam Hellman, an experienced construction engineer from Wisconsin, gave Konrad a tour of the construction site. Hellman was happy to meet a fellow engineer from the copper mines of Pinal County. "I almost took a job in Morenci a few years ago but decided that this project was more secure and would keep me on a payroll for at least six or seven years. I wasn't too sure if that mine would make a go of it, and with a wife and five kids, I decided to take this job. I'm not sorry I did. The heat can be hellish at times but I'm more than satisfied. We started here in 1903 and if we don't get flooded out again, should complete things by 1910 or so. Take your time in looking around. I think you'll be impressed with what we're doing. By the way, if you're the courageous type, take the stagecoach from here to the Mesa train station; you'll see some spectacular country."

Hellman was right. The quarrying of stone, the actual building of the dam, and the way water was controlled as construction progressed was certainly impressive. Deciding to ride the Tonto Wagon Road, Konrad bid Sam goodbye and joined three passengers on the descent to Apache Junction and Mesa. Barely into the drive, they realized they were in for a harrowing experience. The steep grades, dust, sharp turns, and narrow roadbed provided many thrills and the risk of toppling over the unprotected edge of the trail. Below, the deep gorge of the Salt River added to the sense of apprehension; one slip over the edge and the coach and its passengers would plummet down a slope of 500 feet or more to certain death.

All passengers breathed a sigh of relief when they reached the valley floor. Konrad then rode south through the cotton fields of Chandler, crossing the Gila River Indian Reservation and finally connecting with transportation that took him from Casa Grande to Tucson and Ribera. Old friends welcomed the stranger back home before he reopened his office, closed for over three years.

"Konrad, it's good to see you again. I was afraid you were gone for good with that copper mine of yours," Barney Pryor said over dinner at the Whitman Hotel. "Sophie is busy with the baby but should be here shortly as soon as she puts the little guy to sleep. In the meantime, we can talk business. Tent City is still prospering from Bowie River gold even though production is probably off twenty-five percent. Gold strikes in Colorado have attracted some of the local marginal miners but overall, we've nothing to complain about."

Barney's news came as no surprise to Konrad who knew about the continual search for bonanzas that kept miners on the move. It was the Ocotillo Mine that interested him.

"We're down to the 500 foot level at the mine, still following the main ore body," Barney reported. "The grade has tapered off a bit but we're producing around 150 tons per day. Haulage to Copper Flats is sometimes a problem but only because we're short of good teamsters. We train them and the next thing we know, they're off to Bisbee or Tombstone. Growler Creek doesn't supply the kind of entertainment that competes with those two towns. Come up to the mine for a look-see. After all, you're still majority owner. And for the record, ISC smelter is very careful about dumping anything into the river."

As Konrad passed the desk on the way to his room, the clerk handed him a bunch of letters. He glanced at them, noting the one from Zacatecas, Mexico. Ripping open the letter, he eagerly read news from his son Carlos:

"Dear Father—On contacting Britsco Copper Hill Mining Company, I learned you were no longer in their employ and were on your way back to Ribera. If Dr. Rachel Lawson is still in town she can tell you about some of the problems we have down here. The biggest one has been an epidemic caused by the contamination of the water supply. I believe we now have it under control. We've also had a major management shakeup in our silver mining operations after it was discovered that Carlos Ortega and a ring of associates were stealing silver ingots and selling them to crooked brokers."

"But that's not the main reason for my writing. I hope you are interested in returning to Zacatecas for a spell, or maybe for good. We've had to deal with poorly trained miners for years and I've decided to do something about it. I've discussed this with the dean of engineering at the university, and he is very interested in upgrading the schools of mining, geology, and metallurgy. In combining these three disciplines, I've committed to funding a new building and three new professorships. I would like you to meet with Dr. Soledad to suggest how we might accomplish this at a reasonable cost, of course. If we can put a good plan together, we should be able to break ground a year from now. I plan to name the new building after my grandfather, Amelio Rodriguez, but I have not spoken to Dr. Soledad about it."

"As you know, I inherited most of my grandfather's estate and his responsibilities as patron to many, many people. As a result, I feel compelled to stay here; being an absentee owner wouldn't work. Frankly, it's a responsibility I gladly accept. In the short period since my return from New York, I've leaned that I love Mexico and the hacienda. If I can find a way to have Rachel and you join me, my life would be complete."

Konrad retreated to the privacy of his room and smiled as he read the letter a second time, tears streaming down his cheeks.

CHAPTER 60

Konrad and Rachel Meet

RACHEL LAWSON KNOCKED GENTLY BEFORE entering her father's consultation room. She was embarrassed to intrude on a conversation between Ben Lawson and Konrad Bruner. She recognized the German but only knew of him as the man who had become wealthy from gold and silver mining.

"Excuse me, gentlemen. I had no idea you were in conference."

Before she could leave, both men invited her to sit down and join in the conversation. "Rachel, Mr. Bruner is visiting in Ribera before he goes to Mexico to see his son. He's decided to donate some money to the Doctor Gilroy Hospital, but it's better if he tells you his story."

Reserved at first, Konrad soon relaxed and explained how he came by his wealth. "I got my first opportunity when your father was able to talk his brother Tom into letting me become a partner in the Ocotillo Mine. It wasn't anything like it is today, just a short tunnel into a mountain. But your uncle was convinced that it was a major strike. I joined the partnership as a mining engineer and eventually became a twenty-five percent owner in the mine. For over fifteen years now, it's been a steady producer of high-grade ore, and it should continue for at least ten more. When your uncle was killed in the sabotage and explosion, your father's decision to sell out allowed me to increase my ownership share. With some of the profits from the silver mine, I joined up with a young man from New York who was visiting Ribera in the hope of setting up a general store. We bought gold-bearing ground that was next to the existing river deposits of the Bowie River. Peter Hillenbrand was a young man in a hurry. I had examined the area pretty thoroughly and had a good idea of its gold potential, which I shared with Peter. To this day, I can't explain why Peter walked away from our venture but he did, and I became sole owner of a major portion of the placer deposits. Sometimes, luck is more important than technical knowledge. I never heard from Peter Hillenbrand again."

Rachel was mesmerized as Konrad continued. "As a result of my local success, I had visions of becoming a copper baron, which is an entirely different affair. Precious metals are easily converted into cash, but copper mining requires far more investment, patience, and a broad set of skills that I didn't possess, as I soon learned. Finance and managing operations on a grand scale don't suit me. I gave up four years of my life and most of my fortune to find this out. But I met some remarkable people along the way. Your brother Tom is one of them. He has the know-how and ambition to be a corporate copper miner, and I believe he will succeed very well. He's learned how mineral exploration, mining operations, transportation and smelting, and money must all come together if a company is going to succeed. He also works well with people, a necessary trait if one is going to supervise employees and talk to shareholders. I've rambled on for too long, please excuse me."

"Not at all, Mr. Bruner," Rachel replied. "Your story is fascinating, especially when I understand the involvement of my father and late uncle. I've been away from Ribera studying medicine for the past couple of years and never heard about this adventure."

Konrad thanked Rachel for her patience and picked up his story. "Now where was I? Oh yes, several months ago, I decided I wasn't interested in being part of a big, complicated mining company. The Britsco people were kind enough to offer me a consultancy and retention of a small ownership position in the mine, a good deal for both of us. On reflection, I realized how much I owed your father and the town of Ribera for my good fortune. So, I'm making a donation to the hospital that will erase the debt and provide an endowment for the directors."

Ben Lawson interrupted the German, chiding him for his modesty. "Your gift is beyond measure, Konrad. Taking care of our debt relieves us of a major burden, and the endowment will enable us to become one of the best small hospitals in the Southwest."

Konrad thanked Ben Lawson for his kindness and turned his attention to Rachel. "Miss Rachel, you must tell me more about your engagement to my son. He's certainly not the best letter writer in the world, as you probably know, and this development is surprising for sure."

Rachel looked at Konrad in stunned silence, now recognizing that the man sitting across from her was her future father-in-law. Without a word from his son, how had Konrad Bruner learned of her engagement to Carlos?

CHAPTER 61

The Kidnapping

AFTER TALKING WITH KONRAD BRUNER and her father, Rachel accepted the idea of traveling to Zacatecas with Bruner. Beneath his reserved appearance, the engineer was interesting and pleasant to be with. He was also her future father-in-law, and it was time she got to know him. So, Rachel Lawson and Konrad agreed to meet for lunch in El Paso before boarding the train for the ride to the interior of Mexico.

Konrad opened the conversation. "I think you have been wise to work with someone familiar with water purification, delivery systems, and waste removal. It's been a while since I spent any time at the Rodriguez ranch, but I agree that modern sanitation for miners and villagers has been put off for too long. I have no doubt that Carlos will agree to invest the money to do what is necessary. It will protect the health of his employees, but more important, it's the right thing to do. That's obviously his mother's contribution to his gene pool."

The mention of Carlos's mother sparked Rachel's curiosity. "Konrad, tell me about her. What was she like?" the young doctor asked. They left the dining room and retreated to the patio for coffee and dessert. Konrad insisted that Rachel try some marzipan, a sweet made of crushed almond paste and sugar brought to the New World from Spain. "It's very sweet but goes well with the strong Mexican coffee," he added. "Now, to answer your question about Carlos's mother."

"Luisa was the only daughter of Amelio Rodriguez. She was kind, beautiful, and the love of my life. We met after I had left England to work with the patron in his silver mines. It was love at first sight, at least for me. Most of our meetings were chaperoned by an older woman who shadowed us wherever we went. On occasion, we would ride together and talk but always in sight of Anna Maria. We feel deeply in love but could never resolve our differences over her Catholic faith and my ambition to have my own mining company. The local priest was of no help, and Luisa's chaperone did her best to keep us apart. When I left Zacatecas, I had no idea that Luisa was pregnant with Carlos. I only learned of his existence when the patron notified me of Luisa's death in Barcelona, Spain. At the funeral, I learned that his grandfather and a governess, as instructed by Luisa who had joined a convent and left Mexico, had raised my son. You have no idea what it was like to learn that I had fathered a child and lost the most wonderful woman in the world." Tears welled in Konrad's eyes as Rachel hung on his words. "I've never forgiven myself for allowing religious beliefs and foolhardy ambition from marrying someone who I loved with all my heart."

As the train pulled away from the station that afternoon, Rachel thought about Konrad's story. Two people loved each other but conflicting religions, cultural ties, and stubbornness, perhaps equally shared, had ruined their lives. Carlos was undoubtedly raised a Catholic but had never mentioned his religious beliefs. Rachel attended Protestant church services casually but didn't possess strong feelings about religion. Would religion be an issue between them, particularly when it came to raising children? She slept fitfully as the possibility of a disagreement over religion filled her mind.

Barely past dawn, Rachel was awakened by the sound of steel wheels grinding to an abrupt halt. As she lifted the shade to peer outside, she heard Konrad hammering on her compartment door, shouting, "Get dressed quickly; we're being held up by bandits. Hurry, they've taken over the train!"

When the train arrived in Zacatecas, six hours late, Carlos was not overly concerned until he saw his father being helped from the train. His head was heavily bandaged and his arm was held in a sling. One of his eyes was closed with a cut above the brow. Seeing Carlos, Konrad cried out, "I'm so sorry, Carlos! I tried to hold them off but there were too many of them. They've taken Rachel and are holding her for ransom." He then collapsed into Carlos's arms, rasping incoherently about the robbery. The conductor then told Carlos and Lumberto the story of how the train was robbed and Rachel abducted.

"The banditos placed a log across the tracks where we normally slow down; it's a part of the country that is quite desolate. Their leader instructed his men to take the money and jewelry from the passengers, and then went into the sleeping car. He beat Senor Bruner into sub-mission and broke down the door of the lady's compartment and took her prisoner. He rifled through her belongings and discovered that she was betrothed to Carlos Rodriguez Bruner. I heard him shout to his men, 'Julio, tell the others. We've hit the jackpot. The lady's ransom will bring us a fortune.' I'm sorry, but that's all I can tell you. All of this has been reported to the authorities. I pray for her release."

Carlos was frantic and his first thought was to hire a posse and track down the bandits. Lumberto cautioned him against this, however. "No, no, Carlos. We must be patient and carefully think about what to do. I will send three of our best men to locate the kidnappers. If they are politicos, they want money to fight against the government and proba-bly will not harm her."

Near collapse with fear and grief, Carlos agreed to Lumberto's plans. "Get on with it then," he shouted to his trusted friend. "Before I go mad."

Three days after Rachel's abduction, a peasant wearing a white arm-band delivered a note to Carlos from the kidnappers. He'd been picked out of a crowd and paid to deliver the message, nothing more. The ban-dits demanded 500,000 pesos in coin to be delivered by a single, unarmed man to a remote village location. The details of the handover would be specified at a later date. Carlos was commanded to acknowl-edge the message by raising a white flag at the ranch house. This would signify his agreement to the bandits' demands.

Meanwhile, Lumberto's scouts had scoured the countryside where the holdup took place. "All the evidence points to a group of student revolutionaries and farmers who are led by a former army officer by the name of Antonio Gaspar," Lumberto reported back to Carlos. "He's very popular with the people of the area because he usually robs and steals from the government and distributes money and food to the poor. No one we met would admit to seeing a woman with the bandits for fear of jeopardizing their families. But one village elder heard that someone—maybe a woman—had treated a group of sick people in a mountain village. Carlos, I believe Rachel is alive and safe. Just do what they tell you to do; they are ruthless criminals. That's all I can tell you."

Carlos agreed to Gaspar's demands and raised the white flag while Lumberto talked with Felipe Vierra, the man chosen to deliver the money to the specified location. After two exasperating days, the ban-dits delivered a second message to the ranch. On a certain day and time, the ransom money was to be dropped off at a village plaza and left next to a fountain. All villagers would have been evacuated and local police bribed to stay at least five miles away. The money would be picked up, counted, and Rachel released at a different location and time. Colonel Antonio Gaspar, commander of the First Revolutionary Brigade of Mexico, signed the note. As instructed, Carlos raised a white flag to the top of the flagpole, signifying his compliance.

Early the next morning, Carlos received the anticipated directions. At four o'clock that afternoon, Felipe Vierra rode into the deserted village of Santo Domingo and left 500,000 bagged pesos on the steps of the village fountain. Four masked bandits appeared, thanked the courier for being on time and told him to leave; a message would be delivered to the hacienda the following day.

Carlos and Lumberto were pleased to see the safe return of Felipe but were apprehensive over having to wait another day for Rachel's return. They were also disappointed to learn that the thieves wore bandanas that covered their faces and made it impossible to identify them. Would Gaspar keep his word, kill the hostage, or demand more money? Father Petrillo provided the answer the following morning, when he escorted Rachel Lawson to the hacienda, unharmed. "Senor Carlos, we found her this morning, bound and gagged, as we went to fetch water. She's tired and wants to bathe more than anything else, that is, after seeing your first."

Lumberto watched as Carlos and Rachel wept and embraced each other. "Thank God you're safe, Rachel!" Carlos exclaimed. "I never want to go through something like this ever again. Were you treated all right?"

Still shaky from the ordeal, Rachel replied, "They didn't hurt me but at times I thought they were going to. Some of the gang members were bad actors, always eyeing me with lewd grins. The commander made it clear to them that he would not tolerate any harm to me. It was nerve wracking being blindfolded and moved around to a different place every night. I have no idea where they took me after we left the train."

When Rachel went to her room to clean up and rest, Carlos and Lumberto thanked Felipe for a job well done. Lumberto was quietly pleased: Carlos wasn't aware of it yet but men like Felipe were going to be needed to protect the ranch. With talk of revolution blowing through the land, estates the size and wealth of the Rodriguez Bruner spread were vulnerable. Weak or non-existent state militias would not be able to guarantee the safety of the patron and his family. One question remained: how best to deal with Colonel Antonio Gaspar before he spends the 500,000 pesos?

CHAPTER 62

A Family Reunion

AMERICAN INDUSTRY GREW BY LEAPS and bounds as the twentieth century emerged. Andrew Carnegie built steel plants, Rockefeller founded Standard Oil Company, and Henry Ford invented the mass production of automobiles. Railroads and the telephone and telegraph connected the Atlantic and Pacific coasts. The Spanish-American War saw the United States annex the Philippine Islands, Puerto Rico, and Hawaii. Congress funded the construction of a navy—the "great white fleet"—to support America's entrance on the world stage as a power to be reckoned with.

The industrialization was financed by money tycoons from the East and powered by the cheap labor of thousands of immigrants primarily from southern and eastern Europe but also from Asia, the British Isles, and all over the Americas. The newcomers settled in the cities—now electrified—and spread out across the nation to build the railroads, string the telegraph wires, and work in the mines of the West. In the Arizona Territory, mining towns like Bisbee, Jerome, Ray, Globe, and Miami sprang up to meet the demand for the red metal. In a relatively short number of years, the Globe-Miami district became a major world copper producer.

Shannon Lawson's relocation to Globe had been delayed by the arrival of her twin sons, Caleb and Martin. Their births had been eased by the loving care provided by her in-laws, Dr. Ben Lawson and his wife, Kate. During her pregnancy, the young Irish girl's loneliness was eased by her growing friendship with Kate Lawson. After the birth of the boys, Kate and Shannon shifted their thoughts to Tom and Shannon's move to the mining town. Tom Lawson claimed that housing for his wife and young family was non-existent but Kate Lawson believed otherwise. Tired of her son's excuses, she decided it was best if she, Shannon, and the boys—now three months old—moved north and found their own housing.

Upon their arrival in Globe, Kate and Shannon booked rooms in the Highland Hotel and began their search. After a week of asking questions, walking up and down muddy streets, and checking out leads, they found a two-storied house vacated only a day before and took over the first floor. Kate Lawson scoured the town for bedding, cribs, furniture, and kitchen equipment, and inside of a week, the family declared 14 Elm Street to be their new home. Only then did Kate suggest that Shannon leave a note at the Britsco office announcing their arrival.

Tom Lawson was confused and annoyed when he received the message that his family was in town. He couldn't believe his wife had brought his infant sons north and couldn't fathom why his mother had gotten involved. He was also upset that their arrival in Globe was going to take attention away from the demands of the mine.

Tom realized he was in trouble when he knocked at the door of 14 Elm Street. "Tom, you've been up here for over a year while your wife waited for you to locate a house," his mother scolded. "Your brief visits to Ribera only increased her loneliness and frustration. I can see that Globe is a noisy, crowded town filled with rowdy miners, but I can't help but think that you didn't work very hard to take care of your family. No excuses, son. We found this place in less than a week, and while it's not a paradise, it will allow you to be with your wife and children. Now, you better make peace with Shannon and get to know your boys. And learn to appreciate that your wife is a wonderful person. You're a lucky man."

Tom walked to the rear of the house where his wife and Caleb and Martin were fast asleep. Gently tapping Shannon's shoulder, Tom met his wife's silent stare. Furious, she admonished, "Don't you start telling me about how overworked you are at the mine because I'm not interested. What I want from you is help getting us settled in this house and getting a room fixed up for your mother. We need a bed, a mattress, a chest of drawers, and a small table to start. We were able to find this house without too much trouble; I'd expect you to outfit a room without too much of a problem. You owe her a lot, Tom. She's been an angel to the boys and me. Without her, I think I would have been on my way back to Scotland long ago."

Realizing the severity of the situation, Tom quietly decided to do as he was told. "I'm sorry Shannon. I've missed you terribly." The crying of two hungry babies interrupted Tom and Shannon's embrace. The speed with which she broke away from his hold told Tom that his sons had priority for Shannon's attention. Times have changed, he contemplated.

Geoffrey Gibbons, whose wife had been in Globe for six months, only smiled when Tom told him that he would be going home for dinner at the end of the day. The two men agreed that when the railroad was completed to the staging area, they would proceed on building a company town with housing for bachelors, families, a general store, a first aid station, and a school. A church would be left for the general population to decide on.

In 1909, the first train belched and chugged into the Britsco mine property. All the hard work of B.J., Konrad, Geoffrey, and Tom, supported by Scottish money, began to show the wisdom of developing Copper Hill into Britsco Copper Hill Mining Company, Ltd. While the mine was still not breaking even, Geoffrey Gibbons was confident that under Tom's leadership, Britsco had a successful operation and that it was time for him and his wife to return home. With mixed emotions, the Gibbons left by train for New York and the ship that would take them to Glasgow.

Tom's first independent move as manager was to create two new management positions to run underground operations and above ground ore handling, crushing, and transportation. Tom shifted his attention to the construction of the town and meeting with Dan Jackling, the successful engineer from Utah who had revolutionized mining and milling low-grade copper ores. Jackling's visit confirmed that in all likelihood, huge quantities of low-grade porphyry-type ores underlay the enriched copper near the surface. The visitor also influenced Tom to consider a new extraction-floatation process and the construction of a company-owned smelter.

As building began on the town, Tom began spending more time on the job and missing dinner meals at home. At first, Shannon said nothing and hoped it was only temporary. But when it persisted, Kate Lawson decided it was time for a talk with her son.

"Tom, it's easy to see that you've accomplished a lot and have a big job running Britsco's operations here. And the construction of a town is a new venture for you. I've only been here a month or so but in watching how Geoffrey did things, I came away impressed with the way he balanced business demands with family obligations. I also got to know his wife Corliss and listened to some of her observations. They were a lovely couple with experience living in a variety of conditions in several countries. I think you have to review your role as general manager and father and husband. Shannon hasn't said a word to me, but I've noticed that you seem to be focused more on your job to the detriment of your marital responsibilities. You've been missing dinner again, far too often."

Tom bristled at his mother's remarks but thought better of telling her to mind her own business. Kate Lawson continued. "You're up at dawn, gone for the day, and sometimes bring home paperwork to do before retiring. Shannon has been far more patient about this behavior than I would be. All she seems to do is wash clothes, feed the babies, clean house, and prepare meals for a husband who never shows up to eat them."

"Mother, I work hard because I'm learning on the job and someone has to do it. And you can tell Shannon if she has something on her mind, she should come to me and not go running to you."

"Tom, for someone as smart as you, you're acting like a complete blockhead. Shannon isn't complaining to me; I just see it in her eyes and how tired she is. I'm leaving here in a week to get back home and she'll have her hands full. Now think about how you're going to help her. Think about your wonderful wife and two adorable boys. Think about what is really important to you."

Tom digested his mother's remarks and had to admit she was right. He pondered his problem for a few days and then, one early evening, asked Shannon to join him for dinner while Kate tended to the children.

"Shannon, Mom is leaving in a few days and I know it's not going to be easy for you without help. I've hired Mrs. McGonigle to help you during the mornings. If that works out to your satisfaction, we can extend her hours. Unless it's an emergency, I'll be home by six o'clock in the evening to join you and the boys for dinner. The promotion of the two men to run the mine and my selection of a construction chief should give me the time to manage my home life a little better. I've also authorized the building of a brick house for us; I'll show you the plans tomorrow. I'm interested in what ideas you might have."

Over a warm piece of apple pie and coffee, Shannon Lawson smiled at her husband and remarked, "Well, Tom, it sounds like a major change for you; all I can say is, I'll believe it when I see it. I hope you mean what you say because the past few months have been almost impossible. The boys will be happy to see their father again."

As night approached, Tom and Shannon viewed the sunset of pink, blue, and gold streaks intermingled with puffy clouds. Holding hands, the young lass from Ireland by way of Glasgow silently thanked Kate Lawson for her understanding, wisdom, and ability to get a clear message across to her son. Somehow, this time, I think he listened, Shannon thought.

CHAPTER 63

Lieutenant Booker's
Redemption

SERGEANT MAJOR LEON PETER DIXON hadn't seen Lieutenant Vince Booker in several years. As he rode toward the main house of the Volunteer Ranch, his gaze caught several hands busy herding cattle and an expanse of land planted with wheat, corn, and vegetables. With all the trouble the lieutenant had with Caleb Benson and Major Garrison, the old pony soldier hadn't done too badly for himself. With a spread like this, I'd retire from Uncle Sam myself, the sergeant thought.

Sam Ortiz met Dixon as he got off his horse and walked to the ranch house. "Mrs. Booker is in the library and Mr. Booker is in town; he should be back in an hour or so. If you'd like, I could go into town and tell him you're here, sir."

"No thanks, Sam. Just let Mrs. Booker know that Sergeant Major Dixon from Fort Gore is here to see her and Mr. Booker." When Sam gave the news to Barbara Booker, she asked him to usher the soldier to the library and have Betty Ortiz serve coffee and some of her best cookies.

Sitting near a fire in the library, Leon Dixon was impressed with shelves filled with leather-bound books, silver spurs, army pictures, and Indian memorabilia. He was even more taken with the warmth and grace of Barbara Booker. As Dixon fought to balance his coffee cup and saucer on his knee, Barbara inquired, "To what do we owe this visit, sergeant? Vince hasn't seen anyone from the fort since his retirement. He will be so pleased to see you."

Dixon squirmed in his chair, searching for a tactful answer. He hadn't expected to be explaining anything to the lieutenant's wife without Vince being there. "I think it would be best to wait for your husband, Mrs. Booker. But I will say this: It's news from Colonel Burlingame that the lieutenant will be happy to hear."

Before he was forced to give any details, Vince Booker walked into the room, grinning. "What a sight for sore eyes! How in hell are you, Leon? And what brings you to the Volunteer Ranch?" Sergeant Major Dixon withdrew an official letter from a leather map case embossed with crossed cavalry swords. "Well, lieutenant, now that you're a civilian, I'm gonna' call you Vince." Handing the letter to the retired soldier, he went on to explain. "Colonel Burlingame had planned to deliver this message personally but he's tied up with Washington brass and politicians who are visiting the Salt River Dam construction. Some of them are also here looking over prospects for the Territory becoming a state. I'm sure you understand that if he could be here, he would."

"This here fancy box contains a medal that goes with a letter of commendation for your work on the San Carlos Indian Reservation, three, four years ago. More important to you though is the story that goes along with it. After your run-in and retirement, the colonel appointed Lieutenant Masterson to head up a board of inquiry to get to the bottom of illegal whiskey sales to the Indians. Masterson didn't make much of a fuss at first, but checked out post supply records, investigated the death of Limping Bear, and reviewed notes left by Reverend Hugh Packard, the Methodist minister. He then interviewed a whole bunch of Apaches and found that Caleb Benson was the front man for selling whiskey. He gradually collected enough evidence to convince Colonel Burlingame that Caleb was responsible for making and selling whiskey. Benson was tough to crack but Masterson was relentless and had the goods on him. Threatened with expulsion and a prison term in Yuma, Benson finally broke down and implicated Major Garrison as his partner. By shorting food and supplies due the Indians, they stole goods and sold them off the reservation. The whiskey business was where they really made big money, though."

"Benson's confession nailed Garrison. At first, the colonel couldn't believe that a fellow West Pointer could be involved in such an operation. When the major was trapped into lying, the colonel convened a general court martial. The trial went on for several weeks and Garrison was found guilty. He received a dishonorable discharge, forfeiture of pay, and ten years of hard labor at Leavenworth. The sad ending was the humiliation suffered by his family. Mrs. Garrison was a fine lady and didn't deserve that kind of treatment. Disgraced, she went back to her family home in Virginia with her children."

Caleb Benson didn't get off easily. He bribed a sentry in an attempt to escape from the guardhouse but didn't get very far. Figuring to sneak across the reservation, he was caught by some Apache braves. I won't go into the details in front of Mrs. Booker; let's just say that he died a very slow death, Apache style."

When Sergeant Dixon finished his story, Vince Booker stood up and slowly walked to the fire. Leaning on the mantle, he turned to speak. "Leon, I can't say I'm sorry for Benson and Garrison; they got what they deserved. It's a tragedy that so many Indians got sick, went blind, or died by drinking their rotgut whiskey. I can't help but think if they'd been caught earlier, I'd still be in the army and not standing here with my wife, Barbara Casey Booker. Sometimes, things do turn out for the better. I consider myself one doggone lucky guy."

As Barbara looked at her husband, she smiled and remembered their meeting at the horse trough in Tucson. Yes, she agreed, sometimes a person's misfortune does turn out for the better.

CHAPTER 64

Carlos Calls on the Mayor

GRADUALLY, RACHEL BEGAN TO FEEL better. But the kidnapping ordeal would not go away entirely. Sometimes, in the middle of the night, she would awake, convinced she was blindfolded and being moved to a new, secret location. She kept these episodes to herself believing they would fade with time. She tried hard to think about other things such as the water purification project for the villages or getting married to Carlos and adjusting to ranch life in Mexico.

One of the adjustments was the restriction placed on her freedom to travel whenever and wherever she wished. Reluctantly, Rachel accepted Carlos's demand that she never ride alone to the lake and reservoir or the fifteen miles to Zacatecas. Her recuperation had many benefits, however. Rachel began to get acquainted with the servant staff and the cooking artistry of Luz Ruiz, chief cook for many years in the Rodriguez household. Having mastered conversational Spanish, she was able to follow Luz's instructions on the basics of Mexican cuisine. To Rachel, it was miraculous what Luz could do with rice, beans, tortillas, chilies, and salsa sauce.

Rachel also had time to get to know her future father-in-law. Over morning coffee the two shared their recollection of the train robbery and Rachel's abduction. Konrad still felt guilty for not protecting Rachel. They also discussed and compared life in Arizona, Michigan, and Mexico and Konrad's student days in Germany. They talked at length about the water project and the suggestions offered by Dr. Julio Gelvan of El Paso.

"Konrad, you didn't fail me when Colonel Gaspar and the bandits took over the train. There were too many of them; they were well armed and had the advantage of surprise. We should be happy that you didn't have a pistol handy to fight them off; both of us could have been killed.

And you know that Carlos and Lumberto agree with me, so please try to put any feelings of guilt out of your mind. Besides, we've got plenty of work to do here before you take on responsibilities at the University of Zacatecas. That reminds me, how is that going?"

Konrad smiled at Rachel's question. "It's interesting, Rachel. I've had to compare my own education in Germany with Carlos's schooling at Columbia with how the Mexicans approach things. There have been many changes in course work requirements due to advances in technology. The university here in Zacatecas has a strong reputation in medicine and law but has not kept up in engineering. Mining company support has been poor in spite of the fact that they need people schooled in mining and metallurgy. It's something we have to address if we wish to meet world standards. I think Carlos has the right idea of joining mining, metallurgy, and geology into one college. We will build a separate building with laboratories and make it large enough for future expansion. Eventually, we'll have a doctoral program. It's a very ambitious plan but we have the support of Dr. Soledad who will probably retire before the project is completed. With committed funding, it should be a first class operation in five to ten years."

"With your educational background and experience, it seems to me that you'd be the logical successor to Dr. Soledad," Rachel offered.

"Thank you for the endorsement, Rachel, but before that happens I will probably have to earn a Ph.D. to make sure the academic community fully accepts me as the new dean. Dr. Soledad believes I can write my thesis on the Britsco Copper Hill Mining Company, spend a year in residence at the University of Guanajato, and fulfill the requirements for a Ph.D. degree. Once we break ground on the building, I will move to Guanajato to begin my studies. I'm actually looking forward to the challenge, and it's not that far away from the ranch. I'll be visiting the school next month to meet with the faculty to get a class schedule, meet my advisor, and receive an orientation on teaching a few undergraduate students."

"That certainly sounds exciting, Konrad. I'm glad I asked. Carlos is so wrapped up in the construction of the waterworks that I sometimes feel he's not telling me much about what's going on." Konrad picked up on the barb but decided to say nothing.

Meanwhile, Carlos had hired two student engineers from the University of Zacatecas to supervise the digging of trenches, mixing concrete, and building covered water trenches from the reservoir to the central water purification plant. They were following Dr. Gelvan's instructions and blue prints to clarify, filtrate, and disinfect water by the addition of chlorine. Carlos was satisfied that the project was well under control and would soon provide clean water to the villagers.

Enjoying a pit barbecue dinner, Carlos, Rachel, and Konrad conversed about the progress being made at the ranch. While pleased that the water project was going well, Rachel was more than a little annoyed that Carlos had not mentioned anything about wedding plans nor paid much attention to her in the past two weeks. A second glass of wine encouraged her to quip, "That all sounds great, Carlos, but when do you think you'll have time to talk about a wedding date, or is one going to take place at all?"

Carlos ignited like a firecracker. "Had you been in the field working with us you'd know that it hasn't been easy, especially with the delays on cement deliveries. And don't be so self-indulgent; it's time we put the train robbery and kidnapping behind us. And as far as a wedding is concerned, I'm ready to talk about it any time you are. You haven't said a word in weeks about any wedding."

Embarrassed to be caught in a cross fire of words between two people he loved dearly, Konrad looked at Carlos and then at Rachel, stood up, and excused himself for the evening.

"Now you've upset Konrad and chased him away from what was a nice evening," Rachel scolded. "And I resent you accusing me of still moping about the kidnapping. But the truth is I still have nightmares about it. I just can't believe you'd be so insensitive." Upset, Rachel attempted to get up but knocked over her wine glass, the red liquid splashing on her embroidered white blouse. "Now see what you've done! And don't' worry about any wedding date; I don't care if it ever happens." In tears, Rachel ran from the patio leaving Carlos speechless and bewildered. He could only shake his head as he stared into the dying charcoal embers.

The following morning, Carlos awoke early and went to the kitchen in search of Rachel. "No, senor, she is not here," replied Luz Ruiz. "I fed her fresh bread and some coffee and she left just as the sun was coming up. She didn't have her doctor's satchel with her. I think she was on her way to the stables since she was dressed for riding."

Damn that woman, Carlos muttered to himself. Angry that Rachel had disobeyed his command to never go to the reservoir or lake alone he called for Lumberto and Felipe to meet him at the stables as soon as possible. He waited for ten minutes before Felipe showed up still sleepy but ready to help the patron. "Lumberto is up on his land looking for a building site; I don't expect him until tomorrow, senor. Should I get someone else?"

"No, we'll make do," Carlos responded. The two men left the ranch, spread out from the streambed, and agreed to meet at the reservoir in two hours. If Rachel was located safe and sound, the finder was to fire two shots, then return to the hacienda with the doctor. Upset and worried for Rachel's safety, Carlos whipped his horse and took off in search of her. After riding the high ground west of the streambed, he saw the valley basin in view. His hope of finding Rachel faded as he saw no sign of his fiancée. Trying to decide whether she went north to the mountain lake, had an accident, or was taken by kidnappers again, he was close to panic when he heard two shots ring out.

Returning to the main house, he saw Felipe and Rachel enjoying a cool drink on the patio. As Felipe stood up to welcome the patron, Rachel said, "I was looking over the ditching and concrete work. The two men from the university were kind enough to show me around before Felipe arrived. I'm sorry I caused any problem. I just didn't see any need for an escort when I was so close to home. Besides, I carry a six-shooter with me now in case I run into a rattler or some other varmint. And I can shoot, too."

Carlos thanked Felipe again for finding Rachel and escorting her back to the hacienda. When his most trusted ranch hand departed, Carlos turned his attention to Rachel who sat quietly, cool and composed.

"Rachel, please look at me." As she shifted her eyes toward him, Carlos apologized for his comments of the previous evening. "You haven't seen much of Zacatecas, and I have a standing invitation from Senor Ernesto Nunez and his wife to tour the historic district anytime, at our convenience. We could go by horseback and be back here before sundown. I think you'd like Yvette Nunez and I know she's anxious to meet you. She's a charming lady whose family goes back to the original Spanish conquistadors.

Arriving in the ancient city center, Rachel was surprised to see buildings dating back to the 1600s, a magnificent cathedral, and a bustling community of thousands of people buying and selling in the open air market. She was also pleased to learn that Carlos had not exaggerated the friendliness of Yvette Nunez. Her surprises continued when she met Senor Nunez, the mayor of Zacatecas, waiting for her and Carlos in a small chapel that had two small stained glass windows, an altar, and three rows of empty oak pews. What is going on? she thought. Candles burned on either side of the altar and white flowers adorned a pair of tall pedestals. As the mayor suggested they hold hands, he placed them on an old, leather bible. Rachel turned to Carlos and whispered, "What is this all about?" Deadpan, Carlos whispered back, "Quiet, Rachel, we're getting married."

The marriage ceremony was brief and legal by Mexican law. After placing a gold band on Rachel's finger, Carlos kissed his bride, smiled broadly, and said, "And now, Mrs. Rodriguez Bruner, let's join Yvette and Ernesto for a toast before we get back to the ranch." The mayor and his wife guided the couple to an enclosed patio where toasts were exchanged and a mariachi band played traditional wedding songs.

The mayor provided a two-person carriage drawn by two horses for the newlyweds. A member of the city cavalry provided security as Rachel and Carlos made their way to the Rodriguez estate. "Carlos, this afternoon seems unreal to me. Is this some kind of joke? I insist that you stop the foolishness right now. Are we really married?"

Laughing, Carlos looked at his bride. "Believe me, Rachel, we are legally married. The civil ceremony was performed by the magistrate of Zacatecas and witnessed by Senora Nunez. An artist who specializes in wedding certificates is preparing the formal documents. Trust me, we are married and we'll sleep tonight as man and wife."

With flushed cheeks, Rachel replied, "I'm looking forward to it, darling, but what prompted you to engage the services of the mayor?"

"I've been talking to Father Petrillo for over a month about our marriage and after many discussions, I concluded that his way wasn't going to work for us. He insisted that you convert to Catholicism and receive baptism and special instructions, a process that would take months. He also insisted that we sign papers promising that all our children be raised in the Catholic faith. That got me thinking about my father's mistake in not marrying my mother. I decided I wasn't going to repeat that error; I simply love you too much. Whatever we decide for our children will be our decision; Father Petrillo isn't going to run our lives. He's upset with me but I suspect he'll get over it in time."

Rachel looked at her husband with new respect. As she examined her wedding ring, she laughingly said, "I had dreams of a big wedding with fancy gowns, bridesmaids, organ music, hymns, and a mountain of flowers. I expect my mother will be a little disappointed but I'm more than pleased with today's ceremony. Thank you, Carlos."

CHAPTER 65

Statehood

"BETWEEN THE BOOZE, BEER, CHAMPAGNE, and the parade from the Ford Hotel, I feel like I've been run over by a stampeding herd of cattle," Henry Dempsey quipped as he and his wife, Dolores, sat on the porch of their Phoenix home after a late night celebration. After many years of trying, the Territory of Arizona gained statehood on the morning of February 15, 1912, one day after President William Howard Taft signed the proclamation admitting Arizona as the forty-eighth state.

"Well, Henry, I didn't see anyone holding a gun to your head and forcing you to load up on all the free liquor," Dolores said. Henry Dempsey could only wince at his wife's barb, not expecting any sympathy for the night of carousing during which his wife had probably sipped one glass of champagne.

Draining a second cup of coffee laced with a good measure of whiskey, the lawyer squinted into the early morning sun. "It's been a memorable ten years, my dear. It's a damn shame that Don couldn't be here to celebrate the completion of the dam and the growth of the town. We sure had some ups and downs. Remember when President McKinley came out here in 1901 to look things over and how we thought we had statehood in the bag? By the time he got back to Washington, he'd forgotten most of the promises we thought we'd heard."

"Yes, Henry, I do remember, but I don't think we should overlook Congress authorizing the construction of the dam and funding the project a couple of years later." Laughing, Delores added, "Then we found out that no money had been appropriated for building a road from the

Salt River valley to the dam site. That realization brought the community together, however. Why, in less than two years and $500,000 later, we built thirty-five miles of roadway from the Mesa railhead to the dam. It also employed over four hundred Apache and Pima Indians during construction."

"I have to concede that point, Dolores. The dam has been of vital importance in controlling the Salt, Verde and Gila rivers watershed. Today, farmers in the valley grown corn, wheat, melons, cotton, and citrus fruits. Almost anything will grow here providing you have the water to irrigate the crops. Better still, we now have the ability to control flooding, store water, and release it during droughts. And to top that off, we'll soon be able to generate 36,000 kilowatts of low-cost electricity."

Just then, a familiar figure rode up to the Dempsey house. "Good morning," Eric Steinmark called out. Tieing up his horse, he climbed the four stairs to the porch, spurs clanking and gleaming in the sun. Taking a comfortable seat near the couple, Eric accepted a mug of coffee from Dolores Dempsey. "Wasn't that some party last night? Dolores, I wanted to let you know that our work in building a herd of Herefords on the Circle S Ranch has paid off to the point that I'm leaving Tempe to move to the country permanently. I'm kinda' wrapping things up now and expect to be on my way within the month. Madi and her husband Jack will take over the family farm and let Mom take it easy."

"You haven't done much with the land you and Don bought next to my place years ago. I'm asking you to consider selling out or perhaps leasing the acreage. I sure need the pastureland. Or you might be ready to get back to ranching now that all the political stuff with statehood is behind us. I've got the stock to get you started and there are plenty of people ready to buy our beef. The whole area of Globe-Miami and Superior is booming with people coming in to work in the copper mines. Down the road in Clifton-Morenci, there's more of the same. You couldn't pick a better time to get started in the cattle business. It wouldn't be retirement but it sure would be a change of pace for you and Henry. Lord knows, you've earned it after all the hard work you put in on the Salt River Dam project and winning statehood. I'll be around for a couple of more weeks. If you have a notion to get into ranching on some of the best beef pastureland in the state, let me know."

As they watched Eric canter down the road, Dolores turned to her husband. "Henry, maybe Eric's got something we should look into. Arizona's a state now and the dam is built. It might well be time for us to consider a new, different venture." Henry played with his empty coffee cup and replied, "I don't know anything about raising cattle but if you think it's worth a try, I'm willing to give it a go. Heck, there's always work for a lawyer doing wills, settling estates, and making real estate deals."

Dolores Dempsey sighed deeply and remembered her childhood on the River Bend Ranch. "I've been thinking about the political work that went into gaining statehood and completing the irrigation project. Remember the trips to Washington and the near miss of our joining with New Mexico to be one state with the capital in Sante Fe? We can be thankful that Joe Foraker of Ohio required approval by each territory and Arizona voters said no, five to one. By 1910 we got Congressional approval to form our own constitution and state government."

"By then, we got involved with the recall of members of the judiciary and President Taft vetoing our admission. Senator William Alden Smith saved our bacon with a new amendment, excepting the judges from the recall provision. Actually, I liked Beveridge of Indiana, Joe Foraker, and Hamilton of Michigan but it wasn't easy to get them to agree on something we were looking for. What concerns me is the whole unpredictability of the process and never being sure of much of anything. And women aren't overly welcome when it comes to the horse trading that goes on."

"That leads into what will probably be Arizona's next step as a new state. We'll need two senators and a representative in Washington and then a whole host of positions to be filled at the state level. With all the work we've done in the past, I wouldn't be surprised if Governor George W.P. Hunt offers us positions in his new administration. Before all that happens I want him to know that I am finished with any new project and have no interest in state politics. If you feel the same way, I think we should convey that message to his chief of staff."

"Dolores, you're way ahead of me again and I think you're right on all counts. I've had my fill of volunteering. It's time for some of the younger and more ambitious people to take over." Chuckling to himself, Henry Dempsey knew that he could very easily do without smoke-filled backrooms and endless debates.

"Henry, once we are cleared with the governor let's invite Eric Steinmark over for dinner and get his thoughts on starting a beef cattle ranch. He's been at it part-time for six or seven years and knows the territory. And, by the way, you're going to need some cowboy clothes, boots, and lessons on roping." Clicking their mugs together, the Dempseys were filled with the excitement of a new adventure.

EPILOGUE

RON BANNISTER, EDITOR THE *RIBERA Territorial* knew a good news story when he saw one. Now that he owned the paper and had monthly payments due to the previous owner, he was anxious to capitalize on the situation before him. Surveying the crowd, he was able to identify several of the people who had built the town and a few who had gone away from Ribera to enjoy greater wealth and prominence. Today's event—a funeral for one of the town's leading citizens—was more of a celebration than a typical mourning for the deceased. This was the day for flowery eulogies, remembrances, and meeting with old friends. Ron had visions of a special edition with numerous pictures to honor the life of a person known to all in Ribera and Tent City.

Garland Newport, age 86, had died on May 12, 1915. She passed away in her sleep after what appeared to be a heart attack. Her life encompassed the history of Ribera from a small ranch community to a town of over 4,000 people. Her philanthropy was without parallel. The Doc Gilroy Hospital, the 500-acre Ribera Park, and the inclusion of riverfront property owed their existence to her foresighted generosity.

The huge expanse of property adjacent to the River Bend Ranch, guaranteed to remain forever wild, was a testimonial to Garland and her daughter Dolores's love and appreciation of nature. Ron's vision was to produce a commemorative booklet of the matriarch that people in Ribera would be happy to buy and read.

Nearby, he could see Doctor Ben Lawson and his wife Kate conversing with their son Sam and his wife Bonnie. Sam and Bonnie had developed part of the old ranch property into apple, pear, and peach orchards and prospered mightily in doing so. They also provided much of the community with wheat, barley, beans, and a wide assortment of vegetables. They were probably talking about new contracts they had with the army to supply beef and horses to troops stationed close to the border with Mexico. Ron thought about talking to the army commander to see if the reported turmoil in Mexico City was as serious as he'd heard; it seemed that Mexico had a new president every year with power struggles continuing among various factions. Pancho Villa, one of the trio reaching for control, was both popular and hated by many along the border.

Spotting Konrad Bruner and Rachel Lawson and her husband, Carlos Rodriguez Bruner, Bannister walked over to them and introduced himself. On inquiring about happenings in Mexico, the two men remarked that things were relatively quiet in the interior. "Yes, American troops had occupied Vera Cruz for a while and landed in Tampico for a brief spell, but the struggle to see who will win the presidency is the key issue," Carlos offered. "In the meantime, we hope the revolutionaries will stay away from Zacatecas. But we have trained our militia to protect my family and our silver properties. I don't think the revolutionaries are interested in harming the students or faculty at the university; even the most ignorant guerilla respects education."

Carlos's wife, Rachel chimed in. "Yes, I agree with Carlos. We are well positioned to protect our sons, and the government has done a good job of maintaining security on the railroads. Our trip up here was uneventful, not like the problem Konrad and I had several years ago."

Dr. Bruner volunteered that the University of Zacatecas had built a very successful College of Mining, Geology, and Metallurgy and that it would be world class in a few years. "It appears that we will be mining copper in Cananea, Sonora, in the very near future, which should boost our programs significantly. Everything I see and hear tells me that Mexico will be a major producer of silver, gold, and copper in the future. Hopefully, some of this national treasure will provide our people with good jobs and a better standard of living."

One of the highlights of the funeral service was the eulogy delivered by Soleado Booker, recipient of a scholarship awarded by the River Bend Ranch Foundation. She gave a detailed review of her years as an anthropology student at the University of Arizona and her plans to continue her study of the Navajo and Apache nations with graduate work at the University of New Mexico. Her appreciation of the scholarship was an excellent example of the benefit of investing in the young people of the state. Dolores Richmond Dempsey was tearfully grateful for the remarks made by the youngster.

A small group clustered near the bridge dedicated to the memory of Greg Newport. Identifying Dolores and her husband Henry Dempsey, Ron extended his condolences and joined the group that included Tom Lawson and his wife, Shannon, and Barney Pryor and his wife, Sophie. "Dolores, you must be very proud of your mother's foresight and generosity to the community. You folks are a significant part of the memoir I'm producing to commemorate this occasion. Garland Newport's life follows the history of Ribera to where it stands today. And you and your husband Henry have been pioneers in the development of the Arizona Territory into a state. That too will figure in the story I'm going to write."

As the Dempseys excused themselves to greet other guests, the editor turned his attention to Tom and Shannon Lawson and Barney and Sophie Pryor. "I pretty much know the story of the Pryors in Ribera: the Whitman Hotel fire, the rebuilding, Barney's connection with the Ocotillo silver mine, and the purchase of Barbara Booker's general store and its expansion to rival Levy's in Tucson and Goldwater's in Phoenix. But while you're here Tom, I'd like to hear your thoughts on what's happening in the mining industry in the state."

"Well, Mr. Bannister, as I'm sure you already know, gold and silver production has given way to copper mining and its byproducts. People tend to forget that gold, silver, and molybdenum accompany copper in its natural state. New floatation techniques allow us to recover the more valuable elements and prolong the life of our properties. Clifton-Morenci, Globe, Miami, Superior, and Ray are important mines that make Arizona a world leader in copper production. And we can't overlook Jerome, Bisbee, and Bagdad. But most important, Jackling's technical developments at Bingham Canyon, Utah, offer us working mines for many years to come. The major fly in the ointment is the expansion of unions that threaten the profitability of our operations. If it were to continue, we will see serious labor strife and the possibility of strikes and bloodshed. Some of these people are socialists, and I for one will not deal with them."

Ron turned to Barney and Sophie Pryor for comment on Tom's assessment of the mining industry and unionization of the work force but the couple didn't offer anything. "Phoenix has attracted several of our citizens to leave Ribera for opportunities in farming, copper mining, and railroading but you two have decided to stay here and raise a family. What made you decide to do that?"

Sophie looked at her husband for a moment and then answered Ron's question. "You're a relative newcomer here, Mr. Bannister, so it's understandable that you don't know the answer to that question. Ribera has succeeded because it enjoys a diverse economy that is constantly evolving. Garland Newport and her husband were ranchers and Doc and Kate Lawson have followed in their footsteps. But now the ranch also contains fruit orchards, a sawmill, a forest preserve, and a park. And Garland, with the help of Brad Scoville, Barney, and Doc Lawson built us a medical center that is the envy of many larger towns in the state. The railroad was instrumental in enabling us to expand the hotel and help us establish our place as a destination resort. People now come here for long weekends or for weeks at a time to enjoy the mild, four-season climate and to hunt, fish, and hike in the wooded areas. But most of all, Ribera sits on the Bowie River, which flows year round and is well managed by a board of directors. We have the late Don Richmond to thank for that. As time goes by and the population increases, management of the state's water resources will command intense scrutiny as adequate water is not guaranteed in Arizona. That's about it, Ron. Now, you'll have to excuse me as I have to look after our two children."

Barney Pryor looked at Ron Bannister and smiled. "Looking at the real significance of today, I'd be inclined to mention the women who helped build this town. Garland was the pioneer but she had some strong followers. Barbara Casey Booker, Kate Lawson, and Sophie were major contributors to the success of Ribera. That's probably a story all of its own. And judging by what I heard today from young Soleado Booker, the next generation seems to be coming on strong." After listening to Barney's remarks, Ron Bannister closed his notebook, recognizing he had more than enough for his tribute to Garland Newport and the town. "Barney, I think you just about got it right. Thanks."